# LAWD,
## MO'DRAMA

sW

OTHER BOOKS BY TINA BROOKS McKINNEY
*All That Drama*

# LAWD,
## MO' DRAMA

# TINA BROOKS MCKINNEY

SBI

STREBOR BOOKS

NEW YORK  LONDON  TORONTO  SYDNEY

Strebor Books
P.O. Box 6505
Largo, MD 20792
http://www.streborbooks.com

*Lawd, Mo Drama* © 2007 by Tina Brooks McKinney

ISBN-13 978-1-59309-052-4
ISBN-10      1-59309-052-8
LCCN 2005920448

Cover design: www.mariondesigns.com

First Strebor Books trade paperback edition April 2007

10   9   8   7   6   5   4   3   2

Manufactured in the United States of America

For information regarding special discounts for bulk purchases,
please contact Simon & Schuster Special Sales at 1-800-456-6798
or business@simonandschuster.com

# DEDICATION

To Jimmy Hurd, author of *Turnaround* and *Ice Dancer*:
your genius with a pen will be missed—you really left us too soon.

If I'd known I was in the presence of an angel waiting to ascend,
I would have been more proactive to spend time with you.
All I know is that you touched my life in a brief period of time and
I feel cheated. I wish I could go back to the day I first met you
and surround myself in your warmth. But I can't, you're now
a shining star for all of us, showing us the way. Damn, Jimmy,
I miss you, I ain't even gonna lie. But you taught me something
in your passing. I will never take life for granted and I will never,
ever pass over an opportunity to tell someone how much they
mean to me. You will never know how much you meant to me.
You left too soon.
I love you !

# ACKNOWLEDGMENTS

Once again, I must thank God first for showing me the way to this literary world. As a child, I always loved to read so I thank him for giving me the courage to go one step further. With that said I of course would like to thank Zane and the Strebor staff for believing in me. Charmaine, you deserve a special shout-out for all your hard work and efforts on our behalf. I can't thank you enough. Pardon the length of these acknowledgements but I have a whole lot of folks that I need to thank and some I want to put on blast!

I also can't help but to thank my husband, William, for putting up with me always focused on this laptop every night and never complaining out loud about it. My children, Shannan and Estrell, thanks for showing up at my signings and telling everyone that will stand still about my book. My sister, Theresa, for all delightful flyers and the love you show me. My mother, Judy, and my father, Ivor, I got nothing but love for both of you! It's been a long road but I am beginning to see the light. Special shouts out to my long-time friends Angie, Val, Andrea, high school friends Launa, Tammy, Lessia, Muriel and Wanda for always having my back, I do appreciate ya'll.

Tee C. Royal is another shining star in my book. She is one of the "real" people in this industry that ain't in it for the money but for the love of books.

To Shelley Halima, Harold Turley, Darrien Lee, Allison Hobbs and Nane Quartay, I love you all and I can't thank you enough for taking my late-night calls and support. Shelley, you've become more than just a writer friend, you're more like a sista. In fact, I send the entire Strebor family a group hug, too! Remember to share the word, not just about your book, about all of our books. Special thanks to J. Marie Darden for editing *Lawd, Mo' Drama*. As far as edits go, I had a lot of help, Kathy Shewbart, Gail McFarland, Jo Marie and Lenora Harrison. I hope I got everyone, if I forgot anyone charge it to the brain, not my heart!

Cory and Heather Buford, how loudly can I say I love you for the web design that you did for me. If anyone is looking for a great web design team that is not trying to rip you off, please check out csr@gwmo.com! You won't be sorry.

Greatest appreciation goes out to my strong supporters, Muriel Broomfield, Dee Ford, Craig Barnett, Sam Willis, Mike Ray and Ronny Napier—Powertalk-FM, Kim Sims, Donna Cager, Dionne McKenzie, Marvin Meadows, Vanessa (I don't know your last name but you sold the hell out of my books) and Lawd knows there are others but my mind froze. To those I didn't mention you know I love you. Carla M. Walker and Tina R. Hayes for all that you have done for me and your fight against haterism, coming from a circle close to you! Janet my sister, I love you girl, C. Lindsay, (another writer ready to explode), VJ, another sister in spirit. Porchia Foxx, I miss your presence in our lives and can't wait to hear you again on the radio. That other fool is driving me crazy! Thanks to you, Porchia, I have learned to make my haters my motivators!

To all the reading/writing groups that I belong to, thank you. Special shouts out to Raw4all, Passion for Reading, Sexy Ebony Readers, APOOO, GAAL Book Club, The Sunshine Boys and a host of others, thank you for your support, I could not have made it without you and my heart is full when I think of your participation in my success. Also, thanks to all the book clubs that I didn't mention that have showed me love. And I cannot forget Monica, David and the rest of her family that shows up at every Strebor event! I love you guys. Rowenna and Kim, ya'll are off the chain and Stephanie Hester who has been with me from day one.

To my fans, I can't thank you enough for your kind emails and support. I cry at each of the emails that I receive and save them in a scrapbook. I love the interaction with you so please keep it up! Keep writing me and I will keep answering you! And if you're an aspiring writer, just do it! Love you all.

To fellow authors, T.L. Garner, Cydney Rax, Trista Russell, LaTanya Williams, Thomas Green, Gayle Sloan, Sybil Barkley, Allisha Yvonne, Vanessa Johnson, Eric Pete, Lissa Woodson, best of luck to you all! I can't list all the authors who have touched my life as much as I would like but again charge it to running out of room this time.

To my co-workers, Gaynell, Alita, Kelvin, Leslie, Talisa, Diane, Maceo (it's so hard to be you), Bill, Grady, Turtlehead, Sherman and Al, thanks for supporting my book and showing me love.

# Not Alone
## By E

A tragedy has occurred
In this place we call home
A victim of circumstances
Whose cause is unknown

Not quite living
But not quite dead
Food for thought for the person not eating
But seeing this instead

Why did God send my girl this way?

The only changes she'll be seeing
Are in mattress frames,
Room scheme & color decor
But her footprints will never grace this floor
My floor
That I built just for her

Lord

Why me?

I see
My joy, my love, my world
Sitting in her crib dead to my world
No sound, no words
My baby girl

But to the end of her road
I will carry the load
As long as I'm living she'll never be
Alone

## LEAH

I was sick and tired of being sick and tired! My energy was drained. For the first time in my life, I could understand why some women killed their children before turning the guns on themselves. Not that I'd made a conscious decision to do harm to my children. I was beginning to feel that it was the only way out of my current situation.

My mind wandered as I sat at the kitchen table shuffling through a mountain of bills. I arranged the bills in order of importance and then by amounts. Any way I stacked them, I didn't have the money. I picked up the phone to call the mortgage company to request an extension and sighed. I hated making "begging calls," but this time I couldn't put it off. A foreclosure notice was tacked on the door for the entire neighborhood to see. We didn't have anywhere to go, so I had no choice but to grovel.

A bored switchboard operator answered the phone.

"I need to speak with someone about the status of my mortgage," I said, trying to get mileage out of humility.

"Hold on," she said.

I waited through seemingly endless country melodies. Just once, I would have liked to hear a song I could sing along to while I was placed on ignore. I was prepared to stay there a while longer when the line clicked over.

"This is Mrs. Turner. May I help you?"

"Hello." I took a deep breath. "My name is Leah Simmons, and I need to speak to someone about a notice that was posted on my door yesterday."

"What is your account number?"

I could tell by her voice that Mrs. Turner was a sister. I felt like I could be real with her. I read her the number, then held my breath in anticipation.

"What is the name on the account?"

"Um, Kentee Simmons," I mumbled.

"And you are?" She was all business, dashing my hopes for sympathy.

"I'm his wife." I drew another deep breath.

"Mrs. Simmons, I cannot speak to you about this account since your name does not appear on it. You need to have your husband contact this office to discuss the account."

"That's the problem." I began to explain my situation, and I did not bother to hold back the stress and fear I was feeling. I sounded like an imperiled cartoon character to my own ears.

"Mrs., um, Simmons, calm down, please, I can't understand what you're saying," she said with more kindness. I was truly babbling and could not stop my anguished moans.

"My husband left me with three small kids. My oldest is five and the twins are two. We have no food, no money, and now this! I don't know where the hell he is, and I can't wait on him to correct this. My family can't be put out in the street!" I cried. As if slapped, all three children started crying in the background. I rose from the table and stumbled into the bedroom so I could hear what Mrs. Turner was saying. I didn't like leaving my children in a distressed state, but I wasn't able to hear anything above their chorus.

"Hold on," she said, placing me back on hold and forcing me to listen to that awful country music.

While waiting, I tried to compose myself. I absolutely hated having to make that call, and loathed Kentee for putting us in that situation. Before I met Kentee, I had a good job and was doing fine. He talked me into quitting my job and having babies but, at the first sign of trouble, he left our asses. *I wish I had listened to Marie!*

The phone line clicked. "Mrs. Simmons, I need to get a number so I can call you back. I'll try to help you, but you have to understand our rules. If I discuss this loan with you, I'll be terminated. The bank monitors any call over three minutes, so I need to go. I'll phone you on my break," Mrs. Turner said.

Relieved, I gave her my number and prayed that she would call before the phone was disconnected.

Kayla, my oldest child, was banging on the door demanding to be let in. She was my drama queen. I could not have a pity party unless she joined in. Ever since Kentee left me, Kayla cried every time I shed a tear. Even when I snuck into the bathroom for a solitary cry, her radar detected my distress, and she sought me out.

"Lawd Jesus," I lamented. "Can't I have five seconds of peace?" I yelled, hoping Kayla would get the message. It was a silly thought, since Kayla was only five going on six. She understood nothing outside of her own wants and needs. She had matured since the birth of the twins but still required special attention.

The twins were another story. Malik was a dream child and almost a loner. He was content to sit in his room or in the living room playing quietly. He did not like a lot of noise and preferred to do everything himself. Mya, on the other hand, was off the chain! The twins were born two weeks early. I had an emergency C-section because Mya was not in birthing position. She kept getting in Malik's way, so the surgeons had to go in and get them both at the last minute. Malik came out first and they had to fight to get to Mya.

Although the doctors assured me that neither of them had suffered any brain damage, I was beginning to have doubts about Mya. She was not developing as fast as her brother, and she had these inexplicable tantrums that I couldn't understand.

The noise level on the other side of the door was deafening. I opened the door and left the bedroom, realizing that peace would not be found there. Kayla was curled up in a ball in front of the door. I wanted to step over her, but I did not. I helped her up, wiping away her tears. When Kentee left, Kayla had reverted to wetting the bed and her clothes. To avoid embarrassment, I had resorted to putting diapers on her. I needed a conveyor belt to wipe all their butts and keep them clean. I should have also been receiving a residual check from Pampers for all the money I had spent with them.

"I'm hungry, Mommy," Kayla whined.

I glanced at my watch and realized that I had missed fixing their breakfast. It was already lunchtime. The whimpering that normally grated my nerves only shamed me this time. She was right and I was wrong. I led Kayla to a chair and went to look in the cabinets to see what I could fix.

"Mommy," Kayla whispered.

"What?" I mimicked her whisper.

"What's wrong with Mya?"

I was floored. I could not think of a response that would satisfy her. I didn't know my damn self.

"Honey, Mommy doesn't know."

It was not much of a response, but it satisfied her curiosity for the moment. I continued pulling things out of the cabinet. The pickings were slim. I would have to go to the grocery store soon but it was too big of an ordeal; requiring planning and money. Kayla and Malik would be yelling out the things they wanted added to the cart and Mya would scream if anyone looked at her. Because of her heightened sense of smell, she hated all cleaning products and would toss them out of the cart every chance she got; leaving liquid spills up and down the grocery aisles.

I decided to wait on the store until after I dropped the kids off at my mother's. My mind was spinning, and I found no relief. Kayla was right, there was something wrong with Mya and none of the doctors I had taken her to had offered a reasonable diagnosis. I attributed that to not having insurance. The emergency room could only handle so much. Kentee decided to cancel our insurance after the children were born. He claimed he made enough money to pay his bills and that insurance should be called "just in case" because most folks did not use it and never got their money's worth. Although I didn't agree with his premise I could not make him spend his money on things he didn't believe in.

Unlike her brother, Mya still did not sleep through the night. At times during the day she would have these little fits; constantly screaming and kicking. Her fits were not tied to any particular situation; she fell out for no reason. How was I supposed to explain that to Kayla when I didn't understand it myself?

Like a robot, I fixed lunch on autopilot. I did not even remember cleaning up the kitchen. I was worn out and, despite all the love I had in my heart for my children, I had nothing else to give.

I shoved the pile of bills onto the floor and lowered my head to the table. My mind wandered again. I thought of putting an end to all of the pain and frustration. Too tired to think, I waited for the phone to ring and end the suspense that had been building up all day.

Yesterday, while my mother watched the kids, I went to different churches and non-profit agencies trying to get some assistance. I managed to scrounge up $125 from the Salvation Army, $750 from St. Vincent de Paul, and another $500 from various churches. Families in Need was also reviewing my case to see if they could assist me to cover expenses like my light and phone bills. But if I lost the house, I would need that money to cover rental expenses somewhere else.

I felt the tension knot that had formed in the top of my head move closer to the center as I tried to hold back tears. My eyes were already so swollen I doubted they would ever return to normal.

For the life of me, I could not understand how my relationship with Kentee had taken such a drastic turn. Flashes of my life—before and after the children— ran through my brain. *Sure, things were different since we had kids, but I thought he would expect that.* "Was I living in a vacuum where he couldn't see what I was dealing with?" I questioned the walls, but I did not get a response.

I used to greet Kentee naked—or damn near naked—when he came home from work. As long as Kayla was bedded down, I would sit on his lap and feed him his supper. I kept a spotless house and took special care of my appearance.

But that was then, and this is now. After the twins' arrival, Kentee normally came home to find my hair standing on end and the house turned upside down, with no place to walk, let alone sit. And forget about a home-cooked meal. I assumed he understood but, obviously, he didn't.

The shrill ringing of the phone interrupted my musing. A quick glance at the clock told me that I had lost an entire day and had no idea where it had gone.

"Hello," I answered, my voice shaking.

"Mrs. Simmons?"

"This is she."

"This is Mrs. Turner from SunDale Bank. I spoke with you this morning. I did some checking to be certain I relayed the proper information to you. I discovered that I was the loan officer assigned to your husband's account when he first applied for the house you currently reside in. I need to make sure you understand that I have risked my job to call you. I'm doing this because I can relate to your situation. If you tell anyone where you got this information, I'll deny it. Is that clear?"

"I understand. Thank you," I said.

"This isn't the only loan that your husband has with our bank. He has another house over on the south side of Atlanta, and those payments are current."

"Excuse me?" Unable to comprehend what she was trying to tell me, I was fighting the urge to get an attitude with her for bearing the bad news.

"He bought that house a little over six months ago. If I had to guess, I would bet he has set up another household there."

I was so stunned I could not speak.

"Mrs. Simmons, are you there?"

"Uh, yes. I'm sorry. I just caught a curve ball aimed straight at my stomach. Is he aware that his children are about to be put out on the street?" I asked, as if she knew the answer. I felt exactly two inches tall, asking a stranger what was going on with my own husband. But since he wouldn't return my pages or phone calls, I was grasping at any straws I could reach.

Mrs. Turner was feeling my pain. "This is difficult for me to say, and I'm sorry to be the bearer of bad news. When I questioned him about the loan on the house you're living in, he said that you were a renter and he couldn't care less whether you were evicted or not because you weren't paying the rent as agreed."

*Well, I'll just be damned. How the hell was I going to pay rent when he forbade me to work after I had his kids?*

"He's saying that shit because he feels guilty that I caught his lying ass. Now he'd rather avoid me than face me."

I flashed back to a conversation with my old friend, Marie. She had warned me to think twice before I committed to a relationship with Kentee. Lord, I wish I had listened to her. I might not have been going through the current changes. Hindsight is twenty-twenty.

Still stunned, I could not move my lips to ask the questions I really needed the answers to. Realizing that the lady would not stay on the phone with me forever, I grew angry and plunged ahead.

"Renter, my ass! I'm not a renter; that's my husband!" I shouted, my fear turning into unadulterated rage.

Speaking louder and enunciating clearly, as if she were talking to a child, Mrs. Turner said, "I know this, and you know this, but he spoke to me like that wasn't the case. I informed him that if he allowed the house that you're living in to be foreclosed upon he'd permanently damage his credit rating."

"And what did he say?" I demanded, sure that he would at least try to protect his credit rating; if not his own children. I hoped he had said something that would keep us from winding up on the street.

"Hmm...I don't recall," she said, clearly lying, maybe trying to spare me further embarrassment. She changed the subject, putting the focus back on me.

"Look, I don't believe, based on my conversation with your husband, that he's going to be your knight-in-shining-armor. I'm speaking to you woman to woman. My own husband left me high and dry, and to this day, I don't know what happened to him. He could be dead for all I know, and to be honest, I hope he is. Don't waste precious time sitting around waiting for his ass to come back, or for the other shoe to drop."

Mrs. Turner's words hit me like a plank of wood against the forehead. She was right. I was the only person who could rectify this situation, and finally I understood.

"Hey, I appreciate your advice, but I'm still stuck between a rock and a hard place. I have three kids still in diapers. I can't get a job 'cause I can't afford day care. I have less than a thousand dollars to my name, and most of it I got from begging at the local churches here in Peachtree City. What am I supposed to do?" I wailed, no longer able to hold back my feelings.

"Mrs. Simmons, I don't have an answer for that. I wanted to make sure you weren't holding out false hope that your husband's going to fix this. You need to make a way for you and your children because your man isn't going to be there."

I glanced at my watch and realized that we had been talking for over thirty minutes. I needed some time to think about this new information.

Taking a deep breath, I said, "Thanks for everything."

"Hey, I've walked in your shoes before. Thankfully, I didn't have kids! Do yourself a favor. Take the money you do have and try to find some other place to live. I'll lose your paperwork for a few months, but I can't hold it off much longer," Mrs. Turner said, and hung up the phone without waiting for me to utter another word.

I held the phone in my hands and tried to think. The annoying dial tone prompted me to hang up and I finally obeyed. Deep in my heart, I wanted to believe that Kentee would come to his senses and do the right thing, but the evidence did not support this belief. In the meantime, I needed to think about my kids and make preparations for the rest of our lives.

I was hurt that Kentee had chosen to be with another woman. I would gladly take him back, given the opportunity. How stupid was that? But it was the way I felt. He was the first man I had ever loved, and my heart wanted to forgive him for the errors of his dick. Dejected, I realized the situation was out of my hands. The only person I had control of was me, and I couldn't help myself if I didn't make a move, and do it now.

I called my mother to bring her up-to-date, and it was one of the hardest calls I'd had to make. She was supposed to be enjoying her retirement and not worrying about what her grown-ass child was going through.

"Momma, it's Leah. I'm going to need your help with the kids for the next few months while I try to find a job. I found out from the mortgage company that Kentee hasn't been paying the mortgage. They're going to foreclose on this house."

"Oh, Lawd!" she exclaimed. "Has that fool bumped his head? Leaving you there with three children? What the hell is he thinking?"

"I wish I had an answer for that. Sure, we argued when I listened to his voice mail and found out about his pussy on the side, but we agreed to work that out. To be honest, I still feel like he'll come through the door any day now, but I have to prepare for the very real possibility that he won't be coming back."

I could almost hear Momma's wheels spinning. I knew she was thinking that we were going to have to move in with her, but her tiny apartment could never house all of us. I had half a mind to pack the kids up and take them to Kentee's mother, but she was so strung out on crack, I wouldn't be able to sleep at night thinking about what they would be exposed to. Desperate but grateful for small favors, I listened to Mom's sigh, then quickly relayed what Mrs. Turner told me.

"Momma, when I called the bank, I lucked up and got a sympathetic sister who's had similar problems with her husband. She's going to give me a few months to raise enough money to move into an apartment or something. I still want to stay in Peachtree City, if I can, but you know the rents here are pretty high."

"Yes, they are, but maybe you can get some type of assistance; for the children at least." She was trying to be the voice of sanity and reason in my crazy situation. I was so proud of my mother, and I loved her unconditionally. Never in my wildest dreams did I ever envision us relating on this type of level. As a teen, I was a wild one, and she had all but wiped her hands clean of me. I chose a life of sex and drugs, and she wanted nothing to do with me until I turned my life over to God and got my head on straight. Given our past rocky relationship I reveled in our newfound companionship.

"Can I drop the hell's angels off in the morning?" I asked.

"Of course you can. I'll see you then," she said.

"Thank you," I whispered as I hung up the phone, shaking my head. Tears rolled down my cheeks, marking the trail of pain Kentee inflicted. Crying was all I seemed to be able to do and I was sick of it. I was a strong black woman and tears did not come easy. In the past few months I had been stripped of my dignity, pride and control of my life and I didn't like it one bit.

A loud crash shook me from my private hell, followed by a shriek. I raced down the hall and entered the twins' bedroom. Mya was laid out on the carpet, flapping around and banging her head on the floor.

"Stop it!" I yelled, grabbing her and clutching her to my chest. Her brother looked on in fear, as I tried to understand whether I was screaming at my husband or my child.

Mya was so different from her brother, Malik. He was walking now and saying small words. He said "Daddy" the other day, which really pissed me off, since Daddy was nowhere to be found. Mya, on the other hand, had not uttered a word and barely crawled.

# LEAH

I dressed the twins as Kayla put on her clothes. Mya's face was all swollen from where she had banged it on the floor. It hurt my heart to look at her; especially when I knew there was not anything I could do about it.

"What happened?" Momma exclaimed when she took her first look at Mya.

"She was climbing out of her crib and she fell out. Then she started banging her head on the floor."

Momma's head snapped around, and her eyes drilled holes in me. I looked the worse for wear, since I had been up most of the night making sure Mya didn't slip into a coma. I had dark circles under my eyes that no amount of makeup could conceal.

"Girl, you look like you fell out the bed, too." She forced a laugh, but I could tell she was struggling to keep from crying. I managed a tight grin that didn't reach my eyes. *Lord, things had changed so much.*

"I was up all night watching Mya."

"You should have taken her to the emergency room." Momma frowned.

"Momma, you know I can't afford the emergency room. Plus, they would've asked me all kinds of questions about what happened to her. I swear, every time I take her for a physical, they question me about every bump and bruise; as if I would deliberately inflict pain on my own child."

"Well, unfortunately it happens every day, and they're simply trying to be careful. They're just doing their job when they take you through that drill," Momma replied. I placed Mya on the couch and she sat there quietly. She could be so docile one minute and a raving lunatic the next.

I wanted to get mad, but Momma was right. If I were abusing Mya, an emergency room would be the place to catch me. "But if they were doing their job, they'd recognize that something is wrong with Mya; instead of trying to place the blame on me! Hell, if they're doing their jobs, why are there so many children actually being abused and nothing's being done until they die?" I was crumbling under the pressure of it all.

"Look, Leah, I know you're under a lot of strain, but you'll watch your language in my house." She wagged her finger in my face for emphasis.

"I'm sorry. I got carried away, but you haven't been there to see their faces. They make me feel guilty; even though I haven't done anything. I can't be with Mya twenty-four hours a day. Last night, she was sleeping in her crib. I'm gonna have to put a mattress on the floor since this is the second time she's flipped the crib over."

Momma opened her arms, and I gratefully stepped into them, racked with sobs of despair. I stopped slobbering when I realized I was smearing snot all over Momma's blouse. Pulling back, I put down all the bags I still clutched in my hands. Going back to the car, I gathered the rest of their things and opened the childproof door for Kayla and Malik to go in by themselves.

Excusing myself, I went to the bathroom to repair my makeup. I wanted to make a good impression that day and could not afford to appear in my present haphazard state. It had been a long time since I had been out searching for a job, and that wore heavily on my mind.

Kayla immediately went to the living room and turned on the television. She was suffering the most. She was the only one of my children who actually remembered her father. Every time she entered my mother's living room her eyes were drawn to our family picture. I did not know whether to take the picture down or explain the situation. Despite how grown up she acted, I doubted that she was ready to hear the lowdown shit her father did, so I chose to keep that information to myself.

I watched Kayla as she settled on the sofa. Her eyes found the framed picture of our family, and I saw the pain reflected when she saw her father. Her finger reached out to touch his face, and a single tear rolled down her cheek. I had to turn my head away. She was Daddy's girl, and as hard as she tried, she couldn't understand why he wasn't around anymore. Not only was

Kayla missing her father but she had to deal with the twins taking away all the attention that used to be focused on her. Maybe some of that was my fault.

I didn't have the answers. Kissing the kids and my mother, then sneaking out while Mya was quiet was the best that I could do. If Mya sensed I was leaving, she would have a tantrum. I would hate to leave her that way, but I would have to since I was on a mission.

Finding work was not as easy as I thought it would be. Everyone wanted recent work experience and I had been out of the job market for over five years. Nervous and desperate, I called my past employer—White, Muller, & Stevens—to see if they had any openings. However, if they did, the job would be too far away from my Peachtree City home. Kayla would be starting kindergarten, and I did not want to be too far away. Not to mention that raggedy car I was driving would not make the daily commute to downtown Atlanta. But, if they were hiring, I would take the job. The woman I spoke to in human resources said she would check with the hiring partner and get back to me.

It was a long shot, but I could not help hoping and making plans. If I did get my old job back, I could ask my mother to watch the kids while I worked. I could make it to and from work if I did not have to drive so far to get there. But, if I lived closer, maybe I could. I suddenly thought of Sammie. My old friend, Sammie Davis, still lived in Atlanta. My car would make it from her place to what I was praying would be my job. I had not seen Sammie in a few years, not since our friend Marie's funeral, but we had kept in contact over the phone. She was constantly asking me to visit. A visitor was not the same as a roommate, but Sammie was Sammie, and she wouldn't leave me hanging.

Sammie and I had become friends through Marie. After Marie's death, Sammie had become my closest friend besides my mother. I normally didn't bond with women, but Marie was different. She made you love her; whether you wanted to or not. Sammie and I held each other up in the months following Marie's murder, so I had no doubt she would offer to help me.

Momma would keep the kids; they would be safe. I would be working, and everything would be alright. I added that to my silent prayer, flicked my blinker for a left turn, and headed for the Labor Department office. This was an exercise in futility. I was ineligible for unemployment, but in order to get food stamps and WIC assistance, I had to apply.

Climbing from my car, I smoothed my hands over my hips, straightening my skirt. Moving across the crowded parking lot with purpose, I headed for the big glass doors like I knew what I was doing. I did not hesitate because if I took too long, I would lose my nerve and any chance I had of finding the help that I needed.

Taking too long should have been the last of my worries. Two hours and a stack of forms later, I was waiting, turning the pages of *Pandora's Box* and getting the evil eye from the angry little leather-skinned woman haunting the intake desk. I was so immersed in reading that I was annoyed when I finally heard my name.

"Leah Simmons." My name wasn't an invitation or a question; not the way this nerdy little white guy was calling it. My name was a condemnation, an indictment of poverty and, shameful as it was, I followed his tight little blue-shirted back to his narrow cubicle. His mouth was a thin line as he indicated the wooden chair beside his government-issue desk. He slid into a vinyl-covered chair on the other side of the desk and peered at me through over-sized black plastic-framed glasses.

"I'm Mr. Weiner, and I'll be your intake worker. How may I help you?" he piped, and my hope drained clean away when his eyes examined the stack of papers he collected from me. His head went from side to side, giving me the unconscious "no," then, turning a page, he did everything but suck his teeth.

What the hell had I been thinking, hoping to get a sista who may have gone through a similar experience, or a "round the way brother," maybe one raised by a struggling single mother; someone familiar with the nightmare I was living. That would have taken good luck, but luck was having no part of me that day. I could tell by the "seen the movie and the reviews suck" look on Mr. Weiner's face.

He shuffled my papers together and tapped them against his desk. "How may I help you?" he repeated.

"I need to apply for assistance."

"This says your last job was in July 1998." He raised his pale brows and tilted his head at me.

Uncomfortable, I squirmed in my chair. "Yes, sir," I mumbled.

"And, you have three children. Ages five and under."

"Uh. Yes."

"Any other hobbies?" he muttered barely loud enough for me to hear.

"Excuse me?" I said, hoping that he had not gone where I thought he did.

"What about the father? You didn't list his whereabouts or his income."

That was not what he said, but I was not about to start a fight with him because I knew my shit stank. I fidgeted with the flap on my purse as unwanted tears spilled from my eyes.

His words were small daggers thrown at my heart as I struggled to regain my composure. I was not used to asking people for anything. As much as I hated it, being honest was the only way he was going to help me. Sitting taller in my chair, tilting up my chin, I tried to be the confident woman I used to be and answered his question.

"I have no idea where my husband is. I haven't seen or heard from him in over four months. The rat bastard disappeared and, for all I know, he could be dead. I'm a stay-at-home mother, and he left me without any money, in a house that's about to be foreclosed on." As my confession gained momentum, tears streamed out of my eyes.

The nerdy man lowered his glasses from his eyes and handed me a few tissues from the box on his desk. He appeared almost human as I grabbed the tissues and wiped both my nose and eyes. Shame weighed on my shoulders.

He did not comment as he continued to read through my paperwork. I had marked Mya's special needs on the form and, as he read, his face softened. He turned from me and began punching information into his desktop computer. I could do nothing but stare at the back of his sandy-colored head. After several minutes of silence, Mr. Weiner swung around to face me again.

"Unfortunately, according to regulations, you're ineligible for unemployment, but I think you knew that. I've listed you in our data bank and will personally be on the lookout for suitable employment for you. I'm sorry, but it's the best I can do."

I pushed my chair back, attempting to stand, but I didn't have the strength. I didn't know how much more I could take.

"Wait," he hastily spoke as I rose from the chair. "You have other options that you might not be aware of. Your paperwork says you don't have medical insurance." He handed me a form explaining the benefits. I scanned the paper and felt a small measure of relief.

He handed me two more sheets of paper. One was a handwritten note with the name of a day care facility not too far from my house. I stared at him blankly, not understanding where he was coming from.

"I can't afford day care!" I told him, bordering on getting pissed. He leaned in closer to me so no one could overhear.

"This facility was created to ensure adequate day care for the employees of Blank, Rome, and Carpenter. It's a law firm two blocks west of the facility, and they're hiring. With your skills you should be able to get a job as a secretary and have affordable day care as a part of your benefits. I didn't give you this information. You heard about it someplace else, right?"

Comprehension dawned slowly, but I got it. He was giving me a break.

"I'm taking a chance that you need the job more than most and won't let me down." He sat back in his seat with the biggest smile glued to his face, and I was riveted in mine.

"Thank you," was all I could come up with. Fresh tears made their way from my already swollen eyes, and I dabbed at them. I looked at the final paper he had given me. It was from the welfare office. I hated this form the most, but he wrote a personal friend's name on it.

"I'm calling her right now. Her name is Ms. Moore. I'll set up an appointment. Can you go directly from here?"

I drove the three short blocks to her office in a daze. Mr. Weiner was no round the way brother, but I was getting the help I needed.

I asked for Ms. Moore at the intake desk and was led into the supervisor's office. She stood up when I came into the room and greeted me with a warm smile.

"Please, have a seat," she instructed, and I practically fell into the chair.

"Mr. Weiner faxed over your information to me. Unfortunately, there's nothing I can do today to ease your situation. However, I can file emergency papers that'll get you food stamps within forty-eight hours. You'll be receiving seven hundred and fifty dollars a month in food stamps. Of course should you become gainfully employed this amount will be reduced or taken away completely depending on your income. Are any of your children still using formula?"

"No, they all drink regular milk," I replied.

She was banging on her computer the entire time I was talking with her. She pressed papers into my hand, indicated where to sign, and I complied. She detached my temporary WIC card and handed it back to me.

"Is there anything else I can do for you?" she asked with a huge smile.

"Not that I'm aware of," I said, rising to leave. "I can't thank you enough for the help that you've offered me. I truly wasn't expecting this much," I said.

"Mr. Weiner and I try to look out for special cases. What we've done is illegal and we could both lose our jobs, but we believe that, in some cases, rules are meant to be broken."

I sucked in my breath, feeling like I was sucker punched. "Why?"

"Help you?" she nodded and smiled. "We see a lot of people come through these doors. A lot are either strung out on drugs or are plain lazy. Both Mr. Weiner and I have special needs children. We're trying to help those unique persons who didn't give up."

"How can I ever thank you?" I wanted to hug her and fought the impulse, but I did not have to. She approached me and opened her arms, and I went into them.

"Just hang in there and keep in touch," she whispered in my ear. For a brief moment, things did not seem so bleak. As I was leaving the office, she called me back in.

"Leah? I can call you that, can't I?"

"Yes, of course."

"You need to file for child support. Do you know where your husband works?"

"I know where he was working when he left, but I can't get anyone to talk to me over there."

"Come here for a minute. Since you're a state aid recipient, you're required to file for child support. We'll file the papers for you." She handed me another form, and I signed it. "Hey, if push comes to shove, he might come back home; if you hit him hard in his pockets."

That was something that I did not even want to think about. I hated to put Kentee into the system, but he had placed us there without a second thought. Later, pulling into traffic, I suddenly realized that there was no hope for a happy ending for my family.

I stopped by the law firm and inquired about the job opening. Apparently they needed someone badly. I was instructed to wait while they set up the testing area.

The waiting made me nervous. Big beads of sweat broke out all over my body, and I tried to appear calm despite the havoc taking place in my stomach. I went to the bathroom three times and managed to read the same page seven times as I waited for the testing to begin. Stress messed with my bowels and I felt sorry for those who entered the bathroom after me.

I finally heard my name called, so I willed my knees to stop shaking and headed to the test area. First was a spelling test; my weakest skill. For the life of me, I could not understand why we had to be so proficient in spelling in the era of computers. *Hell, if I can make out enough of the word, spell check will correct the shit*, I thought to myself. The typing test was next, then a terminology test, which I felt sure I aced. At my last job, I was about to be promoted to a paralegal, and surprisingly I had retained that knowledge.

"Have a seat in the waiting room, please," the receptionist said when I completed the last test. I sat and thumbed through a copy of the *Atlanta Journal-Constitution* that I had found on the table. I was so nervous, I skimmed the pages barely noticing the words.

Less than ten minutes passed, and the receptionist was calling my name.

"Follow me, please," she said sweetly. She led me down several corridors and past what seemed like a gazillion offices before she stopped in front of a plain oak door. Rapping twice, she turned the knob. The nameplate beside the door read "Anita Blank."

Suppressing the urge to run, I followed her into the office and stood there in front of this tiny black woman who barely could see over her desk. *She needs a booster chair.* I fought the urge to laugh when she sat down and I could barely see her chin.

"Mrs. Simmons, it's a pleasure to meet you," she said and took her seat. She nodded with her head that it was okay for me to sit as well.

"Your test results are quite impressive. I see you haven't worked in a while. Can I contact your last place of employment for a recommendation?" she inquired, all about business.

"Why, of course," I stammered. "My record with White, Muller, & Stevens was impeccable. In fact, at the time I left, I was being considered for a paralegal position. I had completed the necessary classes, but I didn't take the final test," I replied.

"And you turned that down? That's a very prestigious firm."

"I know, but I got married, and my husband didn't want me to work."

"I see," she said, jotting notes on her legal pad. I took a moment to look around her office. It was gorgeous. The room was done in soft neutral colors, with a leather sofa in front of a big bay window and cherry wood furniture. I noticed pictures on her desk of children, hers I presumed, but no husband. Searching for an angle that would give me an edge, I decided honesty was the best policy. I sensed that I was losing her, and I needed her in my corner.

"He left me and I need a job in the worst way!" I blurted. Her eyes rose from the pad she used to take notes and focused in on my face. "I have three children."

"Well, when can you start?"

I stared at her in disbelief. I thought she was about to kick me out of her office when she said, "I see" in a dismissing tone of voice, and here she was asking me when I wanted to start.

"Now, if you'll let me," I said, even though it was three o'clock in the afternoon.

Laughing, she stood up and came toward me. "You can start on Monday," she said, extending her hand to me once again. "Just tell Tracey to give you the employment package, and I'll see you first thing on Monday." She was ushering me to the hallway, and my damn feet were not cooperating. I felt like someone had replaced my high heels with air balloons, and they kept trying to lift me off the floor.

I finally got my feet under control and managed to find my way back to Tracey's desk. She greeted me with the biggest smile and handed me the forms to fill out. "Welcome aboard."

"Hot damn!" I screamed at the sky as I skipped to the car. This day was turning out a lot better than I expected. I had just fastened my seatbelt when I realized I did not even know what time to come in. Leaving my purse on the seat and the keys in the ignition, I raced back to the building, snatched open the door, and dashed back into the office, looking like a crazy woman.

"What time?" I gasped. It was a short run but I was out of practice.

"Eight o'clock," Tracey responded, struggling to hold back her laughter. I bowed out the door thanking her as I went. Things were looking up at last. "See you."

I was so excited that I didn't see the red light that I ran, but I noticed the blue lights flashing in my rearview mirror; especially with the help of that loud-ass siren.

"Fuck!" I slammed my hand on the steering wheel in frustration. "Why, Lord? Can't I just have one good day?" I screamed, searching my purse for my license.

# LEAH

The officer took his sweet time getting out of the car, and it was making me crazy. I self-consciously smoothed out my wayward hair and licked my suddenly chapped lips.

When he did exit the car, I almost wet myself. Adonis himself could not have been finer! He was tall, brown-skinned with a tiny diamond in his left ear, and drop-dead gorgeous. His eyes practically drilled a hole in me, and his body was to die for. His arms were long and thick, and I envisioned them holding me down while he sexed my body. I stopped myself from looking at his thighs because it would have been on then. My overheated twat started smoking and I could feel it trying to reel him in before he even got to the car. *Sweet Jesus*, I thought, trying to fan the fire burning between my thighs.

This was the first time I had ever gotten stopped by the police, and while I was slightly afraid, I thanked God for this piece of eye candy. Regardless of the ticket, this officer would be the subject of all too many fantasies in the coming nights.

Without being asked, I handed him my license and registration. My eyes could not leave his thick, full, and wet magnificent lips. I could actually taste them and that started my mouth watering. I used the sleeve of my dress to wipe my lips. I could not talk to this man, because I might tell him exactly what I was thinking. Instead, I wanted to gaze at him and etch a picture of his body onto my mind.

The muscles in his arms were testing the strength of the blue fabric covering them. I could identify each tendon in his hands and fought myself not to reach out and touch. I imagined his voice would be deep, but I was totally unprepared for the melodic baritone that came out of those perfect lips.

"Did you realize that you ran a red light?" he asked, looking me over.

I turned my head away from his eyes. I felt myself drowning in them. I shook my head to clear my thoughts.

"To be honest, Officer, I didn't notice until you pulled behind me. I'm sorry. I've been having a very bad month I just got some great news and I was excited. I know that's not a good excuse, but it's the truth." I hung my head, even though looking away was hard to do.

"So, what's the news?" he said, looking at his pad. I do not know what it was about the man other than his good looks, but I wanted to be honest with him. Without hesitation I recounted my situation. Hell, he might even feel sorry for me, and if he was single, we might be able to hook up.

"Several months ago, my husband left me with no money and three small children. Our house is being foreclosed on, and I've been out today looking for work. My good news is that I found a job." Wow, saying it out loud to another human being made me feel even happier than when I got the job.

He stopped writing on his pad, lowering his massive arms to his sides. *He must be a body builder*, I thought.

"You did have a good day," he stated.

"It's been a great day. That is, until now," I said.

"Oh, you didn't want to meet me?" he asked with a twinkle in his eyes and a slight smile on his lovely lips.

"Shoot, I'd want to meet you anytime, but my financial situation is so bad, a ticket is the last thing I need!" I realized he was flirting with me.

"What ticket?" he said, giving me back my license and registration along with a piece of paper with his name and phone number.

Shocked, I stared dumbly at the piece of paper in my hand. I looked up into his deep brown eyes, and he smiled; showing off a perfect set of pearly whites.

"Are you all right to drive now? I don't want to have to follow you home to make sure you don't continue to ignore red lights and things like that. I'd hate for something to happen to you before we get a chance to know each other," he said, stepping away from the car.

My hands trembled as I pulled into the flow of traffic. I didn't even tell him my name, I thought, before I realized he knew everything about me since I had given him my license.

"Hope your day gets better and better!" he shouted to my receding taillights. I squealed with joy as I drove the few blocks to Momma's house.

## LEAH

Momma looked worse for wear when I got to her house shortly after four p.m. It was a fulltime job taking care of three children, and I could relate. Thankfully, now that I had a job that included day care, I would not have to bother her as much. She pushed us out of the house so quickly, I did not have a chance to tell her all my good news.

At home I fixed a quick supper and I was busting at the seams wanting to share my joy. Then I briefly thought of Marie and became sad. We had only been friends for a few years, but she was the closest friend I had. Old anger surged through my veins when I recalled her senseless murder. She was killed by her boyfriend who then turned the gun on himself. Thoughts of Marie brought me back to Sammie.

I retrieved the cordless phone from the kitchen and went into my room to call Sammie. I needed to tell someone about my day, and Sammie was an excellent choice. She understood adversity and was herself a survivor. She always had some type of drama going on that took my mind off my own problems.

"Hey!" she said as soon as she answered the phone.

I felt a smile cross my lips. I assumed she would be happy to hear from me, but I did not expect this enthusiasm.

"Hey, yourself." I laughed.

"Oh, Leah, I'm sorry, gurl. I was expecting a call at six, and I was shocked thinking he was actually on time," she said, laughing herself. "What's going on?"

"Do I need to hang up? I don't wanna block a booty call," I said, giggling.

"Shit, that's what call waiting is for. If he calls, I'll hit you back!"

"Some things never change. I needed to hear a friendly voice."

"Uh-oh. What's going on now? Did the bastard come running back with some wild-ass excuse?" She was suddenly serious.

"Naw, I still ain't heard from him. But I know he ain't dead!"

"How's that?"

"I called the mortgage company because I got a notice posted on the door for foreclosure. The rat bastard hasn't been paying the note!"

"Aw damn, Leah. What are you going to do?"

"The only thing I can do. Move! I lucked up and this sista took pity on me. She was the loan officer, and she told me Kentee bought another house about six months ago. Of course he's current with that. He told her I was a renter! Can you believe that shit?"

"Damn, he's got some fucking nerve. He's going straight to hell on a silver bullet!" she said with attitude.

"Yeah, but in the meantime, we've got to live."

We were both quiet for a few minutes, contemplating the gravity of the situation.

"Damn, Kentee has it going on like that? Can he afford two house notes?" she asked.

"He's only paying one, remember?"

"Oh, my bad. But still, gurl, he has to be making some big paper to even qualify for two mortgages. Most people can't qualify for two cars, let alone houses."

"He must have it going on, but he never hipped me to it. I scrimped and saved, thinking we were on such a tight budget, and he's been living large."

"I don't even know what to say about this," Sammie empathized.

"You could start by saying that it's all my fault. I should've been more responsible in our relationship and our finances. When it came down to the money, I threw blinders on. I never knew how much money he made and, to be honest, I didn't care as long as he took care of home."

"I understand. I've been there and I was burned by it, too."

"But, Sammie, the reality is, even if I knew what he was making on his day job, he did so much stuff outside of work tax-free," I said.

"What about his clothes? Did he ever come back and get them?"

"Naw, I even counted the number of drawers he left. Nothing's been taken. I want to change the locks on the door, but I don't have the money."

"Yeah, gurl, I don't blame ya. Listen, I've got a few bucks. How 'bout I go pick up a lock and we change it? It shouldn't be that hard," she volunteered.

"Hell, yeah! I'd hate to have him come here when I'm not home. The way I feel right now, he has no right to anything he left in this house!"

"Give me an hour or two and I'll be over," she promised, hanging up the phone.

I sat on my bed, smiling to myself and saying private thanks for my network of friends and family. Without them, I did not think I would have been able to make it.

I checked my answering machine and saw the number from my old job. They had called back but they were not hiring. The next two messages were hang-ups. The numbers were blocked on my caller ID.

Getting up quickly, I went to check on the kids. They had been quiet for a change, and that was not always a good thing in our household.

As expected, Kayla was glued to the television, and Malik was attempting to color in his book. Most of his markings made it on the floor instead of the book.

Mya was sitting in the same place where I had left her. She rarely bothered to play with toys. She took no interest in playing with her brother or older sister. And when she did show an interest in a toy, it was usually one that someone else was playing with, and she fought like a wildcat to get it.

I surveyed our home, realizing it would take a lot of work to pack up all that stuff by myself. I moved from the living room; trying to judge how many boxes I would need. I walked through the foyer that led to the garage door. The garage itself would be a big chore. It was so full of tools that I could not even park my car inside. A light bulb flashed in my head. Kentee had swiped these tools from his day job and used them on the side to make extra money. Although I knew little about what the tools were for, some of them were quite expensive.

I wandered through the garage inspecting each piece; even though I was ignorant as to its purpose. I began to realize that I was sitting on a gold mine and didn't even know it. I made a mental note to ask Sammie about the treasure trove when she got there. If anybody would know how to hock stuff it would be Sammie.

I went back into the house with a little pep in my step. *If I can sell this stuff for at least a couple of thousand, I can make enough to move and get some work done on my car.*

I ran bath water for Kayla and laid out clothes for all the children for the morning. Mya was still on the floor staring into space, so I felt reasonably safe in the bathroom with Kayla. She bathed quickly because she did not want to miss the last cartoon before bedtime.

I washed Malik in short order. He was a no-nonsense bather. He did not like baths, but he knew from experience he would not win by fighting me. He allowed me to do what needed to be done so he could get back to playing.

Mya was the hard one. She detested having her clothes off and hated the water even more. Bathing her was pure hell, and it took all of my energy to get it done. Some nights I did not have the energy for it, but that night I was determined to give her a bath and do her hair. She fought me like a grown-ass woman, striking out and slapping me in the face.

My face stung where her little hands struck, and I had to fight the urge to hold her tiny head under the water. "Come on, God, give me a break! Can't you see I need a little help here?" I roared, and it sucked the fight right out of Mya. She lay in my arms like a rag doll. Stunned, I finished her bath and, wrapping her in a towel, carried her into her bedroom. She cooperated as I put on her nightclothes, and sat up straight and tall as I brushed her silky hair, twisting it into two long braids down her back. Tying her head with a scarf, I laid her down on the pallet I had made for her on the floor. She did not utter a peep when I kissed her goodnight and turned off the light. Before shutting the door, I turned on the nightlight. Basking in the warm glow of my success, I called to Malik.

"Come on, little man!" I yelled.

Kayla was another story. She was working my last nerve. She wanted me to talk to her before turning out the lights.

"Mommy, do you think Daddy knows I've been a good girl?"

I wanted to stomp my feet and flap my arms in exasperation, but instead I put on my patient face and tried to speak without losing my cool.

"I'm sure he does, honey." I never wanted to lie to my children, and lately that was all I was doing.

"I've been trying real hard! Does he know I'm about to go to big-girl school?"

"Yes, baby. He knows you're going to be six in a few weeks and you'll be off to big-girl school carrying your own book bag and lunch box!" I tried to sound as excited as she was.

"Will he be here when I go to school?"

"I honestly don't know, sugar. The important thing is that you know your father loves you; no matter where he is." I hated myself for the lie I told.

"Then why doesn't he come see me?" A single tear slid down my daughter's cheek. I could not form a response to her cry. Although she cried less and less, she was still a sad little girl when it came to her father. So far, I had refused to bad mouth her dad, but each day it was getting harder and harder. It was only a matter of time before I unleashed a load of fury and frustration on an innocent ear.

"I can't answer that, sweetheart. Daddy needs time alone to think. I'm sure he'll call you one day soon," I falsely promised. Kissing Kayla good-night, I turned out the light and shut the door. I had not eased her mind, but there was little else I could do to satisfy her. The doorbell rang. I assumed it was Sammie so I rushed to the door, not wanting the noise to wake Mya.

Sammie came in, loaded down with bags. She had stopped at the liquor store. I was thankful because my kids had taxed all my senses. I did not drink often, but trying times call for desperate measures. We hugged each other, and I motioned her to keep her voice down. We went into the kitchen to unload the packages.

Getting right to work, Sammie peeled open the protective package the lock came in and started reading the instructions as I prepared cocktails. I was so ready for a drink that I was almost drooling. We toasted, and I gulped my drink. It burned all the way down; its warmth creeping down my spine.

"Gurl, I can't ever thank you enough for this," I said, spreading my arms wide. "As much as I wanted to change the locks, I needed this drink more.

Did you get your phone call?" I asked while she continued studying the directions. She brought all kinds of tools with her, and it reminded me of the stash in the garage. "Hey, I need to ask your advice when you're done." She looked up from the directions with a frown of frustration. "Dayum, my bad. Why you got to eye me like that?"

"Because I can't walk and talk at the same time. Figure out what you want me to do, and I'll concentrate on that."

"Sorry to bumrush you, but I know you have a schedule to keep. Kentee left a whole lot of tools. I believe some of them are expensive. Do you know anyone who might be interested in buying them?" I asked.

Sammie held the partially assembled lock in her hand and cocked her head to one side, thinking. I had forgotten how handy Sammie was. When she had had her other car, the old "Flintmobile," she was constantly under the hood fixing one thing or another, and she continued to use those skills.

"What type of tools?" she asked, still not giving me her full attention.

"Plumbing shit, I don't know. You can take a look." I took another sip of my drink.

"If I can't find anyone, Jessie will know of someone."

"Oh, Lawd, you're still fooling around with Jessie?" I was totally dismayed. I did not even want to mess with that fool. I had heard enough horror stories about him. "I don't want to piss you off, but I won't sleep tonight if I don't say this."

"Aw, man!" She tried to shut me up before I started to preach.

"You know where I'm going. Marie would be rolling around in her grave if she knew that you're still dealing with Jessie. That man pimped you, verbally and physically abused you, threatened to kill you, and you're still kicking it with him. That's unacceptable."

"Jessie's not the man he used to be. He's cool. He even got married again, but he still comes around to hit this."

She proudly patted her rotund behind. I shook my head in disgust.

Sammie moved to the door and started taking the existing lock apart while I sat at the table and nursed my drink. My mind was active, and it called up memories that should have been left in Marie's grave. Poor Marie, she fought so hard to keep Sammie on the straight and narrow. Now, despite her best efforts, Sammie was still running amuck. I could not help but to feel that Sammie was disrespecting Marie's memory by even talking with Jessie; let alone fucking him.

"Jessie ain't no good for you," I blurted. "Can't you feel Marie every time you utter his name?" I asked. If she couldn't feel her, I could; enough for the both of us.

Sammie put down her tools and sat on the sofa. Her head rested on her chest, and for a few minutes she didn't speak. Then: "Yeah, I feel her, every day, but she ain't here. Jessie comes through when I need him. I know you don't believe this, but prison changed him. He ain't the abusive man who went to jail in the first place."

"And what changed that?" I found it hard to believe a leopard could change his spots.

"Probably a big burly roommate named Bubba." Sammie cracked up with laughter. I laughed with her because it was probably true. As the laughter died, Sammie got serious.

"I can understand your reluctance to involve Jessie in your life, so you have to answer a few questions. Do you really need to hock this stuff now? Why not move it so he can't get to it?"

"Damn, why didn't I think of that?" I replied. "I really need the money the tools will bring, but I want to also teach that bastard a lesson he won't soon forget."

"You didn't think of it because your ass has too many other things on your brain." She snickered and deep-sixed the remainder of her drink.

Spurred into action, I called my next-door neighbor, James, who had been itching to get in my panties.

"James, it's Leah. I need a favor. Can you come over here?"

"What's up?" he asked in his thick New York drawl. He appeared nonchalant but I knew that he was curious about my late-night call.

"I'll explain when you get here," I told him.

He was at the door almost before I could get the phone back on its cradle. For a moment, I worried about the possessive three-ton bitch he had left at home, but since he did not appear worried, I decided not to give her a second thought. On the other hand, he was obviously thinking about me. He was more than willing to do what I asked and helped me store all of the tools in his truck.

While James and I unloaded the garage, Sammie finished with the locks. When we were finished, I gave James a kiss on the cheek, and he groped my ass while I was within touching distance. James was a good-looking man, but the heman-sized woman living with him killed any desire I might have felt toward him.

I pulled my car into the now empty garage and closed the door. The final thing we did was change the password on the garage door. I did not have to worry about Kentee using his remote for the garage since he had lost it a while ago. For the moment, I felt safe.

"Thanks, Sammie, I couldn't have done this without you. I still need you to hock the tools to raise money for my move," I told her.

Getting her drink on, Sammie barely paid me any mind as she tried calling her male peeps to line up a date for later on. I could not help but laugh at her as she pulled out her Bible-sized little black book. She thumbed through the pages; dialing number after number until she made a score. I wasn't mad at her. I wished I had my own black book.

It had been over six months since I had had my coals stoked, and I was feeling it. That was a long time for someone who was used to get it on the regular. I sucked on my own drink, feeling lightheaded and slightly pissed. Didn't I deserve happiness, too? Obviously not!

"So, have you heard from Tyson?" I asked Sammie when she hung up the phone.

She was grinning from ear to ear. "Yeah, as a matter of fact, I did. He got married and they're expecting my first grandchild."

"Where's he stationed?" I asked.

"He's in Virginia Beach. I went up to see him last week, and they're doing good."

"And your mother?" I asked, thinking all was well in Sammie World. "How is she?"

Sammie's face changed immediately, and I was sorry that I had brought her up. I assumed that time had healed all the old wounds but, obviously, I was wrong.

"Sammie, I'm sorry. I wasn't thinking."

"Gurl, don't sweat it. Althea's going to be Althea. I haven't really heard from her directly in over a year, but she still keeps in contact with Tyson. When she gets upset, she's like a dog with a bone. I hate that woman."

"Sammie, hate is a strong word for your mother," I admonished, forgetting the low down I had gotten from Marie about Sammie's relationship with her mother.

"Shit, she started it. She blames me for everything that went wrong in her life. She even blames me for Kendall's and Marie's deaths. Hell, she didn't even like Marie, but she told Tyson that if Marie hadn't gotten hooked up with me she'd still be alive. The truth is, she had a problem with me from birth. She made my life hell and sold me off in marriage to Jessie as long as he took me out of state. What kind of mother would do that to her child?"

Sammie could not hold back the tears that unexpectedly stung her eyes. I wrapped my arms around her massive shoulders and we cried together for our fallen friend. It had been two years since Marie was killed, and her death was still a very tender subject for all of us who loved her. But the memories were complicated because Marie nursed us both through our individual trials and tribulations.

I pushed myself away from Sammie. "Marie wouldn't want us to cry over her like this. She would want us to celebrate life." I raised my glass toward Sammie in a toast. Sammie wiped her eyes and lifted her glass, but the smile that crossed her lips was not heartfelt.

"That's my Sammie," I said, and we spent the rest of the evening chit-chatting about everything under the sun.

"I have a question I've been meaning to ask you," Sammie said after awhile.

"Shoot," I replied.

"How did you find out Kentee was cheating on you?"

"Initially, I suspected him because of his late hours and overnight business trips. But he made the mistake of leaving his pager here one day when he went to work. It kept going off, and I got curious."

"Gurl, don't tell me you answered his pages!" Sammie whooped out loud.

"No, but I did write down the number that keep popping up. It was the same person every time, and whoever it was called every fifteen minutes."

"Did you ask him about it?"

"Not right away. I pretended ignorance. After about a week, I went in the bathroom and paged his number from my cell phone. I put her number in and put 9-1-1 behind the number. He waited a few minutes and went into the kitchen to get a drink, but I knew he was going to check the page. When he went to bed, I hit redial and got his access code. The rest is history."

"Damn, gurl, you've been watching way too much television." She laughed so loud I was afraid she would wake Mya.

"It got worse. I started checking his voice mail every day, and this heifer would leave him all kinds of sexy messages. I even taped them."

"No, you didn't." Sammie howled.

"Yes, I did! When the shit hit the fan, I needed to have proof. You want the number? You can listen in on his messages, too."

Sammie held out her hand, and I quickly wrote down his voice mail number and the password. She was laughing, her mirth rocking her body. She laughed so hard that the underside of her arms swung wildly. I tried to keep her quiet, for the kids' sakes, but Sammie was not to be cheated out of a good laugh.

"This is rich! I'm going to check it tonight when I get home," she said.

"Check it often. They leave each other all kinds of love messages all day long. It's a wonder he can get any work done, with all the messages she leaves him. Hell, I used to think I was the freak of the week, but apparently the girl has skills."

I tried to sound like this did not hurt me, but talking about it made me feel bad and like less of a woman. Sammie shook her head, then began gathering her stuff.

"Look, gurl, I've got to hit the road. It's a long way home from this god-forsaken town you choose to live in."

"Hey, Peachtree City is the bomb! I have everything I need right here!" I exclaimed.

"Whatever," she replied, following me to the door.

I went to sleep slightly drunk but feeling more secure. I woke sometime around one a.m. with the distinct impression that I was not alone. It took a few minutes before I got my bearings. I thought I heard somebody at the front door, but I quickly dismissed the thought.

Getting up, I went to check on the children first to make sure Mya was not up to anything, and then I checked all the windows and doors. The kids were still tucked in, just as I had left them hours before. I could not shake the nagging feeling that someone had been there. My gut instinct told me to call the police, but I brushed off those feelings and attributed it to the drinking that I had done. Determined to get a few more hours of sleep, I climbed back in bed. I did not have any more dreams, but my sleep was restless.

# SAMMIE

I was grateful to escape Leah's. Thinking about Marie was something I did not like to do. I backed out of Leah's driveway with fresh tears pouring out of my eyes. As much as I loved Marie, my mental health forced me not to dwell in the past. After all, Marie died in my arms, and for a long time I could not forget it.

Every time I closed my eyes, I could hear the shots and the thud of Marie's body hitting the porch. Time stood still as I raced to the door expecting to see Jessie wielding a gun, looking for me. Never in my wildest dreams did I think Marie would be the intended target and the killer would be her own boyfriend. My grief knew no boundaries as I tried to wrestle with it. So I continued to dodge those memories and stray away from conversations that led back to the first friend I ever had. For a minute I was mad at Leah for bringing up the memory of Marie's death. Leah wasn't there to hear the shots; she didn't hold a dying Marie in her arms. I refused to dwell in those memories because those thoughts were detrimental to my health. So I did what any normal person would do, I stuffed them.

"Damn, I straight-up lied," I said, pounding the steering wheel, fighting back more tears. I had not spoken to Tyson since the day he'd left. The only way I knew about his new baby was through my mother, Althea. She could not wait to call me and spread that piece of news. She had left the message on my answering machine.

I picked up my cell phone to call my date for the evening, no longer interested in getting sexed.

"What's up?" Jessie answered. He had the confident air of a man who still controlled me even though he had a wife at home.

"Look, I can't make it tonight." I was praying he would not pitch a fit.

"Bitch, I already paid your ass when you stopped by my shop to get money to help out your pathetic friend. You owe me, and you're going to give it back tonight; in cash or trade!" he declared.

"Jessie, I ain't stiffing you this time. I had a real rough night at Leah's, and I ain't in the mood. If you come by in the morning, I promise I'll make it up to you," I pleaded.

"Wrong, bitch. You'll make it up to me tonight. I'll be at your house in twenty minutes." He slammed down the phone.

I did not want to make him mad. Then he would want to do all the sadistic shit he could not do to his wife, like burn my nipples and bite my clit. I turned up the remainder of the bottle of Hennessey I'd taken over to Leah's house and prayed to get pulled over for drunk driving.

Reflecting, I didn't learn anything from Marie's death and the loss of my child, Kendall. I was still allowing men to control my life, and I felt helpless to do anything about it. I rarely took the trouble to actually analyze my motives, but the long drive back from Peachtree City to Atlanta gave me plenty of time to think.

I turned up the radio so I could drown out my own thoughts, but it was useless. *I should've kept my damn mouth shut about Jessie*, I thought. I did not want to look in Leah's face and see the same reproach I used to see in Marie's face.

Switching gears, I thought about all the stuff Leah had stored in her neighbor's truck. I was going to call an old fuck buddy to see if he knew of a market for the tools. Knowing Jessie, he would want a cut and I would have to pay for it flat on my back. Not to mention the fact that Leah did not like or trust Jessie. Flipping open my phone, I thumbed through my address book for his number. I was dividing my attention between the road and my phone, and not doing a great job at it. I was fucked up, so I did not notice the cop who pulled up behind me until he flashed his bright blue lights.

*Be careful what you pray for*, I thought, as I pulled the car over to the side of the road.

"License and registration, please," the officer said to me. He was a young black guy who looked like he was barely sixteen. I could not tell who was more nervous, him or me.

"I'm sorry, Officer. I was trying to call a friend of mine and the wheel got away from me. I know I should've never been on the phone while driving, but I was lost and trying to get some directions," I said, trying not to expel my hundred-proof breath in his direction.

He waited while I rummaged through my glove compartment for my insurance and registration cards. My license was easier to get since it was the only thing I had in my purse other than lipstick and my cigarettes. I prayed the bottle of Hennessy I had stuffed under the seat would not roll out and show its long neck.

Clearly out of his element, the cop left me sitting in the car and went to radio in my information. Thankfully, I had paid my insurance last week so I did not have to worry about that issue. For a change I had renewed my license on time. There was a time when I drove without either one of them, but today I was legal; at least on paper. He kept me waiting for a good twenty minutes before he came back with his ticket book.

My mind played tricks on me while I waited. I imagined he was waiting for backup. Scared and in dire need to pee, tears flowed unchecked down my cheeks. My hands were shaking and my knees were locked as I finally took my license and registration back from him.

"I'm writing you a citation for failure to maintain the lane. I suggest you take advantage of all the hands-free devices available. It may be inconvenient, but they do save lives," he said, handing me the ticket for my signature.

My drunk ass started to argue with him about barely crossing over the line, but I did not want him calling the cavalry and realizing that I was as drunk as a skunk.

"Thank you, Officer. It won't happen again," I finally said, happy to escape with a ticket.

"Are you trying to get to 285?" he asked me.

I forgot that I had told him I was lost, so his question caught me off guard.

"Yes, sir," I mumbled, still trying to keep my breath from reaching his face. I was sucking on a mint that I had found in the ashtray of my car. It was real foul since it was covered with ashes, but beggars cannot be choosers.

"Follow this road for approximately ten miles. You'll see the exit signs. And stay off the phone," he said, flipping his ticket book closed with a practiced perky snap and turning around to leave.

"Thank you," I said to his back. I felt one of my peeps, either Marie or Kendall, looking out for me, because the young cop had me dead to rights. What was even more sobering was the fact that I knew no one, other than Jessie, who could bail me out if I had been arrested. *Yeah, Jessie would come, but he would make me pay for it for the rest of my life.*

Not wishing to further tempt fate, I pulled off at the next exit and got a motel room. The motel was directly across the street from a liquor store, so I went there and got something else to drink. The Hennessey was not going to last long. If Jessie still wanted to see me, then he was going to have to make the drive to where I was.

I phoned him again as soon as I fixed myself a cocktail and took a shower. The brief encounter with the cop had me sweating like a sow.

"Jessie, I know you're going to be mad, but I got pulled over by the cops when I was driving home. I promised the cop I'd get a motel room for the rest of the night and he decided to give me a ticket."

"Sounds like a bunch of bullshit if you ask me," Jessie snarled.

"If you don't believe me, come to me. I'm at the Holiday Inn Express on Route 216, room 116."

Jessie did not say anything for a moment. I could tell he was trying to figure out if I was telling the truth and I almost started laughing. I tried to mask my amusement by coughing loudly into the phone.

"What's the number to the hotel?" he asked quickly.

"Wait, I'm sure it's on my receipt," I said, putting down the phone to get my purse.

"Hurry up!" He yelled so loud it was as if the phone was still by my ear. I read him the number.

"You probably looked the shit up in the phone book," he sulked.

"Lawd, Jessie. Give me a break. It would've taken a lot longer to look up the number," I said with a sigh. He was messing up my buzz. "If you don't believe me, call back and ask for room 116."

Jessie hung up the phone without another word. I raised my glass to my lips, fully expecting Jessie to call right back. When the call did not come, I began to get a bit more comfortable. Part of me wanted Jessie to come because I knew he would pay the hotel bill, but the part of me that would have to put out was pleased as punch to have outfoxed him tonight.

I sipped my cocktail while I channel-surfed. Before long, I was no longer watching TV. It was watching me. I was rattled from my sleep by the fierce ringing of the phone. Groggy and irritated at being rudely awakened, I snatched up the phone and barked a reply.

"Hello!" I yelled, hoping to bust the caller's eardrums.

"Bitch, who are you hollering at?" Jessie yelled back.

Humbled instantly, I shook my head to clear my thoughts.

"I'm sorry, baby. Someone's been playing on the phone since I checked in. I wanted to ask the manager for a new room, but I didn't want to miss you if you decided to come see me." I was lying through my teeth.

"Then open the motherfucking door."

Stunned, I could not move. Shit, I could not believe his dick led him half-way across the county to find me. This felt like a bad dream, and I wanted desperately to wake up.

"Now, bitch," he growled.

I placed the phone on the bed, whipped back the covers, and snatched open the door, unmindful of the fact I was completely naked. The cool night air caused the hair on my arms and legs to stand up. I looked both left and right and Jessie was nowhere in sight. Rapid breaths exploded from between my clenched teeth. The cool night air, booze, and fear made me lightheaded. I slammed the door and went back to the phone. Jessie was laughing his ass off.

"Ha, ha, ha," I said, not seeing the humor in his sick joke.

"Just checking to make sure you were alone." He hung up the phone. I glanced at the clock, and I got pissed. It was after three in the morning.

"He is one sick fuck!" I shouted to the walls and poured myself another drink. Taking a rather large sip, I shouted at the walls again. "And my name ain't Bitch!"

He rattled my nerves more than I cared to admit. Although Jessie was not as physically abusive as he was when we were married, he still scared me. He only came around me for sex, and he made sure he paid me each and every time. I was beginning to believe that since prison, he could not get it up unless he paid for it.

Sex with Jessie was an adventure. He liked for me to strap on a dildo, and he wanted it up the ass. He even picked out the dildo himself. He also liked to be whipped and purchased a whip and handcuffs that he had left at my house. Heading for bed, I had to admit that I was not partial to the dildo thing, but I loved to whip his ass! I stopped midway between the bed and bathroom and decided to relieve myself while I was still standing.

Misjudging my steps, I stumbled into the bathroom, narrowly missing the tub with my head. I lay on my back against the cold tile flooring, staring at the ceiling, lost in my booze-induced stupor.

*I'll bet I can pee in that toilet from right here! Shoot, if I could twirl multiple pool balls in my twat and predict the order in which they'll come out, surely I can pee in an arc. It's only about five feet. Men do it all the time, and they don't have nearly the muscle coordination that I have.*

I adjusted my position on the cold floor, aiming my twat at the toilet. I positioned my hole in the right direction and focused my alcohol-soaked brain on the task at hand.

"If I do this, I could do it for the *Guinness Book of World Records*," I said, laughing hysterically.

"Concentrate," I whispered and giggled again. I spread my pussy lips and bit down on my lower lip as I aimed at my target. I allowed my mind to become one with the pee and let it loose. Closing my eyes, I envisioned it rising in the air and disappearing in the bowl.

What the hell was I thinking? Not only did I miss the toilet, I peed all over myself! If I did not have to clean the mess up, it might have been comical.

"I'm going to have to practice that," I mumbled as I pulled myself up to my knees, slipping in the process.

"Whew, that was close," I said, looking at the tub that loomed pretty close to my face as I dipped back down. Now that was funny. I turned around and backed my ass on the throne and rested my head on my knees.

Laughter welled up from the bottom of my belly and spread through my throat and out of my mouth. I would never tell anyone what I had done. What seemed so reasonably sane a few minutes ago had become a knee-slapping joke. *Good thing this isn't my apartment*, I thought, as I trudged back to the bed and fell in without even bothering to shower.

# LEAH

I woke Kayla first because she would do most of the work herself while I got dressed. I had a full plate and wanted to get an early start. Malik was next and I left Mya for last since she was the hardest part of my day. As usual, she was not happy about being disturbed, and she fought me all the way. Every time I put one leg in her pants, she would pull it back out.

"Stop," I warned her, smacking at her kicking legs. I knew my actions would be reported to DEFACS if someone other than family witnessed them, but I felt like there was nothing else I could do. It both pained me and satisfied me to give her a taste of what she gave me. I wished that someone could take a walk in my shoes to see what I had to deal with on a day-to-day basis. For some reason, she hated to be naked more than she hated being awakened. It was okay that she kept me up half the night with her tantrums, but let me wake her up and she wanted to act a fool.

"Mya, I love you, honey, but sometimes you make me want to smother you," I said to her as I cuddled her in my arms when she finally calmed down. Today's outburst was relatively mild compared to some of the other mornings we had been through. Dressing Mya was no joke, and I wanted to curl up and get right back in bed after having completed the task.

The second hardest thing was feeding Mya. None of them were picky eaters, but Mya would not eat anything with a sharp corner. I had to cut her food in circles for her to eat it. I purchased a special circle cookie cutter expressly for her. God forbid me giving her a piece of bread without the crust taken off. She would toss the whole thing to the floor and commence screaming.

Mya always seemed to know when I was in a rush, but I finally got her fed.

I wished she would cut the tantrums out altogether so we both could start our day off on a pleasant note.

After clearing up the breakfast dishes, I phoned Momma to see if she was still going to watch the kids while I made my runs.

"Hey, Momma," I said when she picked up the phone.

"Hey, Baby," she replied. Mya chose that moment to exercise her lungs.

"Hush, Mya!" I yelled, frustrated all over again.

"Has she been like that all morning?" Momma asked with a hint of worry in her voice.

"Not really. We fought getting dressed, but she calmed down. She hates it when I get on the phone," I replied.

"That could be it. She requires a lot of attention."

"Who are you telling? I give her all of my attention. I can't have a moment to myself; not even to go take a dump. I have to jump up and see what she's gotten herself into. I'm so tired, Momma," I complained, briefly feeling sorry for myself, but then I remembered the good news.

"You pushed me out so fast yesterday, I didn't even tell you my news! I got a job, and I start on Monday!" I exclaimed, getting excited all over again.

"I can't believe you didn't tell me! I was tired, but not that tired! Where's this job?"

"I know, Momma, I couldn't really believe it myself, so I wanted to savor it. It's a law firm in downtown Peachtree City, and the best part about it is they pay for child care expenses. I need to go over there today and check it out and stuff. I really lucked up; finding something so close to home."

"I could lay you over my knee and spank your behind for keeping this good stuff away from me. Honey, I'm so happy for you!"

"The other thing I need to do is go look at some of the houses they told me about yesterday that are available under something called HUD. It's based on my income, and I was told that because I have three children, the rent would be real cheap."

"When are you bringing them over?" Momma asked, sounding as excited as I felt.

"When you tell me I can. I wanted to get an early start because I don't know how long it's going to take."

"Bring them now. Have they eaten?"

"Yes. Do you want me to bring lunches?" I asked, hoping she would say no since I had not been to the grocery store.

"No, I have something they can eat. Do me a favor. Take a little of your seed money and get your hair and nails done. You need to do something for yourself!"

Prickly tears poked out of the corner of my eyes. "What did I ever do to deserve a mother like you? I love you, Momma!"

"I love you, too, baby girl!"

"And before you know it, I'm gonna stop all this crying. It ain't me and I hate it but I'm not there yet."

I hung up the phone and got the kids loaded up in the car. Running back in the house, I set the alarm, then hurried back to the car. Setting the alarm used to give me some measure of comfort, but since I didn't have enough money to pay the bill, it was a big farce since no one was monitoring the alarm.

I drove the seven miles to my mother's house and dropped the kids off. As usual, Mya had a hissy fit about my leaving her, but I did not have a choice. My first stop was the day care facility. I sat outside and watched to see who was going in and their demeanor. I saw both black and white parents entering the center and, for the most part, the kids behaved like they wanted to be there. That was very important to me. I waited until the last parent had exited the building before going inside. I stopped at the registration desk.

"Hi, may I help you?" the lady sitting at the desk asked me. She had this huge smile on her face that appeared genuine. *Another good point*, I thought. If she had greeted me with a fake smile I would have turned around and left. A day care worker had to love children or nobody was going to be happy. Not the children and certainly not the parents!

"Hi, my name is Leah Simmons, and I'm going to be working at Blank, Rome and Carpenter. I have three children, one age five, going on six, and my twins are two. I'll be needing day care services."

She began pulling out forms, I assumed for registration. "Will your five-year-old be attending school?"

"Yes, so she'll be part-time in the morning and after school. Do you pick up from school, or will I have to arrange transportation?"

"We pick up from several schools. So, the twins will be with us all day."

My collar started to get a little tight. *Now comes the hard part*, I thought to myself. She didn't wait for my answer, and I did not cut her off to give it.

"Before we go further, let me take you on a tour," she said. I followed behind her as we went from one schoolroom setting to another. The classes were small and structured. I saw an art class, reading circle, backyard play area, and a sleepy-eyed circle, complete with sleeping bags and pillows. They also had a kitchen staff to prepare the meals and snacks. In the back of the building was the nurse's office, an isolation room, the director's office, and a break room for the aides. There was another unmarked room that she did not show me.

"What's this room?" I asked.

"The observation room," she replied and continued walking past it. Feeling a little put out because she was withholding information, I dug deeper.

"Can I see it?" I wasn't comfortable with the images that went through my mind when she mentioned an isolation room and an observation room.

"Currently the room is not in use and I don't have keys for it. Let me see if the director's busy. I'll ask him to show it to you." She led me back to the waiting area and indicated I should take a seat.

While I was waiting my mind began to conjure up what could be behind the locked door. Since this was the first time my children would be in day care, I was very apprehensive. I had seen enough stories of day care nightmares on television to last a lifetime. It would be an adjustment for all of us. Kayla was not used to playing with any children other than family members.

Since her siblings were younger, Kayla always got her way. The twins also hardly ever played with anyone else, so it would be new to them as well. Mental pictures of hard steel chairs with handcuffs strapped to them pranced through my head, and it took all my strength not to bolt out the door. I was so deep in thought that I did not hear the director talking to me until I noticed a set of leather loafers standing directly in front of me. I looked up to find another gift from God in the foine department.

"Hi, my name is Mr. Richmond, and I'm the director of this facility."

At first glance he reminded me of Shemar Moore, but more mature. He was impeccably dressed in a gray linen suit and had on a black tie tinged in blue to bring out his royal blue shirt. His eyes were a piercing brown and he had a dimpled smile. He cleared his throat, and I felt stupid for getting caught gawking. He was a fine piece of leather and well put together.

Standing up, I dropped my purse, which I had been holding in my lap. Everything did not fall out of it; just the embarrassing stuff. My lipstick, an old tampon minus the protective wrapper, my birth control pills, and a crumpled condom all rolled in different directions. Dropping to my knees searching for my belongings, I was unmindful of the hard concrete floor as I scrambled to pick up the items. I was humiliated!

He helped me gather my items and I thanked God that he allowed me to scoop up the tampon myself. Way to go, Leah; that was a hell of a way to make a first impression. He was amused by my lack of composure and fought to hide the smile dancing around on the edge of his mouth. My cheeks flamed red. I noticed his extended hand and finally shook it. He told me to follow him and I gladly did so; admiring the view he afforded me. I was so caught up that I bumped into his broad back when he abruptly stopped.

This man had me so off kilter I would have eagerly signed my children up for death camp if he smiled at me. He walked past me and took a seat behind his desk. I sat in one of the two overstuffed burgundy chairs directly in front of his desk. His office was very nicely done in deep earth tones and the carpet was so plush that I wanted to take off my shoes and wiggle my toes in it. He was reading over my application while I continued to look around his office. My eyes locked on his long manicured fingers but stopped when I spotted the gold wedding band.

"Damn," I muttered under my breath.

"Excuse me?" he inquired.

Scared that he may have heard me, I uttered the first thing that came to my mind. "Uh, I broke a nail," I said, holding up a fingernail I had bitten down to a nub that morning. I quickly stuck it in my mouth as if it pained me. *You are so stupid*, I thought to myself. The other nine nails looked as bad as the one in my mouth. I decided I would get my nails done as soon as I left. My nails used to be my pride and joy, along with my hair, but these days I never took my hair out of a ponytail. I put both of my battered hands under my butt and sat on them, waiting for Mr. Richmond to finish reviewing my application.

"Well, Mrs. Simmons, it says you have three children to enroll in our program."

"That is correct," I said, trying to sound more confident than I really was.

"And you had the grand tour, I take it?" he inquired further.

"Yes, all but the locked room."

"I see," he said, frowning.

"You have to understand. My children have never been in a day care environment. In fact, they've never been around anyone else other than my family. I stayed home with my children but circumstances beyond my control are forcing me back into the work force."

"Your oldest will be starting school this year?"

"Yes, she's very excited about it," I said, smiling when I thought about Kayla looking out the window at the big yellow bus that came to pick up the other children in the neighborhood.

"I'll bet." He cleared his throat before he continued. "Will she be riding the bus with the other school aged kids at the center or will you be dropping her off at school?"

"I'd like for her to ride the bus with the other children, if that is okay."

"Sure, that would be fine. You also have a set of twins," he said, looking back down to my paperwork. I did not want to discuss Mya just yet because I did not want to ruin my chances of getting Malik and Kayla in. If push came to shove, I was sure Momma would help me out with Mya, but only as a last resort.

"Malik is the oldest. He came out a full two minutes before Mya. He's a bit of an introvert and likes quiet playing time. He's really smart, too!"

"And Mya?"

"She's a whole different matter altogether. I'll be honest with you. She'll tax your patience to the limits. I deal with her because she's my little girl, but even though she's difficult I don't want her abused. I have to work, but I won't tolerate any threat to my child's well-being."

"Then we're on the same page," he said, closing the folder that was on his desk. "Come with me," he said, pausing to grab a set of keys from his center drawer. I followed him back down the same hallway leading to the locked door.

"We're not using this room anymore, but it was designed with special needs children in mind." He pushed open the heavy wooden door. The room was all white with cheerful decals of Disney characters all over the wall. It was a large airy space that could easily hold twenty children. Looking in from the hallway, I began to realize that this was more like a wing instead of a room.

"Why aren't you using the space anymore?"

Mr. Richmond halted in his steps. He turned to face me. "Currently we don't have any children with those specific needs."

*You do now*, I thought to myself.

Tiny chairs circled miniature tables and stuffed animals were everywhere. A large room beside the play area was completely padded and there was what appeared to be an examination room with several cots. I was impressed, to say the least. I looked at him with questioning eyes.

"We cater to the needs of our children. Whatever the problem, we try to deal with it," he responded. After wandering around for a few more minutes he led me back to his office. I had so many questions, but I liked what I saw at the center.

"I must say that I'm impressed," was all that I could mutter as I sank back down in my original chair opposite his desk.

"This has to be a comfortable fit for all of us as you transition yourself into the work force. Why don't you bring the children over tomorrow for a visit? It'll give them a chance to get used to us before you have to report to work," he suggested.

"Wow, could I?" I asked.

"Can you make it around ten a.m.? All of the children will be settled into their routines, and we'll be able to get acquainted with each other."

"Wonderful," I said, standing up and dumping my purse on the floor again. Not waiting for him to catch its contents, I extended my hand to him and he took it. After I released it, I gathered my belongings with the little pride I had left and tried to make a hasty exit.

"We'll see you in the morning." He nodded his head, barely able to keep in the laughter I saw in his eyes. I left the center mortified but excited at the same time. If I could have done a cartwheel without breaking my damn neck, I would have done two or three. Maybe I was no longer on God's shit list. I was beginning to look forward to the tomorrows of my life instead of thinking about ending my todays.

I stopped at Wal-Mart before going home and purchased a few pairs of stockings and a couple of skirts to spruce up my wardrobe. I decided to go to the beauty shop to get my hair permed. To save money, I had been doing it myself, but I never could do it as well as a real stylist. I also treated myself to a full set of nails and a pedicure. When I was finished, I almost felt beautiful.

I arrived home feeling hopeful, but my mood was spoiled when I checked my messages.

# SAMMIE

Jessie had left at least five messages on my answering machine at work and another ten at home. I was not trying to avoid the unavoidable, but I did not want to get into it with him at work, which pissed him off. I truly expected him to be at my front door when I pulled up, and he surprised me once again with his absence.

I had to pee badly and could not get the key in the lock quick enough. I barely made it to the bathroom, and I gratefully plopped down on the seat and allowed the hot stream to escape. I should have gone before I left work, but I was afraid they would ask me to work late if someone saw me.

I had only been working at Georgia Power for about two months, but I had made a name for myself as a competent secretary. I normally floated from desk to desk when the full-time secretaries took their vacations and spent the rest of my time in the word processing department. The department operated twenty-four hours a day and, as my reputation grew, it was getting harder and harder to get out of the office on time.

Since I was still tired from the night before, I needed to get home on time. So I packed up my things and headed out the door at five p.m. with the rest of the secretaries.

I went to collect my mail from the mailbox after dumping my belongings on the sofa in the living room. The mailbox was crammed full with sale circulars and other junk. I slipped on the slick surface of a postcard, which had dropped unnoticed on the floor.

I picked it up as I headed to the kitchen to find something to eat. The card was from my son, Tyson! My heart slammed against my chest and unwanted fear tore holes into my heart. Through the fear I read the message as tears of joy streamed down my face.

*Mom just thought you'd like to know you're a grandmother. Your granddaughter was born on August 5th, and she weighed in at a healthy eight pounds. She had a full head of black hair, but most of it is gone now. We decided to call her Nicole Ashley, and she's beautiful; just like her mother. Both are doing well. If you'd like to see pictures, call me and I'll send you some. Tyson*

I could not breathe. I never expected to hear from Tyson again and couldn't decide whether to dance or cry, so I did a little of both. I danced until I was dizzy, and when I was finished, I cried big gut-wrenching tears. The tears seemed to cleanse my soul of all the wrong I had done to my children. I wanted to tell everyone but, by the same token, I wanted to tell no one. I was so confused.

I reread the postcard and little things started to jump out at me. I looked at his opening line first, and it hurt me deeply. It had been so long since I heard the word *Mom* coming from the lips of my child that tears began again. I briefly thought of my daughter, Kendall, but her memory was too painful, so I moved on. I recalled how happy I was when I had Tyson. I would finally have someone to love me. I was only a kid myself when I had my children, but Momma never let me be a mother to them. I did not realize how wrong I was until it was too late, as I was ill-equipped to deal with children, and my mother never gave me the chance to grow into motherhood.

I looked at the front of the card, and there was a picture of Virginia Beach on it. Flipping the card back over I noticed there was no return address, but he had included his phone number. I had not seen Tyson since Kendall died, and I had practically forgotten what he looked like. My mother told me he was stationed in Virginia, but she led me to believe that his wife had just got pregnant. The card said that Nicole was born on August 5th, which would make her one month old.

The fact that he had waited a full month to tell me hit me hard, but I could not blame him. I was not a good mother to him and his sister, and I was ready to admit it. But, he had called me Mom, and that proved there was a chance he would allow me to make up for my mistakes. I reached for the phone to lay my heart on the line as it started to ring.

"Oh, now you want to answer the phone, bitch," Jessie snarled. "I've been trying to get in touch with your black ass all day!"

"Uh, I know, but I was so busy at work I couldn't talk to you. I just got here, and I was about to call you," I lied.

"No, you weren't. I seen you when you walked in, and you've been there for thirty minutes!" *Damn, busted again!*

"Well what happened was," I started off, blabbering like an idiot.

"Save it! Open the damn door!" he hollered. I knew he was not playing this time, so I hid my postcard under the sofa cushions and opened the door. He was leaning against the frame of the door with this awful leer on his face.

I remembered when he used to be so handsome, but time and the ravages of drugs and prison had done a number on him. I looked away from his face to my feet. Most days he did not want me looking him in the eyes anyway, and I didn't feel like getting sucker punched that day. I stepped back to allow him to enter. He sauntered in and plopped down on my sofa, putting his feet up on my glass coffee table. I closed the door, leaning back against it while praying for the strength to make it through this session. My heart was heavy, and I didn't have time for Jessie's shit.

Knowing he would not leave until he got what he came for, I started unbuttoning my shirt. I said a prayer that he would cum and go quickly.

"I didn't tell you to do that!" he barked, and my hands froze. I didn't want to piss him off, or he would be there for hours and I would not get the chance to call Tyson.

"What do you want, baby?" I asked, standing with my hands down at my side.

He slowly started to unzip his pants. This was a good sign because I could suck the juice out of his stick in a matter of minutes. Jessie could never last long when I put my full lips around his dick. I grabbed a few scattered pillows off the couch and put them on the floor. Jessie scooted up to make his dick more accessible. I glanced up and his eyes were closed in anticipation.

He smelled faintly of urine, but I blocked it out. Closing my eyes, I ran my tongue up from the base of his penis to the very tip. I ran it down to his full sack, and took each one in my mouth while gently squeezing the tip of his penis with my fingers. When I finished washing his balls I returned my attention to his dick. It was throbbing, and I quickly put the entire thing in my mouth. I worked hard, imagining that I was sucking a blow pop, working my way to the center. I took less than ten deep-throated sucks to get to the center, and he was finished.

He roughly pushed me back from his flaccid dick. I was not surprised by his rough treatment. We had been down this road before. He felt weak when he came, and he detested weakness in himself and in those around him. I would have paid him money to know what went through his mind. Without my asking, he threw two hundred dollars at my head and zipped up his pants.

"See you Wednesday. And don't make me wait!" He snatched open the door and slammed it shut. I got up off the floor and lay facedown on the sofa. Humbled, I got to my knees and prayed to God for guidance. I wanted to take the money and burn it, but I was not a damn fool. I had earned it! I do not remember how long I stayed on my knees, but when I finally stood up, it was dark outside, and I had lost circulation in my legs. I stumbled to the door and locked it. I wanted to call Tyson, but I felt unclean, so I decided to take a shower first. Wiping my foul-tasting mouth with the sleeve of my shirt, I headed to the bathroom. I turned the shower on to get it as hot as I could stand it; even though it was going to wreak havoc on my hair. Thank God for braids.

I peeled off my clothes and left them lying in a pile in the middle of the floor as I stepped into the streaming water. Water flowed through my micro braids as long-ago memories resurfaced. Cleansing my soul, I forgave myself for Marie's death. She was my best friend, shot and killed by her boyfriend, and she had died in my arms. I forgave myself for my daughter, Kendall's death, when she had used my pills to kill herself. I even accepted my role in the demise of my relationship with Tyson.

It was a long shower as I tried to wash away all the wrong I had done. I accepted the pain I had inflicted on my friends and family, and prayed like never before. I prayed that God would give me the strength to begin again, and this time on the right foot. Leaving the shower, I felt rejuvenated and hopeful.

After oiling my damp body, I put on my robe. I went into the kitchen to find something to eat, but my stomach was all in knots. I would find no peace until I had actually talked to Tyson. I pulled the phone close to the sofa and curled my long legs underneath me, taking in deep breaths to calm my nerves. I fished out the postcard I had hidden, quickly punching in the number before I chickened out. It rang four times before Ashley picked up the phone.

"Hello," she said, and I could hear my little grandbaby crying in the background. The sound bought tears to my eyes, and my mouth was suddenly so dry I could not even swallow, let alone talk.

"Hello," she said again, this time with attitude.

"Uh, Ashley, good evening," I said, clearing my throat. I thought about grabbing a drink, but I did not want her to hear the ice cubes rattling in the glass. I was rooted to the sofa.

"Yes," she said, with growing impatience. Nicole was getting louder by the second.

"Uh, this is Tyson's, um, this is Sammie."

I heard a muffled conversation in the background, and the baby immediately stopped crying. Tyson picked up the phone.

"Hello?" he said.

"Tyson, it's Sammie. I got your postcard, and I can't tell you how happy I am for you and Ashley. Was that Nicole crying?" I asked, waving my hands in front of my face to dry up the perspiration that appeared on my forehead.

"Yeah, she's loud, isn't she? She was hungry, and her momma was taking too long," he said, and I could hear Ashley getting ready to fuss her damn self.

"I can't wait to see pictures. Will you send me some?" I asked with my fingers crossed. I hoped he was not playing a sick joke on me.

"You're just getting the postcard?" he asked.

"Yes, just now," I replied.

"I mailed it two weeks ago."

I grabbed the card and saw that he'd sent it to my old address and it had been forwarded.

"Oh, I see. I've moved, and I guess it took the post office a minute to find me," I said, suddenly happy that he had not waited an entire month to tell me about the birth of my grandchild.

"Sending it was Ashley's idea. When you didn't call, I thought…"

"Ouch," I said. "I deserved that and then some. I can't change the past. I was young, dumb and stupid. Your grandmother wouldn't allow me to raise you and when I got the opportunity, I didn't know how. But if you give me a chance, I'll change the things to come."

He didn't answer me right away, and I was afraid he had hung up on me. After a few more minutes of silence, he said, "What's your new address?"

I gave it to him and we talked. It was not the heartfelt reunion I had hoped for, but it was a start. I went to the kitchen and fixed a much-needed drink. I wanted to ask Tyson if I could come see the baby, but I felt it was too soon. Not to mention the fact that I was new on the job and had not earned any vacation time yet.

I made my way back to the sofa and noticed the money Jessie had left balled up on the floor. I decided to take a hundred dollars of the money to open up a bank account for Nicole. I would use my social security number to open the account, but I would get it transferred as soon as I could. It would be my first order of business in the morning before something else came up preventing me from doing it, and once I got Tyson's address, I would mail the passbook to him. I was so happy I felt like I would split into a million pieces if I did not talk to someone.

Feeling great, I called Leah to tell her my good news, but she did not answer the phone. I finished my drink and went to bed.

# LEAH

The message light on my answering machine was blinking furiously when I got home. After getting my nails done, a perm, and my eyebrows arched, I left the salon feeling like a million bucks. I had dipped into my nest egg, but with the way things were going, I felt like we were going to be okay.

"Now it's you who looks like something the dog drug home," I said when Momma answered the door earlier.

"That child of yours wore me out today. I lucked up when she cried herself to sleep," my unsmiling mother said.

"I'm sorry. She has days like this, and I can't explain it to people when they ask me."

"It's not your fault. You're working on finding out what's wrong with her. That's the first step."

"Exactly, and I think I'm on the way to doing just that. Momma, you should see this day care center. It's beautiful, and I have such a positive vibe about the place. I feel like they can actually help Mya!"

"How do they plan on doing that?"

"They have an entire medical wing, with doctors on staff. I'm taking the kids over there tomorrow to get them used to the place," I said excitedly.

"Sounds good, baby," she said, finally looking at my hair. "Oh, look at you. Now you're looking like my baby again," she said, kissing me on the cheek. I grabbed her in a full-bodied hug. Kayla came tearing down the hall screaming my name. I had kept my voice down to have some quiet time with Momma, but apparently the cat was out of the bag.

"Oh, Mommy's pretty," Kayla said, playing in my long brown hair that reached halfway down my shoulders. She told me I looked beautiful, and I actually felt like I was.

"Momma, I gotta run. Get your things, Kayla," I instructed as I packed up her brother and sister. Kissing my mother on the cheek, I left and drove home still basking in the glow of a pleasant day.

Once I got the kids settled, I planned on calling Sammie to see if she had any luck with the tools. Momma had had a rough day with Mya, and it showed in her eyes. Mya's face was distant and remote. Mya beat her head twice on the floor and spent the next three hours crying after I left.

In a few days I would know if my application was accepted for the house, and I would start work on Monday. I had three hundred fifty dollars left from the money I had received from the church, some food stamps I could sell if things got tight, and the potential for more money from the tools James was holding for me.

It was well after nine that night before I got my alone time. I pressed "play" on my answering machine as I sat down at the kitchen table.

"Where the fuck are my tools?" Kentee's angry voice shouted at me from my answering machine. His voice was so loud it felt like the machine was vibrating. Startled at hearing his voice for the first time in months, I struggled to breathe. "You better not have fucked with them. I'm coming over there tomorrow and they better be there!" There was a loud click.

*Coming over here?* I thought. *That explained why I had felt so uneasy the other day. The bastard had been in the house! How? I had the locks changed!* The second message started to play.

"Leah, don't fuck with me!" The phone went dead. I grabbed the phone to call James to get the tools back before Kentee came back around. The third message began to play, and I stopped the machine. I didn't need to hear one more threat from Kentee. *Fuck the tools. With the money I'd be making, I didn't need his stinking tools. I'd file for child support and alimony and hit his ass where it hurt; his wallet.*

"May I speak to James, please," I said when his Sumo Wrestler wannabe girlfriend answered the phone.

"Telephone!" she yelled.

"Yeah?" James said.

"James, I need to get the tools back into the garage tonight."

James did not utter a sound.

"James?" I said with a sinking feeling in my gut.

"Uh, I thought you came and got them. When I checked the truck this morning it was empty."

"How the hell could I have gotten them when they were in your truck in your locked garage?" I yelled at him.

"I didn't take them. I swear!"

"I didn't say you took them, but where else could they be? I'm not stupid, and I don't appreciate anyone trying to play me for a fucking dummy! You had possession of the tools, and unless you want me to call all my cousins and their friends to come kick your ass, you better return them. No, I have a better idea. I'll tell Kentee you stole them, and we'll see what happens then." I stomped my feet in irritation. I was bluffing big time, but he did not know me well enough to realize it. I wished I had that kind of backup because I would have had Kentee's ass kicked.

"Uh, Leah, wait."

"Wait hell! I'm not taking an ass-whipping unless I get something out the deal. You better ask your dyke girlfriend, or whoever else has access to your garage, where the fucking tools are, or the next visit you receive will be from Kentee!" I slammed down the phone.

Stunned by this new twist of events, I did not know what to do first. I picked up the phone to make sure Sammie was not involved in the removal of the tools, and paced the floor as her phone rang.

"Hello," Sammie's seductive voice serenaded me. "Sorry I can't come to the phone, but if you leave your name and number, I'll make it worth your while!"

"Damn," I said, slamming down the phone without leaving a message. She had caller ID, and if she was anywhere near the phone she would call me back soon. In the meantime my wheels were still turning. Grabbing the phone again, I banged out Kentee's voice mail number. After a brief message, I began to rant.

"Oh, so the dead finally rises. How dare you fucking call my house cussing me when you broke in here in the first place? I filed a police report for the television, DVD player, and the stereo. And I know you took the fucking tools, too, so don't try to play like you've been the victim!" I was lying my ass off, but he did not need to know it. "Well, you had better fence that shit fast, you lowlife, deadbeat fucker, before the cops find you!" I hung up the phone, pissed enough to blow smoke out of my nose.

I was lying my ass off but I knew that Kentee would not want the cops involved in his life, so I sat by the phone waiting to hear back from him. Even though it was still his house and he did not technically break in, he would do what he had to do to keep the peace.

It did not take long for the phone to ring, and for Kentee's name to appear on the caller ID. I did not answer it because I was still too angry with him. I waited until I saw the blinking light on my answering machine before I mashed the button to listen to his message.

"Hey, baby, I know I have some explaining to do, but I couldn't face you. I still love you and the kids, but I wasn't cut out for family life. I felt like I was being tortured every night when I came home. I was wrong for bolting without talking to you first. Don't do nothing stupid like calling the cops before I've had a chance to talk to you, okay? I'll call you back in fifteen minutes. Please answer the phone," he said.

*Well, ain't that a bitch. He wants to be my baby now! He said he ain't cut out for family life, but he's shacked up with some stank heifer? How stupid does he think I am?*

He used the same charming baritone voice that talked me out of my panties on the night we had met, and I had to harden my heart against falling for that shit again.

The most surprising thing, though, was the realization that, despite all the stress and pain, I still loved the rat bastard. He was the love of my life, and I had not figured out how I was going to deal with those feelings.

When the phone rang again, my heart made the decision my brain refused to. All he had to say was, "Baby, I wanna come home," and it would be on!

"Hello," I said in my most seductive voice, not even checking the caller ID.

"Why didn't you leave a message?" Sammie smacked her gum loudly in my ear.

Disappointed, I tried not to let Sammie know she was not who I was expecting.

"Gurl, please. I knew you'd hit me back as soon as you saw my number pop up." I laughed to mask the tears I wanted to shed.

"I just got off work. What's up?"

"Gurl, issues! Either James stole those tools, or Kentee broke into his garage and took them!"

"The slimy bastard!"

"I know that's right. You didn't tell anyone about them, did you?"

"Naw, Jessie was tripping when I didn't see him, so I didn't even mention it. To be honest, I forgot all about them until now."

"Shit, part of me was hoping you did get someone to get them. I could use the money. So either James is trying to fuck me, or Kentee has them. I called James and threatened to have his ass kicked, and I told Kentee I'd called the cops on him for breaking in. I accused Kentee of stealing my television and DVD player. I accused him of stealing my stuff because the police are more than likely to believe a woman over a man; just in case Kentee insists on filing a countersuit for theft. And, if that happens, I'll need to stash the goods at your house."

Her silence told me that I could not count on Sammie for help. She had her own dealings with the "popo" and I could not get mad at her for not wanting to be involved in my drama. Was it a vague threat? Did I have any merit? Hell no, but the implied threat was enough. Shrugging my shoulders, I mentally devised Plan C.

"What are you doing?" I asked.

"Nothing right now."

"Can you come over? I met this cop the other day. I'm going to call him and ask him to stop by. I really don't want to be alone with him."

"Why?"

"'Cause my ass is so horny I might jump his bones as soon as he walks through the door!" I replied as Sammie squealed with laughter.

"Have you already invited him? I'd hate to drive all the way out there for nothing."

"Oh, so I'm nothing now?" I said jokingly.

"Naw, gurl. You know what I meant."

"I was just kidding. Hold tight and let me call him. I'll hit you back."

"Okay, but don't be all damn night. If I don't come out there, I'm sure I can find something else to do with my evening. I can't wait until you get a babysitter so we can hang out. Tonight's Chippendale night at the Mirage, and I'm going."

"Chippendale night?"

"Gurl, you've been shut in far too long! Male strippers and I'm here to tell you they are fine!"

"Wow, I've never been before. I need to have my ass somewhere to see niggas slinging dick! But in all honesty, that's the last thing I need to see. I might grab hold of one or two, and won't want to give them back," I said, laughing. "Give me a few, but I'll call you back either way."

"Alright." Sammie was still laughing as she hung up the phone.

In spite of the cool air flowing through the vents of my air conditioner, icy sweat broke out on my brow as I located Coy's numbers. It had been several years since I had phoned a man other than my husband, and I was truly out of practice. Coy gave me two numbers, but he did not tell me which was which. I hoped the first number was his cell because I really wanted him to come over tonight. He answered on the second ring. *Please remember me*, I silently prayed.

"Yello?"

"Um…hello. Um, Coy, this is Leah. We met a few days ago. Do you remember?"

"Of course, beautiful. How could I forget?"

Flattered, I paused to mop my moisture-beaded brow before going on.

"I hate to call begging, but I need your help. I realize I don't know you, but I have a situation going on. I need to get a jump on it right now before it escalates and gets ugly. Could you come over to my house?"

"Now?"

"As soon as you can. It's important, but not life-threatening."

"Should I throw on my uniform? Today was my off day, and I just got home from the gym."

"I don't know. Could you bring it? After I explain, you decide whether it might help the situation. You can change here if necessary."

"I thought I'd have to wait a while before I could change clothes in your house" He chuckled. I chuckled also, getting a visual of him naked. I was not giving him a whole lot of information, but he still agreed to come.

"Let me jump in the shower. I should be there in forty-five minutes."

"Thanks, Coy." I exhaled the breath I had been holding.

"Hey, don't thank me yet. I haven't done anything. See ya in a few." After he hung up the phone, I dialed Sammie back and asked if she could be there in an hour. This would give me enough time to explain the situation without giving me *any* time for slippage out of the panties! I was horny as hell and did not trust myself enough to be alone with a foine man. I was thankful I had taken the time to get my hair and nails done; just in case I slipped and fell.

For the next thirty minutes I ran around the house hiding things that should have been put away. It was not the best camouflage job, but it would have to do.

With less than fifteen minutes to spare, I raced into my bedroom to change clothes. I selected a form-fitting pair of black jeans and a square cut T-shirt that implied cleavage without shining a spotlight on my breasts. My nipples showed clearly through the thin cotton fabric. I tried thinking about taxes to make those suckers go down, but it did not work. I was touching up my makeup and applying perfume when the doorbell rang.

I flew to the door, hoping to catch him before he rang it again. The children were asleep and I wanted to keep it that way. After inquiring who it was, I snatched open the door. Coy looked better in blue jeans than he did in uniform. The long sleeves of his uniform had hid his bulging biceps, which were now clearly displayed by his muscle shirt. The tight fit of his jeans accented his meaty thighs.

*Sweet Jesus*, I thought, as I stepped back to allow him to come in. A rich, musky sent floated under my nostrils, and I had to stop myself from following it. I was so glad Sammie was on her way because I was having difficulty understanding the need to keep my hands to myself. This guy was fucking gorgeous.

"Hey, sunshine!" he said as I closed the door firmly behind him. I rested against it as I checked out his "phat" behind.

"Hi, yourself," I managed to get out of my suddenly dry lips. "I was about to get a Coke. Can I get you anything?"

"A Coke will be fine for now. Do you have any beer?"

"Sure, if you like Bud."

"Let's deal with the situation first; then I'll take a beer."

"Okay, be right back. Have a seat."

I switched into the kitchen as I waved him toward the sofa. Earlier, I had turned on a soft jazz station, but I should have put on some foot-tapping rap music to get rid of the sexual images playing out in my head. As I reentered the room, I began explaining my situation.

"I told you that my husband left me and my children for another woman, and I hadn't heard from him in more than six months. He called for the first time today."

"Damn, baby girl," was all he could say, shaking his head. He took his glass from my extended hand and placed it on the glass cocktail table in front of him.

"This was my past; up until the day I met you. Since then, I'm looking forward to a new job and possibly another place to stay; one that's nicer than this dump!"

"I'm listening," he said, raising his glass to take his first sip of soda.

"I was angry about my situation and my girlfriend, who's on the way over here by the way, and decided to hit my husband where it hurt; in his wallet."

"How so?" he asked.

"When Kentee left, he took some clothes and all the money in our joint bank account. He left a shit load of plumbing tools in the garage that I intended to sell. Before you say anything, I realize I was wrong, but I wasn't thinking clearly. I had a complete stranger tell me that my husband has another family in Clayton County."

He chuckled. "So, you were going to have a *Waiting to Exhale* Moment?"

My shoulders bunched up and my hands balled into tight knots. I started to kick his ass out, but I guess he read my mind.

"Wait, Leah. I'm not here to judge you." Coy raised his hands in the air to stop me from blowing up.

"Thanks. Anyway, my girlfriend helped me change the locks on the doors, and I asked my neighbor to store the tools in his truck until I could find a buyer for them."

"Okay," he said, gazing into my eyes and making me lose my train of thought.

"You're going to have to stop looking at me until I finish this story," I said, batting my eyes.

"Oh, my bad. I didn't realize I had that effect on you."

I chose to ignore his statement; no matter how true it was.

"When I got home today, there was a message on my answering machine from my husband asking about the tools. He said that if I don't give them back, he's going to hurt me, and I'm scared. The problem is my neighbor, all of a sudden, doesn't know where the tools are. He says they must've gotten stolen from his locked garage."

"Oh, give me a break," Coy said.

"That's what I said. The second part of the problem is that I'm sure Kentee was in here the other day; even though I changed the locks. That's the only way he'd know the tools are gone."

"Whew!" Coy said. "Okay, let me think about this for a minute." He sipped his Coke. The only sounds in the room were the clinking of ice cubes in our glasses and the soft jazz playing on the stereo.

"Did I tell you how pretty you look?" he asked, throwing me completely off guard and causing me to blush.

"No, you didn't, but thank you. You're looking mighty nice yourself," I replied, meaning every word.

"OK, back to business. I can talk to the neighbor and see what he says, and we'll take it from there, but I have a feeling the tools you disposed of were previously stolen. I've got hot sheets in my car and, if I'm not mistaken, a large number of tools were taken over the last few months." Standing up, he put his glass on the coaster and headed toward the door. For a crazy moment, I thought he was leaving.

"Let me get my uniform and pay a friendly visit to your neighbor." He left the house, then came back in the door talking.

"I'm not a lawyer, but you do have rights since you're still legally married to him. The law won't force him to continue to pay the mortgage until you go through the abandonment case, but if what you're telling me is true, the house will be foreclosed on before you can get on the docket. Since you're not feeling safe, I'd suggest the first thing you do is file a restraining order against your husband."

"I can do that even though my name is not on anything?" I miserably asked. "He told the mortgage company I was a renter." I looked at my watch and realized Sammie was late.

"That's actually good news; believe it or not."

"How so?" I was clearly confused.

"Has he served you with eviction papers?"

"No, of course not. His children live here," I stated indignantly.

"Wait, let me finish. As a tenant, he can't drop a bomb on you like this. He has to give you more notice than the sheriff knocking on the door. That's straight up scandalous if that's what he's intending. Did he contact you at all?"

"No, tonight was the first time I heard from him since the day he left to go to work six months ago!"

"Good. Now, as far as the tools, does he have a bill of sale for them?"

"I've searched every piece of paper he left and I can't find it. Maybe he has it with him but, somehow, I doubt it."

"That's even better. If he asks you again, your response should be, 'What tools?' I want you to go to the courthouse in the morning and file that order. Play the tape for them. That's your protection if he tries to come back into the house. Tell them that you're afraid for the lives of your children and for yourself. Save all future messages from him, in case it winds up in court, but somehow I don't get that feeling. What I'm about to say, you didn't hear from me, okay?"

"Sure," I eagerly answered.

"Under no circumstances admit that there were ever tools in the garage. If he wants to be Billy Bad Ass, tell him to file a police report, and I'll handle the rest. Once we file the order, if he tries to enter again, we have him in violation of the restraining order."

I breathed my first sigh of relief.

"That sounds good, but will it work?"

"It will, if you follow my lead. I could get my ass in a sling for telling you this stuff, but I like you, and I hate to see a woman put through some bullshit 'cause of a stupid ass nigger following his dick around. Next question, how well do you know your friend? Would she have been involved in the removal of the tools?"

"No, not at all. Sammie and I have been friends for years. She wouldn't backstab me like that. Now, she might try to steal my man, but something like this? Naw, no way!"

The doorbell rang and I quickly jumped up from the sofa to grab it before Sammie laid on it. She came in talking. She was dressed in a short white dress that made me want to cover my eyes and pray for her soul.

Sammie was such a beautiful woman, but her style of dress left a lot to be desired. She could have taken lessons from other large women who dress more appropriately for their size, but Sammie was all about flaunting her stuff. Her makeup was done to perfection, and I chose to focus on that instead of her skimpy attire. I glanced at Coy. His mouth was wide open. Shutting the door, I turned to Sammie and made the introductions.

"Sammie, meet Coy. Coy, meet Sammie."

"Damn, gurl, where you been hiding him?" she said, sitting across from him on the love seat. Her legs were slightly parted, and for a moment Coy's eyes lingered on the split.

Clearing my throat, I said, "Earth to Coy!" to bring him back into our conversation.

He shook his head and looked back at me with a sheepish grin. I threw dagger-like looks at Sammie for showing up in her hoochie momma outfit.

"Where the hell are you going?" I asked with attitude.

"Gurl, I told you it's Chippendale Night! I got to shake what my momma gave me!"

"Gurl, your momma didn't give you all that. You grew it on your own!"

"Oh, you got jokes," Sammie said, slightly pissed off.

"Oh, you mentioned it, but with all that's been going on, I forgot! We were just discussing the tools and their whereabouts."

"OK," she said, gazing at Coy like he was the last lollipop in the country.

"Look, let me change. I'm going to pay your neighbor a visit to see if I can jog his memory; possibly scope out his garage. Where's the bathroom?"

I directed him. While he was gone, Sammie started pumping me with questions.

"Gurl, if I had a nigger that fine in my living room, the last thing I'd do is call for backup. I'd have his ass backed up against the top side of my mattress!" she said with a throaty laugh. "His ass would be calling for backup!"

"As if that thought didn't cross my mind! Gurl, please, it was all I could do not to touch those muscles!"

"Heifer, please. When God gave out looks, brotherman was standing in line three or four times!" she said, raising her hand for a high-five. I damn near slapped it off because she was so very right about Coy. He had it going on in all directions. He was great to look at, and he was not an asshole. I hated that I had to involve him in my drama, but I needed help.

# LEAH

Coy came out of the bathroom and I swear to God, Sammie and I were panting for breath. I felt like he had taken all the oxygen out of the room, and we were struggling to use the little left in our lungs. All of a sudden I was pissed that Sammie was there. He was oblivious to our stares and all about business.

"Leah, I'll be back. Can you name any of the stuff that was in the garage?"

"He had an industrial-sized sewer trencher, pipe cutters, and some other stuff that I had no idea what he used them for. All I know is that it looked expensive; especially the electric stuff."

"That's good enough. Be back in a few. If all goes well, you'll get either the tools or the money. If things don't go okay, will you back me up if the shit starts to stink?"

"Of course," Sammie and I both responded.

Driving his official police vehicle, he drove next door as I watched from the window. After a few minutes of brief conversation, I saw Coy enter James' house.

"Gurl, does he have any brothers? I don't care if they're ninety with one foot in the grave and the other on a banana peel, as long as they look like him!" Sammie raved.

"I don't know. This is the first time I've spoken to him since we met. I was so wrapped up in this shit that I didn't get the 4-1-1. I just hope his ass is single and that bulge in the front of those jeans wasn't made by a wad of Kleenex!"

"Gurl, I know what Kleenex looks like. That's Grade-A beef up in there! Do you still need me around? I have to find my own beef jerky for tonight, if you know what I mean!"

"I hear ya. Thanks for coming by. If he's talking right, I'll handle my business!" I said, slapping fives with her again.

"Don't forget to ask about the brother thang or someone else that looks as good as he does. He's got my pussy wet!"

"Gurl, you're too much! I'll call ya."

I was embarrassed by Sammie's vulgar words. Sammie never failed to shock me with her candor.

My own shit was wet, but I was not about to admit that to Sammie. I liked Sammie because she believed in keeping it real, but I was not verbal about animal attraction and fucking. Although the tapes played in my mind, I would never let anyone see my show.

Coy came back an hour later waving a wad of green bills with a smile on his face. "When you go file the restraining order, you might want to stop by the bank and open up an account!"

"You're kidding me? How much did you get?" I was elated.

"Seven thousand five hundred dollars," he said with a broad grin.

He handed me the money, and my hands trembled as I accepted it. That would be more than enough money for me to move and to have a little nest egg to fall back on in hard times. I was calculating all the things that we needed and was not paying much attention to Coy.

"Leah," Coy said, snapping his fingers in front of my face.

"Sit down." I did what I was told to do without any further questions.

"Your neighbor did try to screw you. He sold the tools to a fence and he agreed to roll on him, if I left him out of it. That's fine, but the bigger problem is that the tools were stolen. I have a sheet on them in the car. Some of them had been engraved, but I'm ninety-eight percent sure that these tools are the ones. I'm going to check your husband's record out to see if he worked at the locations of the thefts. If he did, I'm going to have to bring your husband in. Are you okay with that? He could be facing some big time since the amount involved is considered grand theft. Are you okay with that?"

"Wait, I'll be right back," I said, going into the kitchen and grabbing two beers. All of a sudden I needed one. I handed him one and sat back down beside him.

"Let me make sure I understand you. You're asking me if it's okay to put the man who left my kids and me for another woman with no food, no money, and a piece of car that's about to fall apart in jail? A man who was about to see his family put out in the street with no remorse? A man who told me that no wife of his will ever work and then leaves her? Are you talking about the same man who called and threatened my life? Oh, hell yeah! I'm down, all right," I said as I raised my beer to clink with his.

"Hey, where's your friend?" he asked, looking around.

"She had to leave, but she made me promise to ask if you had a brother or a friend that looked as good as you. I told her she couldn't have you!" I giggled.

"That's rich. You tell her that I don't have any brothers, and my closest friend is married. It's a shame, 'cause he likes his women big, too!"

"And you? How do you like your women?" I asked, wanting to get closer, but afraid of being rejected.

"There's nothing wrong with a little meat on the bones, but I don't want to have to roll my woman in flour to find the wet spot." He laughed.

I once thought that Kentee was the best lover in the world but I quickly learned he was just humping in the dark. Coy's eyes swept over me as I attempted to turn out the light. He reached over and grabbed my hand before I could flip the switch. Startled, I looked at him and saw the hot lust in his eyes. Never in my life, had I been fucked with the lights on and the images that flashed across my mind, I must say, well, it made me hot.

"Turn around." His voice was heavy.

Nervously, I twirled around, licking my lips, hoping Coy would not notice my imperfections.

"Slow down, baby, what's the rush?"

I stood rooted to the floor, unsure what he actually wanted from me. Slowly, I raised my hands over my sagging breasts as he motioned for me to turn around. I followed the slow rotation of his fingers with my eyes as I slowly spun in front of him.

"Leah. Drop your hands. I want to see you."

My cheeks flushed red as I realized I was naked in front of a man that wasn't my husband and who I had just met a few short days ago. I willed my arms down to my side and closed my eyes pretending this was actually normal.

I completed the turn, and he exhaled.

"You are beautiful."

This melted the ice for me a little.

"Come closer. Step into the light."

"What's the scar on your right shoulder?"

"I ran into the jagged end of a fence when I was twelve playing kick the can with my friends." I laughed as the memories of running around without a care in the world filtered back into my mind.

Coy ran his finger over the raised scar sending shivers down my spine. He licked the scar and stepped back to see even more of me.

"Your breasts...did you know one is longer than the other?"

I sucked in my breath. Was he making fun of my sagging tits?

"The twins favored the right, while Kayla favored the left."

"I think I like the left one." He stepped forward again and gently fondled my breast. His touch shot liquid pleasure through my pussy. When his tongue replaced his fingers I could feel the moisture dripping down my legs. My nipples snapped to attention, jutting out as he suckled my breast as if expecting to receive the nourishment of my body. A small sigh escaped my lips. Coy stepped away and it was all I could do not to follow him and stick it back in his mouth.

"Spread your legs," he commanded.

I did as he instructed no longer feeling nervous.

"Not that way. Put your leg on the sofa and lean back. I wanna see."

Again, I followed his instructions. His penis was throbbing and I could see the swollen veins running down his shaft.

"What's with the scar on your stomach?"

"It's from my c-section. The twins had to be taken at the last minute."

He ran his finger across my stomach, tracing the edges of my scar, and when he reached the end, he bent down and kissed it, too. I was so caught off guard, by his tenderness. He ran his hands over my waist and on down to my hips, resting his hands there for a brief minute. My mouth became parched and my lips felt dry and cracked. I ran my tongue over them and willed some spit into my mouth.

He dropped to his knees, his face inches from my hot pussy. I expected him to touch me there but he didn't. He maneuvered his body until he was lying flat on his back, looking up at me. For a few seconds, he didn't move and I started to get uncomfortable again. His eyes roamed my body and my pussy screamed at him to get on with the fucking!

He scooted along the carpet until his face was directly under my pussy. He inhaled deeply as he ran his hands up the inside of my thighs as far as he could reach. He then ran them down my outer thighs. He rose up on his elbows for a closer inspection.

"You have some moles."

Oh Lawd, I hate those things. I wanted to have them removed but never seemed to save up enough money to do so. There were three of them. One mole was on the left lip of my pussy and two smaller ones were on the right lip. In all the years of my marriage, I don't believe Kentee even knew they were there because he never took the time to really look at me like this. I lowered my hands, wanting to cover them up and I attempted to put my leg down.

"Don't, Leah! Everything about you is beautiful."

I expected him to kiss the moles as he had done to every other imperfection but he gently turned me over so he could view me from behind. Not wanting to turn my head and look at him, I stared blindly ahead, unsure what to expect.

"You have a wonderful ass." I looked back to see Coy, on his knees palming my ass. He kissed each cheek and I glanced at him to catch the expression on his face. His eyes locked with mine as he licked the crack of my ass.

"Bend over." He didn't have to tell me twice! I was touching my toes like an athlete even though it had been years since I had been in that position. Unused muscles screamed at me, Bitch is you crazy? He ran his tongue from the top of my clit to the crack of my ass and I just wanted to holler. He licked my neck, my back, my pussy and my crack! The lyrics of that song played in my brain. Lick it good! Lick it real good! It had been too long and I felt myself approach the edge of sexual release. I didn't want him to stop but he withdrew his tongue. I felt cheated.

"Will you sit on my face?" Boy, that was a dumb question. I attempted to sit on his tongue, facing his dick so I could taste him as well but he stopped me.

"No, Leah. This is for you." He turned me around and I lowered myself onto his face. My knees sunk into the carpet and grew warm as I rode his face. His hands urged me closer and I briefly wondered weather or not I was smothering him. But it was a fleeting thought as I got into the groove.

Pressure was building up and I struggled to hold it back. "Yes. Oh yeah, baby. I'm almost there, don't stop." I was a frenzy of movement rubbing and mashing my breasts together trying to cram them in my mouth. Despite my best efforts to hold on, I came in Coy's mouth. I attempted to get up so I wouldn't drown him but he held me firmly in place. I arched my neck and let him have it while uttering a low growl.

When I came again, this time crying out in pleasure, he allowed me to move. I rolled over onto my back. He sat up on one arm, using the other to wipe the cum he didn't swallow off his face. He smiled at me.

"I love the way you taste." I could only smile back at him, I was so utterly satisfied. He moved with the grace of a panther and in the blink of an eye, he was over me, lifting my legs off the floor. As he lowered himself he pulled my legs around his waist and plunged into my wet pussy. I could not contain myself as I screamed out his name. He filled me so deeply; I thought he was all up in my stomach instead of my pussy.

Coy pulled out and I thought he was going to stop. I stared at him as if he had lost his damn mind but he was fucking with me as he plunged in even deeper this time. I wrapped my legs around him so tightly I knew that he wouldn't be able to wrench himself free again. My pussy lips clamped down on his dick catching him in its grip. This time, it was Coy's time to scream and I smiled knowing I was returning the pleasure that he was giving me. I came again. My legs relaxed their grip, I was through...but Coy wasn't.

He flipped me over like I weighed 10 pounds instead of 150 and quickly entered me from behind, pounding against my ass and despite my fatigue; I pushed back to meet his every thrust. We were both sweating profusely but his sex was just so... damn... good! His cock throbbed inside me causing my orgasm to scream free and I felt his hot cum explode inside me.

Oh Lawd, no condom! Regret seized me as he rolled off of me. I was a strong advocate of safe sex but this time, we were truly caught up in the moment. Regret gave way to content when I snuggled next to Coy's sleeping form. All I knew was that I just got the fucking of my life. He not only fucked my body, he fucked my mind.

With my arms curled around my midsection, I thought about what had just happened, and I could not help but to browbeat myself. There were so many things that I did not know about Coy, and I had not waited to get those answers before I rolled into bed with him.

*What the hell was I thinking! Shit, I ain't no better than Sammie. He didn't even have to ask for my shit. I was throwing it at him!*

I did not know if he was married or shacking and, at the time, it didn't matter. Now that I was alone with my thoughts, my inner voice told me that I screwed up. I feared Coy would think that I was easy simply because I jumped in the sack with him on the first night. But, there again, as much as I wanted to berate myself for my wanton behavior, I was satisfied, and I deserved to be satisfied!

If he was going to bolt after he got the panties, he would do it, and that was the bottom line. The length of time that we had known each other wasn't going to make a bit of difference if he decided that he only wanted a "Wham bam, thank you, ma'am."

Before Coy left, he assured me that he would call me when he had my husband in custody. I told him that I was going to be busy for most of the day and left it at that.

"Oh, it may take a few days, but if you hear anything else from your husband, save the tape. Don't forget to file the restraining order. If you suspect he's been back over here call me right away, and I will pick him up. I want to go after the fence first. Hopefully he'll roll on your husband."

Coy showed me a few things that I could do to alert me if someone had been in the house.

"I know you've got baby powder, right?"

"Yeah."

I retrieved it. Taking the bottle, he scattered a small amount around the front door since we would be leaving by the garage. He left the bottle by the door, as if I had left in a hurry. He didn't want Kentee getting curious as to why I didn't clean up the mess. We wanted Kentee to show up; not expecting anything. He also suggested sticking a piece of gum under the door in the garage. If it had spread then more than likely the door had been opened. Those were the only entrances that I had to worry about, other than the windows, and he put powder on them.

"Oh, avoid contact with James. If he becomes a problem you have my cell and take my beeper number," he said, grabbing the pad next to the door and jotting down the number.

"How can I ever thank you?" I asked.

"Hey, most of this is my job. The rest is personal. Just stay sweet and safe." He closed the door behind him. "Lock it!" he yelled through the door, and I complied.

I had another full day ahead of me, and I was more than a little tired after last night's antics. If I didn't get all of my business handled tomorrow, I would be screwed for work on Monday.

# SAMMIE

The parking lot at Mirage was jam packed when I parked my 2002 royal blue Mustang in the last available spot. I waited until all arriving partygoers entered the club before I squeezed out of the car. There was no question about it; Mustangs were not built for someone my height and size, but I would not trade my car for the world. It had a convertible top. I loved the feel of the wind rushing past my face. Since this was the last few weeks of Indian Summer, I had taken advantage of the warm breeze as I drove from Peachtree City to the club. It was a hassle to secure the top before going into the club but, by next month, I would be glad that I had indulged myself when we were forced to wear winter coats and stuff.

In a car, I was much like a dog trying to get its head out of the window. I insisted that my car be a five-speed. While most people felt it was a chore to shift gears, I loved it! I needed to feel the horsepower shift underneath me.

As I moved closer to the door, Nick, the bouncer, recognized me and pulled me to the front of the line. Since I was a loyal patron, they had finally gotten my name on the VIP list. It was long overdue, since I paid so much money into the club that I had to add it to my budget as a weekly expense; much like food and shelter. And if I got honest, it was the one bill that I never fell behind on.

Tonight, we were celebrating the homegoing of Cha-Ka-Zulu, the number one Chippendale dancer. His untimely death had taken everyone by surprise. V103, the local radio station, had been advertising a celebration all day long. I was ready to get my party started. As a symbol of respect, everyone was wearing white. He had died over the weekend in a nasty motorcycle accident. The details of his death were still trickling in, but Porsche Foxx, the host from the radio station, wanted us to show out for him.

From Porsche's reports, we learned that he was a newlywed and an expectant father. Although he had recently applied for both life and health insurance, he died before his coverage had become effective. Tonight's party was to raise funds for his widow. I was happy to help out, even though the bouncer told me I did not have to pay the fifteen-dollar admission the rest of the patrons were paying.

For once, the club had as many male patrons as female. I was on the prowl, as visions of Leah's policeman danced through my head. *I sure hope she bones him 'cause if she doesn't, she's a damn fool,* I thought. Normally I would pay for a private lap dance but that night I wanted more than a mere brush with dick.

I was a bit put out when I saw several of my coworkers seated at a table directly in front of the stage. I had talked about the party all day long and none of them had bothered to tell me they were coming. Even though I would not have teamed up with any of them, I still felt slighted. Part of me wanted to pull a chair right up to their table, but I stopped myself from doing it. If they wanted me to join them, they would have invited me. After all, this was my space on the map, and I intended to show them where the real party was. I was on a first-name basis with all of the dancers. I chose a table directly across from their table and acted like I didn't know them from Eve.

Tanisha was the ringleader, and Sherrill and Tanya followed her around like lap dogs. Even when we were at work, you could not approach Sherrill or Tanya and ask for their opinion without Tanisha answering for them. I had a real problem with that. I did not respect any woman who could not speak her own mind.

When I sat down, Tanya nodded her head, but Sherrill did not even raise her eyebrows. For the life of me, I could not understand why they did not like me. Tanya was wearing a white midriff top and a short white skirt. She could have been cute if her teeth weren't so fucked up and if she tamed her nasty attitude. She reminded me of Mr. Ed, the talking horse.

Tanisha was light-skinned with big breasts and hazel-colored eyes. She normally wore her hair in a long bob that she constantly flipped as if to remind herself that she had hair.

Sherrill was petite with a mild manner, but she tended to get loud and obnoxious when she hung around Tanisha. That was the main reason I did not hang around her either. Sherrill, by far, was the best looking, and by herself, she was a decent person, but she allowed other people to influence her decisions. Her biggest problem was that she did not own a brain. She rented one from Tanisha.

For a moment, I considered going to the other side of the room entirely, but they had the best seats in the house, and I refused to be put in the shade 'cause of their dumb asses.

Porsche announced the purpose of the party, and a hat was passed for additional collections. Cha-Ka's wife passed the hat and I could not help but shed a tear or two for her loss. Cha-Ka was a very special person to the audience of the club. He performed a lot of community service work including feeding the hungry with his motorcycle group and Toys for Tots. I guess that's why it pissed me off that those bitches from work didn't give a dime. This ignited a spark that would continue to get fed as the night progressed.

"Hey, ladies, are you ready to get this party started?" Porsche yelled into the microphone.

"Oh, hell, yeah!" I yelled, coming to my feet and clapping. The bitches finally noticed me.

"Oh, snap, Sammie, my home girl, what's up!" Porsche yelled, coming off the stage to give me a hug. "Ya'll know how we do it, and if you don't, listen up. What goes on in the club stays in the club! Do ya'll hear me?"

"Yeah!" I screamed with the crowd.

"Oh, Candy," Porsche said, as the screams died down. "I said, Oh, oh, oh, Candy." The intro to "Candy" by Cameo started playing, and the lights dimmed. Porsche took a seat next to me, and I could feel the hate coming from the next table, and I loved it.

Candy pranced his fine ass on the stage, and it got hot in there. He gyrated his short, thick legs, illustrating sexual moves that made all of our panties wet. He did a handstand, then started doing pushups like he was hitting it for real. "Sweet Jesus!" was the cry from the female population. When he did a one-armed handstand, a few women pretended to faint. He allowed his legs to split, and his toes touched the floor as he balanced himself on his head.

Porsche jumped up and stuck a twenty in his g-string, and I quickly followed suit. His dick was looking us right in the face! Women rushed the stage, trying to get a bird's eye view, but the bitches remained seated. When Candy's show was over, Porsche climbed back on stage.

"Lord, that's all I want! Just give me a limber man!" she shouted to the cheering crowd. Sean, the fireman, was next, but he replaced his rubber hose with his dick. He actually invited members of the audience to touch and suck his hose. Tanya looked like she was about to faint as I headed up to the stage. I had rehearsed this scene before, and I did not actually suck his dick, but I put on such a show you would not have known it unless you were privy to it. We both carried on so badly, you would have thought we were having sex on stage.

I made a point to stare directly into Tanisha's eyes as I backed my thing up on Sean's dick. When we were done, he tongued me down, and I left the stage. This was the only part of the act that was not staged, and I decided he was going to have to do a lot more than that tonight.

"Dayum!" Porsche said as I left the stage. "I ain't even gonna ask you how it felt 'cause I can see it in your face!"

"Hey!" I shouted and sat down.

I kept my eyes front and center and avoided looking over at the bitches. Sean blew me a kiss when he finished collecting all the money thrown on stage.

The next five acts were run together in homage to Cha-Ka. It showcased all the different costumes that he wore and his most outrageous dances. It was so touching that Porsche and I clung together and cried. There was nothing sensual about the dancing because we were all remembering how he had touched our lives with his acts of kindness and generosity.

After that, the rest of the show was a blur. I rose from my seat and started to work the room. I wanted to find a hot body for the night, and I would not find it looking at those dancers. Truth be told, most of them were gay anyway, and by that time I was hotter than a Texas grill at a barbecue.

Before I could make an entire circle of the club, I found an old fuck buddy who I knew could deliver the goods. I told him my new address and phone number and agreed to meet him there within the hour.

I went to the bathroom to freshen up and was stopped from entering it because of a small fight. Tanisha was in a screaming match with some lady, and before I could even understand what was going on, another lady snatched Tanisha up by the hair, then held her by the neck while another girl beat the shit out of her. My gut instinct was to walk away, but I could not stand to see that shit.

Snatching off my earrings, I punched the hell out of the girl holding Tanisha's hair and neck. She stumbled back, then came at me like a banshee. The other girl was wildly throwing punches but hardly made her mark because her eyes were closed. Tanisha was raining blows down on her, and I almost felt sorry for her. The sad part was that, even though we didn't start the fight, we ended it. They ran out of the club in shame. Regardless of who won, management tried to kick me out of the club and revoke my VIP card. Claiming to have left my purse at the table, I used that as an excuse to get with Porsche and straighten out the entire mess.

"Oh, Sammie, I'm so sorry!" Tanisha said.

"It's cool!" I squared it with Porsche. She wouldn't let them evict me like that. I brought too much money to the club. "What the hell was that about?" I asked.

"Hell if I know. I've only seen one of those girls before in my life, and I can't remember where it was. Thanks. My friends took one look and ran out on me," she said.

"No problem. It wasn't how I envisioned my evening, but I was not about to stand by and watch that shit; especially since we work together. I'll see you tomorrow," I said as she turned to leave. My nerves were rattled as I reentered the club and sought out Porsche.

# LEAH

Mya woke up the entire house at about four a.m. She was in her room screaming when I got there, banging her head on the floor. Despite the number of times that I had seen her doing that, it always hurt me. For the life of me, I could not understand what was going on in her head that she felt compelled to try to knock herself out.

She was so intent on hurting herself that she did not miss a beat as I flung open the door. I snatched her up, but she bucked against me as if I was trying to harm her instead of her doing it herself.

"Lord, I wish I could understand!" I screamed at the ceiling. She was such a little thing, but when she got in her moments, she was as strong as a grown man. It took all my strength to keep her from hurting herself even more. She had a huge knot on her forehead, but I had to wait for her to stop fighting before I could get ice for it.

It took the better part of fifteen minutes before I got her calmed down. I kept rubbing her arms and legs, and kissing every part of her body I could reach. Her brother and sister were in the doorway silently crying. They had seen this scenario too often, and there was really nothing that they could say or do to make Mya stop.

"Kayla, baby, get me some ice in a towel," I said when I realized that she was in the room. She ran off to get the ice, and I told Malik to go back to bed.

"Your sister must've had a nightmare. I'll stay with her. You get some sleep," I told him. He reluctantly turned and headed back to his room, but I could hear him crying. I made a mental note to go tuck him in when I finished.

I gathered Mya up and took her back into my bedroom. She was completely still and laid as straight as a piece of wood. She did not even flinch when I put the cold compress on her forehead. Her eyes remained locked and fixed on her demons.

When she stopped whimpering, I went to tuck in Kayla and Malik. Both had fallen asleep, but neither bothered to put covers around themselves. I covered them up and went back to get into bed with Mya. She was in a deep slumber, but her eyes were wide open.

I was so wired that I could not get back to sleep. I got up and ironed all of our clothes and took a bath. I took extra time with my makeup and hair. I wanted to make a good impression; especially since Mya was going to come in so beat up. Looking at her face, I could understand why people thought I abused her, but for the life of me I could not understand what was going on in her brain.

I had taken her to a succession of doctors, and none of them could identify the problem. Something was wrong with my baby, and I was determined to find out what it was.

I let the kids sleep while I fixed bacon and eggs for breakfast. Then one by one I dragged them from the bed and into the bathroom to get dressed. Mya was so listless I was afraid to take her to the day care center, but I had to give them all a chance to get used to it before I dropped them off on Monday.

I pulled into the center about ten-thirty; both Kayla and Malik got excited. They saw the jungle gym in the front yard and assumed they were going to McDonald's. Mya did not put up a fuss as I unloaded her from the car seat. I carried her as Malik and Kayla ran ahead. The lady at the desk remembered me from the day before and came to my rescue. She bent down and talked to Malik and Kayla.

"What's your name?" she asked Kayla.

Smiling broadly, Kayla spelled it for her. The lady wrote her name on a tag and put it on Kayla's shirt. Glowing, Kayla turned around and showed me.

"See, Mommy?" she said with pride.

"Ain't that nice." I struggled to hold back a smile. She was so proud of her handwritten name tag.

Malik grabbed the lady's hand and boldly shouted, "Malik, Malik, Malik!" The lady wrote down his name using a different-colored marker. She stuck on his name tag, and he beamed as well.

"I got one, too!" he shouted, clearly pleased.

"I'm going to take them into the classrooms, but I'm sure Mr. Richmond will want to see your daughter. What's her name?" she asked as she prepared to make her a special name tag.

"It's Mya. M-Y-A," I spelled out to assist her. Small tears formed in Mya's eyes, and I felt it was because she could not tell the lady herself.

"My name's Mrs. Simpson," she said, smiling at Mya. She left us alone as Mya lifted her head to look around at her surroundings. I felt her tense up in my arms, and I waited for her to start screaming, but it didn't happen.

Mr. Richmond came down the hall with a big smile plastered on his face. He stopped in front of us and lifted Mya's head from my shoulder where she buried it when she saw that he was there for her.

"May I?" he asked as he gently lifted her from my arms. Mya surprised me and did not act a fool. She wrapped her legs around his torso as if he were her own daddy. That was a first. Mya did not take to strangers.

"Leave them with us for a few hours. We need to establish a relationship. We want them to be comfortable here. If you can, come back between four and five," he said, winking at me.

I backed out of the door without a peep out of Mya. Checking my watch, I realized that I had a good six hours to kill.

I dropped off my completed child support claim forms that I had filled out in the wee hours of the morning. I also began checking out the other HUD houses that were available. Since I had a little deposit to work with, I was feeling more confident. On every application, I noted the urgency of my need to move. Although I would have liked to move before I started to work, I realized the wheels would not turn so quickly. I did let each realty agent know that if the application was approved, I would have to move and sign all documents on a Saturday. That did not appear to be a problem.

My next stop was the police station. I filed for a restraining order that would keep Kentee away from us until we moved. I had to let them hear the tapes.

That bothered me, but not as much as it would if he came and actually tried to harm us. I was given a case number, and I called Coy to let him know what it was.

"Hey, baby," he said when he answered the phone.

"It's done," I said with a huge sigh.

"Good, because I know where he is. Your man has been busy, and it's only a matter of time before we have him. It's crucial that you let me know if he contacts you, or even worse, if he tries to get in your house."

"Okay," I said.

Coy didn't mention anything about trying to see me again, and that was okay. At least he was still willing to help me.

"What are you doing tonight?" he inquired and my heart soared.

I didn't want to let him know how happy those few words had made me, so I just mumbled, "The same old same old."

"How 'bout I bring some movies and we just chill?"

I paused a few seconds to rethink my plans. I would not be able to chill with him until at least ten p.m. and, by that time, I would be ready for bed. If I wanted to spend any quality time with him, I would need a sitter.

"What time are we talking here?" I asked.

"About seven or eight," he said.

"I'll have to call you back to confirm. I need to see if my mother will keep the kids."

"That's cool. Just hit me back on my cell," he said.

Glancing at my watch, I still had a good three hours left to kill. I decided to pay a visit to Marie's grave. It had been a while and I was feeling guilty.

I sat on the grass facing Marie's grave and I could not stop the tears from falling as I tried to bring her up to speed with all the things that had been happening in my life. It was coming up on the third anniversary of her death and, despite my own problems, I could not rest until I paid my respects.

Marie was the first true friend that I ever had and, even though a number of years had passed, my pain was still as fresh as if she was just taken away from me. For a moment, I could not catch my breath as I rubbed my chest over my aching heart. I remained silent as I collected myself.

Marie's grave was covered in flowers and well-tended. I could see that her children had also visited within the last few days. Through my tears, I saw the picture propped against the headstone as an anguished wail escaped my lips. I reached for the picture with trembling hands. Kiera was wearing a gown and the resemblance to her mother was uncanny. But the biggest surprise was Kendall. He had shot up like a weed and was so handsome.

"Damn, Marie, your ex was only a sperm donor. There ain't no denying that these are your kids!"

I laughed for the first time since I had parked the car. They both were smiling broadly in the picture and I wondered what the occasion was. I turned the picture over but it offered no clues. I made a mental note to call Ms. Morgan when I got home. It had been too long since I had spoken to her and the kids.

"Girl, what can I say? I wish I had listened to you about Kentee. As much as I hate to say it, you were right."

I shook my head and leaned back, staring at the cloudless sky. Bitter memories flooded my mind and I choked back another sob.

"I'm sorry I haven't been to see you in a while but things ain't going so hot for me. I've got three kids now. Did I tell you? Yeah, gurl, I had twins and that shit ain't no joke. Mya and Malik are two. Wow, it's been over two years since I've visited but life is kinda hectic."

I laughed again at my understatement. Who the hell was I fooling? I was ninety-nine percent sure Marie was looking down on me and screaming. She always accused me of walking around in denial and it hurt to know that she was right about that also.

"I do have good news. Motherhood has forced me to grow up. How come you didn't hip me to that shit?" I smiled as a visual of Marie formed in my mind. I wanted to make this an upbeat visit but my problems were weighing me down.

"Who am I kidding?" I raised my hands for emphasis. "Marie, this shit is hard. Mya is special. She demands all my time and energy! Sometimes I feel like giving up. It's no wonder Kentee left me."

I wailed. Ominous thunder rumbled loudly in the sky, causing a chill to run up my spine. My shoulders shook as another burst of tears overcame me. I pulled my legs to my chest and lay my forehead on my knees. I gave up all the pretense and bravado and had a soul-cleansing bawl. Marie knew my heart and, I had no doubt in my mind that she also knew of my troubles.

I was so preoccupied with my thoughts, I did not see the woman who approached Marie's grave from the right. Startled, I swiped at my face attempting to erase the crazy evidence of my pity party.

The woman was very attractive and looked familiar but I could not place her. She carried a small arrangement of pink and purple flowers that she laid on Marie's grave.

"Sorry to interrupt you. I tried to wait until you finished but it seems like you have a lot of catching up to do," she said, taking a few steps backward.

"Oh, that's okay. I thought I had the place to myself."

I rose to my feet. I brushed the dirt from the back of my jeans and attempted to control the wild wisps of hair that had been dancing in the wind. She was casually dressed but her hair was sculptured. I could not shake the feeling that I had seen her before.

We stood there in silence for a few seconds. She lowered her head and closed her eyes. I watched her, trying to figure out where I knew her from. Remembrance danced around the edges of my mind but I could not hold it still long enough to grab it.

She turned to leave. "Have a nice day."

"Wait!" I reached out to touch her arm, stopping short of actually touching her.

She looked down at my hand like it contained a weapon. "Yes?" she inquired in a guarded manner.

I felt real foolish for detaining her. "Your face looks so familiar to me."

"I saw you at Marie's funeral."

"Oh, okay," I replied. I rubbed my hands on the seat of my pants and held out my hand to shake hers.

"My name is Leah," I said, smiling at her. She was obviously a friend of Marie's and any friend of Marie's was a friend of mine.

"Uh. My name is Kia." She seemed uncomfortable as she took my hand and barely closed her fingers around mine.

"Nice to meet you. Your name sounds familiar but I can't place it. Were you a relative of Marie's?"

"Uh. Well. Uh." Her face was getting red and I was sorry I was pressing her for details that she obviously didn't want to give. Strange.

"Please forgive me. I didn't mean to pry. Marie was my best friend and I thought I knew all of her friends," I explained, backing away to give her some space.

A single tear rolled down Kia's face, piquing my curiosity once again as to her relationship with Marie. "She dated my brother," she whispered as she lowered her head.

Realization dawned on me and I struggled to control my emotions. She was the sister of the guy who killed my best friend. No wonder she was uncomfortable. Rage began to build inside my body and my knees trembled. I felt the urge to reach out and snatch a handful of her long brown hair. Standing straighter, I withdrew my hand.

"I see." I turned my back to her to keep from hitting her smack dead in her mouth.

"Wait, please don't prejudge me. I also cared about Marie," she said, as if that would make things any better.

I began to gather my purse and belongings strewn about on the ground. I was hot. I wanted to scream at her and demand that she leave. I wanted to ask her why this had to happen! I wanted to choke the shit out of her!

"Wait," she said again, too loudly for the deserted graveyard. I looked around to see if anyone was watching us.

"What?" I snapped back, only wanting to get as far away from her as I could.

I instantly regretted snapping at her when she started crying harder. I forgot that she had lost someone who she cared about as well. Her shoulders slumped and she swayed on her feet.

"Can we go someplace and talk?"

"About what? There's nothing to talk about."

"Don't you want to know what happened?"

She had me there. I did want to know, more than anything, but I also didn't want to give her any satisfaction.

"Please," she prodded.

Slowly I turned to face her. Her eyes were wide and pleading. Tension drained from my neck and shoulders as I unclenched my hands.

"I'm listening."

"Not here, please. Could we go for coffee or, better yet, a drink?"

I glanced at my watch. I still had a couple of hours before I had to pick up my kids. I was torn between my desire to know and a more overwhelming urge to run. Curiosity won out. I followed her to a small bar and grill on Peachtree Street. We didn't talk until we each had taken a sip of our Long Island iced teas.

"Thank you for coming. I've wanted to contact you for some time but I didn't know how."

"Yeah, everybody that you could have asked is dead," I stated sarcastically.

I didn't mean for it to sound as harsh as it did but I couldn't help it. Neither of us spoke for a minute and I was getting anxious. I looked at my watch and tapped my foot impatiently on the floor.

"You're angry and I can't blame you. I was angry at first."

"You're damn right, I'm angry. Marie was the sweetest person I've ever known. She didn't deserve to die. I'm angry because her children are growing up without a mother!" My voice started to rise and I was getting mad stares from the other patrons. Kia didn't say a word. Her eyes refused to meet mine.

"Marie was good for my brother. He came a long way when he met her."

"A long way? What's that supposed to mean?"

"When his wife left him, he snapped. He lost the will to live. He wouldn't eat or sleep. Hell, he wouldn't even take a bath."

"Obviously we aren't talking about the same man."

"That's why I said Marie was good for him. He started caring about his appearance again. He was getting his life back in order."

"Give me a break. I don't have time for this shit. You're trying to set that nut up to be some sort of saint. In case you don't remember, he shot my friend in cold blood!"

"He wasn't responsible for his actions. He'd only been out of the hospital for two months when they met," she said, trying to keep her voice down so I had to move in closer to hear her.

I took a sip of my drink. "Humph. So I guess next you're going to tell me that he wasn't taking care of your mother."

"Is that what he told her?"

"Hell, yeah. He said that he'd given up his condo and moved in with his mother because ya'll didn't have time for her."

"Ow, that hurts," she responded. Silence filled the space again as I reflected on what she'd said. "Norman lost his condo when he got fired from his job. He wasn't taking care of Momma; it was the other way around. He stayed in that hospital nearly eight months. When he got out, he had to be supervised to make sure he stayed on top of his medicine."

I was stunned. Suddenly I remembered Marie complaining about the fact that Norman never spent the night. She thought he was a momma's boy and couldn't stay out. Things were starting to make sense.

"We didn't find out until after his death that he had stopped taking his medicine and seeing his therapist. We suspect he was with Marie all those times he told us that he was going to the doctor appointments but we'll never know for sure."

I started to get mad all over again. "Why didn't you tell Marie about his history? This entire thing could've turned out differently if you would've shared this information."

"I beat myself up about that at least twice a day. I wanted to tell her but he seemed to be okay. We were all so happy that we overlooked the small signs."

"Dag, he seemed so…uh, normal." I was no longer angry with her. Truth be told, she had lost as much if not more than I had.

"So, do you know what happened to them?"

I shrugged my shoulders. Even though Marie was dead, I was uncomfortable talking about her personal business. I concentrated on the melting ice in my glass as I forced myself to remember.

"Norman started off fine. He was the perfect gentleman and had a way with her kids that really got to Marie. Then he started to change. He was rushing the relationship and that frightened Marie." I considered mentioning the fact that he had a little dick but, at that point, it seemed irrelevant.

"I can imagine how he was acting simply by the things I saw when he'd come home from her house. He was bouncing off the walls, but he was happy."

"Well, he started dropping by unannounced and Marie was real funny about that. She didn't even want me popping up on her so she lost it when he showed up. She tried to discuss it with him and things went downhill from there."

A tear rolled down my cheek and I quickly swiped it away. Kia reached across the table and grabbed my hand, gently squeezing it.

"Thank you. You don't know what it was like not knowing. Norman and I were very close. I thought he told me everything but I guess he decided to keep this to himself. He never let on that they were having problems."

Draining my glass, I stood up to leave. "I've got to pick up my kids. You take care of yourself, okay?"

"You, too, and thanks again."

Kia didn't get up and when I reached the door, I turned back to look at her one more time. She had her head down but I could tell that she was crying. I wanted to go back and comfort her but I was out of time.

I considered going back inside to get her number so we could stay in touch but talked myself out of it. Lawd knows I had enough drama in my life and it would be my luck that she would turn out to be as nutty as her brother.

"Sorry, God, not today," I said, pulling out quickly just in case she was thinking of keeping in contact with me. I had one more hour of freedom left. I had given the center my cell phone number. So far, no one had called me. To say I didn't want to do a drive-by was an understatement. That is why I went to Momma's. She would keep me occupied until it was time to pick them up.

"Those kids are going to be okay; if you will stop smothering them," Momma stated vehemently.

"Oh, you're one to talk. You're still hovering over me," I said with a smile. We had such a good relationship. I could not help thanking God for sending me such a special mother. "Have I told you lately how much I love you?"

She laughed. "Oh hell, what else do you want?"

"Momma, I'm serious! I really appreciate your support. I couldn't have dealt with this without you." I stopped smiling, turning serious. "Do you know that just last week, I contemplated killing us all?"

The room grew silent and, as much as I didn't want to, I forced myself to gaze into her eyes.

"You can't mean that?"

I nodded my head. "It's true. If I'd had a gun, I really think I would've done it. I can't stand to be a burden on anyone. The mere fact that that bastard left us to fend for ourselves made us a target. At the time, I thought it was my only solution. Now, I'm glad that I held on to my faith that God would bring us through this."

"I am too, sugar. I would've hated to have to dig your body up to whip the tar out of you!"

"Oh, I'm better now, but it was rough going. Things seem to be turning around."

"So, do you want to tell me his name?" Momma asked.

Blushing, I lowered my head, avoiding her eyes. I did not realize my emotions were so transparent.

"How could I not notice? This is the first time I've truly seen you smile in years. Whoever he is, he is doing you some good!"

"I just met him, but he seems really nice. He's the police officer who pulled me over the day when I got the job. He wants to come over tonight and watch some movies, but I told him I'd have to let him know. Lord knows I don't want him to see Mya acting out so soon."

"Why not let them stay here with me? I'm not doing anything tonight, and they need to start breaking away from you."

"Momma, you do enough for me. I don't want to take advantage of you!"

"Let me be the judge of when I've had enough. Feed them first and bring them over after they're through. You can get them tomorrow after lunch," she said, giving me my last Saturday free before I started work. I was happy enough to sing but, unfortunately, I couldn't carry a tune in a bucket, so I simply left to go pick up the children.

## SAMMIE

Porsche was talking to someone who had her back to me. She was my height, but she was a slimmer version. When she turned around it was like staring in the mirror at a woman who was at least forty pounds lighter than me. With the exception of the weight, she could have been my twin.

"Holy shit!" we said in unison.

"Damn," Porsche said. "Sammie?" she asked of my double.

"No, my name is Jasmine!"

I started to feel weak in the knees, and looked for something that would support my weight. "Damn, you look like me," I croaked, wiping the perspiration gathering on my forehead.

"Well, I'll just be dipped," Jasmine said, shaking her head. "Is this some kind of trick?"

"I've been talking to her for the last fifteen minutes, thinking she was you! Are you two related?" Porsche asked. *Clearly Porsche had had one too many apple martinis if she mistook the lady she was talking to for me.*

"I've never seen her before in my life!" we both exclaimed. I scratched my eyebrow; a nervous tick I'd had since childhood.

"Excuse me, but we need to talk." Without waiting for Jasmine to reply, I grabbed her elbow.

"Wait, I wanna know, too!" Porsche screamed, starting to follow.

"No!" we said at the same time.

"Sorry, Porsche. We have to figure this out ourselves," I said as we inched our way through the club until we reached a quieter spot. Neither of us wanted to be the first to speak. The shit was so weird that I didn't know where to begin. Then, at the same time, we blurted out, "When is your birthday?" It was so funny that we both burst out laughing.

"Mine is November third," I said.

"Oh shit, so is mine," Jasmine replied. Suddenly this coincidence went to a whole different level.

I felt like I walked into an episode of *The Twilight Zone*. "You look just like me; except about forty pounds lighter."

"What's your mother's name?" Jasmine asked.

"Althea Davis," I responded.

"Nope, that ain't it. Who's your father?"

Tears welled up in my eyes. "To be honest, I don't know. I didn't discover that my stepfather wasn't my father until after his death. I never questioned my mother about my real father."

Jasmine led me from the club. We did not talk again until we got to my car.

"Will your mother answer the question? I think we need to know!" she said.

"I doubt it. What about your mother?"

"Let's go see. Can you take a ride?"

I was eager to get to the bottom of the puzzle. "How about I follow you?"

"No problem. I'm in the next row."

She turned around and got into a really fly convertible. My mind was reeling as I followed her to her mother's house. This was something that you heard about on television but never experienced in life. Simply by looking at Jasmine, I realized that she was related to me, but I still couldn't think of an explanation.

We only drove fifteen minutes before she pulled over in front of a lavish home that sat on at least three acres of land. We parked side by side in the circular driveway. She had to practically pull me from the car to go inside. Jasmine used her key and we entered a wide foyer. I was shaking both inside and out. A woman who was smaller in size hurried out of what I assumed was the family room, took one look at Jasmine and me, and fainted.

"Shit," Jasmine and I said together.

"We're going to have to stop that," Jasmine said, laughing. I think she was enjoying our little episode, but I was having a hard time with it.

"I've been the black sheep for so long, it's time I rubbed some dirt into Momma's face," Jasmine said as she fanned her mother.

The woman's eyes blinked open, and she alternated looking at Jasmine and me. The only word that slipped from her lips was "Fuck!"

That was when I grew convinced that Jasmine was my half-sister. Andrea did not have to explain the story to me; I already knew. It explained why my mother had never told me who my real father was. It also explained her hatred toward me.

"That bastard," Jasmine's mother hissed at me.

"Momma, that's not nice. Sammie never even knew. We only met tonight. She doesn't even know who Daddy was!"

"It doesn't matter. He told me that the bastard died at birth. It's bad enough that hussy went into labor the same day and at the same hospital as me," she spat. If words were weapons, hers could have drawn blood.

"Momma!" Jasmine yelled. "She doesn't deserve this. She's a victim; just like me! We were both deprived of each other when we clearly needed one another. How dare you not tell me that I had a sister! All these years of lone-liness and you could've done something about it! You know how much I wanted a brother or a sister, and you deliberately withheld that information from me. I blame you as much as I blame him! I knew something was missing when you kept buying me shit!"

Stunned, I listened to them go back and forth. *I have a sister after all these years?*

"I didn't tell you because it still hurts me, even though your father is dead! He had an affair with our next-door neighbor and threatened to leave me! It wasn't until he found out that I was pregnant with you that he decided to stay!" she wailed.

"Althea had an affair with a married man?" I asked.

"Yes. She used to be my best friend until she tried to steal my husband," Andrea cried. "I made the mistake of telling her that he wasn't the love of my life, and she stole him. When he was dying, he didn't call out my name, the person who had been here with him for the last thirty-some years of his life. He called hers!"

Shit became clear as she uttered those words. My bitch of a mother had decided to punish my real father by not allowing him to see me. She had not only hurt him, but she had also hurt me. I was never given the chance to know my father, and now they were telling me that he was dead. Althea had some fucking explaining to do, and I intended to catch her ass off-guard the same way I had been.

Jasmine left the room, leaving me alone with Andrea. I was at a loss as to what to say to her. She wore her pain all over her face, and I fought against the impulse to rush her and give her a big hug. Silent tears rolled from her eyes as she glared at me.

"Truth be told, I've hated you ever since I knew that you were going to be born. But, I was wrong. The sin wasn't yours; it was my husband's and your mother's. I was wrong to take my anger out on you. You weren't a willing participant."

"Yeah, I could've used a little sisterly support, but that's in the past. I only want to address the future," I said.

Jasmine came back in the room with a large photo album. "Can I show her pictures?" she asked her mother. Andrea nodded her head in agreement. I saw pictures of a little Jasmine who looked like me, with a father who I never knew and would not get the chance to know.

It was a very emotional moment for all of us. I cried for the man I never knew, and they cried for his deception and their loss as well.

As I was leaving, Andrea stopped me.

"If it means anything to you, he was never the same after he broke up with Althea. I believe he grieved losing her and the fact that he never got the chance to meet you."

"Thanks, that means so much. You have to understand; I was brought up in a home full of hate. The only love I ever received was from my stepfather, but I was deceived. All my life I thought he was my father until he passed away. This whole ordeal is a total shock, and all I really want to do now is punish my mother like she has continuously punished me over the years."

"Uh, I don't know what to say. Part of me wants to inflict the same type of pain on your mother that she bought on me, but I have to ask myself, what purpose will it serve? Daniel is gone. For me, it's over. I lost my husband twice. First time with your mother and second when he died. Now all I want to do is make it right. Can I spend some time with you?" she asked.

Stunned, I didn't know how to respond to her unusual request. I nodded my head as I turned to leave. We had talked until the sun came up and now it was time to get more answers.

"Where are you going?" Jasmine asked.

"To see my mother," I responded, snatching the door and stumbling down the two steps that led out of the house. My eyes were filled with tears born of deprivation. I wanted to crawl into a corner and have a gut-wrenching cry.

"I'm coming with you, and I'm driving. You're in no condition to drive. Plus, I want to meet the heifer who stole a part of our lives!" Jasmine paused and then exclaimed, "Oh, shit!"

"What?"

"I'm sorry about calling your mother a heifer. That wasn't nice."

"But it's true. You'll see; she's a heifer and a bitch!"

I grabbed the handle of the passenger side door of her two-seated convertible. I wanted to sink into the soft leather seats, but I was so angry that I could feel the smoke coming out of my nostrils and ears.

"We missed so much!" Jasmine said, and that was an understatement.

My jaw snapped shut, biting back the hateful comment that was about to spill from my lips. *If only she knew*, I thought to myself. Her childhood was a cakewalk compared to mine.

"Look, I need to prepare you for Momma. I haven't seen her since my daughter's funeral."

"What? You had a child, and she died?" Jasmine shouted in the close confines of the car. Her voice echoed and each reverberation produced another wave of pain.

Dejected, I replied, "Yeah, my fourteen-year-old daughter killed herself. Momma blames me."

"Wait, hold up. Fourteen? We're the same age. When did you have her?"

"I was fourteen when I had my son. Sixteen when I had my daughter. My son is currently in the army."

She shook her head. "Dayum!"

"Anyway, we can talk about that later. My mother called about a month ago to rub it in my face that my son was expecting a child. Luckily for me I wasn't home. My son and I hadn't spoken since he left for the army, and she only called to hurt me. So I promise you, it won't be a happy reunion. She might even cuss at you and throw us both out of the house!"

"I don't have time for that drama. I'm going to support you, and if the bitch says something that I don't like, I'm gonna call her on it. I hope that you won't get mad at me! We have a lot of catching up to do, but I refuse to pussyfoot around with one of the people who kept us apart! They created this shit; not us."

"I agree, but my mother's a different animal. Let me give you some background, so you won't be left with your lip hanging on the ground."

"Okay," she said.

"Momma and I have always had a difficult relationship. I thought she hated me, but I could never prove it. I moved out of her house with the first guy who asked me, and left for California. She convinced me to leave my children with her, which was my initial mistake. They grew up thinking that I was a family member instead of their mother. I'll carry that mistake to the grave with me. It took a long time before they called me Mom!"

"Damn, gurl!" she replied.

"Wait, I ain't finished. While I was away, my husband dragged me through hell. That story is too deep to get into now but I returned to Atlanta when the only father I had ever known passed away. Momma called and demanded that I come home to sign what I assumed was his will. He was dead for six months before I found out.

"Shit." Jasmine turned to look at me, barely missing a car approaching in another lane.

"Gurl, you're just driving away, and I ain't even told you where she lives!" We both burst out laughing. I was such a happy passenger that I didn't even realize we were headed in the wrong direction. "We're going the wrong way. We need to go to Lithonia. Althea lives off South Harriston in Lithonia."

"My bad. I was headed to Boulevard Street, which was where my parents lived before we moved out here. I assumed Althea lived in the same house." Jasmine turned the car around and headed in the opposite direction.

"My dad won this big settlement when he damn near got killed on his job. Instead of investing the money in the bank, my mother insisted that we move out to Stone Mountain. It's not much, but it made her happy at the time."

"I'm sorry if this hurts your feelings, but your mother seems like a real bitter pill to swallow," Jasmine said.

"That's an understatement. She's a bitch on wheels; pure and simple. I won't even bother to lie to you about it because you're about to find out first-hand." A few minutes of silence passed before I had the nerve to continue. "She treated me like shit from the moment I was born. I never understood why, but it became clearer over the years. When my father died, she told me that he wasn't my daddy. All those years I worshiped that man, and he didn't even belong to me."

"Oh, he was yours. He was the only father you knew!"

"Yeah, but it's not the same. I still love and respect him since he was the only person in my immediate family who showed me love, but he wasn't even related to me. I just wasn't sure that his motives were pure. He knew that one way to piss my mother off was by showing me love!"

"That sucks, for real!"

"What was our father like?" I asked, choking up.

"He was a kind and gentle man. He was attentive and loving. I could tell that the relationship with my mother wasn't that strong, but he stuck around, so I guess that counts."

"Yeah, it does." I pouted, feeling sorry for myself. "You know what? I don't want to do this. Confronting my mother is only going to piss her off, and she isn't going to answer any questions. Maybe I should get her alone," I said, fear dissolving my desire for answers.

"Oh, hell no! I want to meet the woman who almost ruined my life and kept my sister from me!" Jasmine angrily declared.

"Your mother had a hand in the deception as well," I said, starting to get mad myself.

"But my mother was a victim. Our father and your mother were the real culprits here. Don't beat yourself up about that! You didn't ask to be born, and that's what you're going to tell your mother, if I have to squeeze your head to make the words come out of your mouth!" she yelled back at me.

When I thought about it, she was right. I had been fighting all my life for my right to live and be happy. Every turn I made, my mother had been obstructing traffic. It was about time I started acting like my life belonged to me. I was going to stand up for me for a change.

"Yeah!" I yelled back, sitting up straight in the passenger seat. I looked over at my half-sister and felt a surge of pride. I had survived against the odds. She didn't know my pain and the things I had to do to survive, but that didn't make me any less worthy.

"Hey, we've got about a fifteen-minute drive. Tell me about you. Momma's surely going to tell you every little nasty detail that I'd like to avoid, so I might as well learn all I can from you."

"Hey, my life ain't been a fairytale, either. I've got my own dirt," Jasmine stated.

"Like what?" I was intrigued by the new twist to the conversation.

"We'll talk about it later. Let's take one drama on at a time. Okay?"

"Bet. I made all my drama, and I can only hope that Momma allows me to tell you myself, in my own time. I don't want to lose you, now that I've found you."

"Fine, we have a pact. If your mother starts off on some dumb shit, other than what we came for, I'm gonna shut her up any way I can. Agreed?"

"Agreed."

"And you can't get mad at what I say because I hate ignorant-ass women!"

"Damn, you sound like you know my mother already," I said, laughing.

"Okay, I have another confession. I once read a letter from your mother to our father. Althea did love him, but she tried to force him into abandoning us, and he wasn't about to do that."

"So, you knew about them?" I asked. "Wow! You know it's hard to imagine my mother loving anything or anybody other than herself!"

We traveled the rest of the way to my mother's house in silence. Anxiety twisted my stomach when we pulled up in the driveway.

"Gurl, you look like you're about to stroke out! Are you okay?" Jasmine asked.

"Yeah, I go through this every time I see my mother. She has this effect on me. And now, with you here, she's surely going to act a fool. You can still turn around, if you want to," I said, shaking my head to ward off unwanted thoughts.

"No, we're about to do this damn thang."

"Don't say I didn't warn you."

"Gurl, I ain't even going to trip off your mother. I just want to meet the woman who caused us so much pain. It'll be okay." She patted my hand as she opened her car door.

I went first, with Jasmine following me. She was hidden behind me, so Althea did not see her when I rang the bell. After two or three rings the overhead light clicked on, and the door opened. Althea was wearing a ratty robe and her hair had a few rollers scattered in its black and gray mess. She had a cigarette hanging out of her mouth and a large stain down the front of the robe.

"What the hell are you doing over here?" she demanded, placing her hands on her hips. "I ain't seen your black ass since that night at the hospital when you killed your daughter!" she exclaimed, rolling her neck for emphasis.

Stunned, but not surprised by the vicious attack, I uttered not a word. Jasmine stepped out from behind me, and my mother visibly paled. The cigarette dropped from her lips and, for the first time in my life, I witnessed my mother speechless. I could imagine her shock at seeing me and Jasmine standing side by side.

Althea stumbled back from the doorway like she was suffering from Fred Sanford's heart attack. Jasmine walked right past her into the house and I quietly followed. There was a tense silence as we stared Althea up and down.

Her house was a mess. Empty beer cans littered the floor, and wrappers from various fast food restaurants littered the tables. All the ashtrays within sight were overflowing, and I detected traces of marijuana in the air.

When I lived here, the place was immaculate. Of course, that was because it was my job to clean it. Out of habit, I started picking up the trash.

"Stop that! I didn't ask for your help. I haven't seen your ass in about three years, and now you wanna bring one of your friends over here without even calling first! What if I had been entertaining?" She jeered.

"Well, it's obvious you're not because you wouldn't be looking like you do if you were!" Jasmine said the words, and my mouth all but hit the floor. No one talked to my mother like that without a severe tongue-lashing. *Althea was the only person I knew who could undress you with her tongue.*

Althea stepped closer to Jasmine. "Who the hell are you?"

"You know damn well who I am! I just had to come and have a look at you! I can't believe my father was gonna leave my mother for you," Jasmine said, snapping her own neck to mimic Althea's earlier motions.

"Oh, I heard about how when a woman sleeps with another woman they start to look alike, but I ain't never seen this shit before," Althea said, laughing.

I was stunned because this was the first time that Althea mentioned my shady past. I was both embarrassed and amused. "Dayum." I stifled the urge to clap my hands. Of course it embarrassed me that she mentioned the women in my past, but the shock factor alone was worth that. This shit was so good, it should have been in the movies. I was turning my head from left to right so I didn't miss a single emotion. On the inside I was cheering Jasmine on, and I wanted her to knock Althea out. I was so excited. I practically forgot Althea was my mother.

"What the hell is the matter with you? Why did you bring this woman to my house?" Althea yelled at me, bringing me out of my reverie.

"That woman is my sister who you knew about and didn't tell me!" I screamed back.

"Uh, uh…" Althea stuttered.

"I've been lonely and afraid all my life, and the one person who could've changed this, didn't." I jammed my hands on my hips.

Althea struck me with the force of a linebacker, knocking us both over the sofa. We struggled to get away from each other. Jasmine stood rooted to the floor in shock. Althea rose first, pushing herself away from me like she had touched raw shit. I got an unwanted glimpse of her breasts while she was righting her robe.

"Sammie!" Jasmine yelled. "Sammie, you better slap that bitch! I don't care if she is your mother. You're a grown-ass woman, and you don't have to take that shit. Hell, if you don't slap her, I will!" Jasmine said, starting around the sofa. As if an invisible rope was pulling my arm, I hauled off and slapped the taste out of Althea's mouth, and it felt good.

*Oh shit*, I said to myself as I shook out my hand. I fully expected Althea to come at me like a banshee, but it didn't happen. Instead, she started to cry softly, then louder as she gained momentum. As much as I wanted to see her reduced to tears, it hurt me to have caused her pain. She was my mother; after all. My short stubby fingerprints were visible on her face.

"You've never been a mother to me. At best all you've been is an incubator, and when my time was done you tossed me out!" My tone of voice forced Althea to take a seat and her body shook with the pain of her sobs. I had finally spoken the truth for once but it didn't feel as good as I thought it would.

"Uh, I'm sorry," I mumbled, taking steps in Althea's direction to give her a hug.

"Don't touch me!" I was stunned at the sheer bitterness in her voice.

This was totally out of control. Jasmine stepped in and sat next to Althea. She placed her arm around her shoulders. Surprisingly, Althea allowed this contact. Feeling out of place, I stepped outside for a much-needed smoke. I was so upset, my entire body was trembling. I pulled a cigarette out of my bra and lit it with the lighter that I also had stashed there. I drew deeply from the cigarette and thought about what had just happened.

"Wow!" That was the only thing that I could say.

Suddenly I heard a very strange sound. It reminded me of the sound that you hear just before someone gets killed in a *Friday The 13th* movie. I looked around the front yard trying to locate the source of the sound, when I heard it again. The hair at the nape of my neck stood up as the sound got closer. Ditching the cigarette, I ran back into the house slamming the door behind me.

The one good thing that I learned from the movies was to run first and ask questions later. I was not going to wait on Jason or Freddie Krueger to come get me!

# LEAH

I left Momma's house; anxious and excited at the same time. It was five p.m. and the children had been at the center the entire day. I was hopeful since no one had called requesting that I pick Mya up. Although I wanted her to be happy at the center, I also felt like I was losing my babies when strangers could keep them occupied for so long without calling for a time out.

I parked the car and entered the day care center and, much to my astonishment, it was quiet. The receptionist told me that Mr. Richmond wanted to see me in his office, and the knot of apprehension in my stomach grew. I followed her down the hall to his office and waited while she went in. She waved me in as she exited, and what I saw brought tears to my eyes.

Mr. Richmond was holding Mya as she slept in his arms. His smile was gentle as he motioned for me to have a seat. I did so, but I could not peel my eyes away from the sight of him holding my child. My heart was doing flips and my hands would not stay still. I gripped the armrests to steady myself in the chair.

"We had an interesting day," he said with the same gentle smile.

"She is a handful, but I warned you," I said defensively. All my hopes that this arrangement would work flew quickly out of his open office window.

"Yes, she is, but she's manageable; with the proper care and attention. I tried to get her to play with the other children, but she seemed more content to hang out with me."

A single tear rolled down my face. "You've been holding her since I left?"

"No, of course not. She acted up when she realized you'd left, but she calmed down when she saw her brother playing with the children. The hardest part of the day was when the other children took their naps. That's when she decided she wanted to play! I brought her in here with me, so the other children could get some rest."

"Well, it was worth a try. I'm sorry that it didn't work out. What about Malik and Kayla? Can they stay? I can try to get my mother to watch Mya until I get on my feet financially," I said with a bowed head.

"What are you talking about?"

"Mya. She's so much work and I'm sure you're too busy to personally baby-sit her," I said heavily.

"She reminds me of my son. She has some problems, but I would no more turn her away than I would any of the other children. I created this center for children like Mya."

"You have a son?" I asked. He hadn't mentioned this when I had taken my initial tour.

"Had. He died. He had some medical problems that we didn't know about. He had several seizures at the day care provider's, and they failed to inform us of them. With early detection, we could've had him hospitalized and quite possibly would've discovered his brain tumor. He would've turned four today, but he died two years ago."

"Oh my God. Why would they keep something like that from his parents?" I exclaimed.

"To be honest, I don't know. I didn't find out about the seizures until the funeral. Given the size of the tumor, I'm surprised he wasn't having them at home as well."

"I don't know what to say," I replied.

"Yeah, it was tough, but I know God has a better plan for my son. Holding Mya reminds me so much of him. You realize that you have your work cut out for you, don't you? Personally, after spending the day with her, I'm convinced that Mya has autism."

"Aut... what?"

"A-u-t-i-s-m. In laymen's terms, autism is a complex developmental disability stemming from a neurological disorder that affects the normal functions of the brain. That would explain her lack of communication skills."

"But, I don't understand why none of the other doctors that I took her to couldn't see that," I said, shocked that there might actually be an explanation for Mya's behavior.

"Those emergency room doctors aren't paid to diagnose her disorder. They're only interested in patching up her wounds and moving on to the next patient."

"But I took her to her regular physician, and he never suggested that her problem could be neurological."

"I can't speculate on that. The good news is that I have a friend who specializes in the treatment of children with autism, and I've taken the liberty of setting up an appointment with him. I have to warn you that this won't be easy. Are you up for it?"

"Yes. This is one reason why I need this job so much. Once I'm enrolled in a health plan, I can afford his services. But I need to get off probation first. Are you saying that your center will keep them?" I asked, fighting to keep from getting my hopes up.

"Yes, of course. Do I have your permission to have my friend look at Mya?"

"By all means, yes," I replied.

"He may want to also look at Malik as well, since they're twins. Would that be a problem?"

"If it will help, you have my full cooperation."

"Diagnosis of autism is a long process involving extensive testing. Sometimes it takes years before they officially declare a child to be autistic. But her prognosis will be much better if we get started treating her early."

He stood up, and I came closer to grab Mya. I got a full whiff of his cologne, and I didn't know what it was, but I liked it.

"Why don't you get the other children? You can get them settled in the car, and I'll bring Mya out to you. I'd hate for her to wake up while you were driving home."

"God, you sound like you've been in a car with us when Mya's all riled up!" I laughed.

"Hey, it's like I told you, I've been there. But I only had one so I can only imagine the chaos you've been experiencing."

I collected Kayla and Malik and, as promised, he brought Mya to the car. She didn't even budge as I strapped her into the seat. He smiled at me as I was leaving and called out, "See you Monday."

Mya did not wake up until we reached home, and she smiled at me for the first time in a week. My heart swelled as I returned her smile. Hope flowed through my veins. I unhooked the child seat and went to open the front door before I started helping the kids out of the car.

I put my key in the lock, but it offered no resistance. Since I was a little crazy about locking doors, I knew right away that something was wrong. I turned the knob to see if that lock was engaged, and the knob turned freely. Stepping away from the door, I back-peddled to the car, climbed in, and slowly backed out the driveway. I searched for my cell phone to call for help.

My fingers wanted to dial 9-1-1, but I called Coy's cell instead. I was hoping that I could get him to swing by and possibly catch Kentee still in the house. I let the phone ring about six times before disconnecting. Desperate, I dialed his pager and put 9-1-1 behind it twice. It did not dawn on me that I had committed the number to memory until I disconnected the call. Despite my fear, I laughed and mouthed the word, "Sprung!"

Coy's call brought me back to the twenty-first century. "Hey, pretty lady, we still on for tonight?" It felt like he was reading my thoughts as I began to blush.

"Yes, but I have a problem. The front door was unlocked when I got home."

"Where are you now? Did you go in the house? Was there anyone in there?"

"Slow down. I'm across the street, watching the house."

"Good. Stay there. I'm not far."

"I don't know if he's in there or not. His car isn't in the driveway."

"That doesn't mean anything. He might have hidden it someplace else in the neighborhood. Wait, won't the alarm go off if someone goes through the front door?"

"Unfortunately, the alarm is just for show. It's not monitored, so I didn't think to change the code on it. If it went off when he went in, it wouldn't notify anyone and he would just turn it off himself." Yet another demonstration of the raggedy nature of my current situation.

"I'm right around the corner. Stay put. I'd like to catch that bastard in your house."

"Me, too," I said. In less than a minute, Coy pulled up behind my car. The kids, with the exception of Mya, were still sleep. Mya was sitting quietly like she knew something I didn't.

Coy jumped out of his car and ran up the driveway in a crouched position. He held up his hands to signal me to stay put, then he pulled his gun out of his holster as he neared the house.

"Be careful," I whispered to his retreating back. He looked so sexy, I forgot about the possible danger he might be in. He stood to the left of the door, pushing it open with his foot.

"Police! I'm advising you to come out with your hands up."

I was too far away to hear whether anyone answered, but no one exited the house. After waiting for a few minutes, he stepped inside. My hands were sweating and my stomach was twisted in apprehension. I didn't exactly know what to wish for.

Coy was gone for almost fifteen minutes. I had gotten out of the car and was halfway across the street when he came out the door. He took one look at me and shook his head.

"I told you to stay in the car!" He wanted to be mad at me, but his lips formed a half smile that disappeared when I asked if all was well.

"I can tell by the look of your bedroom that he's very pissed off at you. I think he may have peed on your pillow!"

"Nasty bastard!" I yelled to the sky, wishing Kentee was still within hearing distance.

"I need to get some techs down here to dust, and to take some samples. I don't want you going in there until we're finished, okay?"

"Okay," I replied.

He walked over to his car and called for backup. I needed to go to the bathroom big time. Checking his watch, Coy returned to my car.

"Are we still getting together tonight?"

"Yeah, my mother agreed to watch the kids. I was just coming home to feed them and grab some clothes."

"Take them to McDonald's, and stop by my house when you're done. I don't know how long I'll be," he said, handing me a key and a scribbled note with directions to his house. "Leave your keys, and I'll lock up when we are done."

"Can I get you to do me another favor?"

"Sure," he replied.

"Can you pull the linen off the bed so my mattress can have a chance to air, and maybe run some water on the sheets?"

"I think my guys are going to want to take the sheets to demonstrate the malice intended toward you. See you in a few," he said, going back to his car to write up his report.

I got in the car and drove like a bat out of hell to get to McDonald's. I had to pee so badly it was making my eyes cross as well as my legs. *He gave me the keys.* I shouted to myself. *Hell, if I wasn't sprung before, I am now!*

After dinner, I allowed the children to play for a while. I didn't want to arrive at Coy's too early because that would allow me time to snoop, and I didn't want to get caught prying. I wanted to time it so I arrived about the same time he did. Even though I wanted to shower and freshen up, I didn't want to give him cause to distrust me. It had been a long time since I had been a guest in a man's home.

My cell phone rang, and I dug deep in my purse to answer it. "Hello," I said, looking around to make sure the children were safe. I didn't have to worry about Mya because she refused to leave my side.

"I want my stuff, bitch!" Kentee screamed at me.

"What stuff? You emptied the house when you left, you cheating bastard!" I shouted right back, despite all the ears that turned to hear my conversation.

"Leah, I'm not playing with you!"

"Fuck, and I'm not playing with you! I don't have anything else left to give you! I filed a restraining order, so you better watch your ass!"

"That's my damn house!" he screamed, causing me to move the phone away, and I knocked some things to the floor in the process.

"Correction, mother fucker. Our home. You left it, and me! If you don't believe that I got a restraining order, come by again. I had the house finger-printed, so I hope your stupid ass wore gloves when you broke in again today!"

My response was met with silence. I didn't have anything else to say to him, so I kept quiet too.

"It ain't over," he finally said and hung up the phone. I angrily gathered up the remains of our meals and threw them in the trash.

"Malik and Kayla, it's time to go." I urged them on. All of a sudden I felt like I was being watched, and the feeling unnerved me. We raced to the car as if we were playing a game of cat and mouse, but for me it wasn't a game.

On the ride to Momma's house, I tried to think of a way to get Kentee to leave me alone. I was moving forward with my life, so I didn't need him lurking in the background. On impulse, I dialed Kentee's mother's house. She answered on the first ring. I had heard rumors that she had given up the crack but I had yet to see for myself.

"Hello," she said, sounding sweet and motherly, but I knew her differently.

"Ms. Simmons, this is Leah. I need some help."

"What are you calling me for?" she demanded, destroying the picture of genteel motherhood.

"Kentee is really scaring me, and I was wondering if you could talk to him," I replied.

"I guess he is scaring you after you put him out and won't allow him to see my grandbabies!"

"Ms. Simmons, I didn't put Kentee out; he left me! He bought another house in southwest Atlanta and he's living there with another woman! This week was the first time I've heard from him in months."

"He said you were going to try to lie to get me in your corner, but it won't work," she snapped back.

"I swear on my mother's life that everything I told you is the truth," I said, shaking my head at Kentee's cowardice. "He wants everyone to think he's the victim, but that isn't the case. The house we're living in is about to be foreclosed on, and your grandbabies and I are going to be put out in the street."

"Well, you aren't welcome here. Kentee said you spent all the money, and it's your fault that he never has anything left to help out his own mother!"

"That's not true. I paid the bills with the money that we had in the checking accounts, but I rarely spent any money on myself! Plus, he drained those accounts when he left. If anyone is to blame, it's your son." I tried to contain my temper. This was useless. "I can see that I'm beating a dead horse, so I'll give up. If you love your son, you'd better advise him to stay away from me. The police are looking for him, and I won't be the one trying to bail him out if he gets himself in trouble!" I disconnected the call after I said my peace. I didn't want to hear any more of her silliness. Kentee had his family believing that I was the bad one. I would find no help in that camp.

I walked inside Momma's house trying to put up a brave front, but I sagged in defeat when I saw her smiling face. I was so tired of pretending that everything would be okay, I just couldn't do it anymore.

"What's wrong, baby?"

"Someone broke into my house and peed on my bed. I know it was Kentee, but when I called his mother she said that *I* took all of our savings and kicked Kentee out," I wailed.

"The whole lot of them is crazy, if you ask me," Mom said as she placed her arms around me.

I could not agree with her more, but the pain was still there. I told her about the destruction in my house and my inability to go home.

"I'm staying at Coy's tonight, but I don't have any toiletries. Do you have an extra toothbrush and paste and maybe some deodorant?"

"Sure, honey. Check the bathroom for whatever you need."

I went in the bathroom and gathered a care package that included soap, toothpaste, clips to pin up my hair, and some lotion.

Noticing the lotion in my hand, Momma said, "Baby, you don't want that cheap stuff. That stuff is sticky. What you need is this!"

She brought her hands from behind her back. She held up all these different products from Victoria's Secret from bath gels to lotions, and a small bottle of perfume. I looked at her and shook my head. She never ceased to amaze me. She put her bounty in a bag and threw in something black that I did not inspect. I gave her Coy's home number; in case she needed to get in contact with me. Kissing her and the kids, I left.

# SAMMIE

I rushed back into Althea's house; expecting the worst. I thought that Jasmine would have jacked her up for all the years of pain and frustration Althea had caused her and her mother, but what I saw truly amazed me. Jasmine was holding my mother in her arms, and both were crying. In all my years, I had never seen my mother cry, and I was outdone.

"Yes, he stayed with my mother, but when I think back on it, he was never happy. My mother used me to keep him, but I think that you always had his heart," Jasmine said.

"He so wanted a child, and I so wanted to give it to him. When I found out that I was pregnant, I was the happiest woman in the world. We planned to announce our intentions the following week, until your mother announced she was also pregnant," Althea cried.

"Oh, now this is making sense," Jasmine said. "You blamed Sammie, an innocent victim, for my father's refusal to leave my mother. You never showed Sammie all the love you had for my father. Do you ever wonder why Sammie is the way she is? Can't you see that she's searching for love in all the wrong places because you've never given her a foundation to find it?"

The room got so quiet, you could hear a pin drop. I was holding my breath, waiting to hear the answer to the question that had plagued me all my life.

After a very long pause, Althea said, "No, I couldn't see anything beyond my pain. Don't get me wrong. My husband was a good man, but I wasn't in love with him. Your father was the only man I ever loved."

Her shoulders shook as fresh tears mixed with the older ones. She clung to Jasmine as she had never clung to me, and that hurt. Envy rose in my heart, and I had to shake it away or I might have turned against Jasmine as well.

"You're so much like your father," Althea said.

Clearly interested, Jasmine asked, "In what way?"

"He had a fire in him that my husband didn't. He never backed down when he thought he was right and we spent more time arguing and making up than agreeing. I loved that about him," she said, dissolving in tears again as Jasmine continued to rock her.

I had just witnessed another revelation. It was quite possible that Althea had never loved me because I had never fought back. I had always accepted whatever was handed to me. I was deep in thought, nearly forgetting that they were in the room until pieces of their conversation drifted back to me. I struggled to pay attention.

Soothing her, Jasmine shook her head. "So you would have him leave my mother, who has never done anything wrong, just so you could be happy? Don't you think that's selfish?"

Part of me wanted to go back outside, but the other part needed to hear this conversation firsthand. Neither of them had yet to acknowledge that I had come back into the room.

"I was young, and the only person who was important to me was him! In hindsight I can see where I was wrong, but back then, no, you and your family didn't matter."

"Not much has changed, has it?" I asked, finally ending the silence that I had maintained for most of my life. My words shocked us all. Until that night, I had never really stood toe-to-toe with Althea.

She started to draw back her shoulders—like she was getting ready to fight with me—but they slumped down again in defeat. I was right and she knew it. This gave me the courage to continue.

"All it's ever been about is you! You had a good man who worshiped the ground you walked on, and you stomped right over him. You had me constantly fighting for your love and attention, yet you ignored my attempts. You deprived me of the love that I could've received from my sister and the knowledge of my real father. If that wasn't bad enough, you concealed the death of the only father I'd ever known for six months! How could you be such a bitter and hateful woman?" I cried, shaking with wrath as tears flowed down my cheeks.

"Sammie, it's all a moot point now," Jasmine said, still stroking Momma's shoulders.

"Don't you dare defend her!" I yelled at Jasmine. "You don't know the hell my life has been."

I felt betrayed. Jasmine was trying to be the peacemaker when I wanted to fight. Althea remained silent as Jasmine drove her points home.

"Sammie, I'm not defending her. I'm just being realistic. We can't change the past. It's done. From this point on, we have to decide how we're going to interact with each other. Althea, you can't cause my mother, Sammie or me any more pain. Daddy's gone, and Sammie and I have found each other. The way I see it, you can either wallow in self-pity and hatred for the rest of your miserable life, or try to pick up the pieces with the only family member you have left. The choice is yours." Jasmine turned to me and said, "I'm ready to go."

Heading toward the door, Jasmine stopped. "And while you're thinking about it, Althea, know that my mother and I have Sammie's back. I won't be deprived of a sister again." She slammed the door as she left.

"Jasmine does have my back," I said out loud, laughing at this revelation.

I followed Jasmine, heading toward the door. I glanced back over my shoulder at my mother, but she did not lift her head as I closed the door firmly behind me. I probably should have said something, but my sister had said it all. Vindicated, I got into her car to ride home.

# LEAH

N*ervous* was not the word I would use to describe my state of mind. *Petrified* was more on point. I had not visited a strange man's house in several years and, judging from the sweat dripping off my brow, it showed.

It took every ounce of courage in my body to will myself from the car. *His house was banging! Whoever said that police officers are overworked and underpaid obviously hasn't swung by Coy's crib, 'cause he has to have bank to be rolling like this. I hope he isn't taking some of the drug money he collects!* I double-checked the address to make sure I was in the right place, and unless he had written down the wrong street, I was where I was supposed to be.

His house was set back about forty-five feet from the curb, and I had to maneuver through his extensive garden before I made it to the front door. It was simply beautiful. I didn't recognize half of the flowers. Momma would have been in heaven over there; running around trying to get cuttings for her own garden.

"What in the hell have I gotten myself into?" I spoke out loud as I approached the ornate double doors. It was the type of property that should have been guarded by two pit bulls. I waited for a minute to see if they would come rushing from the backyard.

My palms were sweating as I raised my hand to press the bell; praying that he was home. As I waited, I peeked at the other homes on the block; noticing that Coy's lawn was the best. I rang the bell again.

I began to second-guess what I was really doing there at Coy's house.

Chances were that Kentee had come and gone and was no longer even thinking about me. *Girl, be honest; you came to get your freak on. Why else would you bring Momma's best lotion?* Laughing, I looked around to see if anyone was watching me.

Sadly, Coy didn't answer the door. I dug deep into my purse; searching for the key. My hands continued to find the same objects so I had to take a seat on one of his porch chairs and dump my purse out. "Finally!" I exclaimed when I spotted his key. I hastily stuffed my belongings back into my purse. I tried to fit the round key in the square hole as I prayed his neighbors were not watching me with high-powered binoculars during my botched entrance into his home.

After several tries, I finally got the door open. His alarm system screeched at me and I repeatedly tried to enter my code into his alarm system. It took a few tries before I remembered that I wasn't in my own home. Luckily I got it right before the alarm alerted the company and they sent the police. *How stupid can you get*, I thought to myself. After I turned off the alarm, I took a few minutes to wander around his home. The silence was deafening.

His taste in furnishings was flawless. I was stunned because he could have easily had his house featured in *Better Homes & Gardens*. He had several pieces of African art that had to be originals, and he showcased them on pedestals. I could not help but to run my fingers along the exquisite curves.

I followed the hallway into his living room. His sofas were creamy white leather, and the plush carpet was creamy white as well. It was so thick and rich, I had to take off my shoes and enjoy it. The fireplace was to die for. It was one of those electric ones that produced the heat and appeared to be real but never used wood. Opposite that was a huge plasma television mounted to the wall. The electronic gadgets in this room were enough to make my head spin.

"Unh, unh, unh," I said to the empty room.

I walked into his kitchen and stopped dead in my tracks. It would have made any woman want to be Betty Crocker. There was a large island in the center of the room and over it hung a wrought iron rack that held various sized copper pots and pans. I always wanted pans such as these, but I didn't want to have to keep up the maintenance of polishing and cleaning them.

The stove was one of those state-of-the-art models that didn't have any burners on them and you turned it on with the touch of a button.

"Brotherman must be able to waltz in the kitchen," I said with a nervous giggle. I draped my body over the island, pretending that Coy was naked; cooking me breakfast as I watched. He was placing delectable items all around my pussy and I was the main course. I was so caught up in my fantasy that I didn't hear Coy come in.

He laughed. "Dang, if I didn't know better, I'd think that you're happy to see me!"

I practically rolled right off the island. Good thing I didn't because his white-tiled floor did not look as comfortable as his creamy rich carpet in the living room.

"Sweet Jesus! You scared the crap out of me!" I said, righting myself and acting like I wasn't smack dab in the middle of a fantasy when he caught me.

His hearty voice vibrated against the walls as he laughed at me. He began unloading all of the tools of his trade on the kitchen table; his gun, radio, beeper, handcuffs, and cell phone. Stripped of his gadgets, he came toward me, making my knees quiver.

"Uh, I was merely visualizing you in the kitchen making breakfast for me in the nude!"

"Breakfast? It's seven at night. Can I make you dinner?" he asked seductively.

"I already ate with the kids," I replied.

"Then can I have dessert?"

Without waiting for a reply, Coy started to unbutton my shirt. He pushed aside the cookbooks he had stacked on the island and gently scooped me up; placing me on top. The polished surface felt cool against my bare back.

"Coy, stop. I want to take a shower first." I felt like I had rolled in the mud; after the day that I'd had.

"No, I wanna taste it all." Coy unzipped my pants and rolled them off my hips. He unfastened my bra in less than two seconds. When he was finished, I was only wearing a recently purchased pink thong.

He eyed me with his bedroom eyes, sending a tingle up my spine and down to my coochie! He licked his thick lips, and I creamed the thin layer of fabric that hid my womanhood from his eyes. I lay there on my elbows and watched him as he slowly undressed. The low light filtering in through the blinds enhanced the muscle tone of his body. His arms practically glistened as he took off his shirt and allowed it to drop to the floor.

My breath caught when his fingers traveled to his belt buckle. He made a big production of swirling his hips as he unleashed the beast and allowed his pants to hit the floor. He stepped out of the puddle they had made on the floor and moved closer to me. I had no idea what he had in mind, but I really didn't care. Two steps before he reached me, he swung to the right and opened the refrigerator.

By this time, my twat was twitching in ecstasy. He showed me his magnificent ass as he bent into the fridge, taking his time with his selections. Part of me wanted to run for cover, and the other part wanted to bitch-slap him for taking so long.

Coy gathered his items and placed them on a side table. He pulled the high stool up in front of the island and started to gently knead my skin. I felt like he had pulled his chair up to the buffet and was about to chow down. He did not disappoint. It was such a deep massage that I allowed my eyes to close. My earlier goosebumps were quickly dissolving.

Homeboy was serving me up. He poured a liberal amount of pineapple juice on my toes, and the shit was cold, but he sucked them dry and left them feeling warm and toasty. I was so glad that I had used the money to get my toes done earlier in the week.

Changing bottles, he moved on, spreading liquid chocolate on my legs. He moved it around the front of each leg and licked every inch of it off. The chocolate was warm, and I could smell it as he licked it up. I wanted to kiss him; savoring the flavor of me in his mouth.

"Lawd Jesus!" I moaned out loud, trying to pull him close enough to stick his dick inside of me, but he would not cooperate. Next, from the fridge he pulled out chopped walnuts, which he spread on top of my vagina. Teasing me, he rubbed a few against my clit and I thought I would lose my mind. He placed a few inside my lips and I waited in anticipation for what was going to happen next.

He sprayed whipped cream over the nuts, and I almost jumped off the island because it was so cold.

"Dayum!" I yelled, as Coy placed a cherry on top. I got nervous when I heard him chomping around my clit but—when it was all said and done—I was not complaining one bit. With his tongue, he washed away most of the nuts and cream, and then he replaced his tongue with is fingers. He finger fucked me and brought me to another orgasm. Lifting me off the island, Coy entered me from behind. His dick was hot and hard as I gripped the island to keep from falling over. Coy moaned deep in his throat and increased his strokes, causing me to scream out his name as I came again. This time, Coy joined me.

Once my breathing was under control, I struggled to find something to say to Coy that would take my mind away from the wanton sex.

"If I get an infection for all that shit you just did to me, I'm going to come looking for you," I said, laughing.

"I was very thorough in cleaning it up. Trust me, baby. You'll be okay. Can you trust me?" he asked with a seductive wink.

Damn, that man was too fine to argue with; not to mention his talented tongue.

"Who decorated this place? I love it," I said, despite the nagging feeling I had that his live-in girlfriend must have done it.

"I did," he proudly stated.

"Oh, really. I thought you were about to tell me about your wife who's vacationing in the Caribbean."

"Trust me, I did this all on my own."

"How long have you been living here?"

"About six months. I'm still working on the rest of the house, but I'm pleased with my progress. I'm taking my time with it. I love antiques so I shop for them about once a month. Right now I'm searching for an antique poster bed for the guest bedroom. I can't do the rest of the room until I find it."

"You sure you don't have a girlfriend stuffed in the closet?"

"Would you like a tour now or you want to wait until later?" he asked, cutting short all further discussion of a girlfriend.

"I can wait. Right now I want to take a nap. You wore a sista out!"

Soft music was playing, but I could not see where it was coming from.

"You relax here. I need to put something else in my belly besides the essence of you!"

Coy left me alone in his bedroom. I turned on the television and—before long—it was watching me.

When Coy came into the room with a plate of something sizzling, all I did was utter, "Oh that's nice," and fall back to sleep.

I awakened with the sun beaming on my eyelids through the blinds. Turning my head, I gazed at Coy's beautiful face. *Damn, there ought to be laws against a man being so foine!*

I was happy to be there, but sad at the same time. Coy was really sweet. In fact, he might have been too sweet. I was stuck between a rock and a hard place. He had never told me how he felt about children, and I had never pressed him. I should have made it clear that I was a package deal before we did the bump and grind. I needed a man for my children and me. Looking around his place, I realized that my kids could never come there for a visit. I would have been too afraid that they would have broken or spilled some-thing.

I rose from the bed, trying not to disturb Coy, but he woke up anyway. "Where are you going?" he asked with a gentle smile on his face.

"I was going to take a shower," I said, resisting the urge to fall back into his arms.

"Be my guest. I'll be right here." He turned over and pulled the covers up to his neck.

His bathroom was off the chain. He had all kinds of scented soaps and lotions and a countertop filled with the latest colognes. Everything in the bathroom was coordinated, and I could tell he had spent a pretty penny in one room alone. He even had the oversized bath sheets that I had always wanted, but could not afford. I stepped into the shower and lathered up; using some of the perfumed soap my mother gave me.

*I could really get used to this type of life*, I thought to myself, but reality struck again when I thought of the kids. Coy was a mystery to me because I had fallen for the dick way too soon. I wanted to get to know him better, and those thoughts made me unhappy. Coy never did join me so without bothering him, I dressed quickly and went home. It was hard leaving him in that big bed by himself, but I had some thinking to do.

As I cleaned up the previous day's mess at home, my mind relived all my conversations with Coy I realized most of them had lacked any real substance. We had mainly talked about my problems and then commenced to fucking.

The doorbell rang as I was putting fresh sheets on my bed. Scared, I rushed to the door and peeped through the eyehole. Coy's stern face greeted me.

"What are you doing here?" I asked him.

"No, the question is, what are *you* doing here?" He pushed me aside and entered; acting all mad and stuff. "The last thing I remember, you were going to take a shower."

"I was, but I needed to come here and clean up before I picked up the kids." That wasn't the real reason that I had left, but it sounded good to me.

"Wrong answer. I hired someone to come clean this up before you got here and—if you had stayed where your black behind should've been—you wouldn't have had to come home to this."

"Coy, I'm sorry. Feelings that I can't describe overwhelmed me. I needed to come home to think!"

"Think about what?"

"About where I am in life, what's going on with my family, and what's going on with you and me," I responded.

"Leah, don't make this complicated. It's too much too soon! I'm attracted to you, and I hope you feel the same way. I'd be lying if I said I didn't have other friends, but you're the person I want to be with. Let's take this one day at a time, okay?"

"I can deal with that, I guess, but I'm not used to this game. I haven't dated in years, and while it appears the rules have changed, no one wants to show them to me," I said dejectedly.

"Nothing changed in the dating game. You simply need to lighten up."

I lowered my head in shame. "But we slept together already, and I don't even know you! I don't want you to think I'm cheap."

"There's nothing cheap about you. Our circumstances might be unusual, but that doesn't change the fact that I like you and I want to spend some time getting to know you." Coy lifted my chin to gaze into my eyes. "Fair enough?"

"That's fair." I closed the distance between us, forgetting all the arguments running through my brain. Suddenly I was so horny you would have assumed I have been sexless for years.

Dragging Coy into my bedroom, I tried to push him back on the bed, but he flipped the script. I lay back on the bed resting on my elbows as he examined the toiletries on my dresser. Finding my oils, he turned around and did a strip tease for me.

"Take off your shirt." He tossed me a bottle of oil. When I got my shirt off, he had more instructions as he fondled his hard dick. "Spread it on your boobs; I want to see them shine."

I poured a liberal amount in my palm and applied it to my breasts, spreading the oil and gently squeezing my tits. He bent down and took each one into his mouth. He pushed them together and his tongue flickered over them, sending shock waves to my pussy.

I reached out to grab him and he said, "No, this one is just for you." He raised his head and kissed me deeply, practically sucking away all of my air.

"Turn over," he mumbled as he rolled me over onto my stomach. Starting at my feet and working his way up to my ass, he massaged me. He paid particular attention to my ass, kneading it like it was dough. My hips involuntarily lifted from the bed; trying to meet his hands and mouth. When I could not stand it any longer, Coy flipped me over and put his tongue on my clit. I could feel his teeth graze my hole, and he bathed me until I exploded in his mouth. I reached out to him again, but he pushed away my hands as he entered me. Every fiber in my body was in tune with his beat, and my hips met his every thrust. I was so eager to get closer to his throbbing dick that my body kept leaving the bed, only to be slammed back against it.

It was a good thing that my closest neighbor was at least a half acre away because I was moaning and yelling to beat the band. Coy continued to grind into me, and I kept giving it back. He sought out my face—which I had purposely turned away—and kissed me. We climaxed together and, afterward, we could only lay in a tangled mess for about five minutes.

"Wow," I said, as I rubbed my forefingers over my nipples; basking in the afterglow. Coy was lying next to me; unmoving except for his heaving chest. We were both spent as we curled up and fell asleep. I completely forgot about picking up the children. All I could say was, "Damn!" Then I decided that I would control the next "sexcapade."

# LEAH

"Where the hell have you been?" Sammie asked when I picked up the phone. I blushed as I recalled the past twelve hours. "I spent the night at Coy's."

"Damn, you let him hit it?"

"This was the second and third time. I thought I told you that already," I said.

"Gurl, please. There's no way I would've forgotten about you getting some dick action? Was he any good?"

"A lady never tells," I replied.

"That means yes. If his shit was raggedy, you would've said so right off the bat!"

"True, but I've got a question."

"Shoot."

"Why do men like to kiss you after they perform oral sex? That seems to turn them on big time and I don't get it."

"It reminds them of two women fucking, and they love that shit. They like to see a woman eating another woman. It's their ultimate fantasy!"

"Yuck! If I wanted to taste pussy, I'd date a woman. I don't want to smell me or taste me. That shit is gross," I said.

"Leah, don't knock the shit until you've tried it. You'd be surprised how good it feels."

Stunned, I could not even answer her.

"Shocked your ass, didn't I? I could've sworn Marie had told you that I've done it both ways. Don't worry; I ain't after your ass. I've walked down that road before, and it ain't all bad."

I was at a loss for words and did not respond.

"Cat got your tongue?" Sammie asked.

"How the hell do I respond to that?" I fired back. "I don't know anything about that shit except the fact that I don't like the smell or taste of pussy; even if it's my own!"

Laughing, Sammie said, "You haven't had the right one!"

"You know what? I've had enough of this conversation. Why were you looking for me?"

I shook my head in disgust. Sammie was right; I should not throw stones at something I had no personal knowledge of, but eating coochie did not interest me in the least.

"Gurl, I've been hunting you down 'cause I found out I've got a sister!"

"A what?"

"S-i-s-t-e-r! You heard me, nigga!"

Sammie knew I hated the N word but I decided to let her slide.

"Damn! How did you find out?"

"I was at the club and ran smack into her. There was no denying the fact that we were sisters; we look just alike."

"That's deep," I replied.

"I knew Momma was creeping, but I didn't realize the man was married. All those years she tried to play like she was holier than thou, to find out this shit!" Sammie snapped.

"Did you speak with your sister?"

"Hell, yeah. First, we went over to her mother's house to get the scoop, and then we went to see Althea!"

"Mo' drama; mo' drama!"

"Yeah, Althea wanted to act the ass until Jasmine set her straight! Jasmine told me to hit Althea, and I cold-cocked her ass!"

"You hit your mother?" I asked, truly appalled.

"Yeah, I slapped the shit out of her, but it wasn't for the way she was acting last night. It was for all the years of pain she's inflicted on me. And you wanna know something? I don't feel a minute of regret. Jasmine was right. Althea blamed me because Jasmine's father wouldn't leave his wife once he found out she was pregnant as well."

"Damn, gurl, this sounds like something out of a soap opera."

"Tell me about it. Jasmine told Althea that she could continue to wallow in self-pity or wake up and recognize the family she still has. The man she loved is gone!"

"I'm sorry, Sammie. That sucks; that you never got the chance to meet him."

"Yes, it does but, on the flip side, I finally have a sister. I want you to meet her."

"I start work tomorrow, but I'll be around in the evening. I can't wait."

"She's a hoot. You'll like her."

"Set it up. Is she anything like you?"

"A little. She's everything I wish I was but I won't say any more until you meet her."

"Cool. I'm dying for details, but I'll give you a break. Girl, did I tell you that Kentee broke in here?"

"No, when?"

"Yesterday. That's why I went to Coy's. He trashed my bedroom and peed on my bed!"

"That rat bastard!"

"I said the same thing. He called me, and I told him I went to the cops. He said it isn't over."

"What's that supposed to mean?"

"I don't know, but tomorrow my first order of business is to find out how quickly I can move. Even if I have to do it in the middle of the week, I'm out of here, and he won't know where to find me."

"Good idea!"

"Hell, I even called his mother to ask her to make him lay off, but he told her some bullshit, and she thinks I'm the bad guy. He told her that I kicked him out and won't let him see his kids."

"He's going to burn in hell for all the lies!"

"Yeah, you are so right but, for now, I just need to get through this."

"When are you seeing lover boy again?"

"Not sure. Coy said he'll call, so I'm just gonna wait him out. I like him, but it's too soon to get seriously involved, and I'm not sure what level of involvement he wants."

"I hear ya. What are you about to do now?"

"I need to go pick up the kids."

"Oh, I was going to ask if you wanted to go grab something to eat."

"I can't today, but thanks for thinking about me. Let me know when I can meet your sister, okay?"

"Sure, I'll holla at you later."

# LEAH

I was more nervous about leaving the children at day care for a full day than I was about starting a new job. They must have sensed my trepidation because—for once—they did not give me any resistance when I was getting them dressed. After taking an unusually long time getting it together, I finally settled on the same navy blue suit I had worn for my interview. It was conservative but sexy. I pulled my shoulder-length hair into a bun and added my glasses to achieve that professional look of corporate America.

Mya waited until I had pulled up at the center to act a fool. She started shouting and beating herself about the head. It appeared that she didn't want to go inside, but I was wrong. She was excited about going back, but her confused mind was sending her mixed signals. The only reason I knew this was because when Mr. Richmond stepped out of his office and grabbed her from my arms, Mya's smile could have brightened a dark room. Malik and Kayla ran off in the direction of their classrooms like they had been attending the center all their lives.

"Wow that was easier than I thought." I turned to leave. "Wait, my contact information is on my application. If I'm not available, I left my mother's number as well. Since this is the first day at work, it might not look good if I get any personal calls; unless it is an emergency," I mumbled, still stressing and using way too many words to make a simple point.

"We'll be fine but, if I need to, I'll call you personally. I've got a little pull with the owner of the firm. Knock 'em dead," Mr. Richmond said, winking as I turned to wave at them both.

I felt ten pounds lighter when I left the center. But as I drove the few short blocks to work, my nervousness returned. I did not doubt my secretarial skills. Getting to know people who would be around me for eight hours a day left a sour taste in my stomach. I hoped there were no drama queens or divas there.

My first few hours were spent filling out health insurance forms and watching orientation films. It was boring, but at least I didn't feel like a guppy in a fish tank. That came later when I was given the grand tour of the building. Our offices occupied four floors of the ten-story building. On my interview I did not question my assignment, but I was pleased to find out that I would be working in the word processing center. Some secretaries had a problem with working in a pool, but I preferred it. It gave me the opportunity to view and participate in all of the firm's different cases.

Most of the work that filtered down to word processing involved legal documents, and I would not have to do daily correspondence, which I found boring and tedious. My supervisor's name was Andrea Brooks. She was a black woman in her mid-to-late fifties who seemed cool enough.

"Leah, there are only two things that will land you on my bad side. The first is lying. I can't stand it, and I never forget it. If something happens that you can't handle, tell me. That's all I ask," she said.

"What's the second thing?" I asked.

"I can't abide by tardiness. I schedule work before you even get here. If you're going to be late, call me so I can adjust my schedule. That's common courtesy."

"I can abide by that. I hate tardiness myself. I typically arrive at work at least half an hour early so I can get a chance to unwind before I have people in my face."

"Sounds like you and I will get along fine. I've prepared a booklet that will show you how we format documents. If you're unsure about anything, anything at all, let me know."

"I will."

Andrea handed that day's assignments. I was a bit rusty in transcription, but she told me to take my time. She didn't give me anything that needed a quick turnaround.

There were three other ladies and one man in the word processing pool, but I didn't try to strike up any conversations. I wanted to do my job and go home; simple as that. Although I was not a standoffish type of person, I wanted to let some time elapse before I cultivated any workplace friendships. My first three assignments were a piece of cake. I had typed petitions before, so I could understand everything on the tapes. Transcription was hard when you had to listen to voices you were not used to, or when the speakers were not comfortable talking into a microphone. I was beginning to feel more at ease.

During my lunch hour, I was reading over my assignments when this woman blew into our work center with a tape. Looking around and only finding me, she approached.

"I need this tape transcribed immediately!" she said without bothering to do introductions.

I glanced at my watch, noting that I had another forty-five minutes left on my lunch hour.

"Ms. Brooks is at lunch, but I'll tell her as soon as she returns."

I went back to reviewing my work.

"I said, I need this immediately," she barked.

"I see," I said, putting my own work aside, trying to act like I gave a shit about what she was saying. She was the type of woman who was used to getting over, and I wasn't about to fall for that shit.

"I'm at lunch right now. As I said, I'll be delighted to let Andrea know that you urgently need this tape transcribed. Other than that, my hands are tied."

"Are you being insubordinate?"

"Not at all. This is my first day so I don't know how they handle emergency requests. I'm not trying to get off on the wrong foot," I replied smugly.

"We'll see about that!" She slammed the tape down on my desk. "Have Andrea call me!"

As she was leaving, the peace I had gathered was shattered.

"What should she call you, bitch?" I said to her retreating figure.

Self-doubt ate away at my tranquility as I debated whether I should start on the tape. After sweating over it for a few minutes, I popped the tape into the transcriber. I assumed it would be an emergency pleading and was surprised to hear it contained only a few PR letters. The kicker was the tape was at least two weeks old. I did the letters but I intended to tell that neck-snapping, teeth-sucking heifer that lack of planning on her part did not constitute an emergency on my end.

"Oh my goodness. You're still here?" Ms. Brooks said, smiling, when she came back into the "barracks," as she affectionately called them.

"You will have to rent a crane to get me from this building before quitting time," I replied, smiling as well. "I did have one problem, and I didn't know how to handle it. This woman stormed in here demanding that I transcribe a tape. I told her I was at lunch, but I'll admit she intimidated me into doing the tape."

"Damn, I see you've met Shonell. She works for one of the senior partners. Between you, me and the wind, I believe she's only getting paid for time on her back. She doesn't do her work and, when she gets called on it, she comes down here and creates a scene. I'm sorry you had to deal with her on your first day."

"She doesn't know I did the transcription yet so, if you want me to, I can erase it like it never happened," I said.

"No, it's okay that you did it, and I'll put in for your overtime since you did it during your lunch hour. I plan to nip this situation in the bud. Every other person in this office is running scared of Shonell because she works for the big dog, but her bulldog tactics won't work in here. I'm going to fire off a memo to the managing partner and inform Shonell that this is the last time she'll be allowed to submit work in this manner. She must've gotten word that there was fresh meat in the house." She chuckled. "All of us old heads know what time it is and don't get sucked into her drama."

"I wish I'd known because I wouldn't have done it. I kept thinking it would be some emergency pleading she needed to have filed this afternoon, so I did it. If I'd known it was a bunch of PR letters I would've let it wait until after I finished my lunch."

"Tell you what. You can knock off an hour early, how is that?"

"Uh, no offense, Ms. Brooks, but I could really use the overtime."

"You'll get your overtime. Don't worry about that."

"Wow, that's nice of you. But will this get me in trouble?"

"You're under my supervision while you're in my department, so no. But from what I'm hearing, I don't think you're going to be here for long. Word in the lunchroom is that they plan to have you work as a floater. This means the only time you'll come in here is when you don't have another desk to cover."

"Darn!" I exclaimed, not wanting to cuss in front of my supervisor. "I like word processing. I get a taste of all different types of law. I hate typing up stupid PR letters. Give me a brief any day!"

"You're just nosey!" Ms. Brooks said, laughing.

I laughed with her because she wasn't even lying. I rose my right hand. "Guilty, your honor!"

"Ms. Thang is going on vacation next week. They'll want you at her desk. After that, I'll see what I can do to get you back here. I like the work I've seen so far, and I could use the company."

I was touched. "Thanks, Ms. Brooks."

We shook hands. "Call me Andrea."

I started for the door but turned back. "Andrea, what will happen to that case I was working on with the lady that stabbed her husband with the fork?"

"It's up for review by the Appeals Court and that process usually takes several months. We should know something by spring."

"Will you let me know when they reach a decision?"

"I will."

## SAMMIE

Rushing to beat the clock, I hit the revolving door and raced to the elevator. I was trying my best not to be late since I had an important meeting with my supervisor that morning. I chastised myself for too much partying and celebrating the night before. But, in the end, I still felt nothing but good stuff. Jasmine had come over. We watched some movies and drank some shooters. Talking to Jasmine was a breath of fresh air to my boring existence.

Jasmine had lived the life that I had always wanted. She had been raised in a loving environment with two affluent parents and yearned for nothing. She had traveled extensively throughout the world and could even speak two languages. I was dually jealous and proud of my sister.

We were watching *Bringing Down The House* on DVD when the door had started to rattle. Startled, I turned to Jasmine as the knocking began. *Oh shit.* I had forgotten that I had a date with Jessie.

"Who the hell is that?" Jasmine asked, turning to face the door. "Somebody obviously has issues with you."

With leaded feet, I walked to the door expecting the worst. Jessie hated to be kept waiting.

"Bitch, you are really tripping," he said as he strolled into my apartment, glaring at me in disgust. He shrugged off his leather coat and shook off the moisture from the light rain that had been falling all day.

"Hi," I muttered, totally embarrassed that he had called me a bitch in front of my sister. Even though we had been talking nonstop since we had met, I had never mentioned my Jessie thing to her.

"Aw, hell, no! No this nigga didn't just come in your house and call you a bitch!" Jasmine said, jumping up from the sofa.

Their eyes locked, and Jasmine had this vicious snarl on her lips. Jessie was stunned into silence. His head kept swinging from me to Jasmine. I chuckled to myself, knowing he was confused.

"Jasmine, meet Jessie. Jessie, my sister, Jasmine." Still too stunned to say anything, Jessie stood there with his mouth open.

"Close your mouth. You don't want a fly in there, do you?" Jasmine said.

I cringed because Jessie hated being the butt of a joke.

"Sister? What the fuck are you talking about?" Jessie shouted. "You ain't got no damn sister!"

"Like hell, she doesn't! Who the fuck are you?" Jasmine demanded.

"He's my ex-husband," I replied.

Jessie shot me an evil look. I walked over to the DVD player and pressed stop. "Jessie, I forgot about asking you to come over. We were just watching a movie. Would you like to stay and watch it?" I really wanted him to leave but tried to act nice.

❂❂❂

"Hell no, I don't wanna watch a movie. You know what I came here to do!" He put his hands on his hips and snapped his neck like an irate woman.

I found an ounce of courage to stand up for myself. "We'll have to re-schedule that."

"Reschedule my ass!" he fired back. "Tell sister dearest that you got something to do!"

"You know what? I don't like your fucking attitude!" Jasmine stood up. She was all business, based on her stance, she must have thought she could take Jessie. "My sister told you she was busy. What part of that sentence did you not understand?" When he didn't respond, she started moving her fingers around in front of Jessie's face. "Can you understand the words that are coming out of my mouth?"

She was so funny that I busted out laughing before I could stop myself. Jessie failed to see the humor.

"Oh, you think this shit is funny?" Jessie reached out and snatched a handful of my hair. "Hell, I'll fuck you both!"

His breath was foul and I could tell that he had been drinking. He pulled tighter on my hair and, for a brief second, Jasmine was paralyzed from the sheer brutality of the attack, but she quickly recovered. My sister took two steps and slammed her fist into Jessie's face. Blood gushed from his nose and he instinctively released my hair. I gulped in a quick breath, amazed at Jasmine's fearlessness and held it until I became lightheaded.

"I'm sorry. Did I break your concentration?" Jasmine said, and I fucking fell out laughing. She'd used a phrase from the movie *Pulp Fiction*. The veins on the sides of Jessie's neck started to bulge, and I thought he was going to stroke out right in front of our eyes. He turned and glared at me as he started to leave. I could not believe what I was seeing! Jessie walking away with his tail tucked between his legs! Un-fucking-believable!

He used one of his bloody hands to grab the door open but shot me one more menacing glare before he left. I rushed behind him and slammed the door before he changed his mind. In my head, I rewound to the moment when Jasmine's hand had connected with Jessie's nose, and I nearly fell over laughing. I had suffered abuse from that man for almost ten years and, in a matter of seconds, my sister had his ass running skeerd!

"Sorry, sis. I didn't mean to hit him like that, but he pushed all of my buttons at the same damn time!"

"Hey, and I ain't mad at ya. I should've done that shit a long time ago. I just didn't know it would be that simple."

I shook my head. If I didn't love and respect my sister before, I did now. She'd shown me a way out of a situation that I thought would haunt me for the rest of my life. I would miss the money Jessie threw my way, but I could do without the physical and mental abuse. As we got closer to the end of the year, I wanted to change my jacked-up thinking and old behavior. I walked back over to the DVD and pressed play; still in a daze.

"Oh, hell no, sistergurl. You're going to have to explain this shit!"

Jasmine hit the off button on the remote that was sitting between us on the sofa. I sat down heavily.

"I'm so embarrassed. I was hoping that you'd never see the part of my life

Jessie represents, but I guess this is yet another prayer that God left unanswered."

"Sammie, when are you going to get it through your thick skull that we're sisters? I'm not here to judge you or make you feel like less than a woman. We've all had our share of shit!"

"Jessie was special to me. He was the first man who said he loved me, but he used me badly. He turned me into a stripper and a prostitute. What else can I say? I thought I loved him and, unfortunately, he showed love with his hands."

Tears streamed down my face. Jasmine scooted closer and wrapped her arms around me. It opened the barriers I held onto in my heart, and I dumped out all my pain on her shoulder.

"Hush, boo. Please don't cry or else I will also," she mumbled into my shirt.

But it was too late; she was crying already. We remained locked together for over fifteen minutes. I told her where my love for Jessie had taken me. It was just a brief overview, but I told her practically everything; even about my encounters with other women. I had planned on keeping that information to myself.

Moving away from her and smiling, I said, "If only I knew I could've busted him in the face to stop him, I would've cold-cocked him ten years ago!"

"Gurl, as big as you are, you could've snatched his scrawny neck right off and shoved it up his ass with no problem!" Jasmine raised her hand for a five, which I gladly slapped.

"Imagine that!" I said as we each shook off the pain and allowed the joy to shine through.

"On a serious tip, why is he still coming around? Aren't you divorced?"

"Yeah, we're divorced and, believe it or not, he's remarried. But when Jessie wants something other than traditional sex, he knocks on my door."

"Damn, gurl! You got gold between those legs?"

"I guess so. He keeps coming back, and he pays me good money, too!"

My current lifestyle relied on financial support from means other than my nine-to-five.

"Hey, we, and let me say it again for your hard-headed ass, *WE* are going to get through this. If you need anything, let me know. I'm not as well off as I used to be, but I've got a little something on the side."

After a rough night of tossing and turning, I made it to my desk with two seconds to spare as my phone rang.

"Sammie, could you please come into my office," Ms. Barker requested.

"On my way." I hung up the phone. I was not nearly as nervous about the meeting as I had been about Jasmine finding out about Jessie.

"Shut the door," Ms. Barker said as I entered her office.

*Damn*, I thought. Maybe I should have been worried, since shutting the door was serious. I tried to think back on all the screw-ups that I had made since my hire date and could not think of anything that would warrant a closed-door session. Hell, this was the longest I had held a position in my life and I thought I was doing a halfway decent job.

Icy fingers of fear pressed against my heart as I waited for her to speak. She had my folder open and was reviewing it.

"Relax, this isn't a bad meeting. It's just a move that I'm concerned about."

I was completely in the dark. "I have no idea what you're talking about."

"I know, and I'm not sure about the underlying reasons either. I've been instructed to switch your assignment from Mrs. Tanner to Mr. Spencer, effective immediately."

"Am I in trouble?" I asked, still not understanding what was really going on here.

"From what I understand, no. As you know, Mr. Spencer is the senior vice president at Georgia Power. He requested you, and it's my job to make sure that he's happy. This means that you're entitled to an initial small raise, if you accept and another one after you complete your six months."

"I don't know what to say. I don't even know the man. Why me?" It felt like a setup.

"I don't have the answers for you. All I know is that if you accept you are to move your things right away to your new office on the twenty-second floor. If I find out anything else, I'll let you know. Congratulations," she said, rising out of her chair and indicating that the meeting was over.

"What are the repercussions if I don't accept?"

"I honestly don't know, but you'd be doing so at your own risk. During my fifteen years here, I've never handled such a request."

Even though I had a million questions, I didn't utter a word as I exited her office. Valerie, the girl I was replacing, was sitting in the waiting room. I looked her in the face, and she glared at me as if I had stolen her man. The shit was so weird!

# LEAH

After a few weeks on the job, I felt elated as I left work. It had been so long since I had been mentally challenged, and I was looking forward to the following week. I gathered up my belongings and joined the cattle call at the elevator. All of the nine-to-fivers were standing around staring at the up and down buttons, waiting to be free of the office. I was the only one who was reluctant to leave because I had been out of the mainstream for so long.

"Night," they all chorused as the elevator arrived and we filed on. The workers acted like they didn't know each other as the elevator began its decent. I was uncomfortable, since I didn't know any of the brown and white faces so near mine. I was parked right beside Shonell and that heifer didn't even bother to say "thank you" or kiss my ass for doing those letters on my first day. She had become my nemesis. The office was large but the gossip was rampant, and I had heard a number of stories about me that she was spreading behind my back. I wanted to confront her ass, but I was still in my six-month probationary period, and I didn't want to jeopardize my job.

I drove the few short blocks to the day care center and spent several moments behind the wheel trying to erase thoughts of the office. I had to switch hats when it came to Mya and, even though I felt reasonably sure that things were going well, you simply never knew with her.

The center was quiet when I entered, and there was no one at the desk. I tiptoed down the hall toward the classrooms; not because I wanted to sneak up on the employees. I hated the rat-a-tat-tat of my heels. I glanced inside as I passed Craig Richmond's office. He was becoming another pillar of strength to me, and I had to check myself on that. I did not want to encourage the connection we had growing and risk it becoming inappropriate. I was relieved he was not in the office.

I turned the corner leading to Kayla's classroom and ran smack into Craig.

"Damn," I uttered before I could check my language.

Laughing out loud, he grabbed my shoulders to steady me, and an electric jolt traversed through my body. Although I had initially thought he was a good-looking man, I had never allowed myself to think of him in a sexual way because he was married; until then. Red splotches marked my cheeks at the mental pictures that played through my head at his touch. He simply chuckled.

"Just the person I was looking for! Come with me."

He pulled my hand and led me back to his office. He was so animated you would have thought someone had lit a match under his ass. I immediately thought something was wrong; my face must have expressed it.

"No, everything went fine today. I wanted to run something by you. Have you ever had Mya's hearing tested?"

"I'm not sure I understand you. The doctors look into her ears every time she has a physical," I answered, not sure where he was going.

"Sorry, I'm babbling here, and you don't know what I'm talking about. Let me start over. I spent some time with Mya today, and she spent a good amount of time with the other children. I noticed that she interacts better with the younger children. She's really responsive to them and they're drawn to her. She exhibits more defiance when she's around the older children."

I had noticed similar behavior from her so I was eager for him to continue. I sat up straighter in the chair. "Please, go on."

"When she got a little out of control today, I took her into the observation room and she immediately calmed down. I was still working and moving around the room and, at certain times, she acted as if she couldn't hear me. It seems that Mya's okay as long as she's not alone. She panics when she can't see you and, if my thoughts are accurate, she also gets upset when she can't hear you."

"Wow, this is kind of making sense. She doesn't get frustrated around her brother and sister and me. It's easier to get her to do something that I want her to do when she's not alone. To be honest, I've never given any thought as to whether she could hear me or not."

"I tried it, Leah, and I think there's a problem. I walked out of Mya's eyesight and she started to whimper. I called to her and she didn't respond. When she saw me, she responded to my words. Now, I'm no doctor, but I think our little Mya can't hear as well as most people. I'm not suggesting that she's deaf, but I do think she has an issue with her hearing. I wanted to ask your permission to have her tested."

"Craig, I'll have Mya tested but I need to start saving some money first. I simply cannot afford it right now. In fact, I've been seriously considering giving Mya up to a group home that's better suited to handle her needs. I hate to admit this, but those thoughts are coming more and more frequently," I said, my shoulders slumping in defeat.

He rose from his desk and came around to comfort me. I could feel his soft hand on my shoulder and, for a brief moment, I wanted to raise my mouth to it. He was such a kind man. I was jealous of his wife!

"Hush, please hush," he said as he rocked me in his arms. He pulled me to my feet and wrapped his arms around me. I was thankful that the door to his office was closed. "I realize things are difficult for you, but please don't rush to judgment until we can find out what's going on."

"But I'm not just taking myself into consideration. Mya's behavior affects our entire family. Kayla and Malik can't have a normal life because of it. If I don't do something soon I'm liable to ruin Mya's life; as well as those of her brother and sister!"

Grabbing my chin in his hands, Craig raised my face so I could look him in the eyes. I was so ashamed of my admission, but it was less shameful than some earlier, desperate thoughts I'd had.

"Can you just trust me?" he asked, looking deeply in my eyes.

Lawd, Jesus, it was hard to look him in the face. He was so damned good-looking. I felt like someone was pricking my skin with a thousand needles. I nodded my head and he kissed me on the lips. It wasn't a deep tongue dance, more like a peck, but it ignited a fire in my blood that caused me to push away from his grasp.

He seemed uncomfortable. "I'm sorry. I had no right to do that."

I walked over to the window to put some distance between us. "It's okay. I was a little surprised."

Clearing his throat, Craig said, "Leah, the center has its own doctors. I thought I had explained that to you when you first came in. If you agree, we can start testing Mya on Monday."

"Wow, I knew you had a doctor, but I assumed it was for kids who might have a cold or some other simple ailment. Certainly not this."

"They can test her hearing. We have all the equipment here to do it."

Tears slipped down my cheeks; I did nothing to stop them. Craig was offering me a ray of hope, and I did not know how to handle this chain of events.

"Hey, I said I was sorry! Why the tears?" Craig asked, moving closer to draw me into an embrace. "This should be good news."

"It is. It's been so long since things have come this close to being okay. I don't know how to handle all this good fortune," I said honestly.

Craig covered my forehead with soft kisses and tenderly caressed my back and shoulders. It felt so good that I forgot that he belonged to someone else. Lawd! This time, I sought out his mouth and kissed him like my next breath depended on it. I felt his dick growing against my leg as he disengaged from the kiss.

Picking up my purse, I mumbled, "Schedule the test and I hope you have a good weekend."

"Good! I'll see you Monday!" he yelled at my departing figure.

I felt like a cheap tramp, and I could not wait to gather the children and get the hell out of the center.

Once again Mya was smiling when I saw her. She was eager for me to pick her up, and she kissed me on the cheek. She didn't even mind when Malik and Kayla also joined in for a group hug. Despite my wanton behavior in Craig's office, I was feeling good about the working-day care thing.

We were in the car and ready to roll when my cellie rang.

"Hello," I chirped, full of cheer. I had just placed the car in reverse, but I had my foot rested on the brake.

"Leah. We got him. He's being held in Fulton County jail, but we have extradition orders when he gets released from Fulton."

My hands started shaking so badly that I could not drive, so I shoved the gear back into park and turned off the ignition. Mixed emotions about Kentee's arrest flooded my brain. On one hand I was happy that he would not be able to provide for his other family but, on the more real tip, I was upset that he would not come back to my family.

"What are the charges in Fulton?"

"Robbery and theft by taking. He won't be arraigned until Wednesday. The results of that trial will tell us when we can get our hands on him. Like I told you before, it's likely your husband's been stealing for some time. The problem was we could never get a bead on him until I dusted your house for prints. His prints match crime scenes that I've visited before. We got him!"

"Good. I'm about to go home. Please call me later."

I didn't want to hear Coy's voice any longer. When he was talking about Kentee it became personal, and I was having my own doubts about setting the law on him. Those thoughts were coming from the right side of my brain, while the left side was saying, "*That's what the motherfucker gets!*"

I started the car again and drove to my house; my mind racing the entire way. Not only was I dealing with Kentee's issues, I was thinking about Mya's test and what that would mean to our family. If Craig could help me help Mya, it would improve my whole family structure. As it was, Kayla and Malik were held back from a lot of activities because of their sister. My mind said fuck Kentee and his trivial shit but he was, after all, the father of my children and my husband. Dismissing him was easier said than done.

## LEAH

The message light was blinking on my answering machine when I entered the house. It showed a total of five calls. I waited until I got the children settled before I listened to them. The first three were from Kentee; mostly begging me to come down to the police station to post bail.

"With what and for what?" I wailed at the machine. Even though I still had the lion's share of the money from his stolen equipment, I would rather pee on it and set it on fire before I gave a penny of it to assist him. He had shown his lack of love and affection for us all when he left us alone. His messages did nothing but anger me.

In the fourth message, he had the audacity to be belligerent. "Bitch, how are you going to charge me with breaking and entering into my own house? I'll see your ass when I get out!"

I marveled at the contrast between the first three "I love you and I'm sorry" calls and the fourth one where his true colors were revealed. Shaking my head, I poised my finger to delete the fifth message; assuming it was also from Kentee.

"Ms. Simmons, this is Kimberly Carter from Gateway regarding your recent application for housing. We've approved your application and I'm calling to find out when you'd like to take occupancy. Please give me a call at 5-5-5-3-8-1-5. Have a good day."

*Oh shit!* I thought to myself. The Gateway was the nicest of the three subdivisions I had visited. I glanced at my watch as I dialed her number. There was a good chance that she would be gone for the day but I decided to try my luck. If there was no answer, I would leave a message and follow up on Monday.

An out-of-breath woman answered the phone after the fifth ring. "Gateway. Kim speaking. How may I help you?" Ms. Carter said.

"Hello, this is Leah Simmons. You left a message on my answering machine, and I'm returning your call," I said, sucking in my breath.

"Oh, Ms. Simmons, thanks for calling back." I could hear paperwork rustling as she asked me to hold for a few seconds. "I wanted to find out if you were still interested in the house and when you might be planning on moving?" she said.

I attempted to sound nonchalant about the matter. "When will it be available?"

"It's ready now. Let me know when you want to take possession, and I can start the paperwork."

My nonchalance flew out the window and excitement flew in. "Would tomorrow be too soon? I'd have to move in piece by piece, a little at a time but..."

"That's cool with me. Once I turn over the keys to you, it's on you when you move. I'll be in the office at nine o'clock. We can sign the papers then."

I waited until she had hung up before I started dancing all around the house. This was the second piece of good news of the day. I was on overload. Exhausted, I sank onto a stool at the kitchen counter to analyze how different my life was than a few short weeks ago.

I had to share this information, so I immediately called Sammie. Lately our lives seemed to be running parallel, and she was the one I wanted to share my good news with first. I picked up the phone to dial, but the dial tone was gone.

"Hello," I said, getting ready to push the off button on the cordless phone I was holding.

"Hey," Sammie said.

"Gurl, this shit is weird. I was picking up the phone to call you!"

"Uh oh," she said and it sobered me as well. Too many good things were happening and I knew beyond a shadow of a doubt that it was being orchestrated somewhere else.

"Marie," we said in unison.

"No doubt about it," Sammie said. "I can see good things happening to one of us over a period of time."

"Yeah, but this shit is unreal! Earlier, I got a call that they locked up Kentee, and I just found out that I got the house I wanted. I can start moving in tomorrow. Which, of course, leads to another request. Can you help me?"

"Sure, gurl, I got you. I was calling to tell you that Jasmine punched Jessie in the nose. I think she broke his shit!"

"Get the hell out of here! Where did they meet up?"

"He came over last night while we were watching movies and started making his usual demands. Jazz hauled off and popped him. I wish you could've seen that shit! Jessie practically crawled, dragging his ass out the door, with his tail between his legs," she said, laughing.

"Oh, my God! I would've paid dearly to have seen that shit," I replied, laughing as well.

"Gurl, I was there, and I still don't believe the shit. He punked out so fast, it was comical. Can you believe I allowed that bastard to beat up on me all those years, and all I had to do was smack his ass and he would have left me alone?"

"Gurl, Marie is working overtime on our asses! She said to me one day that if you whipped that black ass one time he wouldn't fuck with you no more." I clutched my arms around my chest. I felt like I was not alone in the kitchen, and I kept looking around for the source of my discomfort. Seeing no one, I assumed what I had originally thought; that Marie was looking out from up in heaven.

"There's something else I wanted to tell you. Althea called and she's cooking me dinner tonight."

"Oh, snap!" I responded for lack of a better response.

"So, if my ass turns up sick, dead, or shut in, check her ass out first!"

"And you know this! Can she cook?"

"Beats the shit out of me. I can't remember a single meal she ever prepared. When I lived with her she didn't cook a thing. She had a maid and a cook—me!"

"Gurl, you're going to have to call me when you get done and tell me how it went."

"She even told me to invite Jasmine but I want to feel her out before I suck Jazz in that mess. She might nut up when I get there, and I don't want any witnesses when I punch her ass out," Sammie said.

"Good idea. From the limited amount I know about your mother, she's likely to say anything."

"You ain't even lying. She already came out the bag on Jasmine once, and once was enough."

"Well, I've got to go. I need to fix supper and start packing. I also need to call my mother and let her know we'll be moving."

"Oh, okay. I'll holla at you later," Sammie said.

"Sammie, wait. I forgot to tell you that they arrested Kentee!"

"Damn, gurl. You did tell me but, if it makes you feel better, I'll play along! Dang, gurl, for real?" she said, mocking me.

"Sorry; too much excitement. He left four messages on my machine. Three to apologize for leaving me and asking to come back, after I post bail, of course, and the fourth one cussing me out for having his ass arrested for breaking into the house."

"The Lord watches out for damn dummies and fools, and I swear your husband wears both of those hats," Sammie said.

"He sure does. Did you ever listen to his voice mail? I'm about to call now and see what kind of response he's getting from the heifer he left me for."

"Gurl, I forgot all about it until now. I'm gonna call before I head over to Althea's. Check you later," she said, hanging up the phone.

# SAMMIE

Laughing out loud, I called the number that Leah had given me. I entered the password and Kentee's sexy voice filled my ears. As far as I was concerned, he wasn't much in the looks department, but the brotha had a voice that would make your panties fall off. He had two new messages and a host of old ones. Since I wanted to hear the dirt, I decided to listen to the old messages first.

"Hey, baby, it's me. I woke up and reached for you; only to come up empty. How could you sex me so good and leave without giving me a chance to get seconds? Oh, that was so good I can't stop touching myself; wishing the hands that I felt on my clit were yours! Um, I'm so hot and horny." The message beeped and cut her off in mid-sentence.

*Damn*, I thought to myself as I saved the number in my phone. I was definitely going to come back and listen when I had more time. He had that heifer trained to give him phone sex. She had such a sexy voice, it was getting me all wet.

It had been a moment since I had been with a woman, but I hadn't forgotten the thrill and the feel of a woman's touch. Most times thoughts of another woman shamed me, and I tried to believe that I had forgotten my past, but every now and then a voice would do something to make me crave a soft touch.

I replayed the message, and this time I allowed my fingers to wander over my body as I listened to her sexy voice. I began to daydream, thinking about the first time I had felt a woman's touch. Jessie had wanted to humiliate me, so he paid a stripper to come on to me while I was performing in a club. It backfired when he found out I actually enjoyed it.

I often thought about trying it again, but I didn't know how to approach a woman, so I let those thoughts linger unanswered in my mind. Shaking my head, I got ready to visit Althea. I gathered up my things and headed over to her house.

I was nervous as a cat in a room full of rocking chairs as I knocked on Althea's door. Her house had represented nothing but pain for me throughout my entire life. I had to fight my feet to keep them moving straight ahead. I willed my hand to actually ring the bell and prayed she would not answer; despite the twenty-minute ride.

She opened it like she had been standing on the other side waiting for me. She pushed open the screen and waved me in. I felt like a prisoner walking the green mile to execution.

"Dinner's almost ready. I kept it simple," Althea said.

"What are we having?" I scanned her house and immediately noticed that she had cleaned up the pre-existing mess. Althea had also gotten her hair and nails done; looking more like the mother I remembered.

"I fried up some chicken and made some potato salad. How's Jasmine? I'm sorry she couldn't make it."

"Oh, she's fine. She told me to ask you for a rain check."

"Uh, sure," she said, walking to the kitchen.

I didn't know what to do, so I just stood in the spot she left me in. This side of Althea was so new that I wasn't sure how to act.

"Can I help do anything?" I asked, wanting to keep occupied.

"You can get out some glasses and pour the drinks. I've got some lemonade in the frig and some beer. I'll have lemonade."

"Do you mind if I have a beer?" I was strongly in need of something to relax my racing heart.

"Sure. No problem."

She finished bringing the food to the table as I got the glasses. I came into the room as she was sitting down and handed her the drink. I eyed the food carefully; it looked delicious.

"Wow, that sure does look good!"

I pulled out a seat across from her. Althea smiled at me, and I thought I would faint. She reached across the table so we could say grace.

"Heavenly Father," she began, and my mind left my body. I had never heard Althea say a prayer in my life, and I was having a difficult time accepting this dinner invitation. I could not remember a thing she said, but I knew the prayer was over when she released my hand.

Her grasp was firm and soothing. Usually, when I was allowed to touch her, she reminded me of a wet fish. Tonight she actually felt like a warm and loving human being. I waited until she had fixed her plate before I started loading mine down. I was hungry, and the food smelled too good.

We ate in an uncomfortable silence for about fifteen minutes. For the life of me I could not think of anything to say to her. She must have been struggling also.

I noticed her glass was nearly empty. "Would you like more lemonade?"

"No, in fact, I think I'll have a beer with you."

She smiled as I got up and bought one for both of us.

"Althea… uh, Mom, this is good. Thanks for having me," I said.

"Thanks? It was long overdue. Even though I hated the fact Jasmine was out there, I'm glad you two met and she was able to make me see the errors of my ways."

I was so stunned that I could not speak. Althea put down her fork and looked me in the face.

"I can't make up for all the years of pain I've caused you, nor can I erase all the negative things I've done. I wanna try to make things better for us in the future; in the little time I have left. Can I do that?"

I did not answer her right away because I didn't know what that meant. After looking into her eyes and noticing the tears forming, my heart melted. I wanted to rush to her and give her a hug, but I held back. I nodded and she picked up her fork and continued eating like nothing had happened.

Pieces of her speech trickled down to my brain. "Little time you have left?" I asked.

"This invitation has nothing to do with the news I received recently. It's time we became friends, but my doctor told me that I have a brain tumor yesterday. It's inoperable. So, I'm counting my days and taking advantage of every opportunity I have left and I decided to move. This house has too many memories for me. I'm getting older and I want a simpler lifestyle. I've seen a house for sale in South Carolina, and I'm going this weekend to put a deposit on it."

*What the fuck? Is she just playing me? Why is she revealing all of this now? What am I supposed to say? Is this the part where I ask her to come live with me? Oh, hell no. But…what if it's true?*

"Wow, I don't know what to say!" I said. "Why South Carolina?"

I was harboring too much pain from my childhood to feel sadness, but I could not help the feelings of remorse for what could have been had things been normal between us.

"Say that you'll come to visit before it's too late."

"Of course, I'll come if; you want me to." I fought back tears. I didn't know why I felt like crying. Althea was never there for me but, if it was true, it was still sad. Even though I hardly ever came over to her house, at least I knew where to find her.

"Finish your supper," she instructed, and I complied. The food that had tasted so wonderful to me a few minutes earlier had transformed into shit. I finished the meal and even had a slice of carrot cake, but my heart was not in it.

I helped her clean up, and then I told her I had to go.

"Let me know if you do decide to move. I'll come over and help you pack; if you want," I said, looking at my feet and completely ignoring her statement about the tumor.

"Sure, I could use the help," she said as I walked out the door. I wanted to hug her, but she didn't appear like she wanted to be touched. She gave me a photo album, which contained pictures of my stepfather and my real father whose love would remain a mystery to me.

"They would have wanted you to have these. Your stepfather loved you very much, and your father wanted the opportunity to love you, but I denied him," Althea said.

I felt like the room was closing in on me, and I could not wait to escape

Althea's home. I appreciated her gesture but I needed some space to think things over.

"Wow," was the only thing I could say when I got back to the car. I wanted to call Jasmine but decided to wait until I got home. My mind was already wandering, and I needed to pay attention to the road. I stopped off at the liquor store before going home; it was going to be one of those nights.

I considered calling up some able-bodied dick to release some of the tension mounting in my body.

I immediately fixed a drink when I got home. Kicking off my shoes, I curled up on the sofa before dialing Jasmine. Her answering machine answered, and I had no choice but to leave a message.

"Gurl, I just got back from dinner with Althea. It was crazy, and I need to talk about it ASAP. Hit me back when you get some time. I'm about to get sloppy drunk," I announced, hanging up the phone. I called Leah next; she didn't answer, either. "Damn," I said to the empty room.

I thumbed through the phone book, came across Tyson's number, and called before I could talk myself out of it.

"Hello," he said. I could hear my grandchild crying in the background.

"Hey, what are you doing to my grandchild?" I asked jokingly.

"She's just hungry and her momma ain't fast enough," he responded with a laugh. "Thanks for the money you sent; it came in handy. Children are expensive."

"I know that's right. I'm gonna try to send some more when things get better for me."

"Well, we appreciated it. When are you coming to visit?"

"In a few months, I have to make sure your grandmother gets settled first."

"Althea? What do you mean, settled? I didn't even know you two talked."

"It's kind of a long story, but I ran into a woman who looked just like me. We started talking, and I found out she's my half-sister. We confronted your grandmother, and one thing led to another. I just came back from having dinner with her. Did you know that she has a brain tumor?"

"Althea or your sister?"

"OK, I'm rambling, so let me back up. Althea called and invited me to dinner. She said she has a brain tumor. She's thinking about moving to South Carolina."

"Why?"

"That's what I said. Her mind is made up, though, and she plans on going up there this weekend and putting in a bid for a house. I offered to help her pack and stuff."

"This is too deep." The noise level in his house decreased, and I could tell my grandbaby was eating at last. "You have a sister?"

"Yeah, ain't that a bitch? Momma was sleeping around with a married man, and he got his wife pregnant at the same time she got pregnant with me. We could've been twins," I said with pride.

After a few seconds of uncomfortable silence, I told Tyson I had to go.

"Damn, wait! So you're telling me Althea's not the saint she pretended to be?"

"No, she's not. Hell, I could've told you that. I wouldn't have gone as far as guessing that she was screwing a married man, but I knew something wasn't right with her."

"That explains a lot of things," he said, and it opened up another folder in my life that I wanted to forget. "Things sure do change fast in your world, but that's nothing new, is it?"

"Hey, my phone is ringing," I said, clearly lying but needing to get off the phone. Life was whacking me in the face, and I didn't want him to hear me cry. Althea's words didn't register until I repeated them to Tyson. *My momma just told me she's dying and all I could say was, "I will help you pack!"*

"Oh, okay. No problem. I sent you some more pictures of the baby. You should have them in a day or two."

"I have the other ones on my desk," I said, wondering whether he picked up on my anguish as well.

"She's really growing. I can't wait for you to see her. She looks like me when I was a baby; especially her ears. They stick out from her head," he said, laughing.

"That is so wonderful. You take care of that family, and I'll talk to you soon."

"Night, Mom," he said and hung up. It had been so long since he had called me "Mom" that it caused me to cry uncontrollably. The good tears mixed with the bad when I thought back to Althea.

## LEAH

I finally got the kids to bed, and I was in my room going through my dresser discarding clothes and folding up the ones that I wanted to take with me. The room was a mess, but I wanted to pack up enough stuff that night so I could haul it to my new house. I could not do children's room while they were sleeping. I first packed the last of Kentee's clothes and planned to take them to his mother's. This was very painful for me because I always assumed we would have worked this out by now. Those thoughts were dashed when I got word he was in jail. He would never forgive me for bringing "the man" into our relationship.

My phone rang and it startled me. I raced to get it before it woke up Mya. "Hello," I said, out of breath.

"Bitch!" a female voice screamed at me.

"Excuse me? Who the fuck are you?" I stared at the phone like the caller's face would be revealed.

"You had my man locked up?" she screeched at me.

"That man belonged to me until your whorish ass came along," I said, realizing who I was speaking to.

"If you were handling your business he wouldn't have come my way."

"I was handling my business. His kids are my business." I balled my hands into fists. I glanced at the caller ID and realized that this dumb heifer didn't even block it when she called. "Tarcia," I said in disgust.

"How the hell do you know my name?"

"'Cause your dumb ass didn't block your name and number before you dialed. Plus, I know a lot about you," I replied, fucking with her mind.

"Yeah, well, you're going to have to straighten this shit out for Kentee!"

"I don't have to do a motherfucking thing but pay taxes and die!" I said, screaming back at her.

"You stole his tools, and now he can't post bond!"

"And your point is? Why should I help him out? You handle your business and get your man out!" I snapped and slammed down the phone.

She called me right back.

"Bitch, don't you hang up on me!"

"I've got your bitch! If you call my fucking house one more time, I'm gonna have your ass arrested next!" I banged down the phone again. That heifer had some nerve; calling my house and cussing me. She had ruined my marriage; not the other way around. I wish she would have brought her trifling ass over to my house because I would have pulled every strand of hair out of her head. I blocked her number on my phone and went back to packing, but my heart wasn't in it. I was so pissed that I wanted to scream.

I went into the kitchen and poured myself a drink. I didn't want to do it because I had so much work to do but I could think of nothing else besides fucking that would take my mind off my problems. I wanted to call Coy, but I was hesitant to do it. I was always calling him, and I wanted him to make the next move. My thoughts went to Craig. He was one sexy guy, and I wondered about him and his marriage. He never talked about his wife, and I found that strange; especially after we had shared a kiss. I respected the vows of marriage enough to attempt to keep my distance from him, but I could not deny that he turned me on hot.

Picking up the phone, I dialed my mother.

"Hey, baby," she answered.

"Hey. Listen, the house came through, and I can pick up the keys tomorrow. Can I ask a favor, please?"

"Sure, what is it?"

"I need to drop the kids off at your house in the morning so I can move as much stuff as I can. They arrested Kentee, and I feel the need to move from here quickly. He was still coming in here when I wasn't home, and I don't like it."

"Sure, bring them over," she said, and I exhaled.

"Thanks, Momma! It's so hard to do anything when they're awake, but when they sleep I'm afraid to make too much noise and wake them up; especially Mya."

I was so blessed to have her as a mother. Our past had been rough, but we were making it through. I had been a terrible child. I had played hooky from school, stolen money out of her purse, and done drugs. Through it all, she had stood by me, and I still felt her love. The fact that she was still speaking to me was a testament to her good character.

Momma had an addiction problem years ago, so she regularly attended AA meetings. With her encouragement, I had joined as well. I'm a firm believer in addiction being hereditary. At those meetings, I had met a woman named Vee whose spirit was wonderful. She had brought so much into the meetings that I could not help but to befriend her. I had invited her to stay with my mother and me while she straightened out her legal problems.

Momma didn't complain about Vee coming to live with us, and I was thankful. But problems arose when I loaned Momma's car to Vee, and she went out on a binge and totaled it. Momma and I had gone through some shit. Since I had let her have the keys, I could not claim the vehicle as stolen. Although Momma never pointed the finger, I had learned a valuable lesson; never lend anything that you can't afford to replace. Vee had burned us and, fortunately, my mother had forgiven me.

I put together some more of the boxes that I had gotten from the grocery store and started loading them down with clothes. I was going to have to ask Coy if I could use his truck, and I had already made plans to transfer my phone and cable television services. Things were definitely looking up.

Since the kids had started school and day care, I hadn't had any more mishaps with Mya. She was compliant and offered no resistance. She was sleeping throughout the night and she was more amenable at home. I said a silent prayer of thanks for the center and hoped that we were close to finding an answer to Mya's troubles.

I sought the phone and found it under several piles of clothes. I was curious to find out how Sammie had made out with her mother. This was such an unexpected turn of events. I wished the best for Sammie, and I was hoping that this was what she needed to get her life back on track. The phone was off the hook when I finally located it, and I saw that two new phone calls had gone directly to voice mail. One was from Sammie and the other was from Coy.

It had been a few days since I had talked to him about anything else but Kentee, and knowing that he called made me feel happy. The last thing that I wanted to do was to fall for him and not have my feelings reciprocated. I listened to my messages and decided to call Sammie first.

"What's up?" I asked.

"I'm working on a serious drunk right about now," Sammie responded.

"Why, things didn't go well with your mother?"

"It went better than well. I can't understand where she's coming from, and it is making me uneasy. She's planning on moving to South Carolina."

"Who the hell lives in South Carolina?"

"Nobody; that's the point. She wants a fresh start with no memories plaguing her."

"Running away from one's problems is never the answer. Changing locations to better your life rarely works because you're taking the biggest part of the problem with you. Yourself!"

"I know that's right, but I guess she'll have to discover that on her own. I'm just grateful that we're going to work on a relationship. I've always envied what you and your mother have. There's a second part to this problem, and I don't know if I believe it or not. She says she has an inoperable brain tumor."

"Say what?"

"That's what she said, and I don't know how to feel about it. Part of me wants to be happy that her life isn't peaches and cream, but the other part wants to spend as much time with her as I can while she's still able."

"How are you going to do that if she moves?"

"That's my point! I'm going to call her tomorrow and ask her to reconsider. But I also want to talk to her doctor and make sure she's telling the truth!"

"She would lie about that kind of shit?" I asked in amazement.

"I wouldn't put it past her."

We both fell silent.

"Gurl, I called your husband's pager, and that shit is off the chain."

"Ain't it? I listened to his calls from jail, and he's not a happy camper. His whore had the nerve to call me up today and demand that I bail her man out!"

"No way! Is that bitch crazy?"

"Obviously. He can rot in hell as far as I'm concerned."

"After what he's put you through, I don't blame you." She yawned and I followed suit.

"Why did you have to start that shit?" I stifled another yawn that threatened to escape.

"I'm sorry, gurlfriend; I couldn't help it."

"That's something I always couldn't understand. Why is a yawn so contagious? I mean, all you have to do is yawn and everyone around you yawns as well. That's some funny shit."

"Yeah; one of life's mysteries. Gurl, I'm going to turn in. I'll be there in the morning to help you move."

"I was hoping you'd say that. I can use all the help I can get. I've got a lot of shit up in this house."

"Later," she said, hanging up the phone.

*She's a good friend*, I said to myself. Most people would have made me beg for help. I finished packing up the last of the items in my bedroom that I would need immediately for the house. And I even got ambitious and packed up the bathrooms and the kitchen. All in all, I was happy with my achievement.

I called Coy before I called it a night but only got his answering machine. For a minute I wondered where he was, but couldn't do anything about that, so I went to sleep. I left a message that I would be moving in the morning and that I could use his help.

# LEAH

I stumbled through the next day as I signed the papers and gave my five-hundred-dollar deposit.

"The lights and water are already on, but you'll need to have them switched over in your name," I was told.

"No problem. I'll start moving right away. Are there any restrictions?"

"Not really. Since these are houses instead of apartments you're pretty much free to do what you want. We do require that you keep up the grounds and maybe plant some flowers."

"I'd love to. I have quite a green thumb; if I do say so myself. Thanks," I said turning to leave. I was so excited I didn't know whether to shit or go blind. I called Sammie to see if I could get her to move the boxes that were already stacked by the front door while I cleaned out the house. She agreed to come by as soon as she shook the cobwebs off her brain. I also called Coy to see if we could use his truck. With his assistance I could get the lion's share of my things moved that day.

"Hey, beautiful," he answered when I hit up his cell phone number.

"Hi. I hate to be a pain in the butt, but I got a house today, and I wanted to start moving some things. Can you help me?"

"Just say the word. Do I need to bring backup?" he asked, causing me to smile. He was really a sweet man.

"Would that be too much to ask? I have Sammie coming over but, if I could get the muscle, I'll get her to help me pack while you guys move the stuff in."

"Only if I can help christen the place later," he replied, sparking a fire in my pussy.

"I wouldn't have it any other way!" I exclaimed.

"Okay, let me check with my boy. Greg has been dying to meet your wild friend anyway, so I won't have to twist his arm to come. We should be at your place by eleven-thirty, and you can give me the directions."

"Oh, you've been discussing my friends, huh?"

"Uh. Well. See what happened was…"

Amused at his lack of words, I just laughed.

"Don't sweat it. I don't know what I'd do without you," I said in earnest.

"Oh, I'm quite sure you can figure out a way to repay me," he said, and I seconded that emotion.

"Is your boy the married guy you told me about?"

"Uh. Yeah."

"Okay, just checking."

The rest of the morning flew by quickly. I had more than enough boxes ready by the time Coy and company arrived.

He arrived first and he looked better than he had ever looked. He had on a denim outfit and his shirt was opened to reveal his hairy chest. It was all I could do not to jump his ass and throw him to the floor. The man just exuded sex!

"Damn," I said, not bothering to check the wave of sexual energy he brought to the room. "I might just have to kick Sammie's ass when she gets one look at you. I ain't playing that sharing shit."

Laughing out loud, Coy responded, "I told you how I feel about that. You got this," he said, grabbing hold of his balls and shaking them at me. Normally I found that type of action offensive, but I was feeling those nuts!

"Okay, don't make me have to cut them off or something like that!" I laughed.

"Ouch! Women joke about that shit, but I'm here to tell you we don't find that shit funny," he said, now shielding his member instead of flaunting it.

"I had a friend who glued her boyfriend's dick to his stomach. He woke up and peed in his own face!"

"Now see, I would've had to shoot her ass!"

"I think homeboy wanted to shoot her, too, but she left town!"

"I would've put out an APB on her!" he said, still clutching his balls protectively. I walked over to him and removed his hand, gently squeezing them.

"I won't hurt these for all the tea in China. I just want to make your balls happy."

"Now that's what I am talking about," he said, grabbing me and kissing me deeply. He practically sucked away all of my air, and I came up gasping for breath.

"Dayum," I said, punching him lightly on his shoulder.

"Stay tuned; it gets better," he said, patting me on the butt as I turned to leave. I was about to reply when the doorbell rang. I swung open the door expecting Sammie, but meeting Coy's friend instead. *Oh my God*, I thought to myself. He was gorgeous.

"What up?" he said, raising his hand in greeting. I was speechless. His body was clearly designed by God, but I could tell immediately his mind was created by Mattel. He was definitely a piece of eye candy, but I was not fooled by his physical attributes. I needed to be able to have a serious conversation with my partner as well, and this guy was all about the physical.

Coy stepped around me and grabbed his boy around the shoulders. "Hey, man. Thanks for coming. This is my friend, Leah. Come on in!"

"She ain't for me?" he said, looking me up and down.

"Nah, nigga. She's mine," he said, and they high-fived.

Sammie chose that moment to knock on the door, which was ajar. She wore a hoochie dress that clung to her body and left nothing to the imagination. I shook my head at her choice of clothing, but that was Sammie.

Stepping forward, I took the bull by the horns and proceeded to make introductions.

"Coy, you met Sammie already and this is his friend, Greg," I said.

Sammie hardly paid Coy any attention, and I was glad about that. *I would hate to have to get into a fight with her big ass*, I thought to myself. Her eyes were glued to Greg, and he was not paying us any attention either.

"Hi," she said, coming into the room switching hips and throwing up flumes of perfume. She looked and smelled good, but I didn't need her to show up like this. I wanted her help first and then, if she happened to make a love connection, so be it.

"Damn, baby. I'm feeling that dress," Greg said, taking Sammie's hand in his and kissing it. I rolled my eyes at Coy and stepped away from the door. Sammie turned to greet me; I hoped she could tell I was pissed.

"Hey," she said, fanning herself.

"How the hell are you going to help dressed like that?" I said, not bothering to conceal the contempt in my voice.

"Oh, I've got a change of clothes in the car. This is what I wore to work," she said.

"Where the hell do you work?" both Coy and Greg chimed in, and I could not stifle my laughter.

"Wouldn't you like to know," she sheepishly replied, not bothered by the gaping stares. She turned around and strutted to her car with Greg ogling her ass.

"Hummm, I could work with that," Greg said, closing his eyes and crossing his heart. Who he was praying to was a mystery to me, but it got us all laughing.

"Negro, we're here to work. Let's break down the beds first. Leah has some more boxes to pack. Right, baby?"

"Yeah, the ones by the door are ready, but Sammie and I are going to finish packing up the kids' rooms."

Coy led Greg back into my room, and I could hear them joking as they took apart the furniture. Even though I had not planned to move actual furniture that day, I had to take advantage of the free labor. I didn't know Coy's or Greg's future availability so Coy had rented a larger moving truck on his way there

Sammie came back into the house and changed into some tired spandex pants and a short t-shirt. Greg would find it exciting but, for Coy and me, it was disgusting. I didn't need to see the outline of the crack in her pussy, and I knew enough of Coy to know that he would be equally disgusted. She had swept her long braids into a ponytail that she had slung to one side of her head.

My assessment of Coy was not too far off the mark. "That is entirely too much information," Coy said when he witnessed Sammie bent over a box. But it was just the right incentive for Greg. He started hefting boxes like he was on a time limit.

They cleared my living room of all the packed boxes as well as the furniture in all the kids' rooms and my room in record time. They were coming back for the living room furniture while I finished folding the clothes that I had hastily emptied out of the drawers. I had no idea they were planning on moving as much stuff as they had, but I was pleased. If I could get the big stuff, I could make separate trips back during the week for the smaller things. I was feeling pressed to move since I didn't know how long the police would be holding Kentee, and I wanted to be long gone before he was released.

Sammie did more flirting than she did packing. She must have gone into the bathroom fifteen times to spray on more perfume. As it was, she had on enough to choke a maggot.

"Damn, Sammie. What the hell are you trying to do, kill me? That man knows you're here. You don't have to try to kill off the roaches with all that perfume you're wearing. I feel like I ought to have on a fucking gas mask!"

"Oh, my bad. My sinuses are acting up, so I couldn't smell it," she said, going back to the bathroom. Throwing my hands up in the air, I walked around in circles. Feeling frustrated, I started flinging shit in a box.

"I'll just sort it out later," I said in disgust.

Sammie came back in the room, and it was evident that she had tried to wipe off some of the additional spray, but it didn't help much; her clothes reeked of it.

"Do you really think he noticed? He is so damn fine!"

"He ain't blind. You've been putting your ass up in his face since you got here," I said, laughing. "But I have to tell you; he's married."

She winked at me. "Hey, I don't want him until death do us part. I only want one night."

At first I wanted to get pissed, but then I had to realize who I was getting pissed at. There was no shame in Sammie's game. She saw something she wanted and went for it. Thank God she was leaving Coy alone because I might have had to fight her for him. I was really feeling Coy but I was a little gun-shy around him. I had yet to whip it on him because I just didn't want my feelings all out getting trashed so soon after Kentee.

Looking at the clock still mounted on the wall, I realized it was close to nine p.m. When Coy and Greg returned from their last trip to my new home, I called it a night. Since I no longer had a bed, we all traveled to my new home and spent another hour setting up the beds and making it usable for the evening. While Coy and I put fresh linens on the beds, Sammie and Greg got acquainted.

# SAMMIE

"So, beautiful, where have you been all my life?" Greg asked.

"Wow, you reached back for that line. How about telling me how you really feel?" I giggled.

"I don't know if you can handle how Big Daddy really feels."

"Try me!"

He grinned wildly. "I'd like to take you somewhere and suck the lint out of your toes."

"Yuck! Is that supposed to turn me on?" Greg's face fell when he figured out that I wasn't amused. "Oh, man, I'm gonna have to work on you," I said in despair, hitting my hand up against my head.

"What, you wouldn't like your toes sucked?"

"I didn't say that, but if you're trying to get in my personal space you have to be more creative; more daring. Stimulate my mind and my body will follow."

Taking a few minutes to think about it, Greg was stuck on stupid about how to proceed. I could tell he had never had to work this hard for the panties, and he was about to give up. I had probably insulted his best line.

"Do you ever dream about making love?" he asked, taking another stab at it.

"Oh, all the time!" I replied.

"Well, let me make your dreams come true," he said suddenly, feeling proud of himself while patting himself on the back for his snappy recovery.

"Shit," I said. "Let's switch roles. I'll be you and you be me, okay?"

"Uh. Sure."

"Hi, my name is Greg, a.k.a. the dream maker."

"Hi, my name is Sammie; nice to meet you. I'm curious about your alias. What does that mean?"

"Anything you want it to. Tell me your wildest fantasy, and I'll make it come true."

"Damn. Does that shit work?" he asked, perplexed as if I had written out some sort of genetic code.

"Try it and see."

"Sammie, I have this strong desire to make your fantasies come true. Tell me what would be your ultimate fantasy?"

"I would like... No, I would love..." I said, getting closer to him so I could whisper in his ear.

"Yes, my sweet. What is it?"

I could see him growing stiff in his pants at the feel of my warm breath on his ear. I suddenly wanted him to slam me back on the sofa while ramming his dick up my ass.

"My ultimate fantasy is to get fucked in a graveyard!" I said.

Greg's manhood instantly deflated.

"A graveyard? Are you fucking serious?" he said, getting pissed. He probably had visions of chocolate syrup and whipped cream and I wanted to fuck in a damn graveyard.

"Yeah, that's my fantasy," I said with this special smile and a wink. Despite his initial misgivings he started to look interested.

"Are you scared?" I asked, knowing full well that he was. Most black people feared the graveyard at night but I was not one of them. I'd had my most vigorous workouts in the graveyard and wanted to know if he was a man or a mouse. This usually gave me the quickest answer. If he was a mouse, he wasn't for me anyway, but if he wanted to get his freak on as much as I did, he would immediately step up to the plate.

"Hell no, I'm not scared!"

He was lying. He didn't like the idea one bit, but was not going to admit it to me. He probably had avoided the cemetery until it was his time to either visit or become a resident. But I could tell that my idea, as audacious as it sounded, was beginning to have some appeal.

"What if we get arrested?"

"You're a cop. Can't you fix it?"

"Damn, you've thought of everything, haven't you?" he said, clearly amazed that he was having this discussion at all. Even though he probably still thought it was nuts, he was obviously intrigued at the sheer boldness of the move. I did not ask him if he was married, if he had AIDS, or any other disease; I simply wanted to fuck in a graveyard.

"How will we get in?" he asked, still trying to reason out my plan.

"I have bolt cutters in my truck."

"Damn, you are serious, aren't you?"

"As a heart attack!" I exclaimed.

I sealed the deal when I reached between my legs, rubbed my pussy and stuck my finger in his mouth. His erection was the proof I needed. End of discussion!

I got up and went to inform Leah that Greg and I would be leaving.

"Gurl, we are rolling. I'll holler at you tomorrow." I winked at Leah and waved at Coy.

"Greg is leaving also?" Coy asked with this big-ass smile on his face. He knew the deal, and he could only shake his head.

"Yeah, he said he'd catch up with you at work." I shut the door behind me, cutting off further conversation.

"Oh my God!" I said, clearly amazed at how swiftly Sammie had worked. I had heard about her exploits from Marie, but had never witnessed her going for the kill myself.

"Ouch! I think she's about to hurt my boy!" Coy said, laughing.

"Yeah, I hope his insurance is up-to-date!" I responded, sitting on the edge of the bed. I was a little bent out of shape about the way Sammie had behaved. This was the first time she had met Greg, and she was already leaving to go fuck him. I hoped Coy wouldn't judge me by the company I kept, but then I had a reality check. I had slept with Coy just as quickly so I could not stand in judgment of Sammie.

He shook his head. "Yeah, I'd hate to inform his wife that he'd given his life but not in the line of duty."

"How long has he been married?"

"About fifteen years, but he ain't the loyal type," he admitted.

"Coy, please don't judge me by the actions of my friends," I said.

"Baby, relax. What we have is more than mere sex. I recognize what I have right here. Let's just take it a day at a time."

I searched his face to see if he was giving me lip service. If he was, it didn't show. His look and demeanor appeared legit.

"I don't know about Sammie sometimes. She's had a rough life and defines her happiness by who she's with. Sometimes I want to get mad, but I honestly don't think she knows any better. Sammie's been searching for love ever since I met her."

"How did you two meet? You've got me curious now."

I glanced at my watch. "Wow, do you have the time? It's already late."

"Tomorrow is Sunday, and we can finish getting things straight in the morning. Let's take a shower and you can tell me while we bathe," he suggested. I agreed and went to make sure the house was locked up, making a mental note to change the locks. This was my own personal quirk, and I would not be able to sleep well in the house until I did. Luckily, with Coy there I would feel a little safer.

I located the box of bathroom stuff and laid out enough for us to take a shower and lotion each other down. When I returned to the bedroom he had the shower going and was already under the flow.

The master bathroom was huge. It had twin sinks and a shower big enough for two with a little bench to sit down on if you felt compelled to. He was sitting on the bench, and I slipped down between his legs letting the warm water pelt the back of my head.

Taking his dick into my mouth, I gently sucked it. It grew as he grabbed my head and held it in position. He was not forceful in his grasp, and I appreciated it. There was nothing I hated more than a man who tried to ram his dick down my throat, trying to meet my tonsils. He gently pressed his hips toward my mouth as I sucked deeper and deeper. When I thought he could not handle anymore and was about to spill his load, I got up and mounted him. I was so hot it did not take long before we both climaxed.

Shaking, he lifted me off of him and said, "Damn."

"I'm sorry. I lost control," I said, feeling a tad embarrassed.

"I ain't mad at ya, but my whole body is tingling. Oh, I still want to hear about you and Sammie."

"Oh that wasn't an excuse not to talk about it, because I want to. I just got distracted," I said with a smile.

I grabbed the soap and a fresh washcloth and began to lather it as I started to speak.

"I met Sammie through a friend I used to work with. Her name was Marie. She and Sammie had been friends for years when I met them. I couldn't wait to meet her after hearing some of her hilarious stories from Marie."

"So, why haven't I met Marie?" he said as I applied the lather to his chest, gently massaging his skin as I rubbed. My hand paused and for a moment I could not move it.

"She was killed by her ex-boyfriend," I replied sadly. "That's another reason why I took Kentee's threats so seriously."

"Damn, boo, I'm sorry," he said. He took the washcloth from me and began washing my chest. He took his time over my ample breasts and sucked them; soap and all.

"It was tough going for a while, and Sammie was the closest tie I had to Marie. Marie was a very special person; more like a caregiver. Everyone who knew her felt a special connection and she intuitively knew when you were in distress. She would call at the damndest times just to say hi, and it was usually during my darkest hours!"

"Wow, she sounds really special," he said, as the cloth traveled lower to my thighs. He turned me around and pushed down my shoulders so I was seated on the bench as he lifted up my legs and carefully washed them.

"Sammie used to make her so mad, but she always wound up forgiving her. That was just how Marie was. She left behind two children. It was so sad. Her mother is raising the children, and I still try to visit them. Marie would have been so proud of them."

Coy was paying so much attention to bathing my pussy that I thought he was not interested in the story, so I stopped talking. He instantly looked up into my eyes.

"Why did you stop?"

"I thought I was boring you."

"Didn't I say I wanted to hear it? I'm a cop; I can multi-task," he said, winking.

"Oh, okay. I didn't know the hell Sammie had put Marie through because she didn't tell me most of it. Sammie told me when we got together after the funeral. She bears a lot of weight on her heart because she believes Marie would still be here if she hadn't been spending so much of her time worrying about Sammie's drama."

"Oh, drama! This is getting better. Let's get into the bed because my skin is starting to wrinkle," he said, pulling me off my seat and pushing me out the shower door. We left huge puddles on the floor, but this was the type of water I didn't mind cleaning up later.

After drying off, we both raced to the bedroom and climbed under the covers.

I hadn't bothered turning on the heat. When I was firmly snuggled in his arms, I continued the story.

"Sammie has a past that includes a drug-addicted, abusive husband. He moved her halfway across the country, away from her family and children."

"Wait, she left her kids for a man?" Coy asked in shock.

"Yeah, but she was young and dumb, and I'm constantly discovering that there's more to the story. Anyway, after they'd been in California for a while he started making her strip. She was scared and in love, so she did it. When she stopped earning the money he needed her to make, he started dancing. It was a real freak fest."

"Sounds like it," he said, totally engrossed in the story.

"Jessie started Sammie in a new career as a prostitute."

"Okay, you're losing me now. I stretched my imagination to believe that someone would throw money at her for taking off her clothes, but now you want me to believe that someone would pay to do the naked nasty with her, too? Nope, I ain't feeling that!"

"Where's your friend at now?" I asked.

"Damn, I forgot all about him! I guess you've got a point. But I know my boy ain't paying for it! Different strokes for different folks."

"I guess you could say Sammie can work that ass!" I giggled. "Just remember that I neither endorse nor criticize Sammie's behavior. She's driven by her own demons and, little by little, she's filling in the gaps for me. Enough talking, it's almost midnight and we both have to get up early tomorrow."

"Okay, boo. Turn over and press that fine booty against me so I can go to sleep. Good-night," he said, kissing me on the forehead.

Turning over, I nestled against his now firm dick. "You behave now. I don't want to have to get back into the shower!"

"I'll be good. My johnson is just reacting to your warmth!"

We fell asleep shortly, but my dreams were less than peaceful. I dreamed of Marie and made a vow to spend some time if I could with her mother and my godchildren. We still kept in touch by phone, but the way I was feeling required a personal visit.

# SAMMIE

Oakland Cemetery was pitch black with no surrounding streetlights to illuminate the gates. I chose to drive and allow Greg some time to get into the moment. The roads leading down to the gates were void of moving traffic.

Even though this was not the first time I had visited the graveyard at night, it was the first time I had taken a newbie. I usually reserved this special treat for my regular fuck buddies, but I was looking forward to turning Greg out on this sacred turf. I reached across the seat and grabbed his thigh to make sure he was still with me. I got out of the car and he followed me.

"Dang, boo; you sure are quiet," I said, knowing full well he was about to change his mind. I could identify with his fear, since I remembered my first time with reverence. As long as he didn't haul ass off running, I was sure he would enjoy the experience as much as I would. The sounds of chirping crickets and other insects were the only noise we heard other than our breathing.

"Wait here while I get what we need," I said, popping the trunk. Inside I had blankets, a flashlight, and some mace. I always traveled prepared for my special games. I took variety in sex to a whole new level, and although I should have been ashamed, I wasn't.

Greg was in shape, so the uphill climb did not affect him. On the other hand, my big ass was struggling with every step. The only exercise I received was in my arms, moving from hand to mouth. I almost wanted to turn around, but I was so excited I had to see this through.

"I'm still here, but I don't think this is such a good plan. When you think about it, it's sick and perverted. Don't tell me you were just sitting around the house and said to yourself, 'I wanna get laid in a graveyard'!"

Laughing loudly, I said, "No, it wasn't like that. I saw it on television, and haven't been able to get it out of my mind."

"What the hell were you watching?" he mumbled under his breath.

"What did you say?"

"Nothing."

"I want to hear what you have to say when we're done," I said, smiling.

Leah wanted to know why my men kept coming back, and I wanted to tell her but I didn't want her to look at me differently. My secret: I brought adventure to fucking! Fucking was an art that I had perfected over the years. Sure, I still had sex, but when I wanted to be fucked, the script was written and directed by me. Greg was going to be my co-star that night. He had the proper equipment, and with a little training he would grab the Emmy. I was going after my nut. If he didn't get his before I got mine, shame on his ass! In this debut, first one across the finish line would be the winner!

For a moment I reflected on what we were about to do. *Maybe I am sick*, I thought but dismissed the idea.

"You ready?" I asked.

"Uh...sure," he said.

"Don't forget the bolt cutters," I said, and he hurried back to the car to claim them. The bolt cutters were a bold move and something I had used before. In the past, admittance to the graveyard was often a problem. I didn't know I would wind up there that night, but I kept them in the car just in case.

"What did you bring them for? No one locks up the cemetery, because the residents aren't going anywhere," Greg said.

"True but this is the hood! They lock everything. This is more to keep folks out than in."

I tried not to let him hear me huffing and puffing with each step, but he was probably in touch with all the neighboring sounds and I sounded like a freight train. I could tell he was afraid, and it just heightened my sexual attraction.

At the entrance gate, I handed him the items I was carrying and held my hands out for the bolt cutters.

"I can do it," he said.

"Nope. If we do get caught you can always claim you caught me breaking in and were taking me in for questioning." I said.

He shook his head. "Damn, where do you come up with this shit?"

"I have a very active imagination."

"No shit," he muttered, still shaking his head. I could not tell if he was trying to talk himself out of going through with it or if he was really starting to feel the vibe pulsating all around us. He looked on as I tried several times to cut the thick chain.

I was a big woman and thought cutting a chain would be easy, but I forgot most of the muscles in my arms had been dormant for so long, they had forgotten their purpose. After struggling for over three minutes, I managed to snap the link and pushed the gate wide enough for us to enter.

Once we were inside, I threw the chain back around the fence to make it appear secure at casual inspection. Even though it was pitch black in the yard I did not turn on the flashlight until we were several feet from the fence. I was holding on to Greg's hand, and I could feel the tremors emanating from his body. This excited me even more, and I prayed he would make it to the gravesite I wanted to lie on.

Fucking in a graveyard is exciting enough, but it takes that excitement to another level when you know who is buried beneath you. I was looking for the grave of my tenth grade sex education teacher. His name was Raymond Hunter, and he had been the source of many late-night masturbation sessions among the girls. I thought it was only fitting that he should squirm like I did when he talked about penetration and ovulation to us!

Greg did not utter a word as I practically dragged him into the middle of the graveyard. I had gotten a map several months ago from the curator and knew exactly where I wanted to go. Greg's hand had started sweating, and a few times it slipped from my grasp. Despite his misgivings, he continued to follow me.

I finally located the site and was touched to see all the fresh flowers on the grave. After laying down the blanket, I took several of the roses and stripped them of their petals, tossing them on our blanket. I doused the light and walked toward Greg. My hands found him before he could flee, and I could tell from every taut muscle in his body that that was exactly what he was about to do.

"I thought you weren't a chicken shit," I chided while running my hands up his muscular thighs. His body was good and tight. "You must work out!" I said, pressing my breasts against his chest. His lips were trembling as I gently nibbled on them. He grunted in response.

I started unbuttoning his shirt, and he neither helped me nor stopped me. When the wide expanse of his chest was exposed I started trailing my tongue all over it. His taut nipples were pert and seemed to like the mixture of my hot breath and the cooling night temperature.

I slid off his shirt; never taking my lips off his body. The shirt hit the blanket, and I used my foot to push it to the side. I didn't want to be lying on his Phat Farm shirt when we finally connected. My hands traveled to his firm waist and below. His groan deepened. I toyed with his belt buckle, drawing out the moment when I would take down his pants.

Suddenly I pushed him away, and he stumbled but did not fall. I took off my top and unhooked my bra, allowing my breasts to burst forth. Even though I could not see his facial expression, his eyes were undoubtedly glued to them. I lifted them up and as he bent forward I placed the left one in his mouth. His lips immediately closed around the nipple, but I withdrew it before he could really get into it.

I took that same nipple and placed it in my own mouth, making greedy sucking sounds that had to be driving him wild. He reached out to touch me, and I smacked away his hand.

"In time. In time," I said.

Carefully, I got down on my knees. The ground was hard and rocky underneath the blanket, but I was so intent on pleasing Greg that I hardly noticed. Again I grabbed his belt buckle; undoing it this time. He sucked in a deep breath as I unzipped his pants and eased them down his legs. I paused long enough to unlace his shoes and slide them from his feet; careful to pile his stuff together in case we had to get dressed in a hurry.

I blew on his enlarged dick, and he let out the oxygen he had been holding as I stifled a laugh. He didn't seem scared then. I shimmied out of my stretch pants and knelt naked before him. For a brief moment I turned on the flashlight so he would know where everything was, and then I quickly turned it off.

Before he could move, I took him in my mouth, swallowing the entire thing. I wished I could have seen his face when I did it. It took years of practice to be able to take in a man of considerable size, and Greg's size was nothing to scoff at. Inside my mouth he got larger and I fingered his balls to increase his pleasure.

I massaged his butt cheeks with one hand, pulling him deeper into my mouth with the other. I could tell he was about to blow, and I didn't want it to happen until I crossed the finish line. I abruptly removed my mouth and pulled him down on the ground.

"Wow," he said as I directed him to my special place. When he entered I automatically tightened up on his dick, catching him in a vise grip.

"Oh God," he moaned, and I increased the grip. When he pulled back, I sucked him in further. I could suck a marble off the floor with my pussy from two inches away, so he wasn't going anywhere.

I started moving my hips; preparing for my final approach. With each thrust I was getting closer to the finish line, and I held him firmly against me so he would not move and cause me to lose my momentum. I held him so tight it was a wonder he could breathe, but he did his part and kept pounding into my hot spot. We came together as he dropped his full weight on me. For added measure, I gripped his now softened dick twice more before I allowed him to roll off me.

With this one act of sex I knew who was in control of our budding relationship. He looked like he was about to call his wife and tell her he was never coming home, but I didn't want him for that. He would be good for getting rid of some frustrations, but I was not ready to get back into a steady romance. For the first time in my life I was having some fun, and I was not letting go of my freedom.

"Damn, gurl!" he said when he was able to catch his breath.

I chuckled. "Still think this shit is sick?"

He slowly groped for his clothes. "Yeah, but I must admit that I enjoyed it!"

I had forgotten that fear usually besieged me once I had gotten my nut but now it was nagging me to get the hell out of the graveyard! Greg was languid and taking entirely too long to get dressed! If he could have taken a nap, I think he would have.

"Hey, look. We better move it. It doesn't pay to stay here this long," I said, already pulling at the blanket he was still sitting on. He jumped up like I had stung him and started helping me get my stuff. He led the way back to the car, a lot more confident then when he first entered through the gates.

We walked back as silently as we had come in, but the tone was different. All of a sudden he was acting cocky, and it turned me off. Both of us were locked into our own thoughts, and this made me a bit uncomfortable. I tossed the blankets back in the trunk and drove him back to Leah's house.

I remembered how abruptly we had left Leah's house, and regrets began to seep in, ruining any sexual gratification I had initially felt.

"Oh, God," I moaned.

"What's wrong?" Greg asked.

"What are we going to tell them?" I uttered.

"Nothing. You just drop me off at my car and we drive away."

"You don't want to go back in?"

"For what? Knowing Coy, they're getting busy anyway. You're worrying about the wrong thing. Sammie, we're grown and we don't have to answer to anyone but God."

I was not sure I believed his easy answer to a delicate situation, but it was the only remedy I could think of. I would eventually tell Leah about my evening, as I was sure she would tell me about hers with Coy, but, for that night, I did not want to confess my sins.

When we arrived at Greg's car, he asked for my number and gave me a pager number to reach him. He still had not mentioned the fact that he was married, and I did not question him about it. I wanted to get away from him because I was suddenly feeling like a tramp. I cried all the way home. I wanted to stop the vicious cycle my life had become, but I simply didn't know how.

## LEAH

On Monday morning, I woke up with a start when I realized that the alarm did not go off. Coy and I had spent Sunday arranging furniture and making the new house into a home. We cleared out the remaining items in my old house, and I was officially moved in. To celebrate we made love in every room in the house, and I loved every minute of it. Of course, he ended up staying over again, and now I had overslept.

"You can use the guest bathroom. There are towels somewhere but you're going to have to find them yourself. I've got to find some clothes to wear." I rushed into the bathroom, slamming the door behind me.

It was a mistake to entertain Coy for two nights in a row, but we were having such a good time, I wasn't ready for it to end. If I made it to work on time I would declare it worth it, but if I arrived late, I would probably be mad at him. I jumped in the shower, allowing the water to run through my hair. I would have no choice but to put my hair in a ponytail, and the warm water helped to smooth out the knots.

I tried to wash my face and brush my teeth at the same time. I briefly wondered what Coy was doing, but I didn't have time to check. I still had to find my underwear! Quickly brushing my hair, I raced from the bathroom with twenty minutes to spare.

Coy stood grinning before me. He had ironed a pair of charcoal slacks and a white shirt for me. He had even found the box that held my underwear. Kissing him on his cheek, I snatched the clothing and put it on.

"Thanks, baby. If you hadn't helped me, I would've been late. Can you lock up when you leave? I've got to go."

Not waiting for a reply, I kissed him again on the cheek and flew out the door. It was only after I was a few blocks away that I had misgivings about leaving him in my house to snoop.

I didn't have much to hide since he had already seen most of my dirty business when he investigated my house after Kentee broken in, but it was still the principle. I was getting so comfortable with Coy, and he had not yet told me his intentions. That was the same mistake I had made with Kentee, and I didn't want to travel that road again.

"I'll talk to him tonight," I said to myself.

Even though I had revealed a lot of the stuff that had happened in my life to him, we still had not discussed his role. I wanted a man in my life, but Coy would have to understand that I had kids; one with special needs. I needed to find out if he wanted to be involved or not; I needed to know so I could keep a tight reign on my feelings.

I arrived at work with ten minutes to spare and used the time to phone my mother. I had originally planned on stopping over at her house before coming to work. As I approached the building I dialed her on my cell.

"Hey, Momma," I said cheerfully to hide my discomfort.

"Hey, baby. We're all okay. I thought you were coming over here before you went to work."

"I was, but we didn't get finished until late and my stupid alarm clock didn't go off. I just made it to work, and I really had to rush to get in here on time."

"I'll drop Kayla off at school and the twins at day care in about half an hour. Go ahead. I don't want you late for work, either."

"I don't know what I'd do without you," I said as I dashed into the building. When I rounded the first corner I slowed to a casual stroll like I had been there all along. I popped my head in to say hi to Ms. Brooks before going to my assigned desk.

"Hey, I was looking for you," she said.

"Oh really, why?" I inquired, nervously.

"I've heard some good feedback on you. If you aren't busy this morning, I could really use your help on a few projects."

"Let me check in and see what's going on, and I'll come back," I said, relieved it was good news. I knocked on Mr. Lyons's door, but he didn't answer and, since I did not see any work in my in-basket, I dashed back down the hall.

Putting my purse in my desk, I walked to the employee lounge and got a cup of coffee before I headed back to word processing to see what Ms. Brooks had for me to do. I was careful not to spill any of the black coffee on my favorite blouse.

Thinking about my blouse, I remembered Coy's kindness that morning by finding me something to wear and ironing it for me. *I could get used to that sort of treatment*, I thought to myself.

"What's going on?" I asked Andrea when I popped my head back in the door.

"Two interrogatories and a brief," she replied. "I'm shorthanded today. I thought Tarcia was coming back, but she called in with a family emergency."

*When I heard the name Tarcia the hairs on the nape of my neck stood up, but I wasn't sure why. Where had I heard that name before?*

"Who's Tarcia?" I asked, assuming that I had met everyone who worked in the department.

"She was on her honeymoon when you started, so you haven't met her yet. She's a nice girl, but I think she's having some personal problems."

"What's the brief about?" I asked, trying to shake the uneasiness I felt.

"It's juicy. The wife is on trial for attempted murder. She stuck a fork in her husband's throat when she found him in bed with her sister."

I giggled with excitement. "Gimme!"

"Somehow I knew you'd say that!" Andrea said. "I knew it would get you!" Pretending to snatch the brief and the remains of my coffee, I made it back to my desk still laughing. She was a nice lady, and I had enjoyed getting to know her.

This was going to be a long week because Mr. Lyons was not actively involved in the legal aspect of the job. His duties were merely administrative, and I hated that shit. Just listening to his droll voice on the tape recorded last week let me know what I was in store for. I was just there to answer the phones, confirm or deny appointments, and transcribe whatever letters he had dictated. The job was a piece of cake but was not one I would want full-time. I liked to be kept busy and, based on what I had seen thus far, it would not happen there. I planned to make use of my connection with Andrea to keep myself occupied for the week. If not, I would resort to reading the phone book to stay awake.

I turned on my computer. While it was booting up, I called Coy's cell to thank him.

"Hello, sexy," he said when he answered the phone.

"Hi, yourself. Did I thank you for this morning and last night and the night before that?"

"For what?"

"Oh, you know what I mean," I said. "Were you late?"

"Naw. As soon as I get in that car, I'm officially on duty. I missed roll call, but Greg clocked me in."

"Oh God! Greg! Did he tell you what happened between him and Sammie on Saturday night?"

"I haven't seen him yet, but he sure was in a good mood when I spoke to him!"

"Lawd have mercy! I've got to get busy; I have a domestic violence brief to prepare. Call me later, if you can."

"Bye baby."

Hanging up the phone, I plugged in my headset and began the transcription process. I felt like I had slipped back in time to the days when Marie was working right around the corner from me. I quickly pushed that thought out of my mind as I commenced to transcribing the defense of yet another woman done wrong by yet another man.

For the next few hours I typed a case law that argued for keeping the young black woman from either dying in prison or by lethal injection. When I was finished, I was so intrigued by the case that I trotted down the hall to find Andrea to see if she would let me read the depositions.

"Don't tell me you're done with the brief," Andrea said, laughing. "You truly are a hard worker, and I can't wait to make my recommendation to keep you in my department!"

"Oh, thank you. That's so kind of you. I like to keep busy, and there's something about criminal law that makes it easy. It's almost like reading a book."

"I know how you feel. That's what got me in this field in the first place; being nosey."

"The brief was very compelling, but it's left me with more questions than answers. Can I read the depositions?"

"Wow. This is the first time I've been asked that one. I don't see why not. If someone questions it, tell them to see me."

"I'm not going to tell anyone. I just want to know."

"I believe you; it's a matter of confidentiality. But since you're now an employee of the firm, you're bound by the laws of confidentiality; just like the lawyers representing the case. Since this case is going to trial soon, you'll be seeing more and more of it. I'll request the preliminary file that'll give you the background information. We had to really fight to get it. Mrs. Phillips is a pro-bono nut, and the other partners didn't want her to take on a case of this magnitude and not generate any income to the firm. She was adamant about it and won them over."

"That's very charitable! I'd better get back to my desk before Mr. Lyons gets in. What's he like, anyway?"

"A strange bird," she replied with a smile. "But you'll be able to handle him; if you can fight him off."

"Oh no, not one of those," I said. I was not afraid of those types of employers. I made it clear up front, I was being paid to type and answer the phone. Anything outside of that was extra and they couldn't afford it. "Do you have anything else you need me to do?"

"I still have one set of interrogatories, but that's all for now."

Holding out my hand, I took the tiny tape and went back to my desk. I took the long way back to my desk, trying to get a feel for my co-workers. Most had their heads covered with headsets and, although they waved, I did not feel any special vibe from them. Humming softly, I went back to my desk.

Thoughts of the case were still plaguing me. I could relate to it since I was victimized myself by a selfish man. Mrs. Phillips' line of defense was that her client had temporarily gone insane and could not be held accountable for her actions. I wanted to know exactly what had driven her to the point of sticking a fork into her husband's throat.

Before I could get the headphones on my ears, the phone rang. "Mr. Lyons' office," I said in my most professional voice.

"Is he in?" a young female voice responded.

"No, I'm sorry. Mr. Lyons is out of the office at the moment. May I take a message?" I said with my pen poised.

"Where is he?" the voice persisted.

"Ms...uh, if you'd kindly leave a message I'll be delighted to give it to him when he returns." I tried to be as polite and as firm as I could be.

"Where is Shonell?" the caller demanded.

"She's on vacation, and I'm filling in."

"Shit," the caller said and hung up the phone.

Stunned at the anger in the lady's voice, I held the phone for a few seconds, staring at it. Before I could place it in the cradle good, it rang again. I punched the second line and said, "Mr. Lyons' office, can I help you?"

Again the voice was female and she asked the same question.

"Is he in?"

"No, Mr. Lyons is not in the office at this time. Can I take a message and have him return your call?"

"No, I need to speak with him right away!" the caller responded.

"I understand. When I hear from him, I'll be happy to give him the message."

"Where is he?"

"He had a court appointment this morning, and hopefully he'll be in as soon as it is over," I lied.

"Oh, okay. Ask him to call Kathy."

"I'll be sure to give him the message," I said, shaking my head as I hung up the phone. I put my headphones back on and started typing. Lunch came and went without my knowing it. When I finally unplugged myself, it was two p.m. Stretching, I decided to find Andrea and tell her that I had worked through yet another lunch hour. I was about to walk away when the phone rang again.

"I want Ray," a nagging and uppity-sounding voice said.

"Excuse me?" I asked, not knowing who she was talking about. I flipped open the phone directory to scan the names of employees but came up blank.

"Shonell?"

"No, this is Leah. Shonell is on vacation," I replied, remembering that Mr. Lyons' first name was Ray.

"I want to speak to my husband, Raymond Lyons," she said, dragging out each syllable like I could not understand English.

"Mrs. Lyons, I'm sorry. I just started in this department today, and I didn't know Mr. Lyons' first name. In fact, I've never met him. He hasn't been in the office yet, but I do expect him."

There was a long moment of silence, and I didn't know whether she had hung up or not.

"Hello?" I inquired.

"Never mind. Please disregard the call," she said, clearly pissed off, and hung up.

*This shit ain't for me*, I thought to myself. I had finished the interrogatories and I took them back to Andrea.

"Uh oh, you don't look like a happy camper," she said.

"I'm not. Mr. Lyons hasn't been in all day, and I've been fielding questions on his whereabouts, and I don't have a clue where he is. At the very least, he could call me and tell me what to say. I don't want to get into any trouble for saying the wrong thing. This is making me very uneasy."

She patted me on the back. "Calm down. I'll handle any flack for this. He should've left word that he wasn't going to be in; or called you at the very least. This won't come back to haunt you. I promise."

"Thanks."

"Did you get lunch?"

"No, I lost track of time," I responded with a grin. *I just wanted to finish this boring project, hoping for something else with more meat.*

"Come on. I haven't had lunch either. Let's go grab a quick burger, and we can get to know each other a little better."

"Okay, let me grab my purse," I said. I was not exactly looking forward to lunch with Andrea, but she had been good to me thus far. I didn't want her too far up in my business, so I planned to speak only when spoken to and avoid references to my personal life.

## SAMMIE

I hadn't seen or spoken to Leah in over a month. I had allowed the stress of my new job and my active sex life to keep me from my dear friend. If I was being really honest with myself, I had to admit those were the same excuses I had used for my shameless behavior the last time I had seen her, on the day she moved. I was still stepping out with Greg, but he was beginning to get on my last nerve.

Greg was ready to leave his wife and start shacking with me, and I wasn't trying to hear that. He was fun and all that, but he was so predictable. I controlled the sex in our relationship; including the creativeness of it. Quite frankly, I wanted more in a man. I wanted him to make me weak in the knees and not the other way around.

He wanted it every night, but I was feeding him with a long-handled spoon. He seemed like small fish when I compared him to my new boss. This man was not only foine, but he also had money, and those two things went well together in my book. So far, all we had done was flirt, but I could tell I was wearing down his resistance. He was Italian with dark wavy hair, and I couldn't wait to run my fingers through it. But when his blue eyes struck my dark brown ones, I was convinced to have him; if only for one time.

I had never made it with a white man with money, and I was anxious to turn him out. I was beginning to think he was receptive, since he had stopped dictating into his handheld tape recorder and suggested that his flow would be more natural if I used my shorthand skills.

I had not used my shorthand in a number of years, but he didn't seem to mind. He didn't flow much better in person than he did on tape, but, hey, I was cool with that. When he started to get ahead of me, I would drop my pencil and bend down low enough for him to glimpse my boobs or part my legs so he could see my underwear. That would slow his roll in a hurry, and he would stumble over words and often ask me to repeat what he had said. In fact, he was so slow I was able to write it out in longhand.

"Ms. Davis, I need to dictate a letter," Mr. Spencer said into the speaker that was on my desk.

"I'll be right in," I said, feeling excited because I wasn't wearing any underwear that day. This sneak-a-peek shit was taking too long for me, and I wanted to put the game in motion for real. I smoothed down any wayward hairs and applied another coat of lipstick on my already ruby red lips. I dabbed a few drops of perfume on my earlobes and another two on the insides of my thighs. I jumped up from my desk and rushed into his office, only to return to my desk to grab my steno pad.

Flipping though the used pages on my pad, I wrote today's date on the first blank one. I crossed my legs and licked the tip of my pen, knowing full well he was watching.

"I'm ready," I said in a seductive voice.

He stuttered, trying to find his train of thought. "Uh...ah..., this is a letter, to...uh..."

I uncrossed my legs and left them open. He could not regain his composure.

"Enough is enough," I said, slapping my pad on his desk. I shut and locked his door and turned to face him. "You want to hit this, don't you?"

He did not respond, and I was getting a little ticked off.

"You've been sniffing around me for a couple of weeks, and I've been trying to let you know it was okay, but I see I'm going to have to break it down for you. Do you want to hit this?" I asked, turning around and revealing my near naked ass.

Looking at him over my shoulder I saw him jump up from his desk and hurriedly tug at his belt. That in itself was a warning sign that he would be a two-minute brother. My fantasies had worked him up to at least ten minutes, and I had half a mind to pull down my skirt and say, "Syke."

He slipped his hands underneath my skirt. "Damn," he said.

Paralyzed, I allowed him to continue to stroke my moist center. He backed me up to the desk and instructed me to sit on it. Sitting in his chair, he lifted my legs and placed them on his thighs. He parted my lips and placed his hot tongue on my throbbing clit. I could not stifle the moan. He nibbled and sucked until I thought I could not stand it any more.

Pulling me closer to the edge of the desk, he quickly stood up, unzipping his pants. He donned a condom and dipped his exquisite dick into my dripping pussy.

"Lord have mercy," I moaned out loud.

He grabbed my legs and wrapped them around his waist and I pushed with all my might to get every inch of him inside of me.

My eyes rolled back in my head, and I felt like I had left my body. *Nothing this illicit should feel so fucking good,* I thought. He clutched me tighter as we prepared to climax, and I strove to ride the tide of his dick!

Our eyes locked as we rode that wave together. Then, satisfied, we disengaged. He gave me a towel that he had in his desk drawer and I wiped up the excess that dripped from my pussy as he gave me this "and you know this" grin. The phone stopped me from acknowledging his prowess. He gave me another look that said, "Aren't you going to get that?"

I snatched up the phone, suddenly feeling very ashamed of myself. I listened for a few seconds and placed the caller on hold.

"Your wife is on line one," I said, giving him the evil eye as I climbed off his desk. I closed the door behind me, but it was loud enough to let him know I didn't appreciate the way he had treated me. His face was beet red, and his eyes would not meet mine.

"Thank God it's Friday!" I screamed when I got inside my car. It had been a long week, and I was looking forward to some down time. The twins were getting along well at the day care center, Kayla has adjusted to being away from her siblings while she was in school and I had Craig Richmond to thank. At lunch today, I had bought him a card telling him just how much I appreciated the extra care he was giving Mya.

Every night for the past two months when I picked the children up, I always found Mya in his office. For the first time in her life, she seemed content. Her behavior had even improved at home, and I was beginning to feel like a normal life was achievable for us.

I hadn't heard any more from Coy about Kentee; except a brief message on my answering machine earlier that day stating that he was out on bond. It was a good thing my number had been changed, and we had moved from what I now deemed "his house." Since Kentee lived on the other side of town with his girlfriend, I felt confident I would not run into him or his family during the course of our daily lives.

As a getaway, Coy had invited me to take a trip with him the following day and I had already cleared it with Momma to watch the kids. I was starting to feel like a young adult; instead of an indentured slave. I pulled into the day care center full of inner joy, and I was looking forward to a quiet night with the kids.

The center was quiet for a Friday and, as I was accustomed to doing, I stopped by Craig's office first to collect Mya, but the door was shut. Hesitating for a few minutes, I knocked on the door.

"Come in," Craig said, and I could not help but smile. God had really delivered blessings to my family lately. My smile quickly disappeared when I walked into his office and noticed his somber face.

"Oh, Lord," I said as my entire body started to shake. I'd had this nagging fear that something was wrong all day but had refused to entertain the thought.

"Leah, please sit down," he said, rising out of his chair.

"What happened?" I asked, unable to contain the fear racing through my blood.

"Mya had a rough afternoon," he said.

Frantic, I looked around his office for my daughter. I had deluded myself into thinking my troubles with Mya were over since she seemed to be doing so well at the center.

"Where is she?" My voice rose along with my anxiety level.

"She's resting right now. She sure has a lot of fight in her," he said, rubbing his jaw.

"Why didn't you call me?" I asked, wanting to get pissed at someone, and it didn't really matter who.

"It happened about an hour ago. She was having a really good day until then. She actually played with the other children and even napped when they did. Normally, I take her out of the class at naptime because she's too wired to nap with the other children."

When I didn't respond, he continued.

"I usually take her to the observation wing with me, and she stays there or in here until you come to get her."

"I knew she was spending a lot of time with you, but I didn't realize just how much."

"I don't mind at all. While she plays, I work on whatever I have going at the moment. Have you seen her drawings?"

"Her what?" I asked, like he was talking French or some other foreign language.

"Her drawings. That's what she does when she's with me."

He reached into his desk drawer and pulled out ten pictures that Mya had drawn. She was no Michelangelo but she did have talent. I had never given her a crayon before because I didn't want her writing on the walls.

"Mya did this?"

"Yeah, she did. Most of them were done the first day she was here but she does at least one a day for me."

Craig smiled as I reviewed each picture in awe. If he hadn't told me Mya had drawn them, I would have sworn they were drawn by a child at least ten years old instead of two. There was so much attention to detail. She had even drawn our family, minus her father, and that picture made my heart ache.

"What happened today?" I asked when I could finally tear my eyes away from the pictures.

"To be honest, I don't know. When I went to get her at naptime, she was already asleep. I saw no need to wake her, so I instructed Beverly, the teacher, to call me when she woke up. Since she never napped with the other students, I wanted to be there. Beverly got busy with the other students and, before she knew it, Mya was up."

"I can't take this; tell me what happened," I cried to him.

"I'll have to let Beverly tell you. I wasn't in the room, so anything I could tell you would be hearsay." He punched two digits into the phone. "Ms. Simmons is here. Can you get someone to sit with the kids and come into my office?"

"Right away, Mr. Richmond," she said over the speaker, then hung up.

Craig tried to be reassuring. "Leah, calm down. We both knew this wasn't going to be easy."

"Are you giving up on Mya?" I asked, giving voice to my worst fear.

"Of course not, I've grown attached to those kids; especially Mya. I can't turn my back because we've hit a bump in the road. If I was that kind of man, I wouldn't have started this center in the first place." He reached across the table to squeeze my clenched hands. He drew back his hand when his office door opened and Beverly entered.

"Hi, Ms. Simmons," she said as she took the other vacant chair in the office.

"Please, call me Leah," I said, trying to diffuse the tension in the air.

"Please tell Ms. Simmons what happened when Mya woke up from her nap," Craig said with a smile.

"She woke up screaming. She was one of the last ones to wake, and it took me a moment to get to her. By the time I did, she had scratched up her face pretty good and was banging her head against the floor. It shocked me because she was sleeping so well," she said, wringing her own hands in torment.

I gave her hand an understanding pat. Mya's outbreaks often took me off guard as well, and she was my child. I understood how quickly Mya could change from sugar to shit.

"She banged her head quiet a few times before I could restrain her and all the other kids were in hysterics. Mr. Richmond was finally able to get her to stop," she said, nodding her head at Craig for approval.

"Thanks, Beverly. I can take it from here," he said, dismissing her.

She got up from her seat and left the room, but not without saying, "I'm sorry."

"There is one more thing I would like to discuss before you go see to Mya. I got the results from her hearing test today and it confirmed my suspicions that Mya is not hearing as she should be. Our doctors recommend that she be fitted for a hearing aid." Craig handed me the results and I scanned the pages but I could not concentrate on the words.

I rose from my chair. "I need to see Mya."

"Of course, but we need to plan a course of action."

I sat back down. "Course of action?"

"Yes, there's something else going on that we're not aware of and we need to address it as soon as possible."

"Hell, I could've told you that! I've taken her to every doctor I could think of—at least the ones I could afford—and they aren't telling me anything. If you have some miracle up your sleeve, by all means, tell me!"

"I know what you mean. When my son was sick we took him to doctor after doctor and they couldn't tell us what was wrong until it was too late. I don't want to wait this one out. Your daughter's very special. I want to take her to the doctor my son saw for an assessment. We can't afford to wait on our doctors to get back to us."

"A specialist? I can't afford it!" I said, wanting to call the words back but facing the hard reality of my life.

"Leah, you have insurance now. They'll pay for it. If they don't, I will. I'm still waiting for our doctor's assessment of Mya. Just give me permission to set it up and I'll handle the rest. The only thing I need from you is a permission slip to take her to the specialist and an authorization for the testing."

"Will they hurt her?"

"No, of course not. Don't forget I love that little lady also," he replied with another smile that was beginning to melt my heart.

"Where do I sign?" I asked, relieved I was no longer alone in the situation.

Craig gave me all the paperwork and told me to bring it back on Monday. I went to get the kids and I cringed when I saw Mya's face. I knew how brutal she could be to herself but it did not lessen the shock or the anguish I felt when I saw her.

"Oh, baby," I said, gathering up her tiny body in my arms and taking her to the car. I vowed before God, I would do anything He wanted if He would just protect my baby from herself.

"Good night, Leah. We'll see you all on Monday," Craig said. "If you need anything over the weekend, here's my number. Just give me a call," he said, handing me his business card with a personal number scribbled on the back.

"Thank you," I said, leading the other kids to the car.

## SAMMIE

Work was a struggle that day and I didn't want to deal with it. I had toyed with the idea of calling in but, since I had recently received a promotion, it would have been a bad idea. So, I kept to myself, did my job and, when the day was over, I did the happy dance all the way to the car. Conveniently enough, the boss man didn't show up. He was probably as ashamed of his behavior as I was of mine.

Pulling out my cell phone, I decided to hit Jasmine up to see what she had planned for the evening. Eyeing my phone, I was surprised to see that I had a message. I was anal about my phone and refused to turn it off during the day; even though it was against company policy. Instead, I kept it on vibrate, stuffed it in my bra, but I had forgotten to put it on vibrate that day. I hit the button to hear the recorded message. It was from Greg and my heart could not make up its mind whether it wanted to gallop full speed ahead or stop altogether.

"Hey, gurl, how was your day? I was just checking in to see what you've got planned for the weekend and to make sure everything is going well. Hit me back when you get the chance. I get off at six."

Stalling, I called Jasmine first to see what she had going on.

"Hey, sis," she said, answering the phone.

"What's up?" I asked, smiling at her greeting. I was getting used to having a sister around and I felt like she enjoyed it as well.

"Just chilling," she replied.

"You hanging tonight?" I asked, hoping that she would have some time to spend with me. If she was busy, I would end up calling Greg and I knew what time that would be. Not that Greg was a bad lay; I just didn't want to encourage a relationship with him when we were strictly about fucking.

"I really haven't made up my mind yet. What do you have in mind?"

"I was hoping you'd want to go out and party a little. I heard on the radio that Frank Ski is having his five-year anniversary party at different clubs all over the city. We could hit a few and get our groove on." I snapped my fingers to the imaginary music in my head.

"Hey, I also heard about that. I'm down. We have to get there early. On the radio, they said to come right after work. How quickly can you get ready?"

"I'm almost home. I need to take a bird bath and throw on my clothes."

"What does that mean? How long?"

"One hour, tops!"

"Cool, I'll pick you up."

I raced into my apartment and started tearing through my closet looking for something to wear. My choices were limited and I was disgusted. I opted not to bathe, and dashed back out to the mall to pick up a little sumthing, sumthing. Since my hair was still in braids, I didn't have to fool with it. Throwing on a wraparound dress and stuffing some shoes in a bag, I raced out of the house in less than fifteen minutes.

I had acquired my gift of shopping from Marie. She was the only woman I knew who could visit the mall on her lunch hour and come back with ten outfits. I couldn't pick mine out nearly as fast but I was getting better.

On the way to the mall, I called Leah to see if Greg had blabbed his mouth to her new friend. She answered the phone sounding very depressed.

"Aw damn, gurl, you sound like someone just ran over your dildo with a cement truck!" I said.

"Gurl, if I wasn't so depressed that would be funny. Plus, Negro, I'm mad at you. I ain't heard from your ass in over a month. What's up with that?" she said, not even pretending to be amused.

"What's wrong, boo? Is Coy acting the fool?" I asked, trying to change the subject.

"Naw, it's not Coy. It's Mya. I thought she was doing so much better since she started at the center but she had one of her fits today and it threw me for a loop. She's been doing really well and I thought the dumb stuff was behind us!"

"Damn, since you haven't mentioned anything else about her, I assumed she was adapting well."

"Negro, please! I ain't talked to your ass!"

"Anyway," I replied with attitude.

"Craig, the director, said she had a great day but when she woke up from her nap, she started scratching herself and banging her head on the floor. She looks terrible, Sammie. Her head is all swollen and her lips are cracked."

"Wow! There is one consolation that comes out of this," I said.

"What's that?" she asked, clearly not able to see any saving grace out of her daughter's trying to take out her own face.

"She did it in front of witnesses who can testify, if necessary, that you're not abusing your child!"

"You know, you're right but it doesn't make it any easier to deal with. She's resting now."

"I'm headed to the mall to get a little sumthing to wear to the club. Jasmine and I are hanging with Frank Ski and his morning show crew."

"Sounds like fun. I wish I could come. Hell, if anyone needs to let their hair down, it's me!"

"I know that's right! Why don't you ask your mother to watch the kids?"

"She's watching them tomorrow. Coy's taking me on an all-day outing."

"Oh, this sounds serious. Where are you two going?" I asked, pulling into the parking lot at the mall.

"Don't know; it's a surprise. Hell anywhere will be different for me. I rarely have a chance to interact with adults outside of work and talking with you and Momma."

"Lawd, I'm so happy those days are over for me!"

She killed my mood. "So what's up with you and Greg?"

"Why? What did he say?" I asked, feeling scared. I didn't want Leah to know about the graveyard.

"Hey, I haven't spoken to him." I could see her holding her hands up in the air.

"Oh, I thought maybe Coy talked to him and told you something. Look, I'm at the mall so I've gotta dash. I have forty minutes to find an outfit and make it back to the house. Jasmine is picking me up."

"Ya'll two are doing the damn thing, aren't you?"

"Yeah, gurl, and it feels good! Talk to you later."

Clicking off the phone, I raced to the little hoochie boutique that carried plus sizes. After flinging several dresses to the side, I found a short, pink spandex dress that would go well with the black sandals I had brought with me. The dress had a halter top cut low in the front, and even lower in the back. I wouldn't be able to wear a bra, but I was not bothered. Despite my size, I frequently went braless. The dress had a split up the back that stopped dangerously close to the bottom of my butt cheeks, and I had to have it.

The price almost made me put it back on the rack but, as I admired myself in the mirror, I realized I would be wearing it when I left the mall.

I had exactly fifteen minutes to get back to my house before Jasmine arrived. I quickly charged the dress and strutted out of the mall, ignoring the stares.

In the car, I pulled out my cell phone again and dialed Greg's saved number. He answered on the first ring like he was holding his phone in his hands.

"Hi, it's Sammie. Is this a bad time?"

"No, ah, I was about to uh, make a call. Yeah, make a call," he stumbled, trying to convince himself into a lie.

"Oh, want me to try you later?"

"Naw, I'm cool. What's up?"

"I'm about to hang out with my sister. We're going to celebrate Frank Ski's anniversary."

"Oh. I was kind of hoping we could hang out tonight," he said, clearly dejected.

"Sorry, boo. Why don't you run by the club? We're hitting Visions for happy hour; then we'll following the crowd until we get tired."

"After thinking for a few seconds, Greg said, "No, I don't think so. I have a lot of things I need to do in the morning."

"Dang, you're going to miss me in this sexy ass dress!" I sighed. All my assets were hanging out, and I wanted him to see me.

He suddenly grew interested. "Is it hot?"

"Like an oven baking biscuits!" I smoothed out the wrinkles that formed as I sat down.

"What time will you be there?" I could envision the drool coming out of his mouth.

"My sister is picking me up in about ten minutes, so we should be there in about an hour."

"Cool, see you then," he said.

For a few minutes I regretted extending the invite, but I wanted him to see me all dolled up. Plus, since he was married, he could not hang out long anyway. I was riding with my sister, so there was little chance I would leave the club and wind up in the backseat of some car with him. I vowed not to do that; no matter how good he looked.

I made it home with two minutes to spare. I raced back in the house to hide the clothes I had worn to the store, but Jasmine blew the horn before I could stash the bag. Grabbing my small clutch, I rushed out of the house. I didn't want to keep my sister waiting.

"Hey, sis!" I exclaimed as Jasmine leaned over and opened her car door. Her dress was as conservative as mine was provocative. From what I could see, it was a short clingy number, but she was not exposing her DD-sized breasts.

"I'm loving that dress," she said, flashing me a beautiful smile. She had the most perfect teeth that I had ever seen on someone who wasn't a celebrity. Her mouth could have been on a poster for a dentistry school.

"Let's do the damn thing!" I hollered as I folded my body into her little sports car. Even though it was early November, she still had the top down and the weather was cooperating.

Turning down the radio to be heard over the air rushing through the car, Jasmine said, "I invited a male friend of mine to stop by; I hope you don't mind." She snuck a glance at me.

"Of course not. I did, too," I said, giggling.

"This is scary; we are thinking alike."

She was right; our outlooks on life were very similar. The main difference between Jasmine and me was her obvious self-love. I hoped that, by hanging around with her more, I would be as comfortable in my skin as she was in hers. Although she was not as big as me, she was as tall, and that was hard on a woman. It was no fun going on a date with a man who barely reached your shoulders.

"You know V-103 is going to have a pajama party tomorrow night," Jasmine said.

"I heard. That sounds like it's going to be a lot of fun."

"I went last year and had a ball. Do you want to go?"

"Uh, I haven't even thought about it."

"Think about it. I want to go, and I can't think of anyone else I would want to attend it with."

*Shit, that means back to the store I go*, I thought to myself. I didn't wear pajamas and preferred to sleep in the nude; even if I was sleeping alone.

"We could make a day of it. We could go to Natalie's Boutique for the right sumthing sumthing and head over to the party afterwards. I already have a room at the hotel where the party is located, so we don't have to worry about parking or driving home," she said, laughing at the shocked look on my face.

"Dayum, sis! You've got it like that? Those rooms are going for about a buck fifty a night!" I exclaimed, thinking about the bills that I could pay with that money. Turning down an invite like that was not in my plans.

"I'm in!" I shouted, and we high-fived. We were about a few blocks from the club, and I started to get nervous. Part of me wanted Greg to be there; another part didn't. I was also nervous that Jasmine was going to get all the attention, and I would wind up holding her purse while she danced the night away.

"Why so gloomy, sis?" she asked, picking up on my despondent mood.

"Oh, nothing," I said, looking out the window, pretending to admire the scenery.

Mentally, I was comparing myself to Jasmine. To be honest, I did not like the differences. While we looked exactly alike in the face and we were both tall, that is where the resemblance ended. She was a good size fourteen and I was a twenty. My own hair was short and, at the moment, I chose to wear braids, but she had long flowing locks that she didn't have to pay for! For a brief moment I wanted to snatch them out by the roots, and I immediately felt ashamed.

Shaking my head, I tried to rid my mind of those ugly thoughts. *She's your sister, for Christ's sake.* Jasmine turned up the music as we pulled into the parking lot of Visions; a new club in Buckhead. She wanted people to turn heads to see who was riding in such a flashy car with the awesome sound system. Again, jealousy ate away at me, but I remembered that the last time I had allowed that bastard jealousy into my life it had almost cost me the best friend in the whole world. I was not about to lose my sister to that green-eyed beast.

People were lined up in front of the club like it was the first of the month and they were handing out vouchers for free food. My feet were already hurting from the shoes that I had chosen to wear, and I did not like the idea of standing out front of the club for over an hour before gaining admittance. But Jasmine pulled a fast one and we soon were walking into the club ahead of everyone else.

"I got the hook up," she said, winking at me as we waltzed past the crowd of pissed-off people. "Let the party begin!"

I echoed her sentiments. I had never been to the club before and it lived up to its name from the second we walked in the door. Everywhere I looked, I saw my reflection and those of the other party people who were also coming in.

Frank himself was at the door handing out apple martinis to all the ladies, and I eagerly grabbed one from him. Before I could edge my way past him, I grabbed another. I needed to lighten my mood. If it had to be alcohol induced, so be it!

## LEAH

I made a quick meal salad for the kids when we arrived home. We were all so hungry that we tore into the meal like it was steak and baked potatoes instead of ground beef and lettuce. Everyone ate with relish; except Mya. She was withdrawn and kept crying silently for no apparent reason. Shooing the other children off to their rooms, I picked Mya up and held her in my lap.

"What's wrong, boo?" I asked her as my own tears spilled out of my eyes. She looked at me but, as usual, she did not say anything. She laid her head on my shoulder and, after about ten minutes, she fell asleep.

The fits had taken a lot out of her. It would probably take her all weekend to recover from the energy she had expended. My heart was full when I went to lay her down in my bed. After one of her events, I rarely let her sleep in her own room. I wanted to be there; in case she had another one during the night.

She did not utter a sound as I undressed her and pulled the covers up to her neck. I bent down and kissed her on her forehead but I was sure she did not feel it. Turning off the light, I went back into the living room to finish unpacking the last of the boxes from our move.

I looked around my house, and it was beginning to look like a home I could be proud of. I had arranged our meager furnishings to create a warm environment and could not wait to really start entertaining. Part of me wanted Kentee to see how we had come up, but I quickly erased the thought.

My thoughts wandered to Coy and to doubts I had begun to have about our relationship. We were supposed to go on a day trip the following day. I was getting up extra early to drop the kids off at Momma's. Thinking of Coy must have conjured him up because the phone rang.

"Hello," I said, barely containing my smile.

"Hey, sunshine! I don't have but a minute; I had to work over tonight. I want to make sure we're still on for tomorrow."

"Sure," I responded, nodding my head like he could see it.

"Cool, I'll be there to pick you up at nine o'clock, okay?"

"I have no idea where we're going. How should I dress?"

"Naked." He laughed. "Just kidding! Be warm and comfortable. I heard the weather report and it's finally gonna start feeling like fall."

"Are we going to be outside?" I asked, trying to get a feel for where we were going.

"Only if you want to be. Just wear a sweater or a jacket for the morning. If you get too warm, you can take it off. I'm wearing some jeans and a tee shirt."

"Oh, okay," I responded, wondering where I was going to get a pair of jeans from since I didn't have any in my closet.

"Gotta run; the sergeant is calling me," he said, hanging up.

When he was gone I realized he didn't even ask about how my day had gone. I didn't get to tell him about Mya, or anything else, and it was beginning to bother me. I was going to have to speak to him about my children. So far, the only time we had gotten together was when I had a babysitter. In the beginning, that was fine, but I needed to know where he thought we were headed. If he wanted a relationship, it was a package deal. I could not continue to ask Momma to watch the kids every time he wanted to see me.

"Why are you thinking about this now?" I asked out loud. I didn't have any answers; only a ton of questions. After the day I'd had, I craved the strong arms of a man who would comfort me as I cried on his shoulder. That would not be happening that night, and it made me mad.

The phone rang, shaking me from my daydreams. I worried about the sound waking Mya up as I quickly ran into the kitchen to stop it.

"Hello," I whispered, even though the kids were in their own rooms.

"Hey, sugar, it's Momma."

"Hi, are you okay?" I asked, scared since she was calling so late. She normally went to bed around eight and it was well after nine.

"I had a rough day, had a headache I could not shake, but otherwise I'm okay."

"Is your pressure up?" I asked, worried that the devil was trying to take yet another person I loved away from me. Momma always had high blood pressure, but she was very good about taking her medicine.

"No, I don't think it's my pressure. I'm just tired. I'll take Mya 'cause I know you won't find anyone outside of the family to watch her, but I was hoping you could find someone else to watch Malik and Kayla."

My mind started spinning as I contemplated an eleventh hour save for my plans. I didn't want to cancel my date. I needed the downtime but I could not immediately think of anyone I trusted who would be willing to stay with my children.

"I'm sorry, baby. I just don't feel up to all three of them," she said, pleading for understanding.

"Wait, Momma, I have an idea."

"What?"

"I'll call you back." I hung up the phone without waiting for her to answer. I suddenly remembered that the next day was their cousin's birthday. They had been invited to the party; even though Kentee and I were broken up. His sister and I had always been close, so I decided to call her to see if that relationship had been ruined along with the marriage. "What do I have to lose," I mumbled to myself.

"Clo, it's Leah," I said when she answered the phone.

"Damn, gurl, where you been? Just because you're leaving my sorry-ass brother doesn't mean you can't stay in contact with me!"

"Oh my God! I thought you were mad at me, too. I talked to your mother several weeks ago, and she cussed me out. She believed I kicked Kentee out, and she didn't want to talk to me."

"You didn't kick him out?" she said in shock.

"No, he left me without even leaving a note! I found out from the company that held the mortgage on the house that he was living somewhere else."

"Aw damn, that ain't what I heard," she said, sucking her teeth.

"Well, now you've heard it from the horse's mouth. The kids and I were about to be put out in the street because Kentee stopped paying the mortgage the day he left. He told the bank officer we were renters who wouldn't move out, and he didn't care what happened to us!"

"That doesn't sound like my brother!"

"Ask him," I said. "I don't have anything to hide, so I welcome the chance to clear my name of the lies he's telling your family."

"Damn. When you put it like that, I can't help but to believe you. Are you coming to the party tomorrow?"

"I don't think it would be appropriate; since most of your family believes him, but I would like Malik and Kayla to come. The only problem is I would have to drop them off early in the morning; like eight a.m. They were going to spend the day with their grandmother until I remembered the party." I told that lie without even batting an eye; just like she'd accepted the lies her brother told her without ever asking me.

"No problem, because I'll already be up. We have a clown and a magician coming, so I need to set it up. Keira still doesn't know she's having a big birthday party. She thinks we're going out to Chuck E. Cheese's."

"Damn, I hate that I'm going to miss it," I said, even though I was actually thrilled I would be somewhere else. "There's a second part to this request. I recently started a new job, and I have a training conference out of town. I'll be back tomorrow night but I'm not sure what time. Can you either keep them for the night or take them to my mother's house when they pluck your last nerve?"

"Gurl, they can stay here. It's been so long since I've seen them that I'm looking forward to it. And, if I know Keira, she'd punch holes in my tires if I tried to cut their visit short. Your daughter is the only cousin she has her age."

"So true. Thanks, gurl. I really appreciate it," I said. "When I get set up, I'll invite you and the kids over. You're right. Just because my marriage to your brother is over, that doesn't mean we can't stay in contact."

"My brother's shit is his shit! He's a grown-ass man. I ain't got no beef with you, and that's the bottom line."

"Cool, I'll see you in the morning," I said, hanging up the phone.

Now all I had to do was pack their overnight bags and set the clock to get up early in the morning to drop them off. My excitement at the prospect of having an entire day off without children, along with Coy's surprise, kept my heart rate up as I raced around the house to get ready. I needed to calm the hell down, so I paused in the kitchen and poured myself a glass of wine. I turned on the radio to a jazz station and sat down to enjoy the drink.

The last two months had been a whirlwind of activity. I had met a man, gotten a job and a new home, and finally had a glimmer of hope. I reminded myself to thank God for the bounty He was bestowing on me. Silently, I sank to my knees to give Him the props He deserved. I stayed on my knees so long that they hurt.

Getting up, I drained my glass and poured another; taking it with me into my bedroom. I surveyed my wardrobe, trying to figure out what I was going to wear since I would not have time to stop at the store. I settled on a light-weight blue jogging suit. It wasn't jeans, but it was relaxed wear.

My hair looked like it would hold up for another day; if I could manage to sleep with my head hanging off the bed. Sipping my wine, I sat back down on the bed and thumbed through the latest issue of *Sister 2 Sister* magazine. I wasn't really reading the articles; just looking at the pictures. Weariness from the long day at work and the wine began to take their effect on me, and I decided it was time to shower and hit the sack. I needed to be fresh for the morning. I lingered inside the shower. Detaching the showerhead, I used the warm spray to wash away all the fatigue from the day, and I inadvertently allowed the stream to hit my clit. It was like a jolt of electricity. This startled me and I pulled the showerhead away like it was alive.

Laughing out loud at my silliness, I continued washing myself, but I could not forget how wonderful the water had felt on my now throbbing clit. Spreading my legs wider, I applied the water again and allowed myself to relax and enjoy the feelings I was experiencing.

"Ohhh," I moaned as my feelings intensified. I slipped two fingers into my wet pussy and let my muscles suck them in further. "Damn," I purred as I increased the tempo of my fingers, making sure to keep the water steadily aimed at my clit. I lifted my leg onto the bench; allowing myself better access, and my hips rocked to the rhythm I had created. I had never masturbated before and, now that I knew it felt so good, it was going to be tough not to keep doing it again and again.

As I moaned one final time, my body shuddered, and all the pressure building up inside of me rolled down my legs. A slow smile spread across my face as I replaced the showerhead and once again grabbed soap and a washcloth, cleaning up the evidence of my personal gratification. It didn't feel as good as when I had Coy inside of me, but it certainly did the trick for the time being.

Leaving the shower, I curled up in bed and fell quickly asleep as the TV news droned on in the background. My dreams were of knights-in-shining-armor and everlasting love. They were so vivid, I woke the next morning believing it could be possible.

# SAMMIE

"I'm skeerd of you," I said to Jasmine as we were shown to VIP tables in Frank Ski's personal section. Cristal was flowing from a fountain in the center of the room.

"The DJ Buddy used to have a thing for me. It didn't work out but he still kept me in the loop so I had the best of both worlds. Buddy Love and I fooled around for a minute and he still wants some of this puddin', so I can usually get in most places without a thang," she said, laughing. We were early, and most of the VIP section was deserted, but I still felt uncomfortable. Most of the people who were going to be seated in that particular section could afford to be there. I was robbing Peter to pay Paul just for showing up!

"Dang, gurl, I knew you were rolling, but I didn't know it was like this," I said in awe. I continued having doubts about my being there; until Buddy Love rolled into the spot. He was a big man but he was fine as can be and he wore the biggest smile on his face. He was the type of guy you wanted to hug to your chest and smother.

"What up, gurl?" he asked when he saw Jasmine with the biggest smile on his face. He turned and glanced at me, and his head swung back, doing a double take. "Dayum, what the hell?" he asked, looking back at Jasmine for an explanation.

"This is my sister," she said, smiling. That broke the ice for me, and I was able to relax a little bit.

"I thought I was looking at the Doublemint twins," he said, laughing. He extended his hand. "I'm Buddy."

I blushed. "Sammie."

"You're just as fine as your sister, and she sho did whip my ass! Are you nicer?" he asked.

"It depends." I blushed again. Buddy's good humor was infectious.

"And she's got some spice to her." He winked at Jasmine. "I've got to go set up, but don't you two beauties go anywhere. I want to get the chance to know this fine sister of yours," he said.

"What's up with him?" I asked as soon as he was out of earshot.

"Oh, just a toy. You can play with him if you want to because I'm done. As long as he continues to treat me right, he can still call himself my friend," she said, looking around the club as it rapidly filled up.

"So, you won't mind if I spend a little time with him?" I asked. I was feeling that charcoal brother.

"Naw, sis. He's all yours; if you want him."

She was discarding him way too quickly. "What's wrong with him?"

"Nothing. Buddy was a means to get here. I was never feeling him; only what he could do for me," she said earnestly.

"Cool. We'll see if he really wants to play," I said.

"Shit, yeah, he's old news. We haven't been together in years, but he keeps extending invitations, trying to get me back, but I've moved on. Wait until you see my new man!" she stated confidently. I had forgotten all about Greg until she mentioned her date.

"Hey, let me take a stroll around the club. My friend Greg isn't going to know to look for me hanging with the big dogs!"

She waved me away. "I hear ya. If you see a tall, brown-skinned man with short wavy hair and green eyes, tell him Jasmine is looking for him!"

"Hell, if I fall upon that nigga, I'm keeping him for myself!" I rushed away from the table with her in hot pursuit.

All eyes were on us when we left the VIP section, and I didn't know if it was because we were actually looking good or because of where we were coming from. Jasmine went one way and I went the other, each of us looking for our man of the hour. I hadn't traveled far before I ran up on Jasmine's man.

"Jazz?" he asked when he grabbed my elbow in passing. I wasn't even looking for him; I was so intent on finding Greg.

"Nope," I said, pulling my arm away before I looked him in the face. "Oh,

I'm sorry. You must be the man Jasmine is looking for. I'm her sister," I said with pride.

He shook his head. "Damn, I didn't even know she had a sister!"

"Neither did she," I replied. "I know where she is, so follow me." I continued walking around the club looking for Greg with Jasmine's man in tow. I didn't ask his name, and he didn't bother to give it to me. We met Jasmine and Greg back where we first started, and we all burst out laughing. I hugged Greg, and she hugged her man.

"Sammie, meet Carlos," she said, and I shook his offered hand. Turning to Greg, I said, "Greg, meet Jasmine, my sister, and her friend, Carlos."

Bewildered, Greg shook Jasmine's hand and nodded to Carlos. There was a tense moment of silence as the men eyed each other, and Jasmine and I could not help but to laugh. They were acting the same way Jazz and I had when we first met each other.

"We're sitting over there," Jasmine pointed, and I followed her lead; leaving the men to follow. Jasmine pulled me up close to her and said, "He's cute."

I struggled to keep from smiling.

"Gurl, if you weren't my sister, I would've thrown Carlos down on the floor, and we'd be doing the nasty right now!" He was definitely a piece of eye candy. Although Greg was fine, he did not have the sleek confidence Carlos had.

As we sat down, the waitress came over to take our orders. I pulled my chair up closer to Greg, and he whispered in my ear.

"I didn't know you had a sister. Damn. Ya'll look just alike," he said.

"There's a lot about me you don't know," I said with a wink.

He placed his hands over mine. "I'm beginning to see."

I looked across the table and winked at Jasmine. She was playing with Carlos under the table, and I could tell he was both loving it and hating it at the same time because we were there.

"Hey, do you want us to get our own table?" I asked them.

Carlos looked like he wanted to say yes, but Jasmine quickly spoke up. "Nonsense. We came out to be together, didn't we?"

"Yes, we did!" I said excitedly, secretly pleased she would not put me on the back burner because her man had shown up. I would have to find out the details about him when we got back to my house.

When Carlos learned we were not going away, he decided to loosen up and enjoy himself. After the first ten minutes of utter silence, we all started to have a good time. It could have been the booze, but I think it was our wicked conversations and flirtation that finally melted the ice.

Jasmine introduced us to the entire cast from the Frank Ski and Wanda Morning Show. I was nervous about meeting on-air personalities, but they were really nice. They all seemed to know Jasmine, and I envied her. She was leading the life I always felt I should have but, for once, I put aside my envy and felt proud that she was my sister.

We danced the night away and, before I knew it, it was time to go home. If Greg expected to jump my bones, I dashed those hopes when I told him that I rode with Jasmine. As we were leaving the club, Buddy Love grabbed my arm.

"Hey, we didn't get a chance to talk. Are you coming to the pajama party tomorrow, or should I say tonight?"

Surprised at his boldness, I tried to hide the blush that crept up to my cheeks. "Uh, yeah. Jasmine and I will be there."

I could tell Greg was surprised by this admission, but he did not break his stride. The only indication I had that he was taken off guard was the raising of his eyebrows.

"Good, I'll see you both then," Buddy said.

"All right then," I said and allowed Greg to escort me out of the club. Once outside, Greg let me know he was not happy about the latest turn of events.

"Damn, gurl; you are full of surprises," he said, fighting to keep his voice down so that Jasmine and Carlos could not hear him.

"What?" I answered innocently.

"You... you...," he stuttered.

"Spit it out," I said, starting to get an attitude.

"Nothing," he mumbled when he detected the tone of my voice. "I'm sorry. I just wanted to spend some quality time with you," he said, trying to cover his real feelings.

"Hey, I'm sorry about tonight. By the time I got your call I had already made plans to hang out with Jasmine. I wanted to see you, too, so I thought I could combine the two."

"Don't worry about it. I'm cool. When can I see you again?"

"Monday would be good. When we get back on Sunday I'm going to be bone tired."

"I'll bet." I could tell he regretted saying it as soon as the words had left his lips.

"Excuse me?" I placed my hands on my hips.

"Nothing. Look, I had a good time. I'll call you tomorrow." He kissed me on the cheek and turned to leave.

"Bye, Greg!" Jasmine yelled to his retreating back.

He threw up his hand without turning around. Carlos had already left, and we waited until we got in the car before both of us fell out laughing.

"Gurl, that is one pissed-off nigga," Jasmine said.

"You ain't lying a bit," I said, also laughing.

"Homeboy looked like he wanted to take out a chain and tie it around your neck," she said as she started up the car. The annoying thing was that she was right.

"Gurl, it ain't even like that. We just met; really. I don't get with him that often."

"Then you must have put it on his ass 'cause that nigga is sprung."

"You think so?"

"No doubt. And you must have sparked some interest in Buddy 'cause he caught me going to the bathroom, asking me fifty thousand questions about you!"

"For real?"

"Yeah," she responded.

"So, what's up with that?"

"Girl, I done told ya; Buddy's old news. If you like him, go for it. My feelings won't be hurt in the least."

"What's wrong with him?" I asked again with renewed interest.

"Nothing, we simply met at the wrong time in our lives, and I don't believe in going backward."

"And you would be cool with it if I gave him a little play?"

"Hell yeah. He ain't my man and never was. What are you going to do about Greg? He seems like he's ready to fight for ya."

"He don't have no legs to stand on until he gets rid of his wife," I said.

"Oh, I hear ya. Then go for yours," she said.

We rode the rest of the way home in silence; each of us lost in our own thoughts. When she pulled up in front of my house, I was reluctant to get out.

"Jazz, you ain't mad at me about dating a married man, are you?" I asked, nervous about her response.

"Hell no, Sammie. I ain't into judging people. We all do things we feel we have to do, or want to do. Whatever happens, you're my sister. Plus, Carlos is married, too," she said, laughing. I gave her a hug, and we made plans to go to the store together to shop for our outfits for later on.

## LEAH

The damn alarm clock ejected me from my peaceful slumber, and I fought to find the right button to turn it off.

"Good Lawd," I said when I finally located the right button. I stretched sleepily and willed my body to an upright position. *Today is my day.* This would be the first day since the birth of my children—other than the weekend of my move—that I would be allowed to think only of myself, and I was looking forward to it. Mya was still in bed, and I left her there.

Racing out of the bed, I ran my shower and went to wake up Kayla to get her started getting dressed.

"Hey, sleepyhead. Wake up. Today is Keira's birthday party," I told her and, instead of complaining, she climbed right out of bed.

"Can we spend the night, Mommy?"

"Yes, you can," I said, as happy as she was.

While she was taking her shower, I took my own. By the time I had my clothes on, it was time to wake up Malik. He also responded to my prompts about the party at his cousin's and gave me no trouble getting dressed. I used the time while he was in the shower to put on my makeup and said a silent prayer that Mya would be as cooperative. As it turned out, she was still tired from yesterday, so she offered me no resistance while I bathed and clothed her.

I fed the kids a quick breakfast and ran around the house collecting the last-minute items that I needed to stuff in their bags. At seven-thirty we were ready to leave the house. I dropped Mya off first. She was sleeping off and on during the drive, and I prayed she would stay that way for most of the day. The last thing I wanted was to receive a frantic call from Momma urging me to come right away; especially since I did not know where Coy and I were going.

Momma was waiting in the living room when I turned the lock, and she took the sleeping Mya from my arms and put her into her bed.

"She looks worn out," Momma said.

"She is. Hopefully she'll have a good day. I don't know where we're going, but I promise I'll have my cell phone on."

"We'll be okay." She smiled. I kissed her on the cheek and thanked her again for giving up her day so I could have fun.

I quickly dropped off Kayla and Malik; promising to spend more time with them when I came to pick them up. I was still sticking to the lie that I had a meeting out of town that was driving me to hurry. Driving back home, I was a whirlwind of emotions. I was looking forward to my date but still apprehensive about Kayla and Malik being with my in-laws and Mya being at my mother's. My apprehension disappeared when I saw Coy's truck parked in my driveway.

"Hey, sunshine," he said as he got out of the truck to greet me. He had on a pair of tight jeans with creases so sharp they could have cut butter. His thighs practically bulged out of them.

I planted a kiss on his lips. "Hey, yourself."

"You ready?"

"I need to jet inside to get my bag and lock the house down," I said, practically skipping inside. My fantasy date had begun.

He stood behind me as I locked up the house, and I got into his truck. Inside he had a pillow and blanket.

"Go to sleep," he instructed and, at his command, I made myself comfortable. "We'll stop in a couple of hours for breakfast."

"A couple of hours? Where are we going?"

"That's for me to know and you to find out!" He pulled the blanket up over my shoulders.

Surprisingly, I fell asleep. I woke when we pulled into a Waffle House. The clock on the dashboard said ten-thirty so I had been asleep for over two hours.

"Damn, baby, you were calling hogs like you haven't slept in a week." Coy laughed as he took the keys out of the ignition.

"No, I wasn't! I don't snore!"

"If you say so, but I had to turn up the radio to hear the announcer," he said, still laughing.

I grabbed my purse, and we went inside the diner to eat.

"Where are we?" I asked, knowing full well he was not going to tell me.

"Waffle House," he said with a smug smile.

"Oh, you got jokes, ha ha ha."

He ordered for the both of us, and I was pleased with his selection, but I could not possibly eat it all. I also ordered a cup of coffee to clear the cobwebs from my brain. He was looking so handsome that I just wanted to dart into a motel room and quench the fire building inside of me.

He paid the check, and got back into the truck. Now I was wide-eyed and bushy-tailed. He could not get me to go back to sleep unless he drugged me, so he had to contend with my questions for the duration of the ride. Coy had me puzzled. Despite the time I had spent with him, I didn't know what he wanted from me. I wanted whatever he was offering and I allowed those things to endear him to me.

"I can't figure you out," I said with a sigh.

"What's to figure?" he said, stealing a glance at me.

"What are we doing?"

"Going to have some fun and enjoy ourselves."

"But, why me?" I asked, still perplexed.

"Why not you?" he answered.

"You're not going to make this easy, are you?"

"Leah, relax and have fun. Don't try to analyze things. Just go with it, okay?"

"Okay."

We left the highway at an exit called Shorter. I still had no idea where we were going until we stopped at the dog track.

"What is this?" I asked.

"Have you ever been to the dog track?"

"No, what is it?" I was feeling disappointed because I didn't think watching a bunch of dogs would be any fun. I thought a dog track was where owners went to show off their dogs.

"What about horse racing? Ever been there?"

"Never, but it sounds like fun," I answered.

"Then you'll enjoy this, too," he said, undoing his seatbelt. I did the same and followed him to the gates for admission. I was looking around in shock. I never knew people raced dogs for money!

"Is this legal?" I whispered, preparing to hide my face from the camera mounted over the gate.

"Leah, shut your mouth. I'm a cop. What would I look like taking you somewhere that wasn't legal? You'll enjoy it, baby. Just sit back and watch a few races to get a feel for how it's done, okay?"

"Okay," I said as the announcer broadcast the first race. I could feel the excitement when the dogs pranced out on the field and we were given a chance to look at them.

"You okay?" he asked, wrapping his arms around my shoulders.

"Yeah, five, three, one," I whispered in his ear.

"What is that, a bet?" he asked, stunned I was ready to bet so soon.

"I think so. I have a feeling," I responded.

"I'll be right back. I would let you place the bet, but they can confuse you if you don't know what you're doing. The next one, I want you to go with me."

"Okay."

I watched the dogs being led to the starting gate with growing trepidation. I didn't know what to expect. The people around me were all calling out their chosen dogs and I regretted saying my bet to Coy without listening to what seemed to be old pros at the betting process.

He came back with a large soda and a bag of popcorn; just as they announced final call for bets. Coy handed me a ticket, but I could not make heads or tails out of it. He held a similar ticket in his hands.

"Here comes Betty!" the announcer yelled, and I looked to Coy for an explanation since I had no clue who the fuck Betty was.

"See that little mechanical rabbit running around the track? That's Betty."

"Oh, I thought I was gonna have to fight a heifer," I answered as the dogs flew from the starting gate. I found myself on the edge of the seat; alternating between looking to see who was in the lead and hiding my face in Coy's shirt wanting to be surprised. It was a photo finish, and when it was all said and done, we had won $2,333.

"Damn, baby; you won!  Look at the scoreboard!" he exclaimed.

I saw the numbers flash across the screen, but it was all Greek to me.

"How much did we win?" I asked, dumbly still trying to make out the board.

"You won $2,333!" he exclaimed.

"Wait, how could I win that much money, when I didn't even bet?"

"Give me two dollars," he instructed, and I pulled them from my battered wallet.

"It's all yours! Go get your winnings," he said happily and took me up to a window to collect on my ticket. The dogs finished in the exact order I had called them. I had to fill out forms so the IRS could tax the money, but I was not mad about it. I bet on several other races, but none of those winnings matched the first one. In the end I came home with about $2,800 and Coy won about $1,000. I was so excited I could barely contain myself.

"Is this money really mine?" I asked Coy once we were back inside his truck and headed home.

"They were your bets so, yes, sweetheart, it's yours.  I have to remember to bring you with me all the time because this is the most money I've ever won here or anywhere else," he said, laughing.

We stopped at a quaint restaurant about ten miles from my house for a cozy candlelit dinner. Without warning, I realized that I was falling in love with Coy. He was showing me a side of life I didn't even know existed. I leaned over the table to give him a big kiss. I had to tell him what I was feeling.

"You keep this up and I just might fall in love with ya!" I said jokingly.

He did not respond. In fact, he got quiet for the remainder of dinner and during the ride home, until we were almost at my house.

Out of nowhere we saw a deer on the side of the road. Innocently, I said, "Look, a deer!"

You would have thought I had rolled down the window and called his ass because he ran right in front of the truck and stopped! Coy slammed on the brakes, but it was useless. We were going too fast, and the deer, blinded by the light, froze. A scream burst from my throat and echoed through the cab of the truck. In the next instant, shattered glass fell into my lap, and I could see the deer's tiny feet trying to free itself from the windshield. Not wanting to get kicked, Coy yelled at me.

"Get out of the truck!"

He didn't have to tell me twice. The kicking legs damn near knocked me in the face. Surprisingly, the deer managed to free himself from the windshield and run off into the forest.

"Damn," Coy said as he inspected the damage to his truck. His mood had gone from sugar to shit, and there was nothing I could think to say to him that would make the situation any better.

"Wanna write him a ticket?" I asked in a joking manner.

His head snapped around, and he glared at me like he hated me. "Why did you have to call him?"

"Surely you must be kidding. That deer couldn't have possibly heard me and, even if it did, it's a wild animal. Do you really think it would've come?" I didn't bother to hold back my laughter, which only made Coy angrier. Brushing off the seats, we got back into the truck and drove the rest of the way to my house in silence.

"I had a great time today, and I can't begin to thank you. Sorry about your truck," I said, edging my way out of the truck.

"Me, too!" he said, not giving me a chance to finish my sentence. I didn't know if he was responding to my comment about the fun we had or the damage to his truck. And he clearly missed the hint I was giving him about how I was going to show my appreciation. He did not budge from his seat as I closed the door, nor did he even acknowledge the fact I had left. He was clearly in a black funk, and I was starting to get a little pissed myself. He acted like it was my fault that the deer had challenged his truck.

"You're not coming in?" I asked, shocked he would go through all that trouble and not want to spend the night.

"I have to be up early in the morning trying to get this fixed, so I better get on home," he said.

"Why can't you leave from here, like you did the last time? The children aren't here, and I promise not to touch you; unless you want to be touched," I said, remembering the words he had to me during our first encounter. I was struggling hard not to get an attitude since he did give me a picture-perfect date; up until Bambi ruined it!

I could see the signs of struggle written all over his face. For a moment I grew worried, until he switched off the ignition and followed me into the house. When we got inside, I forgot about his indecision about coming in, but I should have paid attention.

I took a shower and washed away the road grime that had accumulated on my skin. When I was done, he did the same. As he emerged from the shower, I pushed him onto the bed. "I know you have to go to sleep, so I won't jump you; I just want you to relax," I whispered in his ear.

I took some oil that grew hot when you rubbed your hands together and began rubbing it on him, working all of the muscles in his back and arms. I worked my way down his muscular thighs to his toes. When I was finished, I asked him to flip over, and he readily complied. I started at the bottom of his feet and worked my way up to his neck. Throughout the entire process he remained silent and, sadly enough, his dick remained limp. I did not give it much thought as I snuggled up next to him and fell into a deep sleep.

When I awoke a few hours later, Coy was gone without a trace.

# SAMMIE

For a change, I picked up Jasmine from her house to go shopping. I stopped in the house and gave her mother a hug and kiss. As before, she treated me like I was her own daughter and told us both to have fun when we left.

Jasmine was waving a gold card over her head as we turned onto I-20; headed to Stonecrest Mall.

"Charge it!" she yelled, imitating Wilma Flintstone from the cartoons of our youth.

"Girl, you are out the box!" I exclaimed as we giggled like teenagers.

"Have you decided what you're going to wear?"

"I haven't decided whether I'm going for warm or sexy."

She laughed. "Girl, with all those honies who'll be there tonight, I'd beat your ass if you tried to pull out some flannel shit!"

"Oh, it's all going to be about sexy tonight. I wanna meet a man who'll pay my rent!"

"Now, that's what I'm talking about," she said, raising her hand to high-five me. I pulled in Stonecrest and tried to locate a parking space that wasn't two miles from the mall. Up and down the aisles I drove until I found a spot right in front of the mall entrance.

"What did you do, call and tell them to save this spot?" I asked.

"And you know this," she said, joking.

We walked into the mall; still giggling and acting like kids. We fell up into Natalie's Boutique and tore at the racks like we were in Jim's Bargain Basement. We were flinging shit like we were in the living room and the stuff already belonged to us. I gathered up three outfits and hurried to the dressing room. They were all long negligees with deep slits. My favorite was a dark green negligee with a matching robe.

Jasmine picked three short teddies with matching robes, including a dark green one, wanting to dress similar but different. We decided we looked too cute to leave them there. We also found some green high-heeled slippers to match. Jasmine picked up the tab for our outfits, and I could not tell her how much I appreciated the gesture.

I purchased earrings and the accessories for our hair. We also stopped by a Bovanti's and had our faces made up and eyebrows arched.

"Sistagurl, we're ready now!" Jasmine said, admiring our reflections in the mirror. I was starting to get excited about that night's events.

"Let's get something to eat," I suggested, and we went to nearby Bugaboo's for an afternoon snack.

"What time is check-in?" I asked in between stuffing my face with spinach dip and chips.

Looking at her watch, she said, "Anytime now. What do you have to do when we get back home?"

"Nothing, really; I packed a bag this morning before we left. How about you?" I asked, still stuffing my face.

"Just grabbing a bag, too. I don't want to work up a sweat because I don't want to have to refresh my makeup!"

"I hear ya," I replied.

We finished up our meal, talking smack and giggling. After paying for the check, we went back to my house and collected my bags.

"Damn, gurl! What the hell do you have in this suitcase?"

"My stuff!" I said, growing defensive about all the shit I was taking with me for an overnight stay. Staying in hotels overnight was not something I was used to. Most times—during my prostitution days—I only stayed for a few hours or, at the very least, checked in with just the clothes on my back.

"I'm only kidding you, gurl. I've got as much shit in my bag as you do!"

Breathing a sigh of relief, I struggled to get the bag out the door without falling over. I locked up and drove back to her house. We had already decided we would show up at the hotel in her car. It was a statement kind of thing.

"Gurl, can you imagine coming to the party tonight and not having a room? Those heifers waiting outside to get in are going to freeze, and all we have to do is come down on the elevator!" she said.

"I know that's right. It's about fifty degrees now. After the sun goes down, it's going to be on. Every woman in that place is going to have her nipples standing up because of the chill."

"Girl, you are too crazy!" she said, laughing, and pushing down her own nipples that started to stand up under the thin fabric of the shirt she was wearing.

"Damn, gurl. What you thinking about?" I asked.

"None ya," she responded.

"So, is Carlos coming tonight?" I asked, hoping she would say "no" since I hadn't asked Greg to tag along.

"I don't bring sand to the beach," she said with much head and attitude.

"I hear you. I didn't even answer my phone today because I didn't want to hear no mouth about tonight. Are we getting the special treatment tonight, too?"

"Of course. That's the only way I roll," she said. We laughed so much and for so long, my jaws were hurting.

"Hey, let's hit the bar and get our drink on!"

"Let me change my shoes. These motherfuckers felt good in the store; now they feel like they're attacking me."

"You ain't lying about that! I had some shoes last month that turned on me. Hurting feet is an awful feeling. I bought them on my lunch hour, and I did the nigga thing and wore them out the store, leaving my old ones in a trashcan by the door. Those shoes hurt me so bad, I had to take a cab back to work!"

"What did you do with the shoes?" she asked.

"Took them back to the store the next day. I went home barefoot. The lady at the store tried to clown on me since I had worn the shoes. I said, 'Bitch, please! How else am I going to find out if they hurt, unless I wear them?' I told her she had two choices: Give my money back and take her shoes, or I would go to the bank and stop payment on the check, and she wouldn't have the shoes or the cash!"

Jasmine laughed. "And she brought that?"

"I had to roll my neck and bat my eyes a few times, but when I started balling up my hands into fists, she hurried up to the register."

"Too funny. Come on, gurl, I'm feeling a little parched."

Grabbing our purses, we deposited our bags in the room and headed up to the top floor of the hotel for drinks. The view was beautiful.

Over drinks, we really got to know each other.

"I've told you so much about me yet you rarely talk about you. What's up with that?"

"There's really not a lot to tell. I'm recently divorced and trying to make up my mind what I want to do with the rest of my life," she said with a weak smile.

"How long were you married?"

"Ten years."

"No kids?"

"Nope. Warren told me he couldn't have kids. I accepted it; even though I wanted them. It took me ten years to find out that he had fathered children outside of our marriage, and that he had given me an STD that prevented me from ever having kids." Jasmine took a long gulp of her drink and signaled the bartender for another.

"Wow, that's deep," I said.

"I've always wanted kids, and the slimy bastard took that away from me. I wasted ten good years with him, and that's why I don't feel bad for taking him for half of what he's worth on paper!"

"Sure, you're right." I raised my glass in salute to her statement as we both smiled at each other.

"When he lies down with another woman, he's going to think twice about that half shit! Technically, I won't have to work for the rest of my life; if I don't get silly."

"Gurl, I could use a relationship like that! I'm broke on payday most of the time!"

"You're so crazy!"

"Have you ever thought about getting your own place?"

"I thought about it, but right now I'm cool. Mom was lonely and so was I.

It really is a win-win situation, she ain't up in my business and I ain't up in hers."

"Wow, I cannot even imagine living with Althea again."

I finished my drink, and we ordered another round. We spent awhile admiring the scenery and acting stupid like two sisters who love each other are supposed to do.

"I need to call Leah and see what she's into. She'd love something like this, but I doubt if she can get a babysitter."

"When are you going to introduce me to your friend?"

"To be honest, I wanna enjoy you myself, before I bring someone else into the circle."

"Are you serious? I'm going to be around for the rest of our lives. I want to know some of the people you invite into *your* circle of friends."

"I'm being selfish, aren't I? I keep thinking that if you meet Leah you'll like her better than me, and I don't think I could handle it," I said lightly, but I was totally serious.

"Gurl, shut up! We're sisters! Nothing can come between us! Call your friend and see if she can hang with the big dogs. There's more than enough room in our suite, and I'm sure I can get another ticket for her."

"Oh, okay," I said, dialing Leah's number. As luck would have it, all I got was her answering machine. Most days since the birth of the twins, she often didn't answer the phone or call me back until several hours had passed. She didn't want to answer the phone if the kids were acting a fool.

"She didn't answer, but she'll hit me back when she gets a moment."

"Let's go get ready for our night of fun!"

"I'm right behind ya!"

It was almost eight by the time Leah hit me back, and we were about to go out the door.

"What's up, my nigga?" I asked when I recognized her name on the caller ID.

"Girl, talk about drama, I've had my hands full for the last few days!"

"Look, Leah, I'm about to roll out. I called you to see if you wanted to come to a party with Jasmine and me."

"Darn, I can't. I'm waiting for my sister-in-law to drop off Kayla and Malik, and then I have to go get Mya. Where's the party?" she asked and I could tell she was pouting by her voice.

"It's the big party they've been advertising on the radio for Frank Ski's fifth anniversary! We're about to go to the pajama party!" I was feeling happy just to be in my skin.

"Damn, gurl! I'd shoot someone to get to go to that party! How come you didn't tell me sooner?" she demanded.

"Jasmine only told me about it last night. She has VIP passes, and I asked her if you could come."

"Damn, I guess I'm going to be depressed for the rest of the weekend!"

"I'm sorry, boo, but at least I tried!"

"Yeah, you did. Take pictures if you can, and call me tomorrow with the dirt."

"I'll call with the dirt, but cameras aren't allowed. They have a sign posted at the door. What happens at the PJ party stays at the PJ party. I've got my cell phone camera; in case I see something nice," I said, laughing.

Hanging up the phone, I could not help but feel sorry for Leah. Her life had taken a drastic change since the birth of her twins, and she hardly got any downtime.

"Is she coming?" Jasmine asked as I turned around to leave the room.

"Naw, she has babysitter woes. That girl's got it rough since that bastard husband ran off with another woman, leaving her with those three kids. If I was more domesticated, I'd volunteer to baby-sit sometimes, but hell, to be honest, I didn't do such a hot job with my own kids, so I doubt I'd do much good with hers."

"I love kids. Maybe once we get to know each other, she'll allow me to watch her kids for her."

"Oh, honey, I'm sure she will. That child is on overload! Her youngest daughter is a special needs child, so it won't be a walk in the park. That little girl can be vicious."

"Special needs? What does that mean?" she asked perplexed.

"They haven't clinically diagnosed her yet, but she has these fits where she falls out all over the floor, banging her face into whatever she can, until she either passes out or someone has enough strength to stop her."

"Damn, gurl! That's deep! How old is Leah?"

"She'll be turning thirty-two in a few weeks. Hey, I have an idea. Why don't we throw her a little party? She has a lot to celebrate. She recently got a new job and a new home!"

"I'm down, but let's discuss this after we get our groove on!"

"Hey!" I shouted, raising my hands in the air, ready to shake what my momma gave me.

## LEAH

It had been six lonely days since I had heard from Coy. I continued to sniff the pillow he last laid his head upon, but his scent was long gone. I had repeatedly called him on both his home phone and cell, but he did not return my calls. I had no idea why he had placed me on terminal ignore status and didn't know how to find out.

It was the weekend once again, I had no plans for the next two days, and the thought depressed me. In the short time I had known Coy, he would fill my weekends with his spontaneity. I missed the late-night booty calls and the stolen moments when he phoned me at work just to tell me he was thinking about me.

Stretching, I decided I would wash the sheets that day. I had savored our smells long enough but other familiar smells had long since replaced the spicy aroma of his cologne. I felt a hollow pain in my heart. There was more to Coy than met the eye, and I was having a hard time trying to handle his apparent dismissal of me.

My moods kept changing. When he first disappeared, I assumed he was involved in an undercover sting operation. I believed this lie for about twenty-four hours, and then I assumed it was another woman. The thing that made his silence so hard to understand was the fact we had been open and honest about our relationship. Or at least I was. The other thing that made it hard was that, up until the car accident, every time had been perfect.

In addition, my birthday was approaching and the added aggravation I was receiving from Kentee and his family was wearing me down.

When my sister-in-law had dropped off Kayla and Malik last weekend, I was surprised to learn that Kentee had also attended the party. He was talking smack about getting back together with his family, and everyone believed he was sincere; especially Kayla. She came home with all this talk about what her daddy said. I was shocked that he had filled her head with empty promises.

The bottom line was he was talking shit in front of his family, but he had yet to discuss any of his plans with me. The bad news was that Kayla had given him our new unlisted phone number, and his dumb ass was using it frequently to harass me; not to discuss reconciliation. When I really thought about it, I could not blame her. So I tried to ignore the apparent pain in her eyes when she did not hear from her father when she wanted to. She expected him to be walking in the door at any moment, and that it was not happening fast enough for her, so she started making up shit.

"Mommy!" Kayla screamed as she raced down the hallway into the kitchen. "Guess what Daddy said? He's going to be home by my birthday and he's going to take me shopping!" Kayla jumped up and down in excitement. My blood started to boil, and I could not figure out who I was angrier with, Kentee for filling her head with bullshit, or me for not straight-out telling her that her father was full of it.

This was another aspect of child rearing that my mother had neglected to educate me about. She had never blasted my absentee father, and I was so sure that he had done some shit that would have made me mad. I found myself emulating her actions; even though my gut told me to dash that fire.

"That's nice, honey," I said between clenched teeth. It was a good thing Kentee was not in the room, or I would have shoved a spoon up his ass and fed him his own shit!

"I'm so happy I saw my daddy," she said, beaming from ear-to-ear like it had happened the previous night instead of a week earlier.

"Did your daddy tell you where he's been?" I asked sweetly, still gritting my teeth.

"He's been away on impotent buzness," she said with immense authority as she struggled over the large words. I fought back against saying anything about the heifer he was staying with on the other side of town or his short stint in jail.

"I told Daddy about my new school and our new house and everything. He said he wanted to see where we lived, so I showed him!" she declared.

"I'll be damned!" I said loudly, before I could stop myself.

This was the first time that she had divulged that information. I wanted to make sure it was the truth and not make-believe.

"You showed Daddy our new house?"

"Uh huh," she said, smiling.

"But you were over your aunt's house, and you don't know how to get here," I said, shaking my head to dispel my gathering thoughts.

"Yes, I do. Auntie lives on Baker Street. That's 24.5 miles from here; off Fairview Road."

I was so shocked. She could have blown me over with a sneeze.

"Where did you learn that?"

"It was on the invitation," she said with the biggest smile. Hitting myself on the head in frustration, I remember giving Kayla the invitation to play with, and it had directions to her aunt's house with a map. To make Kayla happy, I had marked on the map where we lived so she would know how far we would have to travel to see her cousins.

My own child leaking information to the enemy wasted all the trouble I had gone through to keep where we lived a secret. I fought to keep from strangling her on the spot.

"Baby, I was trying to surprise your daddy with our new house, and you spoiled it," I said.

Tears welled up in her eyes and dripped on her plump cheeks. Her shoulders quaked and her little hands balled into fists.

"I'm... I'm... sorry, Mommy," she wailed.

Instantly, I felt ashamed for beating up on her; especially since I knew how sensitive she was. I was blaming her for doing what little children do; telling every damn thing they know.

I scooped her up and smothered her with a massive hug. I kissed her all over her face and neck.

"Sweetheart, it's okay; Momma isn't mad at you," I said, wiping away her tears. I made a solemn vow not to use my anger at that deadbeat husband of mine against my children. Kentee would expose himself eventually without any help from me.

Kayla's small arms were wrapped around my neck so tight that I could barely breathe. She let me go when the phone rang. Lately, she had become a phone hag, and she struggled to get free to answer it.

"Hello," she said like she had not just been in the depths of despair.

"Oh, okay. I'll get her," she answered. Acting proper, she handed the phone to me. "It's for you," she said and skipped down the hall.

I was so stunned by her mannerisms that all I could do was shake my head.

"Hello," I answered.

"Hey, gurl. What's up?" Sammie said.

"Nothing, gurl, just another day in the life of Leah. What's up with you?"

"We'll tell you when we get there. We're having an impromptu birthday party for you today. We know you can't get out of the house, so we're bring-ing the party to you!"

"Oh my goodness!" I exclaimed. "We?"

"My sister is coming with me. She wanted to meet you, and she suggested the party!"

Laughing, I said, "My birthday isn't for two weeks!"

"I know, but you're so close to Thanksgiving that we decided to do it early. Do you have plans for the evening?"

"Uh, no. When are you coming?" I asked, looking around the living room, assessing the damage.

"Open the door," she responded. Gasping, I hung up the phone and rushed to the door. Sammie and a woman who could only be her twin stood on the doorstep. The resemblance was uncanny, and I kept looking from one to the other with my mouth hanging open.

"Damn, Sammie; it looks like you were cloned!"

Jasmine stepped forward and grabbed my neck, giving me a kiss on my cheek.

"My sister told me you were good peeps, so consider yourself a friend of mine," Jasmine said.

They had really surprised me. Sammie pulled the door shut after they brought in the bags they had with them.

Among the things they'd bought was a big cake and I was down with that. The cake came with enough candles to burn down the White House. I was so overwhelmed by their kindness.

I could not hold back the gratitude I was feeling. A few moments earlier, I was contemplating genocide again, and now I was about to party hardy.

"Lawd Jesus! You don't know how much I needed to see a friendly face!" I said happily.

"Where are them bad-ass children?" Sammie asked.

"Trust me; they're not far away. I'm shocked that Kayla didn't run her fast ass down here to see who'd come in."

Glancing at my watch, I realized her favorite cartoon was on, so she probably didn't even hear me open the door.

Sammie and Jasmine put down the bags, and Sammie went to the refrigerator and pulled out some ice trays to fix cocktails. Jasmine went to the phone and called Pizza Hut to order the food.

"Damn, how long have you two been planning this?"

"We decided a couple of weeks ago when we called you about joining us at the PJ party. We knew that you wouldn't be able to skip out on the kids, so we brought the party to you!" Sammie said.

She passed out glasses to everyone, and we had a toast to the new "old ass" in the group.

"Here's to the old, soon-to-be crippled lady in blue," Sammie said, raising her glass.

"Look, beotches! No matter how old I get, you two cows will be older!" I snapped back.

"Oh, damn." Jasmine laughed. "She got us on that one." We all cracked up.

"What happened at the party?" I asked as we sat down to talk.

"It was crunk up in there!" Sammie and Jasmine said in unison. Their voices were so similar, I kept doing doubletakes to see who was talking. The main difference between them was that Sammie was heavier than Jasmine. Other than that they were practically identical.

"I feel like I'm drunk and seeing double and I haven't even tasted my drink! What is this, anyway?" I asked, holding up my glass for inspection. The drink was a pretty pink color and had a little umbrella in it.

"Cosmopolitan!" they shouted in unison, which caused us all to bust out laughing and Kayla to run down the stairs to see what was going on. She stopped short when she saw Jasmine. Her mouth dropped to form a large O, and she keep looking back and forth between Sammie and Jasmine, trying to understand what she was seeing.

"Kayla, this is Jasmine. She's Sammie's sister," I said, trying not to laugh at her bewilderment.

"How come my sister don't look like me?" Kayla asked.

"Your sister is a lot younger than you are. Give her time," I said.

"Hi," Kayla said, coming over to me and burying her face in my chest. She could be shy at times around strangers.

"Gurl, if you don't get your narrow behind over here and give me a kiss, I'll have to take back the present Ms. Jasmine and I bought you."

"Present!" she exclaimed, clapping her hands and jumping up and down. "Gimme, gimme!"

"Kayla! You know better than that," I said firmly.

"Sorry," she said, hiding her face but peeking nevertheless.

"I'm still waiting on my hug," Sammie said.

Kayla shuffled over to Sammie and gave her a big hug. Jasmine held out her arms to be hugged as well, and reluctantly she hugged her also. From behind her back Jasmine produced a bag that held stuffed toys for all three of the children.

"Give one to your brother and the other to your sister, okay?" Jasmine asked.

"Okay," she said, turning to leave.

"Excuse me, missy," I said.

"Thank you," she said and took off running down the hall.

"We've got something for the birthday girl, too." I started bouncing up and down, clapping my hands.

"Gimme, gimme!" I exclaimed and we all busted out laughing.

"Leah, I know your momma taught you better than that!" Sammie shouted as she handed me a flat envelope. The envelope contained a gift certificate to Xceptional Designs, a full-scale beauty salon. It entitled me to a full day of beauty.

"Oh my goodness! I can't thank you two enough," I said.

"Thank Jasmine. You know I'm the broke bitch!" Sammie said.

"But the thought was there, and I don't have the words to say how much this means to me. I was sitting here feeling sorry for myself before ya'll called. This is what I needed!" My voice was cracking.

Sammie looked at me, surely noticing the stress lines around my eyes and the unnatural slump of my shoulders.

"What's wrong, boo?" Sammie asked.

"Men!" I responded, taking a huge gulp of my drink. "You can't live with them, and you can't live without them!"

"I second that," Jasmine said.

"Where is the fine-ass Coy?" Sammie asked.

"Beats the shit out of me! We had this perfect date and bam, now he's M-I-A!"

"M-I-A?" Jasmine asked.

"Missing in Action," Sammie and I shouted as one.

"When was the last time you talked to him?" Jasmine asked.

"Six days, two hours, and forty-three minutes," I said, sighing. "He spent the night after our last date, but he couldn't get it up, and when I woke up, he was gone."

"Do you think he's embarrassed?" Sammie asked.

"At first I did, but he was acting funny way before that. I had to practically beg him to come in when he dropped me off."

"That is strange, 'cause the nigga was sure feeling you! I tried to get his attention and he totally ignored me!"

Draining my glass, I held it up for a refill. Jasmine jumped up to refresh all of our drinks.

"I like her," I whispered to Sammie.

"Yeah, me too!" she responded with a bigger smile.

"So, what's up with Greg? You two been kicking it?"

"Gurl, the nigga is sprung! He calls me fifteen times a day. He's starting to get on my last nerve," Sammie said.

"Girl, he was really tripping when he saw Buddy trying to cut in on his action," Jasmine said, retaking her seat.

"Who the hell is Buddy?" I asked.

"The DJ from the evening show on V-103. I introduced him to Sammie, and he's been running around trying to sniff her dirty drawers."

"Is he cute?" I asked.

"He's alright," they answered again as one.

"Look, ya'll are going to have to stop that Doublemint shit. It's hard enough watching you without ya'll speaking in unison!"

"Sorry. I like the way he rolls. Top of the line, all the way, and he don't mind sharing, if you know what I mean," Sammie said, winking.

"Must be nice," I said, feeling jealous. I was at the age where I should have been partying and having fun but my life was not turning out that way.

"Oh, shit; I forgot to tell you the latest shit! Sammie, you know I took Kayla and Malik over to my sister-in-law's last week when Coy and I went out. Kentee was there. Kayla told her father we moved, gave him our phone number, and showed him where we live!"

"Damn! Has he called you?" Sammie asked.

"Hell yea; talking shit! He told Kayla he was coming back home. Can you believe that shit?"

"Yeah, like bad pennies, their bad asses always show back up. You can walk through a parking lot and never find a dollar but bad pennies are everywhere!"

"You still didn't tell me about the party!" I said.

"Oh, the party," they said, standing up and slapping each other five.

"You missed the throw down of a lifetime!" Sammie continued. "They got buck wild at the PJ party, and it almost turned into a big freak-fest! Those people would've been screwing on the floor if it wasn't for security."

"Damn, and I had to miss it!" I said, feeling sorry for myself once again; even in the company of friends.

"Hey, do you think you can arrange for a sitter for next Friday?" Jasmine asked.

"I don't know. Why?"

"Porsche Fox, from the radio station, is having her birthday party for all the Sagittarians. You're a Sagittarian, and I can get you on her VIP list," she said.

"I don't want to go alone."

"We'll go with you, silly, and if you can't arrange a sitter, you and Sammie can go, and I will watch the kids."

"Gurl, you don't know what you're talking about. Mya can be a real handful!" I said. As if on cue, Mya chose that moment to act out. Jumping up, I raced down the hall to my room, where she had been previously playing. Jasmine and Sammie were quick on my heels.

Mya was laid out on her back on the floor. Her hands were clenched, and she was beating her head on the floor and screaming at the top of her lungs. The pencil she had been drawing with had broken, so I surmised that it was the reason for her little outburst. I snatched her by the shoulders, trying to keep her head from hitting the floor anymore, and tried to rock her into the quiet mode.

I looked up at Jasmine, and saw the same horror in her face that I felt every time Mya acted like that. This fit clearly showed Jasmine that she didn't realize what she was trying to sign up for.

"Sammie, take Jasmine to meet Malik. He's in his room upstairs."

"Sure," Sammie replied, pushing Jasmine out of the room despite her obvious desire to stay.

"Damn, how often does that happen?" Jasmine said.

"This one was mild," Sammie replied as they stood outside my bedroom door, trying to talk low so I could not hear them but I heard every single word.

"And no one knows what triggers this?" Jasmine asked.

"Not so far. Luckily for Leah, she recently enrolled then in a new center that seems to care enough to try to find out what's really going on inside Mya's head."

"She's such a pretty little girl," Jasmine said.

"Yes, she is and, on a good day, she's so sweet! But it's like something is going on in her head that only she can hear," Sammie said.

I heard them finally make it to the steps and head up to Malik's room. I went out into the hallway to see if I could make out the rest of their conversation. My house had some thin-ass walls and voices carried well.

Sammie paused in front of Malik's room and knocked as Kayla came down the hall. She must have still had all three stuffed animals still in her arms because Sammie asked, "Kayla, why didn't you give your brother and sister their toys?"

"I was about to," she said, obviously not happy about being caught acting selfishly.

By that time, I was at the bottom of the steps, watching as well as listening.

"Good, you can give Malik's to him now!" Sammie said.

She marched into Malik's room without knocking and must have thrown the stuffed football player at his head.

"Stop it," Malik whined as if he had not experienced that type of behavior from his sister before.

"Hey, Malik," Sammie said, trying to stop the fight before it happened. I was glad because I had enough to deal with downstairs without having to run interference between my other two children.

"This is my sister, Jasmine. She bought you the stuffed animal."

Malik came out into the hallway to give Sammie a hug and then also hugged Jasmine. "Thank you," he said with his head bowed, not bothering to look at either one of them. They went into his room to look at some of his drawings while I returned to Mya in my room.

The festive mood we tried to create was gone as we gathered in the living room. I was sure the stress was evident on my face.

After several unsuccessful attempts to start up a conversation with either Jasmine or Sammie, I gave up and suggested that we call it a night.

"Look, ya'll, it's getting late and I spent the better part of my morning getting ready for work. Please don't be mad at me for cutting the party short. And thanks so much; you two really made my night," I said, genuinely smiling; even though I felt like crying.

They didn't waste any time in leaving, either, and I felt their relief when I let them off the hook. Bolting the door and turning off the light, I made my way back to Mya for another overnight vigil over her fragile body.

# LEAH

I was running late and feeling the weekend. Briskly brushing my hair back into a makeshift ponytail, I hastily applied my makeup while barking out instructions to Kayla and Malik to hurry. I refused to be late that day because it would be my first day back in the word processing center, and I was looking forward to it.

I had been gaining experience working in different departments all over the firm, but no department had made me as comfortable as the word processing center. Andrea and I had a connection, and I enjoyed the light banter that we shared.

I dropped the kids off at day care without going to each of their individual classes to make sure they were settled, making it to work with only ten minutes to spare.

"Morning," I said as the door to the word processing center closed behind me.

Andrea was happy to see me and gave me a big hug, but the other black lady who was sitting next to where I used to sit merely grunted.

"Welcome back," Andrea said. "I sure did miss you. How was it?"

"It was okay, and I focused on something different every day, but I missed this place!" I laughed.

Andrea turned to the other lady and said, "Tarcia, this is Leah Simmons. She's been here for about two months."

"Hi," I said and still got a grunted response. No smile lit up her eyes as she looked me up and down with disdain. Right that second, I realized that I was going to have problems with her, but had no idea why. She was an okay-looking, dark-skinned sister with a short, natural haircut. Her makeup was artfully applied and, if she didn't have such an evil snarl on her face, she might have even been pretty.

Trying to cover up for Tarcia's rudeness, Andrea started babbling. "Tarcia was on her honeymoon when you started and was only scheduled to be gone for two weeks. Unfortunately, she miscarried while she was away and is just now returning to work."

"Damn, you didn't have to tell her all that," Tarcia said, jumping up from her chair. She walked over to the door, snatching it open. "It's my business, and I decide who hears it, not you!" she said, slamming the door behind her, rattling the glass.

"Lawd, that girl is a hot mess. I don't know how to take her. One minute she's so nice you can eat from her fingers, and the next minute she's trying to gnaw off your arm," Andrea said, shaking her head.

"If she recently lost a baby, I can understand the mood swings," I said, having a moment of sympathy for Tarcia. "I would've hated to lose any one of my children. Was this her only child?"

"Yes. Personally, I think that's why she rushed to marry a guy she hardly knew. And if you want my opinion, things aren't going so well because she's been difficult to work with ever since she came back."

"Well, I'm not trying to get caught up in any drama so, if you don't mind, I'll take the farthest seat from her. She doesn't appear to like me, and I want to keep my distance."

"Sure, make yourself at home. I got the word today that you can stay here, if you want to. You've made quite a name for yourself, and the partners want you to be happy," she said, smiling.

"Oh, I'm happy to be back, and I'd love for this to be my permanent assignment," I said, beaming back at her. I walked past Tarcia's desk, and I suddenly felt like I had been popped with a sledgehammer. On her desk she had a big 8 x 10 picture, obviously from the wedding, that almost made me drop everything I was carrying to the floor.

It wasn't so much her picture but who was in the picture. Her new husband was the father of my children. I was looking at the man I had married six years ago as he gazed into Tarcia's eyes, holding her hand. Bending over as if severely punched in the stomach, I almost managed to make it to my desk without falling down. Time stood still, and I could feel my knees buckling, but I could not stop them from trembling. I collapsed on the floor, hitting my head in the process. *This can't be happening!*

Andrea ran over to me and helped me to a nearby chair.

"Oh dear, are you okay?" she asked, fanning my face.

"Uh, yeah. I just slipped; that's all," I lied, trying to regain control over my emotions.

"You're so pale. Let me get you some water." She rushed out the door to the water cooler.

Things were becoming clearer to me. Kentee loved children. He must have left me when he realized he couldn't handle our own special needs daughter. He was trying to start a new family, and the shit backfired. "No wonder he told Kayla he was coming back home," I said out loud.

Armed with answers to the questions that had been nagging me ever since Kentee had left, I felt calmer. I didn't excuse his behavior, but I understood. Mya was enough to make anyone run for cover, but because she had lived inside of me long before she slipped into this world, I had a bond with her that Kentee could never develop. Finally, it was clear to me that I didn't fail at being a wife. Kentee had failed at being a father.

I managed to get through work without any confrontations with Tarcia. She had to know who I was and that explained her reactions to me. So she kept to herself and so did I. I buried myself in depositions and transcripts, and she carried on lengthy conversations on the phone with Kentee, I assumed. I was the first person to leave at the end of the day. And I couldn't wait to get home and process my new information.

I flew into the day car center and collected the kids, trying to get out before Craig even knew that I was there. As luck would have it, Mya was in his office. I didn't want to see him since we had become rather close over the last few months and he would surely know that I was battling with something.

"Leah, how are you?" he said, putting down the magazine he was reading when I entered his office.

"Oh, I'm making it," I said as I went over to gather Mya up from her nap.

"Let me," he said. Our hands touched when he tried to take Mya from my arms. The jolt that ran through my veins shocked me, and I jumped back as if burned. Clearly he felt it also because he looked startled; almost dropping Mya. He gazed at me with hooded eyes, and I promptly forgot that he was a married man.

"Wow," he said, and I could not raise my eyes from the carpet. He was such a handsome man. I tried not to spend too much time in his company, fearing becoming sexually attracted to him.

"Um, I'll go get Kayla and Malik," I said, backing out of the room.

"Wait, we need to talk about this," he said, stepping too close to me.

"About what?" I said with feigned innocence.

"You know what I'm talking about. Please don't try to downplay it," he said, sounding annoyed.

I looked at Mya's sleeping face, and decided I just didn't have it in me to discuss anything other than going home at the moment.

"Okay, I'll bite. I know exactly what you're talking about, but it's a moot point. You're married and, legally, so am I," I replied.

"Everything isn't as it seems. You don't know my situation," he said.

"And you don't know mine," I said, getting angry.

"Yes, I do," he responded.

"No, you don't. I just found out that the woman my husband left me for works right next to me. I can't deal with any more right now!" I said as my voice rose. I had held in my emotions all day, and I felt on the brink of overload.

"Oh, sweetheart," he said, stepping closer to me. "I didn't know."

"Neither did I," I snapped. "Look, I can't talk right now. I have a lot of thinking to do. Could you take Mya to the car while I get the others?" I backed out of the room.

"Of course," he replied, clearly hurt by my bitter tone. But I could not focus on him right then. I had to get home to have the meltdown that had been brewing all day.

I got Kayla and Malik and was getting them settled in the car when Craig brought out Mya.

"Can I call you tonight?" he asked, and my heart did a leap.

"Uh…yeah, sure," I said and climbed into the car, shutting the door and ending any further conversation. I gunned the engine and raced out of the parking lot.

Even though I was extremely attracted to Craig, I could not afford to risk a relationship with him that could potentially get my children displaced from the center. I agreed to his calling so I could explain my position because I knew that as long as I was looking into his honey-colored eyes, I would not be able to stick by my decisions.

During the short drive home, I rehearsed everything that I was going to say to him. I was so deeply emerged in my thoughts that I did not see Kentee's car until I had pulled into the driveway and he had pulled in behind me; blocking off my escape. I pressed the garage door remote but he was able to scoot under it before it closed.

As I looked at the husband who I hadn't seen in so long, my emotions raged from wanting to slap him to a desire to kiss him to a need to snatch off his dick and set it on fire.

"What are you doing here?" I demanded, placing my hands on my hips and glaring at him. The only thing I didn't do was snap my fingers in front of my face to dismiss him.

"I needed to see you," he said, stepping forward as if to touch me.

I took two steps back and bumped against the car door. My movements woke Kayla, and she bounded out of the car screaming, "Daddy!"

"About what? You didn't want to talk when you left me so why, all of the sudden, do you want to talk?" I asked, turning my back and getting Mya out of her seat. Kayla had wrapped her arms around her daddy's legs, and tears were flowing freely down her cheeks.

"See, Mommy. I told you Daddy was coming home!"

I looked at her with compassion, but I shot him a look that should have melted him into the pavement.

"Sweetheart, your daddy has another home now. *Not to mention another wife.* Let's go in the house. It's cold," I said, hurrying to the door as if Kentee was not even present.

My heart was pounding so loudly in my chest, I could barely hear myself think. Sadly enough, after all the hurt that he had caused me, I was still attracted to him. I fumbled with the keys and went inside, laying Mya on the sofa. I went back to the car to get Malik, who had slept through the entire confrontation until I went to pick him up. He saw his father over my shoulder, but he didn't react one way or the other. That had to hurt Kentee, but he had brought that on himself. I walked past him again and went into the house, after locking my car and grabbing my purse. Briefly, I glanced at Kentee, and he could not even hold up his head.

"Malik? Who is that man?" I asked, pointing to Kentee. Malik looked at him but did not answer; even though he had been at the same party, my son still ignored him like a stranger. "That's pathetic! Your own son doesn't even know who you are!"

Kentee didn't move or acknowledge the dig I had delivered. Part of me wanted to be the bitch, but another part of me, the part that still loved him, wanted to hear from his lips why he had chosen another woman over his family.

"Can Daddy come in?" Kayla asked.

I had to stifle the urge to scream at her. I stopped, contemplating my next move. If I denied Kayla the opportunity to spend time with her father, she would hold it against me. He had me between a rock and a hard place, and he knew it.

"For a little while," I replied.

Kayla pulled her father into the house, upstairs, and down the hall to show him her room. I went into the kitchen to fix us some dinner. I thought Malik and Mya would warm up to their father, but neither paid the other any attention. He spent time playing in the bedroom with Kayla.

The phone rang scaring the hell out of me. "Hello."

"Hey, Leah, did I catch you at a bad time?"

"Craig, we are about to have dinner. Can we possibly talk tomorrow, it's been a long day and I just ain't thinking straight."

"Oh, okay. I will see you tomorrow." I hung up the phone feeling conflicted and angry. I could not wait to take me a hot bath and climb into bed.

I fixed their plates and called Kayla in to eat. She came down the stairs grinning from ear to ear. "Momma, can Daddy eat with us?"

"Daddy isn't hungry, baby. Go sit down in the kitchen and eat before it gets cold," I said, daring him with my eyes to contradict me.

"I'll wait until you finish," Kentee said as he took a seat on my sofa. I was fuming since I hadn't asked his trifling ass to sit down. I waited until Kayla went in the kitchen before I turned my attention to Kentee.

"This is truly foul. How dare you show up here after all this time?"

"You have every right to be mad. I wanted to see you and the children, but I was afraid you would shoot me or something."

"You aren't worth the prison time, or the bullet!"

"Ouch, I deserved that," he said.

"And then some. You left us with no food, money, or explanation. What did I ever do to you to make you treat us that way?" I asked angrily.

"I was confused. I needed to talk to you, and you never had time for me."

"I didn't have time for you? How dare you!"

I went over and slapped him as hard as I could. The force of the blow shocked us both, and I was instantly sorry. Grabbing his jaw, he opened his mouth to speak, but all that escaped was a moan. Without warning, he started to cry uncontrollably.

"I've made a mess out of my life. You're right. My children don't even know me, and I messed over the best relationship I've ever had!"

I was stunned at his tears, and my heart went out to him. I fought to keep from folding him into my arms and telling him it would be okay.

"Kentee, I needed someone, too! Most days I felt like I was going crazy, and you didn't even notice. When you were gone, I had to contend with three kids, two in diapers, and Mya screaming for hours on end. I prayed that you'd come home and help me, but all you did was come in the house and start bitching!" I said, remembering all the pain he had inflicted on us.

"I'm so sorry. I was so used to having you to myself, and I didn't see anything past my needs but, while I was in jail, I realized that I was being selfish and unfair. I tried to reach you, but you had the number changed and you moved," he moaned.

"Well, the last time we spoke you weren't exactly nice," I said. "All those nasty calls you've made since your niece's party. Yet, you were telling everyone else we were getting back together."

"I was afraid," he admitted. I sank down next to him on the sofa, drained of energy. It had been a hell of a day. We sat in an uncomfortable silence.

"Can I start spending time with my children? I don't want them to grow up hating me," he said.

"I won't deny you access to the children, but I do have rules. You're not to take my children around any other woman. And I don't want you dumping them off on your mother. If you want to spend time with them, then you'll be responsible for them. Can you do that?"

"I'll do whatever I have to do to make this right," he said.

"So, what is your other wife going to say about this?" Kentee opened his mouth but closed it again without saying anything.

"What's the matter, cat got your tongue?"

"Leah, what do you want me to say, I fucked up. I'm sorry."

"Sorry can't make this right. You married another woman damnit and you're still married to me."

"That marriage ain't legal and you know it."

"But does Tarcia know it?"

"Uh…no, I told her we were divorced." Frustrated I let out a heavy sigh.

"Why Kentee. I'm so pissed at you I could slap the taste out of your mouth."

"I'm going to fix this. I'm getting it annulled."

"I don't have any faith left in you, but I'm willing to give you a chance for the kids sake, not for yours. If you mess up, just once, we're through with you. You won't ruin their lives like you did mine," I announced.

# SAMMIE

I hadn't heard from Althea in weeks, and it was beginning to bother me. After the dinner we had shared, we had briefly begun to talk at least twice a week, and I was beginning to understand my mother. I had finally realized she was not entirely to blame for her poor child-rearing skills. She only passed on to me what her own mother had taught her. We talked about everything, and she even reached out to Jasmine. From what I was hearing from Jazz, they were also communicating on a regular basis.

Once again, I picked up the phone and dialed Althea's number, but she still didn't answer. I decided to stop by her house on the way home to make sure everything was okay. Until then, I tried to concentrate on the work that had been piling up on my desk.

With the end of the year approaching, my boss had to settle out as many of the personal injury cases as he could. People were a trip. Just because they worked for Georgia Power, they assumed it was a cash cow and decided to sue them for everything from paper cuts to injuries on the job. It didn't bother me since it kept me busy and didn't allow me much time to take personal "dick-tation." Ever since that episode, I had made it clear that it was not going to happen again. I was still smarting from the look he had given me when his wife called. I wasn't ashamed of my behavior because it was a good screw, but I was beginning to want more than an occasional romp in the hay.

I had been spending some time with Buddy, and he was turning out to be a lot of fun. He treated me like a lady, and I was not used to it. We had been out several times, and the subject of sex hadn't even come up. He would show up on my job with flowers and take me to lunch or pick me up in the evening for a quick dinner before he would go on the radio.

What I liked most about our relationship was the shout out he would give me each night before signing off. Staying up until twelve midnight was wearing on my sleeping habits, but I loved the sound of his voice as he said good night to me. While I still gave Greg a roll every now and then, I wasn't on the prowl as much.

Jazz called as I was headed out to lunch.

"Hey, sis," she said, and I smiled into the phone. I still hadn't gotten used to the title.

"What's up?" I answered.

"Nothing; just checking on ya. How's work?"

"Work, child, work. Something you don't know nothing about," I joked.

"Hey, one of us has to keep our pulse on the social world," she replied. "What are you doing after work? Wanna go get something to eat?"

"Can't; got to go over to Althea's and check on her. I haven't heard from her for a minute, and I'm worried."

"Hey, come to think about it, I haven't, either. Have you called her?"

"Yeah, I've been calling her for the last few days, and she won't answer."

"Look, I'm not doing anything. Do you want me to ride over there?"

"Would you? I can't shake this feeling that something isn't right. She keeps a key under the flower pot on the front porch."

"Sure, sis. I've been feeling funny, too, but didn't know why. I'll call you when I get there," she said, hanging up the phone.

I felt better immediately. I had been fighting the urge to leave all morning, and now that Jazz was going over there, I breathed a sigh of relief. There was no way I could make it all the way to her house on my lunch hour and arrive back to work on time. Since I was no longer putting out for the boss, I didn't want to give him any reason to write me up.

## LEAH

I fell asleep with Kentee still in the house, and I was surprised to see that he was still there in the morning, fast asleep on the couch. As uncomfortable as the couch was, I knew he was going to be in some pain when he stood up.

Ignoring him, I went about my ritual of getting ready for work. I turned on the coffeepot and ran my shower. Once he got up, Kentee bathed Kayla and Malik while I handled Mya. She was still withdrawn and did not fight me when I put on her clothes.

I fixed a quick breakfast for the children and savored a cup of coffee while Kentee ironed the clothes he had slept in. He looked preoccupied and said very little which was fine to me. I assumed he was thinking of a lie to tell Tarcia about where he spent the night. Since she was nothing more than a hood rat, I imagined he was going to catch hell when he went home.

"Do you think I can have some of that coffee?" Kentee asked.

I shrugged my shoulders in response. I pointed to the cabinets where all the condiments were kept, then glanced at my watch.

"Take a plastic cup, because we have to be leaving," I said, since I was not about to leave him in my house unattended.

"Uh, okay. Listen, I've been doing a lot of thinking. I want to start paying child support. I can bring some money over this evening after I get off work, maybe bring some Chinese food and...," he said, not finishing his sentence and searching my face for a reaction.

Putting down my cup, I returned his gaze. "What are you doing, Kentee?"

"I'm trying to do the right thing."

"Okay, I'll buy that this time. But I want you to understand you cannot keep rolling in and out of your children's lives. If you are going to be their father, then be their father. I cannot and will not keep picking up the pieces you leave behind."

"I understand. Just give me some time to get my life in order. I'm not going anywhere again."

He got his coffee, said good-bye to the kids, and left. I shook my head at the closed door, but I didn't have a chance to reflect on what was just said or things that he didn't say.

Barking orders, I got the kids out of the house and loaded up in the car. I managed to drop off the children without running into Craig, and I was both happy and disappointed. My thoughts were so muddled that I forgot about having to deal with Tarcia.

She was in rare form that morning, so I made no attempt to speak with her. She had dark circles under her eyes, and they were red-rimmed. She barked at Andrea and gave me the evil eye every time I looked at her. I wanted to opt out of the department for the day, but we were swamped, so I just dug my heels in and concentrated on my work.

It was difficult to concentrate, with her slamming down the phone and shoving things around, but I tried my best to tune her out. I could only surmise that she was calling Kentee, and he was not answering. I wanted to shout out to her, "Been there, done that," but I didn't feel like snatching out her weave. Luckily, she went home sick at lunchtime, and we were all given a reprieve.

"I guess all is not well in paradise," Andrea said, but I just nodded my head; not wanting to get into any discussion about Tarcia and her personal problems. I ate lunch at my desk and lost myself in a novel. My lunch hour flew by, and I finished up the rest of the day working on a deposition that was shaping up to be extremely interesting. I planned on asking Andrea to see the rest of the case file in the morning.

It was a long day, and when it was over I practically skipped to the car. I was looking forward to a nice long bath. If Kentee did show up, maybe I could get him to entertain the children while I finished up my book. Reading was a pastime that I'd had to give up once I had children, and I missed it.

# JASMINE

I called Althea repeatedly as I drove over to her house. My fear was beginning to spiral out of control, and I wasn't sure why. When I got there her car was parked in the driveway, but she did not answer when I rang the bell. After waiting a few minutes, I started pounding on the door so hard that my knuckles hurt. I was hoping that Althea hadn't fallen off the wagon and started drinking again. She had been doing well for the last few months. My biggest fear was that she was drunk and unwilling to answer the phone.

Checking over my shoulder several times to make sure no nosey neighbors were watching me, I retrieved the key that Sammie had told me about. With shaky fingers, I inserted the key in the lock and opened the door.

"Althea!" I yelled out as I stepped into the foyer.

The house was closed and the drapes were all drawn. My voice echoed back, scaring me. I pulled the door closed behind me and stepped further into the house. I smelled old garbage and bacon grease. I wanted to open the windows to air out the house, but first I had to find Althea.

It was possible that she had ridden with someone to the store but, in my gut, I didn't believe it. I started searching the house, calling out every few minutes, hoping she wouldn't come to and shoot me.

"Althea, it's me, Jasmine. Are you here?" I yelled as sweat popped out on my brow. I checked the kitchen and it was empty. The living room was also empty, and so was the bathroom off the living room.

My cell phone rang and scared the shit out of me. I had it tucked in my bra on vibrate, and I almost wet myself. "Shit!" I grabbed at the offending instrument and tried to shut it off. I felt like I was walking among the dead and didn't want to disturb anything.

"Hello," I whispered.

"Hey, baby," Carlos said.

"Look, I'm tied up right now. I'll hit you back," I said, snapping the phone closed and ending the conversation. With my hand still covering my chest, I took deep breaths to calm my nerves. *Baby? That rat bastard cheated on me and now I'm Baby? He'd better save that notice for his wife*, I thought to myself. I leaned against the back of the sofa, wondering what to do next. I hadn't searched the bedrooms yet, and I was afraid to. But since I had come that far, I had to finish. I pushed off the sofa and went in search of Althea's room.

There were three bedrooms, and the center one appeared to be the largest, so I went in there first. I was scarcely breathing when I pushed open the door. The shades were drawn and the room was dim, and I searched for the light switch. The room was clean but the bedding was rumpled.

"Althea?" I asked again, not expecting an answer. I noted that the cordless phone was not in its cradle, and I went on the other side of the bed to see if it had happened to fall on the floor. My heart practically stopped when I saw Althea lying on the floor beside the bed with the phone in her hands. "Althea!"

Falling to my knees, I touched her neck to see if I could feel a pulse while placing my face close enough to see if I could detect her breathing. Her breath was shallow and I snatched the phone from her fingers and quickly punched out 9-1-1.

"Nine-one-one, please state the nature of the emergency," the operator said.

"Yes, I'm at...shit, I don't remember the address but it's on Winters Chapel Road. My stepmother is unconscious and is barely breathing. Please send help!" I said, fighting to keep my composure. Even though Althea was not technically a relative, I had come to think of her as a stepmother.

"Okay, I'm dispatching an ambulance. Please tell me more about the patient. How is she lying?"

"Lying, what are you talking about?" I said, fighting hysteria.

"Is she on her back or her side?" the operator answered without switching beats.

"She's on her side," I responded. "Should I move her?"

"No, leave her where she is. Did you try to wake her?"

"No, she didn't respond to my scream when I found her, so I assumed she wasn't just going to wake up." Now I felt stupid because she might have been drunk and not heard me. I gently shook Althea but she didn't move or make a sound.

"The ambulance is on the way. I want you to keep me informed of her breathing. I'll stay on the line with you until they arrive."

"Okay," I said, still trembling. I grabbed the sheet off the bed and threw it over Althea.

"Her skin is so cold. I put a sheet over her, is that okay?" I asked.

"Yes, but I don't want you to move her body, okay?"

"Yes."

"Do you see anything that might have caused her to fall, or does there appear to have been a struggle in the room?"

"No, the room doesn't look like it's been disturbed," I answered.

There was also no evidence in the room that she had been drinking, and that scared me even more. In the distance I could hear a siren, and I hoped that it was coming there. I opened the front door and left it ajar, then I stayed by Althea's side until the paramedics came into the room. Thanking the operator, I hung up the phone and backed out of the way.

The paramedics were asking me questions that I didn't have answers to, so I punched in Sammie's cell phone number. They had brought in the stretcher and placed Althea on it. She did not come to the entire time. They taped her chest with wires and ran an IV into her arm and also placed an oxygen mask on her face.

"Her vitals are steady but they're low," one of them said to the other, and I willed Sammie to pick up the phone. She answered on the last ring before the phone automatically went to voice mail.

"Hey, where was she?" she asked.

My teeth became locked, and I could not find the words to speak to my sister.

"Jazz, what's wrong?" she said with her voice rising.

"I don't know what's going on, Sammie, but you have to come. She's unconscious, and the paramedics are here. Please hurry!" I said. Turning around to face the paramedics, I asked them, "Where are you taking her?"

"DeKalb Medical," they responded.

"Sammie, they're taking her to DeKalb Medical. I'll ride with her. Please hurry."

"Did you tell them about her brain tumor?"

"Damn, I was so upset, I forgot."

"Tell them and let them know that she's refused treatment for it. I'm on my way," she said.

# SAMMIE

I acted on pure instinct. I could not possibly drive to the hospital by myself, so I called Buddy.

"Hey, baby," he said when he answered his cell phone.

Taking a deep breath, I spoke as normally as I could under the circumstances. "I need your help right away. Are you busy?"

"Not too busy for you. What's up?"

"My mother is ill. They're taking her to DeKalb Medical, and I'm in no condition to drive. Can you come get me?"

"No problem; I'm right around the corner. Meet me in the lobby in about five minutes," he said.

I went to office administration, instead of my boss, to request permission to leave early.

"Ms. Baylor, my mother is ill, and I need to leave. My sister found her unconscious, and they're taking her to DeKalb Medical. I've got to go," I said.

"Of course. Have you informed Mr. Spencer?"

"No, I haven't told anyone. I have a ride picking me up. Please, can I go now? I don't know what's going on, and I'm about to lose it."

"I understand. Please call us and tell us what's going on. My prayers go out to you," she said, and I left her office. I went straight to the elevator without bothering to turn off my PC or anything. I had my purse, and that was all that I needed. My mind was racing. I was scared that I was about to lose the mother who I had finally become close to.

Buddy was in the lobby when I got there, and he ushered me out to his car.

Luckily for me he didn't speak on the way to the hospital since I would have been incapable of coherent thoughts. He got me to the hospital before the ambulance even made it, and we paced the lobby together.

While we waited, I was surprised to see Jasmine's mother burst through the door. She marched right up to me and hugged me. I had been trying to hold my stuff together, but seeing her face caused me to lose all composure. We had a group hug in the lobby as they wheeled my mother in.

"What happened to her?" I asked no one in particular.

Jasmine came in and rushed to her mother to give her a hug. I waited until they finished before I approached Jasmine. My eyes asked all the questions my lips could not form.

"Boo, she's in a coma, but they don't know if it is tumor-related yet. Her doctor is in there with her now," she said, closing her arms around me as I cried for the first time. We cried together until it was time to fill out the insurance forms.

Hospitals are very insensitive. They want to make sure you can afford to pay for their services before they even venture to guess the nature of the problem. I had to check my tongue before I cussed out the heifer behind the desk who was demanding my mother's insurance card. Luckily, Jasmine thought to bring Momma's purse with them.

I helplessly watched them wheel Momma to the back as I filled out countless forms so they could admit her.

*How was I gonna live without the mother I'd just found?*

# LEAH

"Leah, I need your support. Can you come?" Sammie asked when I answered the phone. I was at the center picking up the children.

"What's wrong?"

"It's Althea. She's in a coma, and we're at DeKalb Medical. Can you come?"

"I'll do my best. Let me see who I can get to watch the kids. If I can, you know I'll be there for you," I said, hanging up the phone.

Craig looked at me with questioning eyes as my mind raced through the possibilities. If Kentee was telling the truth, he would be at my house when I got off, but I didn't trust his ass as far as I could throw him.

"I've got a problem. My best friend's mother is in a coma, and she wants me to come to the hospital. I can't possibly take the children with me, so I have to find someone to stay with them until I get back," I said.

"I'll do it," he said without hesitation.

"But they have to eat, and the staff has gone home," I said, thinking his invitation was the best answer to a difficult problem.

"We can order a pizza and wait on you, or I could take them to your house and wait on you," he said. "Whichever you prefer."

"I don't know how long I'll be."

"Then they should be at home, so I can put them to bed. Do you trust me?"

"Of course, with my heart and soul," I responded, giving him a glimpse of how I had been feeling for him since we had first met. I briefly thought about Kentee, but quickly dismissed him. Craig was more qualified to watch the kids than Kentee.

"Kentee wanted to come by tonight to see the kids, but I'll call him and tell him to make it another day. I need to reach the hospital as soon as possible," I said.

"Okay, let me close up shop here, and I'll follow you home."

I called Kentee and explained the situation. He wanted to argue, but I told him I didn't have time for his dumb shit. We left the center together, and I let Craig in the house before taking off for the hospital.

"Make yourself at home," I said as I raced down the walkway to my waiting car. I thought ahead to the possible events that I could walk into at the hospital. I knew Sammie was not ready to lose her mother so quickly after reconnecting with her.

My heart bled for both Sammie and Jasmine because Sammie would lean on Jasmine like a brick pillar until things settled down. I prayed for the best as I raced to the hospital.

# KENTEE

I went home at lunchtime that day and removed my clothing from Tarcia's house. I had been prepared to move back in with Leah when she had pulled this dumb ass-stunt. Knowing that I could not go home to Tarcia, I had no choice but to wait on Leah to get to her house and that just didn't sit right with me.

"She chose a teacher at the day care center to watch my children," I said out loud. I was huffing, puffing, spitting, and grunting when it dawned on me why she had chosen a teacher who had been around my children over me.

"Damn, I really fucked up," I said. I realized that she was doing the only thing that she knew how to do, and I promised myself I would be a better husband and father. I also decided to sit in the truck until she got home and not give her a minute's worth of grief for not letting me stay with the kids. Sure, I could have gone back to Tarcia's house, but I didn't feel like hearing her shit. I needed to be home, and that was the bottom line. So, I snuggled down in the comforter that I kept in the cab of my truck and waited in front of Leah's house.

Tarcia was blowing up my pager, and I didn't have anything to say to her. I would have to face that music soon enough, but I wanted to make sure Leah was okay with my moving in before I severed that tie with Tarcia. Her earlier messages were pleading with me to call her, but sometime after noon she had started threatening me.

I wasn't really worried about her since I had gotten most of my things out of the house before she had arrived home; even though she had ironically left work early as well. The biggest problem that I was facing as far as Tarcia was concerned was the mortgage on the house. I had purchased the house assuming we would be raising a family together. She already had two children from a previous relationship, but when she told me that she was pregnant with my child, she had forced my hand into marrying her. She didn't know that I had discovered that she was never pregnant in the first place. Those thoughts plagued me as I drifted off to sleep.

Bright lights coming down the street woke me up. I glanced at my watch and noticed that it was after midnight. The strange car was still parked in Leah's driveway and the house was dark. Sitting up straight, I winced from the pain in my neck and shoulders. *I can't do this, there's no telling when she will be back.* Starting the car, I drove to a nearby Motel 6 and booked a room for the night. My reconciliation with Leah and my family would have to wait another night. I feel across the bed without bothering to remove my clothes and went right to sleep.

## SAMMIE

"**M**s. Davis, your mother would like to see you now," an elderly white nurse informed me. My friends and family surrounded me as I waited to hear my mother's fate. Thus far, no one had been forthcoming with information, and we were getting weary.

Now that it was time to see my mother, I was scared. I searched the nurse's face for answers, but I found none. Pushing off the chair, I followed her through several long corridors until I arrived at intensive care.

"You only have ten minutes," she said and left me outside the room trying to find the courage to go in. When I did, I was surprised to find my mother awake and looking at me with a smile.

"Hey, baby," she said, and I smiled in return. I was still getting used to our new relationship, so I tended to blush and cry when she addressed me using terms of endearment instead of cursing me.

"Momma, you gave me a scare," I said, placing a gentle kiss on her forehead.

"Who's here with you?"

"Jasmine and her mother are here, so are Leah and Buddy."

"Good, I didn't want you to be alone. Who is Buddy?"

"Someone that I'm dating, Momma. I'm going to bring him by when you get better," I responded.

"Could you ask Jasmine, Leah, and Buddy to come in to see me now?"

"Sure, Momma; anything you want," I said, leaving to summon my friends. At the time I didn't think anything of her request. Momma was always a drama queen, and I thought this was just another one of her acts.

I returned to the waiting room and quickly asked Jazz, Leah, and Buddy to follow me. I didn't want the nurse to catch us because I had already used my allotted ten minutes. We went back to my mother's room, I parted the curtains, and the three of them filed in.

## ALTHEA

"Sammie, wait outside, please; I want to talk to your friends alone," I said. Sammy looked like she wanted to argue with me, but this was my moment; not hers. She backed out of the room looking dissolute.

"Gather around, please. I have much to say and not a lot of time to say it," I whispered.

"Oh stop it, Momma Althea," Jasmine said.

"Hush, child, let me speak. I've let Sammie down all her life. I can't leave this world without knowing that there'll be someone here who'll look out for her when I'm not around."

"You aren't going anywhere," Leah said, grabbing my hand.

"I said hush, damn it!" I said, trying to raise my body off the bed and failing. They all shut up to hear my final words.

"I've been a terrible mother. I allowed my child to suffer and grow up alone. I allowed her children to grow up without their mother. I don't want her to suffer anymore. I'm begging each of you to reach out to my child and love her like I was never able to; until it was too late. Please, I beg you! Don't let her go through this alone. Let her know that I loved her but just didn't know how to show her, okay? Do I have your word?"

"Yes, Momma Althea," they chorused. I searched each of their eyes to make sure that they understood what I was trying to tell them, and finally I closed my eyes for the last time. I had righted a wrong to the best of my ability, and now I could rest.

The machine hooked up to my heart went crazy, and people started streaming into the room. They told Jazz, Leah, and Buddy to leave, and they refused to let Sammie in. I didn't want her to see me go because I know she would have fought with them to save me. The truth was, I was ready to go. I had lived a long life, and it was time to rest.

Despite the pounding they gave my body, I was moving on. My spirit stopped briefly to kiss Sammie's forehead, and I hoped she actually felt it before I floated on to meet my maker. And if she didn't I was sure her friends would tell her how much I loved her.

## EPILOGUE

# JASMINE

It has been three weeks since Althea passed. As evil as that woman was, I still miss her today. When she opened herself up to Sammie and me, I got a glimpse of what my father had seen in her and understood their bond, which had endured through all the years of loneliness and pain. I believe that true love survives; even when one of the parties is no longer present. Althea, even in all her bitterness, gave me hope. My biggest task is to keep Sammie motivated to go forward. Sammie resented the fact that Althea chose to say good-bye to us and not to her, and I am doing everything I can to rectify that.

Sammie finally got to meet her granddaughter Nicole. Tyson brought her to the funeral and Sammie flew back with them to spend a couple of days. That was the best therapy for her. I heard it said that when God closes one door, he opens another and that is the only explanation I have for Tyson's sudden visit. He wasn't particularly close to Althea but he knew his mother needed him. Buddy has been a pillar of strength for Sammie and I feel like it's a matter of time before he places that ring on her finger. She is not the wild and crazy girl that she was when I first met her. Hopefully she will clean up her act. She is learning how to leave the bad boys alone!

Leah is dating Craig. He left his wife and is spending his time with Leah and the children. Luckily for both of them, his wife didn't try to take away the day care center that he operated. Mya still has not been officially diagnosed as autistic, but Leah and Craig are pretty certain it is the cause of her problems. They await the official results. Kentee is still out there doing his thing and hurting most of the women he comes in contact with.

As for me, I am still a rolling stone. In time I hope to find a man who can fulfill my every wish, but until then, ladies, watch your man. I'm on the prowl, and this time, I'm not going to play nice.

### THE END!!!

## Try and Try Again
Lenora Harrison

Maybe you got it
Maybe you don't
Maybe you'll try it
Maybe you won't...
But the next thing you know
Life will have passed you by
And you'll never know the outcome
Because you didn't even try.
So listen up, my friend,
If you have a desire that plagues your thoughts
Or perhaps a dream that tugs at your heart
Don't be like those who wait and wait
Nor like others who only procrastinate
Be like the one who followed the star
Cast fear to the wind! Declare who you are!
Take the first step, and then take two
Believe in yourself and others will too
And even if you fail, you will have succeeded.
Because you will have learned just what you needed...
That the end is never the end
Because as long as you live
You are able to try and try again.

## ABOUT THE AUTHOR

Tina Brooks McKinney was born in Baltimore, Maryland.
She moved to Atlanta, Georgia in 1996 with her two children,
Shannan and Estrell. Once in Atlanta, she met and married her
loving, supportive husband, William. Tina has mad love for Atlanta,
but Baltimore will always be home. Her love for writing is
evident in her novels, *All That Drama* and *Lawd, Mo Drama*.
The characters are vivid and somehow familiar as they take the
reader on a wild ride through domestic dysfunction.

SNEAK PREVIEW! EXCERPT FROM

# Fool, Stop Trippin'

BY TINA BROOKS MCKINNEY

COMING SOON FROM STREBOR BOOKS

**TARCIA**

"I'm telling you, Tarcia, there is something evil at work here."

"What are you talking about, Lasonji?"

"Can't you feel it?"

"Uh, no, I don't feel shit."

"Well, I can. It's like an omni presence and it's weighing down the very air we breathe." She walks around the living room picking up my various knick-knacks dusting them off. I love my cousin dearly, but sometimes she gets on my last nerve. She is two years older than me, but we are still thick as thieves. So when she called and said she needed a place to crash, I didn't hesitate to open my humble abode to her.

"Girl, I done told you I ain't having any of that backwoods mumbo jumbo in my house."

"I ain't brought anything to your house, heifer; this shit was already here when I got here."

"So you say. Just don't start practicing that shit up in here or I'll have to ship your ass straight back to Louisiana."

"Now see, that's some cold shit. I'm trying to help your foolish ass and you got threats."

"Not threats, promises. The first chicken bone I see laying around in a jar with dirt on it, I'm packing your shit and putting you the hell out."

Lasonji gives me a look and I cannot help but to feel a tiny bit nervous. I don't want to piss her off, but I refuse to go back to living in fear of the simplest things that she would construe as evil or vengeful spirits.

I had moved away from Louisiana when I was fifteen and it took me a long time to get that superstitious horseshit out my mind.

"All, I'm saying, Tarcia, it's some strange shit going on here and you would be a fool not to keep an open mind and hear me out."

"Girl, I ain't trying to hurt your feelings or anything but I don't believe in that crap." Lasonji bites her nails as her eyes dart from one corner of the room to the other. I can feel panic emanating from her skin, causing goose bumps to appear on my arms. This is just the type of shit I was worried about when I told her she could stay with me until she gets herself together.

"One day you will learn to be careful about the things that slip out your mouth."

"What's that supposed to mean?"

"If you don't know about something, you should keep your mouth shut, or you may bring unwanted events into your life."

"What did I say?"

"You know exactly what you said and I'm not about to repeat it."

"Okay, whatever." I pick up a magazine off the coffee table, pretending to read it. I flip through the pages, but the images don't register. My mind skips back to those years spent in New Orleans when we had to sprinkle salt over our shoulders to keep the devil from riding our backs. I could almost feel the prickly points of its claws on the base of my neck. This is exactly the type of shit that chased me and Momma from home thirteen years ago. I feel like a teenage girl, instead of a grown woman.

"Tarcia?"

Lasonji's family has been practicing Voodoo ever since we were children. Mom and I were real careful what we said around them as a result. As a child, they had me scared to voice my opinion, but I refuse to cow down in my own home.

"Tarcia!"

Even though I was still young, I felt relief to be away from those old wives tales and the strict religious taboos we were forced to follow.

It was harder on Momma because she had spent her entire life in Louisiana and old habits were hard to break. But she did the best she knew how to do to make a normal life for us in our new home until she was run over by a bus on her way to work.

"Are you listening to me?"

"Huh?" I had blanked out and didn't even know it.

"I'm not asking you to believe in Voodoo, but how do you explain all the shit that keeps happening to you?"

I don't have an immediate answer, but I am unwilling to accept the paranormal as the answer.

"What, cat got your tongue?"

"I was just thinking; that's all."

"Oh, okay. Think on my sista."

When Lasonji goes into the kitchen, I can hear her making a cup of coffee. Even though I want one as well, I don't want her messing with anything that I have to swallow. I chuckle at my foolishness and go into the kitchen to fix my own coffee.

"I would have fixed you one, too, if I had known you wanted some."

"That's alright, girl. I like to do it myself. Most people make it too weak for me anyway. I want my spoon to stand up in the cup by itself."

"Oh, you like it strong, huh?"

"Yeah, the thicker the better." We sit at the table in an uncomfortable silence. I glance through the mail which I had brought in with me earlier, while Lasonji watches the news. I had all but forgotten our conversation of a few minutes before.

◆◆◆

"Girl, look at this; those rent-a-cops are using guns on folks like they asked for this shit to happen." Lasonji is watching the evacuation of the flooded lowlands of the Big Easy.

"Damn, this doesn't make any sense. I heard on the news this morning that black folks were taking advantage of the situation by looting."

"That is not looting; it's called survival. What else did they expect us to do when our own government left us to die?"

"If it was a bunch of white people in those areas, they would have been flown out a week before the storm hit."

"I know that's right."

"I'll admit there may be a few folks wading down the street with TV's, but for the most part, people are trying to get something to barter with for food and water."

"Yeah. It didn't have to come to this."

"You would not believe the conditions we were forced to stay in. I was fortunate, but my heart hurts 'cause those people are my family." Pointing at the TV with one hand, she covers her heart with the other.

"I know that's right. They wait 'til folks are dying, then they want to talk and ask folks to be understanding."

"So folks take matters into their own hands and now they wanna shoot them and shit. Ain't that a bitch?"

"It's a double standard. Had it have been a white person looting the explanation would be different; they would have said they found a box of cornflakes floating down the street."

"With a gallon of milk, eggs and some fresh fruit for dessert, and that would be okay."

"Right. What's the damn difference? They knew those levees were not going to hold and they did nothing to help us."

"It's almost like they wanted everyone to die."

"Naw girl, not everyone. Just the poor black folks who couldn't afford to get out. They forget that it was those same poor black folks who built that city. Don't you find it odd that none of those white communities were affected by the hurricane? It's almost like they planted a bomb and blew up the levees."

"I never thought of it that way. But now that you mention it, that idea fits this destruction better than a natural disaster. It didn't have to be this bad; I blame that damn Bush. He could have made all the difference in the world."

"You ain't even lied. If he had only cared enough about the black folks it would have made a world of a difference."

"I was so glad when you called me and told me you made it out. I just hope the rest of the family was as lucky."

"Yeah, me too. We tried to stick together, but it was impossible. They were yanking children from their parents' arms and putting them on buses. This mess is going to take years to clean up."

"Damn, it's going to take a whole lot of time and money. Look at that house, the only thing left is the roof."

"Girl, that's my street, or it used to be." Our eyes are glued to the grim pictures showing the devastation.

"You know what I think?"

"What?"

"The blacks that do manage to make it out are not going to be able to afford to come back and Whitey will come in and rebuild, making it too expensive for us to live there anymore."

"I know. That's why a lot of the old-timers tried to hang on."

Lasonji had arrived in Atlanta with a few suitcases, a cosmetic case and a few dollars in her purse. Lucky for her, she was able to pack her important papers such as her birth certificate and insurance policies. Others weren't so lucky.

"Now that's what you call some evil shit," I say, pointing at the television. Lasonji looks at me as if I have lost my happy, loving mind.

"I'm going to pretend that I didn't just hear you say that."

"What?"

"Girl, are you trying to compare your life to what happened in New Orleans?"

"I'm not comparing it; I am just saying that bad things happen all the time and it's not Voodoo."

"Tarcia, you may not be trying to piss me off, but you are."

"Why? 'Cause I refuse to accept that my life is being controlled by evil forces and hexes?"

"You know what, this house is too small to be trippin'. We will just agree to disagree. Okay?"

"Okay."

"Besides, Momma always said, 'You make your own bed; you betta know when to lie on it and when to get the hell up.'" I wait for her to say something else but she doesn't. Lasonji takes her cup of coffee, goes to her room, and then shuts the door.

"What the hell is that supposed to mean?" I mumble to myself.

All of a sudden, the milk curdles in my coffee. I use my spoon to try to mix it up, but large clumps of milk float to the top. Spooked, I pour the rest of the coffee down the drain and wash away the clumps of milk that cling to the sink. Trying not to read more into the incident than is really there, I rinse my cup and leave it to dry on the drain board. I just bought that milk yesterday, didn't I?

Opening the refrigerator, I check the date on the milk, but I still have a week left before the expiration date. I shake the carton and it sounds okay, but for some reason I am afraid to open it.

"Girl, stop trippin.'" I walk back to the sink with the milk and pour a small amount. It looks and smells just like milk.

Now that's weird. Shrugging my shoulders, I put the milk back and go back into my room to read a book.

◆◆◆

Alone at last, I take a quick shower and wrap my hair. It has been a long emotional day and I cannot wait to get into bed. Foregoing my usual facial mask, I wash my face and put on my favorite nightgown. It is old as dirt, way too short and had so many holes in it I should've been ashamed to wear it. It is more like a security blanket to me. It was the last thing Momma ever purchased for me. I also have on my trusty wool socks that come up to my knees.

Looking at my reflection, I can't help but laugh. As much as I hate sleeping alone, it is nice to let it all hang out every once in a while. I wouldn't dare dress like this if my boyfriend Kentee was spending the night. He likes to see me in thongs, teddies or naked as the day I was born with my hair hanging freely about my shoulders, so he can play in it while we make love.

I didn't mind his playing in my hair so much when we were caught up in the moment, but the morning after it was a bitch to tame. He liked to curl up behind me breathing on my neck and by morning my hair would be a sweaty, tangled mess. Sometimes, when he was riding me from behind, he held onto my hair like reins, slapping my ass. He also had a tendency to sleep on my hair, holding me hostage until he would roll over. I tried to explain to him how much trouble I went through the next day, but he insisted he didn't want to sleep next to Aunt Jemima.

My vain self would wake up an extra half-hour early just to bump the knots out of my hair and to put on some fresh makeup. Yes, it was a pain in the ass, but I love Kentee so much, it's a small sacrifice to make.

We have been together for almost three years and although our relationship is rocky right now, I have no doubt we will get it together soon. Sooner or later he'll realize I am the only woman for him. Until then, I'll patiently bide my time. Turning away from the mirror, I get in bed and switch on the lamp.

His side of the bed looks so empty. When Kentee first bought a house, I thought we would live in it happily ever after. We even got married, but that didn't last long. Kentee came home one day mad as hell. He said Leah tricked him into believing that she had divorced him when in fact she hadn't, making our marriage null and void. He moved out shortly after that because he didn't want to live with me in sin. Any other man would have said to hell with that, but Kentee isn't just any old man. Unfortunately, he had to sell his house because he could not afford to pay the mortgage, child support and rent at his new apartment. So now I'm living in a two-bedroom apartment, instead of a four-bedroom house.

Over the course of the last two years, I forget my own treachery. Nobody, not even Kentee, knew that I had lied about being pregnant and I intend to keep it that way. Soon, we'll get over our rough spots and will be back together again like it was in the beginning. Satisfied, I turn my attention to the book I have clutched to my chest, losing myself in a fictional world more interesting than my own life.

I wake with a startled feeling more scared than I've ever felt in my life. My heart is beating very fast and I am cold as ice. Pulling the covers up to my neck, I try to calm down as my eyes adjust to the darkness.

"When did I turn out the light?"

Oh great, now I am talking to myself and expecting answers. I have to go to the bathroom, but I am afraid to leave my bed. I lie here until I can't stand it anymore. Rushing from the bed, I run into the adjoining bathroom. In my haste, I bang my toe on the edge of the footboard.

"Shit, piss and corruption." I hop to the toilet grabbing my toe with one hand and swatting away tears with the other. Rocking back and forth, I try to rub the pain away. I'm still frightened, but I need to look at my toe to make sure the nail isn't bleeding. I hobble to the sink and turn on the light, but I can't make my eyes open. I imagine something or someone is staring back at me.

"Oh Lawd, this is getting ridiculous." Peeping, I look at my toe first and a deep sigh escapes my lips. Slowly raising my eyes, I force myself to look in the mirror. "What were you expecting, a shrunken head or something?" My eyes are open so wide, it would be comical if I wasn't so scared. Still cold as the inside of a freezer, I am relieved to find myself alone.

Briefly, I think about crawling in bed with Lasonji like I used to do with Momma when I'd had a bad dream, but I quickly dismiss the thought. She would never let me forget it and it would open the door for more of her voodoo shit. Nope, I will have to deal with this paranoia myself. Turning out the light, I run back to bed; this time mindful of the footboard.

I can't get warm. I light a cigarette, inhaling deeply. Smoking usually calms me but so far it's not working. I can't shake the feeling that I'm being watched...